MW00529054

Claire
At Edisto

Books by Lin Stepp

Novels:
The Foster Girls
Tell Me About Orchard Hollow
For Six Good Reasons
Delia's Place
Second Hand Rose
Down by the River
Makin' Miracles
Saving Laurel Springs
Welcome Back
Daddy's Girl
Lost Inheritance
The Interlude

The Edisto Trilogy:
Claire at Edisto

Christmas Novella:
A Smoky Mountain Gift
In *When the Snow Falls*

Regional Guidebooks
Co-Authored with J.L. Stepp:
The Afternoon Hiker
Discovering Tennessee State Parks

Claire
At Edisto

BOOK 1 OF THE EDISTO TRILOGY

LIN STEPP

MOUNTAIN HILL PRESS

Claire at Edisto
Copyright © 2019 by Lin Stepp
Published by Mountain Hill Press
Email contact: steppcom@aol.com

All rights reserved. No part of this book may be reproduced, stored in a retrieval system or transmitted in any form or by any means—electronic, mechanical photocopying, recording or otherwise—without the prior written consent of the publisher, except in brief quotes used in reviews or as expressly permitted by the 1976 Copyright Act.

This is a work of fiction. Although numerous elements of historical and geographic accuracy are utilized in this and other novels in the Smoky Mountain series, many other specific environs, place names, characters, and incidents are the product of the author's imagination or used fictitiously.

Scripture used in this book, whether quoted or paraphrased by the characters, is taken from the King James Version of the Bible.

Cover design: Katherine E. Stepp
Interior design: J. L. Stepp, Mountain Hill Press
Editor: Elizabeth S. James
Cover photo and map design: Lin M. Stepp

Library of Congress Cataloging-in-Publication Data

Stepp, Lin
Claire at Edisto: First novel in the Edisto trilogy / Lin Stepp

ISBN: 978-0-9985063-7-1
First Mountain Hill Press Trade Paperback Printing: April 2019

eISBN: 978-0-9985063-9-5
First Mountain Hill Press Electronic Edition: April 2019

1. Women—Southern States—Fiction   2. South Carolina—Coastal—Fiction.
3. Contemporary Romance—Inspirational—Fiction.   I. Title

Library of Congress Control Number: 2019931136

This book is dedicated to Babe Hutto, our first "friend" at Edisto. Babe and his wife Gerri lived on The Point on Edisto Island near our favorite beach spots. We met Babe and Gerri in the 1980s when we first visited the island. Babe loved to walk the beach and he always stopped and talked with our family, answering our questions about the island and telling us things to do and see. Every year Babe recognized us and visited with us when we came to the island. A friendship soon developed. Babe walked on the beach with me, took J.L. golfing with him, and he always took time to sit and swap stories and laugh with us. Babe always exemplified the warm and friendly spirit of Edisto that drew us back to the island year after year.

J.L. Stepp (L) and Babe Hutto (R) at Edisto Beach.

ACKNOWLEDGMENTS

"Thankfulness is the beginning of gratitude." – Henri F. Amiel

Thanks to everyone on Edisto Island who shared stories and memories with me on our vacations to the island since the 1980s, helping me to know the island better and making its people and history come alive.

Special gratitude to the Edisto Library and the Edisto Bookstore where I found, bought, or studied many books about Edisto's history....and to all those at the Edisto Museum, local shops, restaurants, marinas, bike shop, resort, and golf club who shared local stories with me and made me feel at home on Edisto.

Thanks to Mr. Bell, who owned Bell Buoy Seafood, for all the great stories and great seafood every summer until his shop closed.

Thanks to Cheryl and Mickey Van Metre, originally from Tennessee, who invited us into their Edisto Island home and shared stories with us about their years on the island.

Thank you, also, to Sergeant Bobby Youmans, Edisto Beach Sheriff's Department, who filled me in on the early history of Edisto's schools, library, sheriff's department, and more, really helping me with my book's story set in 1985.

Last but not least, special thanks to those who work so hard behind the scenes with expertise, dedication, and love to always make my books the best they can be:

     ___ Elizabeth S. James, copyeditor and editorial advisor
     ___ J.L. Stepp, production design and proofing
     ___ Katherine Stepp, cover design and graphics

And to all my fans Thank You for continuing to love my books!
Without you, where would I be?.. .Please keep reading!

To God be the glory, great things He hath done.

A BRIEF EDISTO HISTORY

2000 BC	Archaic cultures inhabited the island
1550s	Edistow Indians lived on the island
1663	SC Colony founded by King of England
	Lord Proprietors granted lands from Charles II
1700-1770s	Plantations grew, importing rice and indigo
1775-1783	Rev War; planters fled; property destroyed
1780s-1860s	Plantations thrived growing cotton
1800s	Edingsville Beach formed for wealthy planters
1861-1865	Civil War years; slaves freed; property destroyed
1870s	Many families returned; cotton still a big crop
1893	Hurricane destroyed Edingsville Beach
1920s	Boll weevil ended cotton production
	Drawbridge to island replaced Dawhoo Ferry
	Intercoastal Waterway dredged, linking rivers
	Truck farming and fishing grew on the island
1925	Resort development on Edisto expanded
	Early cottages built, no electricity or water
1935	Edisto Beach State Park built with CCC help
	Palmetto Boulevard paved for cars
1940	Hurricane destroyed most all homes on Edisto
1941-1945	WWII slowed growth; military patrolled island
	Coast Guard patrolled park; reports of spies
	Edisto S.C. Hwy 174 straightened and paved
1950s	Development on Edisto Beach resumed
1954	Big pier built near park entrance; later burned
1959	Hurricane Gracie did heavy damage
	Groins built to hold sand, stop erosion
1970s	Edisto tourism grew and expanded
1973	Oristo resort and golf course opened
1976	Beach changed fr Charleston to Colleton Co
	Remaining Island stayed in Charleston Co
	Many businesses and beach homes built
1976	Fairfield Resorts bought Oristo Ridge
1993	McKinley Washington replaced drawbridge
2006	Fairfield Resort bought by Wyndham
2008	Botany Bay wildlife preserve opened
	Growth continued with beauty remaining

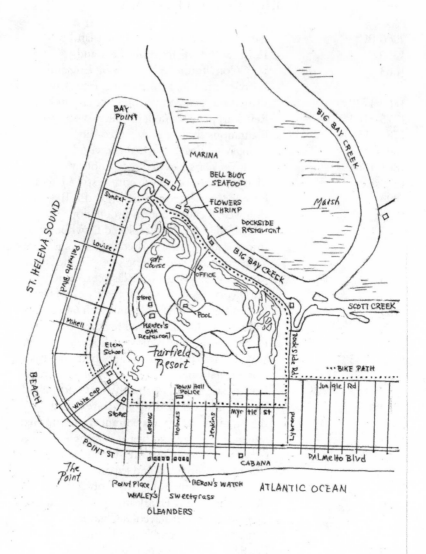

1985 Map of
Edisto Beach

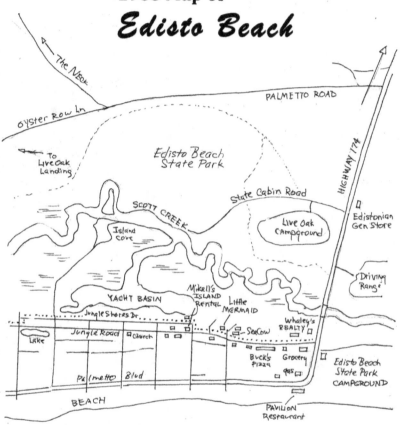

CHAPTER 1

April 1985

Claire couldn't remember how long she'd stood in the same spot. Rain poured down in sheets, dripping off her umbrella, soaking into her shoes, puddling around her feet. Through her tears, she watched the water run in rivers over the freshly covered gravesite in front of her, beating down the remaining flowers not yet removed, pooling in the spots where chairs and tent poles stood earlier. Now and then a rumble of thunder sounded in the background as if angry over the unexpected death of a man so young.

The day had begun sunny and fair, as if to welcome the members of Charles's congregation, their family and friends, coming to fill the sanctuary of the big white-pillared church to pay their respects and say goodbye to a beloved man and minister. The receiving line snaked around the sanctuary and out the front door, and Claire and the girls stood for over two hours speaking to people, being comforted, listening to kind and loving words.

Mary Helen, stoic as a little soldier and so mature and serious for nine, had handled the long hours in the receiving line, and afterwards at the funeral and graveside service, with an amazingly adult manner. Sometimes more so than Claire. Suki, barely five, with her sweet angelic face and sad eyes, captured everyone's heart, even when she grew tired and leaned against Claire's skirts. At one point, as the afternoon grew long, Charles's closest brother Parker moved from his spot down the line of family to come pick Suki up in his arms to hold her, continuing to greet visitors beside Claire, a warm and familiar presence on a hard day.

Hearing footsteps, Claire glanced behind her to see Parker making his way now across the cemetery under a broad black umbrella.

He paused beside her. "I've never understood why women carry such small flimsy umbrellas." He looked pointedly down at her wet skirt and shoes. "They never cover enough in a downpour."

She didn't reply but only sighed, her eyes moving to the grave again. They stood in silence together for a time, the rain providing steady background noise over their thoughts.

Claire reached down to retrieve a red rose from one of the floral arrangements left behind, turning the flower over in her hands. "However did you stand it when Ann died?" she asked at last.

"We bear things because we have no choice to do otherwise," Parker answered.

"You sound like Charles," she said, her voice breaking.

"Charles was a great comfort to me when Ann died three years ago. Actually, three years, six months, and two days ago to be exact." Parker glanced at her. "You gave help and comfort, too. At least we all had warning of Ann's death to come, time to prepare. Unlike this."

Claire thought about his words. "Charles ate breakfast with us as usual that day in the parsonage, promised the girls he'd walk with them into town for an ice cream later in the day." She picked off rose petals to drop them on the grave while she talked. "Most every Saturday he went to the church for a few hours to work on his sermon, to pray in the sanctuary."

"I remember Charles always liked quiet time with God before he preached," Parker added.

"Yes. He walked across the lawn to the church, cutting through the cemetery as always. I remember watching him through the kitchen window where I stood rinsing the breakfast dishes." She paused, thinking back. "As if Charles sensed me there, he turned around to wave and smile at me before heading down the path. It was the last time I saw him alive—walking into the cemetery. Ironic, isn't it?" She choked up.

Parker put a hand on her back in comfort.

"The janitor found him," she said a few minutes later. "Leroy came early to clean up and check on things after a youth event Friday evening. He found Charles slumped over his desk in his office. Leroy thought at first Charles was sleeping."

A crack of lightning interrupted them, followed by a loud roll of thunder, shaking the ground.

Parker glanced toward the sky. "The storm is getting worse. You need to come back now, Claire. Everyone has left the parsonage except the family. And the girls need you."

She nodded, turning to follow him across the cemetery, which lay between the historic Antebellum-style church and the two-storied Victorian parsonage. Sidewalks lined the picturesque downtown street in Sweetwater, Tennessee, where Trinity United Methodist Church had stood since the late 1800s. The church parsonage, donated by a wealthy member in past, lay between the cemetery property and a row of gracious, well-kept, older homes, all with lush yards and mature, shade trees. The white two-storied parsonage, with its gingerbread trim, black shutters, and deep gray roof sat next to a neighboring home painted country blue, with the home across the street a soft buttercup yellow. The many colorful houses, tucked among stately brick or crisp white homes up and down High Street, offered a charming appeal to all who passed by, many of the older homes historically significant.

Parker held the back porch door open for Claire to let her into a sort of mudroom, a nice place to take off wet shoes and coats, with a sink and laundry to one side. The pouring rain outdoors covered the sound of them entering, then stopping to shake out their umbrellas and tuck them into a battered metal stand. Voices floated in from the kitchen, and Claire put a hand on Parker's arm to stop him from opening the door as she heard her mother talking with her sisters.

"I can't believe Claire headed back out in this storm to go to that grave again. It isn't decent," her mother Verna Hampton complained.

"It sounds like something Claire would do," Marilyn added—one of Claire's older twin sisters. "You know she was always odd."

Her mother snorted. "Marrying a minister from some backwoods farm family wasn't the best decision Claire ever made. Just look at this kitchen. Old stove, no dishwasher, only one sink. No help either. I don't know how she has managed to live like this."

Marjorie, Claire's other sister, laughed. "I haven't seen black and white linoleum like this in years. To be frank, most of the furniture in this house is old attic, too, if you know what I mean."

"I did note Claire's handiwork everywhere, though," Marilyn put in. "Homemade curtains, embroidered pillows and samplers, needlework and quilts. She always did sew well."

"Well, what else is there to do in a hick town like this?" Marjorie asked. "I don't see how in the world she stood it these twelve years she's been married to Charles."

"I know this sounds harsh, but maybe in time Charles's death will turn out to be good for Claire," her mother said. "I always told you she married beneath her. Did you hear what his people carried on about endlessly after the funeral this afternoon? Tobacco allotments and chickens. I thought my smile would freeze on my face."

Parker clenched a fist, moving to open the door, but Claire waved a finger of caution to him. "Wait," she whispered.

"Claire won't even get to keep her house," Verna continued. "It's the church's property along with much of the furniture in it."

"Who would want it anyway?" Marjorie added. "Can you believe it only has one and a half bathrooms? One of those little Avery grandsons went out back and peed by the porch because he couldn't wait any longer to get in a bathroom."

The girls giggled.

"Well, it will be a blessing for Claire's girls to gain some advantages and opportunities," her mother pronounced. "The very idea of Charles's parents suggesting Claire and the girls go to live with them on that rural farm of theirs. As if this place isn't backward enough."

"You know Mary Helen acted very grown-up for nine, though,"

Marilyn said, changing the subject. "She handled herself nicely through all this."

"That's Claire's good breeding in her—the Hampton and Wallace bloodlines rising to the occasion." Claire's mother paused a moment. "However, Mary Helen shows a stubborn independent streak that needs work. She's entirely too outspoken for nine years old and shows her intelligence too much for a girl."

"Suki is precious though, isn't she?" interrupted Marjorie. "She looks like Marilyn and I did at that age with her sweet face, fair hair, and big blue eyes."

"She looks like the Wallaces on my side of the family and she's a little beauty already." Verna said the words with pride in her voice. "Please don't call her by that silly pet name though. I don't believe in nicknames. Sarah Katherine is a perfectly fine name. I see no reason to use anything else."

"I'll bet she could be a good strutter, too," Marilyn said. "My girls are already in fifth year and star performers." Marilyn and Marjorie took baton lessons from an early age, marched with the band as majorettes in high school, and won a multitude of awards along the way.

"I heard one of the ladies in the church say Sarah Katherine can already play the piano with an amazing skill for a five-year-old." Marjorie snickered. "She certainly didn't inherit that musical talent or performance poise from Claire. Do you remember how awful Claire was at piano and baton? Fumbling through every recital. So embarrassing."

Claire felt her face flush at the words, and had to put a hand on Parker's arm again to keep him from pushing open the door. "I really need to hear this," she mouthed at him. "They would never say these things in front of me."

He frowned at her, but leaned against the wall again, obviously displeased.

"Claire was an awkward child. It's true," Verna acknowledged. "Particularly in crowds. Always terrified to perform. I never understood that. Too much like her Grandmother Claire Levene

Hampton, Conrad's father's wife. But Claire could paint well like her grandmother."

Claire heard one of them walk across the kitchen before Marjorie replied. "All Claire ever wanted to do was read, sew, and make dinky little art things. She certainly exhibited no social success, so different from Marilyn and me."

In a pause in their conversation, Claire sighed. Marilyn and Marjorie had been cute, short, blond, and popular from the start—just like their mother Verna. Claire, scheduled to be the long-awaited male heir, Conrad Alfred Hampton IV, her name already picked out, had instead been another girl. She caused Verna a difficult birth and became the last child, too. Claire took after the Hampton side of the family in looks, dark-haired, brown-eyed, olive-skinned, and tall—five foot eight now and towering over her diminutive mother and sisters, all only five three.

Unlike her mother and the twins, all cute, buxom, shapely, and extroverted, Claire never enjoyed the social whirl of parties and petticoats or talking on the phone for hours about nothing. Her sisters collected so many friends Claire never even remembered all their names—the same with beaus, clubs, social activities, awards, and achievements. Claire always felt like the black sheep in her own family, known best as "the sister of those cute little Hampton twins."

"I've had enough of this," Parker mouthed to her. He moved to the outside door, opening and slamming it hard enough to be heard.

"It's still raining like cats and dogs outside," he announced in a loud voice, opening the kitchen door to let them into its warmth.

Hearing them come in, Mary Helen ran into the kitchen. And the conversations moved into new directions. Claire was sure her mother and sisters had no idea she'd overheard them talking.

Her parents, of course, expected her to move home to live with them for a time until she could establish a new life for herself and the girls. It seemed sensible on the surface. Her parents owned a lavish home in a fine neighborhood near good schools in Arlington, Virginia, not far from Washington DC and many cultural treasures. With her sisters no longer at home, the house had plenty of room for Claire and the girls, and her parents still employed a housekeeper to ease the load, the same one who'd worked at the house when Claire was a girl.

As Claire's father kindly said earlier that day, "We want to help, Claire. This transition time will be hard for you. You need your family." But many old, unresolved issues still lingered within her family, and if Claire moved home—even for a season—she'd need to deal with them on a regular basis again. Not an easy concept to face.

She pasted on a smile and moved into the living room where all of Charles and Parker's family gathered. They'd left their busy lives for the funeral, Charles's grandparents Clyde and Ida Avery, Charles's mother and father, Thomas and Edith May, and Charles's other brothers—Wylie, Vance, and Jake, their wives, and children. They filled the room with their presence.

Thomas and Edith May Avery birthed five sons, six if you counted Edward who died young. Wylie and Vance lived and worked with their parents and grandparents on the family farm in Blount County near Walland, Tennessee. Jake built on the family land, as well, and worked nearby managing the Walland General Store on the main highway. Only Parker and Charles left to go away to college and make another kind of life, always a sore spot with their parents. Neither Thomas nor Edith May wholeheartedly supported Parker or Charles's career choices or fully approved of their wives, who both came from very different backgrounds and families.

"You know we'll find you and the girls a place with us," Charles's father told Claire at one point. "It might be a bit tight in the big house, with Grandma and Grandpa with us now, but we'll work it out somehow."

Charles's mother smiled at his words and gave Claire a hug. "We'll make a farm girl out of you yet, Claire, just you wait and see. The girls too. You'll all arrive in time to help get the garden in over the summer and to work with the canning and freezing." She'd gone on to reiterate more. Claire knew their love for her and the girls sincere, but even on visits to the Avery farm she'd felt awkward over her lack of knowledge and skills about farm life. In addition, Charles's parents' held views about a girl's place in life very different from Claire's.

Even while Claire smiled and conversed, trying to be pleasing and appreciative to all, she felt like crying. *Why did you die and leave me in this situation?* she asked Charles in her mind. *It wasn't your time. I won't believe that. The girls and I need you. Our life was built around you. Whatever will we do now?*

Charles's family left an hour or two later after sharing from the bounty of dinner provided by the Trinity church family. It took two hours to drive from Sweetwater to the farm. The Averys needed to return home for work the next day, since the funeral had taken place during the workweek. Everyone kindly told Claire, again, that if they could do anything to help her they'd come right away, just to call them. Charles's parents, Thomas and Edith May, assured Claire once more, with her own parents out of hearing, that she was welcome to come and live with them.

"We're only a short distance away," Charles's mother added. "And if you decide to stay here with your church family, where I know you, Charles, and the girls are loved, remember you'll still have family close by. That's important. And you know we love you." Claire did know those words truthful ones, despite any differences. The Averys were good, Godly people.

After a time, Claire's parents and sisters left, as well, to return to their motel on the highway. They'd start home early the next morning to Arlington, expecting Claire to follow when she settled her affairs and the girls finished their school year. Before leaving, Claire's mother talked with the girls about things they would do when they came to live with her. Suki listened somewhat raptly but Claire noticed Mary Helen quieter in her responses.

"You contact me if you need my help with business matters," Claire's father told her, giving her a pat on the back and then a small hug. "We're all so sorry for your loss. Charles was too young to die and I know this is going to be a hard time for you and the girls. But you have your mother and me."

Claire hugged her father, taking in his familiar warmth and smell. She knew he genuinely cared for her. He'd always been somewhat oblivious to the dynamics in the family between she, her mother, and sisters, so lost in his work. Distanced from the emotional content of their lives.

"I'll stay on for a few days to help Claire sort things out," Parker told her father, shaking his hand. "I promised Charles I'd be a support to Claire and the girls if anything ever happened to him. I owe Charles, too, for his kindness and support to me when I lost my wife a number of years ago."

"Loss understands loss," Conrad said, surprising Claire with his insight. "I know you and your brother were close, too, and that you and your wife grew close to Claire and the girls. I remember how they always went down to your beach home in the summers and seemed to enjoy a fine time." He paused. "You and Charles lived together when Charles attended college in DC, if I remember right. Sometimes you came by the house with him when he started seeing Claire. You managed that antiques store in Georgetown after you graduated, Chevalier's. I stopped in there a time or two."

"That's right, sir," Parker said.

"Well, see that Claire gets sensible counsel," he added. "And feel free to call on me for advice or for anything needed. I know Claire is used to Charles managing things. She could do with some help right now. Verna and I will be in Arlington waiting for her when she finalizes her affairs and when she and the girls can close up the house and come home."

He turned to Claire. "I can help you make arrangements for movers when it's closer to the time, and if you need me to fly down and help you drive back home with the girls, you let me know."

"Thank you," she said, tears pooling in her eyes.

"It will be okay in time, girl," he said, his voice softening.

"Conrad, are you ready?" Verna called, coming back in the room with her purse. "We really should be going."

She air kissed Claire's cheeks. "We'll see you soon dear."

Claire stood on the porch to wave to them as they drove away, but all she could think of was the memory of waving for the last time to Charles on Saturday as he walked to the church. *How can this be happening?* she asked herself. Nothing had seemed real since Saturday. Every morning since, Claire kept thinking she would wake up and realize all this tragedy only a bad dream.

CHAPTER 2

Parker expected to stay a night at Claire's for Charles's funeral, two at most, and then to head back to his antiques store in Beaufort. With the weather now warming in early May, the tourists were beginning to arrive in greater numbers along the South Carolina coast and Parker hated to leave his staff to cover the store without him for too long. However, the situation with Claire needed more thought.

He'd assumed Claire had more viable options available for her future. He'd met her father several times in past, even her mother and sisters as they swirled in and out of the house heading to some social event or other when he and Charles stopped by. Their family home was an opulent one, nestled in one of Arlington's most prestigious neighborhoods, and Parker knew Conrad Hampton, Claire's father, was a wealthy and powerful man from old money. Knowing that and remembering the size of their home, he had assumed Claire could move back there for a season with the girls and that her family would support her as she adjusted to Charles's death, moved through her grief, and settled in to what a psychologist friend of his called "a new normal." Now after listening in on the conversation between Claire's mother and sisters he wasn't so sure.

The fact that Claire hadn't seemed shocked by what she overheard bothered him, too. Was she so used to their critical and uncharitable ways she thought little of it? It seemed so. Claire's conversation last night after her family left indicated she still planned to return with the girls to Arlington.

His mind wandered back to visualize his wife Ann, imagining how she'd have handled the same situation. He smiled at the thought. Ann had been a strong, independent woman, sure of herself and of her place in the world, very different from Claire. From a young age, Ann worked at Westcott Antiques, her family's well-established business in downtown Beaufort. At her parents' unexpected death in her late twenties, she took over the management of their store with ease and grace. When Parker met her, on a trip that Ann took to DC, she intimidated him by the strength of her personality. A small conversation trickled back into his memory now.

"I worry about Claire," Ann told him one evening when Charles and Claire were visiting them.

"Why?" he asked. "She and Charles are obviously happy together."

"Yes, that *is* obvious," she replied. "But there's a confidence missing in Claire I'd like to see."

He grinned. "Not everyone can be as confident and strong as you, Ann."

She frowned at him. "I know that, but Claire is too gentle. Too soft and vulnerable in some way. Too unsure of herself."

Parker considered those words in his mind now as he finished shaving and headed into the kitchen to find Claire and the girls. He remembered, too, Charles asking him years ago, as they'd faced Ann's death together, to look after Claire.

"Promise me, Parker," Charles insisted, "that if anything happens to me, you'll take care of Claire."

"Sure," he answered casually.

"No, promise me," he repeated, his dark eyes boring into Parker's.

Parker promised with serious intent then, realizing now some of the concerns Charles worried over at the time. Going to live with either her parents, or with his and Charles's parents, would probably bring Claire and the girls more stress than joy and comfort.

In the kitchen, he found Claire, Mary Helen, and Suki seated around the familiar round oak table in the corner of the room. He settled into Charles's old seat, feeling a little awkward and sad to do so. Claire kept two extra chairs for the kitchen table in the mudroom but they were hardly needed with only four of them eating.

"I just scrambled eggs," Claire told him as she got up to pour him a cup of coffee. "There's bacon on the table, hot biscuits, butter and jelly, and fresh cantaloupe cut up in that blue bowl."

"Looks good," Parker commented.

Mary Helen sent him a thoughtful look, her eyes moving from him to the chair he sat in. He felt sure she was thinking of her father.

The girls' two kittens scampered into the room then, lightening the moment. The little gray tabby pounced on the tail of his yellow tabby sister as they skidded on the linoleum floor.

"Remind me of the names of these two scamps again." Parker grinned.

"Smokey is the gray one. He's mine," Mary Helen told him. "Ginger is the yellow one; she's Suki's kitten. They're almost ten weeks old now."

"Daddy gave us the kittens for Easter." Suki's mouth formed a sad little pout, remembering, but then she giggled with a new thought. "He put bunny ears on them and said they were our Easter bunnies."

As the girls chattered on about the kittens, Parker studied them, noting how much they'd grown since he last saw them. Mary Helen looked a lot like Charles, with rich, dark brown hair, smooth and sleek, and cut in a short bob with long bangs across the forehead. She had chocolate brown eyes and a slightly olive-toned complexion like Claire and Charles—a pretty child, often too serious, but with a touch of fun and mischief that sometimes popped out to delight him. Bright, too, she exhibited wise ways for a child only nine years old. Suki, younger by four years, had pixie angelic looks, fair skin, white blond hair, and deep hyacinth blue eyes. Sweeter by nature than Mary Helen, she was also more emotional. She already had musical gifts surfacing and played piano by ear, with no one quite sure where that latent talent came from.

In a pause in the conversation, Mary Helen put her hands on her hips and frowned suddenly. "Grandmother Hampton said we couldn't bring our kittens to her house. I'm *not* going if we can't take Smokey and Ginger."

Suki teared up. "I'm not going either without Ginger and Smokey. Daddy gave them to us."

Mary Helen sent her mother a stubborn glare. "It was Daddy's last gift to us. That's special. I told Grandmother Hampton that and she said it didn't matter. She said we'd easily find homes for the kittens because they're still little and cute."

Suki began to cry now. "I don't want to give away my kitten and I don't want to move away. I want to stay here."

Parker heard Claire sigh.

"Moving is never easy," he said, trying to help out with the emotional scene.

"Moving is *always* hard, and it's especially hard to leave a place you've known and loved," Claire added softly. "Mary Helen, you were barely two when your daddy came to Trinity Methodist to pastor and Suki, you weren't even born yet."

"This is our special place then," Suki put in. "We need to stay."

"The church owns this house, Suki," Mary Helen explained. "When the bishop decides on a new minister to come, the minister and his family will move into this house. Daddy told me that. He's been here for seven years, longer than most Methodist ministers stay in a church. But he's been growing the church from a little one with problems to a bigger, happier church again. It's probably why he got to stay longer, but he said we'd probably be moving again next year. That he was overdue for a change."

Claire nodded. "We probably would have moved in the next year. Mary Helen is right. But the process to get a new minister for Trinity will take a while. We'll have time to make new plans and plenty of time to pack and get ready to move to your grandmother and grandfather's house."

"I don't *want* to go to Grandmother Hampton's house in Arlington," Mary Helen said. "I don't think she likes me, and she said Suki's name was silly. She told me I'd have to start calling her Sarah Katherine when we moved to her house."

Suki began to cry again. "I don't want to be Sarah Katherine and not Suki anymore."

Seeing the tears start in Claire's eyes now, too, with the girls' unhappiness and so many decisions before her, Parker intervened. "In early summer, all of you always come down to the beach house. You like it there, don't you?"

"I love the beach house!" Mary Helen's face brightened. "We can still go when school's out, can't we Mommy?"

"Please, please," Suki put in.

"Well, I don't know." Claire hesitated. "There's a lot to do getting ready to leave the parsonage and then moving and resettling in Arlington."

Parker stepped into the conversation. "I remember when Ann died, I thought I needed to make a lot of decisions quickly. But a wise friend told me it was better to stop and take my time before making too many big changes. He said I needed time to heal emotionally before making any major moves or decisions. Grieving takes time when you've lost someone you love, Claire. You and the girls don't need too many new changes until you all feel stronger and less sad. I think you should come down to the island and spend the summer at the beach house and heal."

"Oh, boy, can we do that?" Mary Helen all but bounced in her seat.

Suki sent him a worried look. "Can we bring Ginger and Smokey with us?"

"Sure." He smiled at her. "They'll love sitting out on the screened porch and watching the seagulls fly by."

Claire shifted in her seat. "That's a very generous offer, Parker, but I wonder if it's only postponing all the changes we need to begin getting used to."

"Those changes can wait while you take a vacation and begin to feel better. Moving is hard. You could all use a space to recover before you have to face the stresses and changes a move to a new home and place will bring." He lifted his eyebrows on those last words, looking at Claire, knowing she would pick up on what he didn't add to those remarks about the changes moving back with her family would bring for her. "The beach house is familiar to all of you. The girls even have friends there. They know the neighbors. I'll pop down every week to check on you—more often if needed. And you and the girls can come into Beaufort like you always do."

Parker could tell Claire was tempted. "It's a kind offer. I'll think about it." She turned to the girls. "Mary Helen, you need to get your school things together so you can catch the bus on time for school. I'll run Suki to preschool as soon as I clear off the table."

After they left, Parker called the store to check on things at home. His store manager Drake Jenkins assured him all was running smoothly. What few small decisions Parker needed to provide input on, the two resolved quickly.

With time on his hands, Parker wandered around the house for a few minutes. The old Victorian, from another era when homes were built with fewer rooms, had been well kept by the church. A large living room spanned the front of the house with comfortable, worn furniture and an upright piano against one wall. The house had no den so this was where the family gathered and shared their evenings. The downstairs also contained a dining room, kitchen and a large bedroom, designated the guest bedroom, where Parker was staying. There was only a half bath downstairs with one large bathroom upstairs and three more bedrooms. Off the largest upstairs bedroom was a small office, probably intended for a sitting room at one time. Parker made his way there now, since Claire had told him last night she would be glad for him to look through Charles's papers for her and to help her find the important documents she needed.

"Charles always took care of the bills and things," Claire told him, dropping her eyes a little shamefacedly as she spoke the words. "I guess I should have sat down with him to be more familiar with things." She shrugged. "But I was taking care of the house and the children."

Fortunately, the treasurer in Charles's church, Ben Harrison, was also a practicing attorney. He spoke to Parker at the funeral and told him he'd talked with Charles on a number of occasions about his affairs. "I have Charles's will and some other papers he asked me to retain at my office. Perhaps you can come by with Claire to talk with me about these things after the funeral. Charles told me he asked you to be a help to Claire if anything ever happened to him, so I wanted to contact you right away to let you know that. Claire will have worries enough. Please know I will be glad to help in any way I can."

"Thank you," Parker had replied, shaking the man's hand.

"Charles made good provision for his family," Mr. Harrison told him. "Traveling to Haiti and other countries on mission trips, caused him to take out a good life insurance policy, and the Methodist Church provides death benefits for minister's widows and their children. He had some savings, too, although not much. In addition, Claire and the girls will receive social security benefit payments. I think she will be okay. I've seen young women widowed in our church and left with a lot less and with heavy debts, too."

Claire came up to find Parker in Charles's study a short time later.

"Thank you for looking through Charles's things for me. I know they will make more sense to you than me, with you being in business and all." She sat down in a small easy chair in the corner.

Parker told her then about talking to Ben Harrison at the funeral. "He says he thinks you will be okay financially, Claire, and that's good. When we go to talk with him, he can give us more details on everything, let us know what paperwork you need to submit for different things. That will be a real help."

"Yes, he's a kind man and was a good friend of Charles's." A wistful smile touched her face. "The two of them often went fishing together."

"Charles did love to fish." Parker remembered the two of them fishing together many times over their lives. "I think we should call Ben Harrison in a little while and set an appointment—hopefully for tomorrow. I can't stay away from the store too long and I want to help you with what things I can before I need to leave."

"Thank you." She sighed. "I admit to being overwhelmed by it all. I keep thinking every day I'll wake up from this, to find it's only been a bad dream."

"A psychologist friend of mine gave me a book by Elizabeth Kubler Ross after Ann died that discussed the stages of grief following a death. The first is denial, believing somehow it's all a mistake. I remember feeling that way after Ann died, even though I'd known her death was coming. If I can find my copy, I'll send it to you." He shook his head. "All that research and head knowledge seems wiser to me in retrospect. I moved into the next stage of anger really quickly after Ann's death and I stayed there perhaps a little too long."

She looked out the window and then turned her eyes to meet Parker's. "I'm grateful for your help and comfort in this time. I really am. But I'll find my way through this eventually. I have a degree in early childhood education, and I can get a job teaching again. I was working and teaching a kindergarten class when Charles and I met. I haven't worked in a long time, not since Charles and I married, but I've taught the kindergarten class at church, worked in several children's programs and in Bible School. That will count for something, even if it was volunteer work."

"I'm sure it will."

She crossed her arms, frowning at him now. "You shouldn't have offered the beach house to me while the girls were listening, Parker. It will make things more difficult for me."

"Why?" he asked.

"Because the girls will want to come now and because I can't impose on your hospitality to stay at your beach house all summer."

"You used to stay extra weeks in summer with Ann before she died. Many times you and Charles came down to the beach for breaks, too, at other times besides only at Charles's vacation time. You know I never rent the house out and that I own a home in Beaufort. The Edisto house sits empty far too often. Elaine, our realtor and neighbor at the beach, fusses at me about it."

"I remember Elaine. I liked her."

"She'll be tickled if you spend the summer, or even part of the summer. Her girls are close in age to Mary Helen and Suki."

"Yes." Claire smiled. "Elaine's girls Jane and Emma are sweet, too. I always love seeing them, along with Elaine's boys, when we visit."

Parker steepled his fingers, thinking what he wanted to say next. "Look, I know I put you on the spot mentioning the beach house in front of the girls, but I admit I did it on purpose. I wanted to see how the girls would react to the idea, and perhaps I wanted to put a little pressure on you to accept." He paused. "I want you to be happy, Claire. I promised Charles I would look out for your welfare. I'm not totally convinced going to live with your parents would be the best thing for you or for Mary Helen and Suki. I also know you wouldn't be happy at the farm on a permanent basis, although you know Mother and Dad would be glad for you to come. Dad said he told you that."

"He did."

"My folks and my grandparents are good people, but they have limited views and somewhat rigid ideas on many subjects. Because they love their life on the land, they can't imagine why anyone else wouldn't. I suppose we're all like that about the things we love and know best, the things we believe in."

"Yes." She rubbed her arm, uncomfortable, before she brought her eyes to rest on his again. "Look, I'm sorry you overheard my mother and sisters talking about me. I know that made you feel I won't be happy living with them, but you need to realize I'm used to their ways and ideas, just as you are used to your parents limited and sometimes biased views."

He bristled. "Their talk was verbally abusive, Claire."

"Not really." She shrugged. "Besides, I'll only have my mother to deal with at the house now. Plus she is out most days working at the baton studio she, Marjorie, and Marilyn established. Her social life is active and Daddy works long hours. The girls and I will have the house to ourselves much of the time. It won't be so bad, and after I find a job, I can look for a place of our own."

"So you *want* to move back to Arlington? You want the girls to grow up there like you did?"

She glanced out the window again. "It's what I know. Where else can I go? I could stay here, of course. Several members of the church have encouraged me to." She gave him a small smile. "My volunteer work at the church is so extensive that I will be missed."

"I'm sure it's more than that, Claire."

"Yes, I know. I didn't mean to sound petty but I've heard them worrying about who will step in to carry my work roles. I'd agreed to chair Bible School this summer, for example, and someone else's arm will have to be twisted to cover that job now. Among others."

"Have they talked with you about how long you can stay in the parsonage?" he asked.

"An interim pastor is filling in for the rest of the summer, but they are hoping by fall they might get assigned a permanent minister. However, sometimes it takes longer. I do have some time."

Parker brightened. "You see? Coming to the island is the perfect answer for now. You can pack up most of the house, get it ready to move, and come to the beach to stay for a few weeks or more, whatever you decide. I won't pressure you to stay longer than you want to, but I do want you to know you are welcome to stay as long as you like. There's a school on the island, so if you're not sure of your direction, even by fall, you can stay longer. You might even decide coastal living in South Carolina appeals to you. There are lots of schools around Beaufort and Charleston where you could teach. Edisto sits between both cities. I know you're grieving, but I also want you to see you have more options for your life than you might think."

"I admit I hadn't looked beyond the idea of going home to Arlington. I do agree with your mother, though, that living near family is important, especially when you're single." She sighed.

Parker reached a hand across the desk toward her. "I'm family, Claire. I'm Charles's brother. I'm single and lonely, too. It would be good for me to have you and the girls nearby to lighten up my life, to give me some family to think about besides myself."

She reached a hand to take his. "I know you miss Ann. I do, too. You've already been a comfort to me in ways no one else has because you understand loss. And because you knew Charles so well and loved him as we did."

"You'll think about it then?" he asked.

"Yes, I will." She took her hand back and looked at her watch. "If we're lucky Ben Harrison will fit us into his schedule today instead of tomorrow for that appointment. I'll call him and suggest we take him to lunch if that would help. I'd like to find out where I stand financially. It's worried me, I admit, the idea of not being able to take care of the girls. Or having them do without." She looked around the room. "You can see we're not used to a lot. We already live simply. Even if I only receive a small income that is steady, I can manage."

He pushed the phone and Charles's Rolodex toward her. "Ben Harrison's card and phone number is in here. I think you will feel better when you know where you stand."

She glanced toward a photo, on Charles's bookshelf, of she and Charles standing on the beach at Edisto in front of Parker's beach house. "Right now the idea of a few weeks at the beach sounds blissful and healing, I have to admit. I'd like some time to myself to think and come to terms with my new life ahead of me empty of Charles. The girls need that, too. It won't be an easy time, but being at a place like Edisto will help it to hurt less. It's very hard to be too unhappy with the sound of the ocean in the background and the sea air blowing away many of your cares. We always enjoyed such happy times there. And I always came home refreshed."

"Do you want me to stay and help you pack up?"

"No." She shook her head. "Many in the church offered to help with chores like that. I know the women in my church circle will come for a day to work and help me pack. They're a sweet group. Much of it I want to do for myself, though. I'll need to box many items to move later, pack clothes, toys, and other things we'll need at the island. A few of the teenage boys in the church will come and help me pack the station wagon when I'm ready to leave."

"Remember you and the girls have bikes at the island already."

"I remember. We love to bike at Edisto." She tapped a finger on the table. "I'll need to find carriers for the kittens. It would be hard on the girls to leave them behind. Their dad gifted them such a short time ago and made such a fun memory of it for them. You heard them talking about it."

Parker chuckled. "The kittens will probably hate the trip. Cats don't generally like to travel. You might want to consider getting your vet to give you something to make them sleep through most of the journey." A thought came to him. "I can fly up and drive you and the girls down if you like."

"No." She waved her hand. "I can drive to Edisto. I know the way and I used to share the driving with Charles. Besides I need to learn to be independent now, to do more things for myself, but I appreciate the offer."

"You'll call before you come and let me know when you'll arrive?"

"I will." She put a hand to her chin thinking. "The girls have a few more weeks of school, but I might decide to take them out a little early. It's going to be hard being here day after day without Charles. There are too many reminders of him everywhere. A change as soon as we can make one might be best for us. I admit, too, that I'd like some time to strengthen before moving in with my parents again. As you saw, my family can be a little hard to deal with."

Parker decided not to make a comment to that. He'd won in getting Claire to decide to come to Edisto for a space. At least he could feel he'd protected her from harm for a time. Beyond that it would be Claire's call.

CHAPTER 3

After Parker left, Claire spent a few days weeping and wallowing in an unhealthy pity party while the girls were away in school. As a minister's wife, of course, she was expected to handle even her own husband's death with grace. Funny how it had been so much easier to comfort others in their grief and losses in the past—to say all the right things, offer uplifting scriptures and kind words, drop by with a casserole. Now everyone stopped by to visit her instead. Claire would probably have stayed in her pajamas all day, not putting on makeup or brushing her hair, if they hadn't kept arriving regularly, usually bringing food with them. At least she didn't need to worry about meals. The freezer was packed with casseroles and the refrigerator full of salads, vegetable dishes, and desserts. The counters and breadbox groaned with homemade cakes and cookies, certainly appreciated by the girls.

At the end of the week on Saturday, a week after Charles's death, Ben Harrison, the church treasurer, Neal Dawson, one of the trustees, and Lamont Osborn, a member of the church staff-parish relations committee, stopped by the house. Ben had alerted Claire they would come, so she had been expecting them. Despite her loss, the business of the church had to go on.

Fortunately they arrived while the girls were playing across the street with Ruthie and Bea, Claire's neighbor Leona Thomas's girls. Leona had been wonderful helping to support Claire in this hard time, often taking the girls for an outing to keep them occupied or arranging play dates for them.

With all the sweets piled up in the kitchen, Claire brought in a tray of assorted cookies, lemon squares, and glasses of iced tea for the three men before she sat down to join them. A Southern woman—and a pastor's wife—always remembered the social graces.

After a few moments Lamont Osborn cleared his throat. "We wanted to say again on behalf of the church how sorry we are about Charles's death."

"Yes, he was too young to die, much too young. Such a tragedy, such a tragedy," Neal Dawson added, repeating himself as he always did.

Claire bit back a smile.

Ben looked toward the two other men. "As I mentioned earlier to both of you, as Charles's attorney, Claire and I met this week, along with Charles's brother Parker Avery, to talk about her finances and situation. We also spoke about several issues related to the church and about the parsonage."

Lamont leaned toward Claire. "I know you are aware that Pastor Earl Davidson agreed to fill in as interim for the church. He's a retired minister living in Athens, Tennessee—only about twenty minutes down the road—and he agreed to serve at Trinity until a permanent minister can be found. Assignments for the new church year have already been made by the conference and it was expected Charles would remain at Trinity for this upcoming year, but with the situation now, a new minister will be sought. Pastor Davidson agreed to fill in for the year if needed. As you know, he was a friend of Charles's and often came to preach at our church when Charles traveled or went on vacation."

"Earl is a fine man. I'm fond of him," Claire put in. "He stopped by to see me this week and I know he's leading the service tomorrow. It should offer a smooth transition for the church. The people at Trinity already know and genuinely like Earl."

Neal rubbed a hand over the bald spot on his head. "Of course Pastor Davidson won't need the parsonage, since he owns his own home. This is a help, this is a help, at a time like this."

Claire realized they were kindly telling her she didn't need to worry about vacating the parsonage right away. She put a gracious smile on her face. "The girls and I will be going to Charles's brother's beach home for a few weeks of vacation and then moving to Arlington to live with my parents until I can find a home for us. I've already started packing our things, and Parker found a storage facility where I can put any furnishings Charles and I brought with us to Trinity or purchased after we moved here. Since the bulk of the house was already furnished, there are only the bedroom suites upstairs, things in Charles's study, and a few pieces scattered around the house we added. I think Ben and I talked about this earlier in the week."

"Yes we did," Ben affirmed, "and the church would like to make this proposal. They want to pay for the storage of your furnishings until you are ready to move them to Arlington and then pay the moving costs to have them transported. There is extra money in the budget and we would like to do this for you and the girls."

"That's kind of you," Claire said.

Lamont bobbed his head up and down at her response. "Another option is that you can simply leave the furnishings at the parsonage while at the beach and then the movers can take them directly to Arlington when you're ready to move later."

"Parker said you might stay at the beach until fall when it's time for the girls to return to school," Ben added. "It might be easier on you to let your things remain here until you're ready to make a permanent move."

"That could be easier, that could be easier," Neal agreed. "You can take your time with everything since no one will need the house for now."

"Thank you." She smiled at the men, knowing this a hard conversation for them. "Either of those options would be fine with me. Which does the church prefer?"

"Since you ask, it would involve less finances for the household furnishings to stay here until you are ready to make a permanent move," Lamont answered. "The church will keep up the parsonage anyway, and Leroy said to assure you he would look after everything and check on the house if you decide to leave your things here while away."

"This might be easier for you, Claire," Ben added. "You can box up all your smaller possessions and come back to the parsonage later to finish up any final packing before the movers come."

"You have all been very gracious, as has everyone in the church. The girls and I are truly grateful for the love and support we've been given. Thank you." She folded her hands in her lap. "Several women in my circle offered to help me pack and clean at the first of the week. Be assured we'll leave everything neat and orderly." She paused. "If for any reason the parsonage is needed sooner than expected, the church can move our boxes and furnishings to the storage facility at that time. Would that be good?"

They agreed and seemed relieved with her words, probably grateful Claire hadn't broken down like a watering pot to embarrass them. But today, at least, she felt somewhat "wept out" for a time, and she'd already decided in her mind that next week she would pack and get ready to head to Edisto. The memories of Charles stalked her in every corner of the parsonage and at the church, where she was naturally expected to attend every Sunday as long as she lived in Sweetwater. The sooner she could leave the better.

"What did those men want?" Mary Helen asked, coming home as they were getting in their cars to drive away.

"They came to talk to me about when we planned to pack and leave the parsonage," she replied honestly. "It's part of their job."

"What did you tell them?" Mary Helen asked as she and Suki settled onto the living room sofa beside Claire.

"I told them I would be packing this week and that we would be leaving for Edisto on Saturday."

Mary Helen's mouth dropped open. "*Before* school is out?"

"Yes, if it's okay with you girls. It's already May. There's less than a month of school left. I think you can catch up anything you miss. I've already talked to both your teachers."

"Oh, boy!" Mary Helen bounced on her seat. "How long can we

stay? Can we stay all summer like Parker said?"

"We'll stay for a while," Claire answered being purposefully evasive. She knew any specific promise you made to a child was remembered and thrown back to you if you couldn't keep it.

"I love the beach house." Suki clapped her hands with excitement but then her face fell. She looked around the living room and heaved a big sigh. "Maybe it won't seem as sad at the beach. Everywhere here makes me think of Daddy."

"Me, too," Claire said, being honest. "This is a hard time."

"Why did Daddy have to die?" Suki asked. "A lady in the church said God wanted him in heaven. Did he?"

"No, that's stupid," Mary Helen said, scowling. "God doesn't do bad things and hurt people, but the devil does. You know Daddy always told us God is a good God and the devil is a bad devil."

Suki nodded. "I remember, but how come God didn't protect Daddy? He's a minister and everything. He worked for God and he was good."

"Probably more reason the devil came after him," Mary Helen told her. "Daddy told me once the devil doesn't worry much about people he has in his back pocket. Why should he?"

Claire sighed, wrapping her arms around the girls on either side of her. "It's a difficult thing to understand why bad things happen to good people sometimes. We know we live in a fallen world. And as Mary Helen said we know we have an enemy in this world, especially focused on hurting those that belong to God. Sometimes despite all we do to live right, the enemy breaks in somehow and brings hurt."

"Like a robber breaking into a house?"

"Yes, exactly like that. And it's a wrong, illegal thing before God just like it is in the world."

Mary Helen crossed her arms. "I hope God arrests the devil and makes him pay big time for hurting our daddy."

Claire couldn't help a smile. "Me, too."

She changed the subject then. "You girls will need to help me this week after school to pack up your things, to decide what you want to take to the beach house and what to leave here at the parsonage for us to move later."

"Will we get our same rooms at the beach house?" Suki asked.

"Ann made our rooms special for us because she couldn't have any little girls. She told me so," Mary Helen said.

"You remember that?" Claire asked.

"Yes, I loved Ann. She died like Daddy did, and it was sad. I still miss her."

Suki frowned. "I don't remember Ann much."

"You were only two when she died. It would be hard for you to remember much about Ann." Claire smiled at her. "But Ann loved you very much, just as she did Mary Helen. She took much joy and pleasure in fixing up the two upstairs bedrooms so you girls would enjoy staying in them."

Mary Helen smiled. "She bought toys and stuff for us, too. Whenever we came to visit her house she gave us presents, and she brought gifts when she came here to visit. Even on our birthdays and at Christmas she always sent us nice things."

"Ann was a special woman," Claire agreed. "I know, like Parker told us, she'll be happy from heaven knowing we will be staying at her beach house for a while."

"Do you think Daddy will be glad we're going there, too?" Suki asked. "Will he know where we are?"

"Oh, pooh. People in heaven know everything and can see everything," Mary Helen told her. "Daddy said they watch over us down here, too, like the angels do. Daddy will know for sure we're there. He'll go with us, too."

"Why do you think he'll go with us?" Claire asked, curious at this observation.

"Because Daddy told me once, after Ann died, that God would never leave us or forsake us and that Ann never would either. That she'd love me, and Suki, and watch over us forever. He said if anything ever happened to him or to Mommy that you would both always watch over us forever, too." Her voice softened. "I like to think about that, knowing Daddy will always love me and watch over me like he said."

"You can be sure he always will," Claire said, fighting back tears. Claire and the children had many other talks about death through the week. She decided it natural for them to want to talk about it so she didn't discourage their conversations.

"What is heaven like?" Suki asked one day while they were packing up winter clothes and things they wouldn't need at the beach. "What do you think Daddy is doing there?'

"Like the song we sing in Sunday School, heaven is a wonderful place and better than any place we can think of or imagine," Claire answered. "There is no evil there, no sorrow, no hurt or pain. You remember we read in the Bible that even the wolf will lie down with the lamb in heaven and the leopard with the little goats. There will be peace and harmony in heaven among all creation like we've never known here on earth."

"Dogs won't chase cats and try to hurt them in heaven?" Suki asked.

"No, they'll be friends," Claire answered.

"Sometimes dogs and cats are friends here," Mary Helen put in. "Ruthie's dog Sparky is friends with their cat Bouncer. They sleep together and everything."

Claire smiled. "Leona told me they got Sparky as a pup and Bouncer as a little kitten. The two grew up together. Sometimes when animals that are natural enemies grow up together, they bond and become friends."

Suki's eyes lit. "Maybe we should get a puppy right now while Smokey and Ginger are little?"

"And maybe not." Claire laughed. "We're going to have enough trouble packing up two kittens to take to Edisto. Cats don't usually like to travel. They may yowl and be unhappy."

"Me and Suki will play with them and pet them and they'll be okay," Mary Helen said. "And like Parker told us they'll like sitting on the screened porch and watching the sea gulls."

"They like to go outside sometimes, too. Can they go out at the beach house?" Suki asked.

"We'll need to keep them in at first until they adjust to a new place," Claire answered. "Then we can begin to let them out a little and watch them carefully until they feel at home."

"Me and Suki will watch them," Mary Helen assured her. "And we will help you at the beach house and not be a bother."

Claire turned to Mary Helen in surprise. "What brought that statement on?"

"My teacher at school said that me and Suki should be especially nice to you right now because this is a difficult time for you, that we should try not to be a bother and make extra work or trouble for you."

"It's a difficult time for all of us, not just me. We all need to be kind and understanding to each other right now," Claire answered.

"Because sometimes we cry and get sad missing Daddy?" Suki asked.

"Yes," Claire answered, trying not to cry while answering. "Because sometimes we have sad days and cry and miss Daddy."

Suki heaved a very grownup little sigh. "Sometimes I cry at night after you tuck me in and turn off the light because I think about Daddy. I miss him kissing me goodnight and I miss him reading books to me and Mary Helen before bed."

"And always praying with us," Mary Helen added.

Clarie felt guilty at those last words. Charles had always prayed with the girls at night, and she'd been too filled with her own grief and sorrow to remember to pick up that role with them. "I'll start reading books again with both of you at night and praying with you, too. I'm sorry I've forgotten to do that."

"It's okay," Mary Helen told her, pausing as she packed a pile of gloves and winter hats into the cardboard box in front of her. "You've been sad, too. Me and Suki hear you crying at night sometimes."

Claire wasn't sure how to answer.

"It's okay to cry when you're sad and when someone has died," Mary Helen said. "Parker told me that. He cried a lot when Ann died and he said it was okay even for men to cry when they were sad. He cried at Daddy's funeral. I saw him, but I didn't say anything. Bobby John at my class at school said boys that cry are sissies, but I think he's wrong. Parker is smarter than Bobby John. Besides, Daddy sometimes cried, too, before he had to do someone's funeral."

"When you're really sad, your eyes *need* to cry," Suki added.

Claire hugged them both, wondering how she'd have ever gotten through this hard time without them. Often they acted wiser than she did about dealing with death and the sorrow it brought.

As they moved through their final week in Sweetwater, Claire and the girls visited old favorite places and spent time with special friends they might not see again for a long time. Claire put many addresses and phone numbers in her address book, promising to stay in touch.

The women in Claire's circle held a little going away luncheon, complete with small thoughtful presents. Some of the neighbors got together one evening and hosted a potluck dinner to wish them goodbye. Several times Claire remembered the children's words that it was all right to cry when you felt sad. The days since Charles's death had been filled with a lot of tears. Many were shed at Charles's grave. She often walked to his gravestone while the girls were at school and she also took the girls there a last time the night before they headed off to South Carolina.

"Daddy, remember to bring your sun lotion when you come down to the beach with us," Suki told him. "So you won't get burned."

Mary Helen frowned at her. "Spirit beings in heaven don't have regular bodies that get burned. Daddy won't need to wear sun lotion now."

"How do you know?" Suki put her hands on her hips and gave her sister a defiant look. "You've never been to heaven. Maybe Daddy will need sun lotion and flip flops and a swimsuit. How do you know he won't? I think he'll be down on the beach watching out for us so no jellyfishes sting us or so no big waves knock us down. That's what Daddies do, watch after their children. I bet we'll sense him there, too."

"And maybe hear him laugh on the wind," Mary Helen put in softly. She turned her eyes to the grave. "Daddy, you find ways to let us know you're there watching out for us, will you? We'll be thinking about you at the beach and always."

Claire's tears fell again.

Suki looked up at her. "Don't cry to say goodbye to Daddy's grave. He's not there anymore. Just like Jesus in the Bible, he's risen. He's in heaven with God and Jesus. And he's with us wherever we go. That's nice to know, isn't it?"

"Yes," Claire managed to croak out. "Yes, it is, Suki."

Mary Helen came and took her hand. "Remember Daddy said he was going to be transferred from this church and from this place this year? Well, he just got transferred sooner. And now we're all going to Edisto."

CHAPTER 4

Parker glanced at his watch as he drove into Beaufort, South Carolina. The trip from Sweetwater had taken eight hours with stops and lunch along the way. It was nearly five now with traffic growing heavier as people began to head home from work. Parker turned off the highway, driving down lush, tree shaded side streets until he came to Craven Street in the heart of the city. He slowed as he passed Westcott's with its picturesque green door and bay windows loaded with antiques. On the second and third stories of the tall store dark green shutters framed long windows, with the building's architectural details whispering of its age and history.

Westcott Antiques, started by the Westcott family in the late 1800s, sat wedged among a complex of similar historic Southern businesses, along the sidewalk of one of Beaufort's scenic downtown streets. A long covered roof projected over the sidewalk, sheltering the buildings' storefronts from the heat and offering inviting, shady entrances to visitors passing by. Plants and a few pieces of outdoor furniture sat outside the front door of Westcott's today, with the *Open* sign still displayed, so Parker knew his store manager, and long time friend, Drake Jenkins would still be in.

Parker turned his car into a side street off Craven, looking for the narrow driveway that wound behind the complex of business buildings. He angled his Buick Riviera convertible—a new 1985 model he'd indulged in this winter—into a parking spot behind the store, alongside the big van Westcott used to pick up and haul furniture. Parker's new convertible was sportier than most of the cars he'd owned in past—maroon red with a white top. He'd enjoyed it with the weather mild enough most of the year in South Carolina to drive with the top down. Drake called his new car 'the boss's little indulgence' although he could hardly criticize since he drove a sporty Pontiac Firebird.

"Welcome home," Drake said as Parker came into the store. "How was the trip?"

"The funeral was hard. I hated leaving Claire with so many decisions and changes still facing her."

"She's tough," Drake said. "She'll be all right."

Parker lifted an eyebrow.

Drake grinned, leaning against the counter by the register. "Not tough like our Ann, but Claire's tougher than she looks, I think." He'd met Claire many times on their trips to the coast and he'd known Charles well, too.

"I'll miss Charles," Drake added.

Me, too," Parker said. "Has business been good?"

"It has." He glanced at the clock. "It's nearly five. Let's close the store and walk down to Plums for dinner. We can sit outside, enjoy the waterfront while we eat, and catch up. I've been craving some of Plums pan seared crab cakes all day."

"Maybe I should check my phone messages…." Parker glanced toward the office upstairs.

"Nora said to tell you there weren't any calls you needed to answer. She only left a short time ago and said she'd look forward to seeing you tomorrow." Drake grinned as he started counting out the register. "Go pull in those pieces of furniture I put on the sidewalk and turn the sign to *Closed*. We can walk the two blocks to Plums; it won't be too busy yet at five."

It was only a short walk to Plums Restaurant on Bay Street, with its outdoor tables scattered across the back porch and patio behind it, each table with a front row view across the Henry C. Chambers Waterfront Park. The park, stretching from Woods Memorial Bridge to the marina on the river, was a popular spot for locals and tourists, with its walkways lined with coastal palms, deep shade trees, and a profusion of flowers this time of year.

After settling at a table, they placed their dinner orders, Parker opting for crab cakes, too, with a side salad and an order of sweet potato fries.

"Did the Whitehalls decide on some pieces for the remodeling they're doing on their old place on Lady's Island?" Parker asked as their iced tea and salads arrived.

"They did. They bought those Georgian mahogany bedroom pieces we've been sitting on for nearly a year. I can't believe someone hasn't picked them up before. Beautiful wood, oval plate handles, lots of storage in the chest of drawers. The Whitehalls purchased some other pieces, too, a mahogany linen press, an antique clock, and an inlaid desk." He poured a packet of sugar in his tea. "It was a big sale, and they said they may be back. They're really working on the house."

"That's good news." Parker smiled.

"I ran out to that estate sale in the country we'd read about and found a couple of items there I think will sell, too." Drake had an eye for antiques and he enjoyed doing much of the store's buying.

"What did you find?" Parker asked, looking out across the river to watch a boat slide through the water heading toward the marina.

Drake laughed. "I picked up an old U.S. flag."

Parker turned to him, raising a questioning eyebrow.

"Not just *any* flag," Drake told him. "This one was flown over one of the buildings at the Centennial Exposition in Philadelphia in 1876. I got some paperwork verifying that. It's a beauty. The stars spell out 1776 and 1876, commemorating 100 years since the signing of the Declaration of Independence. I'm putting it in the front window to attract attention tomorrow, along with an antique brass cash register I found at the sale. Items like that draw in street traffic for us."

"We don't make much off the tourists with the type of antiques we sell. You know that, Drake. Our store items are generally too high end."

"You never know about people." Drake shrugged. "An old guy in overalls stopped in one day. He'd been down the street touring the Beaufort Arsenal and checking out some of the shops nearby. He saw something in our store window while walking to his car and came in. I'll show you the inventory sheet some day of all he bought."

"It happens sometimes," Parker acknowledged as the waiter brought their food.

They ate for a time in silence, and then Drake waved at some friends he saw coming into the restaurant. A few minutes later the group stopped by to chat and Parker enjoyed watching Drake's charm flash to the surface.

Drake was tall like Parker, five years his senior, his dark hair sprinkled liberally with gray—but in a striking way. Drake was the sort of man, with easy, distinguished looks, that would always draw admiration and command attention because of his natural ease, confidence, and poise. In the store, he always wore clean-cut Southern gentleman suits, usually with a colorful handkerchief of some sort tucked in the pocket. Parker owned suits and often wore them, but he never felt as at ease in them as Drake did. Drake's people, in Atlanta, were moneyed and he'd grown up around fine things. Like Parker, there'd been an expectation for him to follow after his father in the banking business, rather than in farming like Parker's family, but Drake had rebelled and broken away.

"Remind me again how you came to work with Ann and her parents at Westcott," Parker asked as Drake waved goodbye to his friends and turned back to the table.

"What brought that question on?" Drake looked surprised.

"Going to the funeral, seeing my family, remembering how both Charles and I stepped away from our parents' expectations."

"And thinking about Ann?"

Parker rubbed his neck. "It's hard not to do that at a funeral."

Drake glanced out across the water before speaking. "As a Jenkins son I was intended to go into the banking and finance industry with my family. No one ever paid much attention to my passion for fine antiques or to the hours I spent pouring over library books on the subject or wandering through antique stores in our area. I got the appropriate schooling, the degree in business and finance. You know that. But all through college, I poked through antique stores in my spare time, traveled to estate sales. I went to work in the family business but soon hated it. In anger one day I told my dad I wanted to quit."

"What did he say?"

"I remember him responding in a nasty tone of voice, 'And *what* else do you think you could you do?' I snapped back at him, 'Maybe I could work at an antiques store.' I still remember how he laughed and replied 'Now why do you suppose anyone would hire you to do that?'"

Picking at a nail, Drake paused. "In rebellion, I took off on a vacation trip shortly after that to the coast, drawn to Beaufort because of the antiques stores, period homes, and historic buildings. I simply loved the place. I kept dropping in to Westcott's nearly every day. I loved the store, often ended up chatting with customers, looking around, talking to Ann's father. One day he laughed and said, 'Son, if you keep hanging around here much longer, I'm going to have to hire you.'"

Drake smiled, remembering. "I knew he was joking of course, but without thinking, I asked, '*Would* you hire me? I'd like that.'"

Parker chuckled. "And that's how you started working at Westcott's?"

"Yeah. I learned so much from Ann's parents, Vernon and Augusta Westcott. Her father really groomed me in the business, and it wasn't too many years until I was managing the store for them. Ann always worked in the store, even as a girl, but she went off to school, wanting to see a little more of life. Traveled some. But then she had to come home and pick up the reins of Westcott's when her parents were killed in that tragic wreck. She had a rough time for a while, but she was tough and she valued Westcott's. I don't think I remember her taking a vacation after their death until the summer she went to DC to stay with one of her old college girlfriends for a wedding." He grinned at Parker. "I couldn't figure out why she kept staying on and on until she came home all starry-eyed over you."

"She sure intimidated me when I first met her," Parker remembered. "She came into the antiques store in Georgetown, to Chevalier's, where I worked. Like you, I'd studied business in school but kept drifting in interest to the antiquing business. The part time job I held at Chevalier's sucked me in like no other work I'd gotten into before, so I went to work full time there after graduation. I learned the business at Chevalier's and then learned more after I married Ann and came here."

"You've done all right." Drake grinned.

Parker knew he was teasing him with those casual words. Drake had told him he was a natural from the first month at Westcott's.

"I had no idea when I met Ann that she *owned* an antiques store," Parker said, picking up one of the fries left on his plate to nibble on. "She told me she worked at a store in Beaufort, but she left out the small detail that she also owned it."

"You always felt uncomfortable walking into all of Ann's money. With or without the antiques store, Ann would have never needed to worry about money for a moment."

Parker scowled. "I soon learned that *after* I was too deeply in love with Ann to retreat. It was a lot to take in for a small town Tennessee farm boy who'd sampled very little of the wealthy side of life."

Drake laughed. "I remember Ann telling me how your mouth dropped to your feet the first time you saw her big antebellum home here in Beaufort on the Edisto River and then later the beach house down at the island."

"I feel guilty sometimes having inherited it all. As if I shouldn't have."

Drake shook his head. "Let that go, friend. Ann loved you; you loved her. You two were good together. We all saw that. She chose well. You stood by her with great love through her illness, and since her death you've continued to grow the business, used your talents and skills to make Westcott's even stronger and better known than it was before."

"You've helped with that."

"A little," he agreed. "I love Westcott's. So does Nora. We made a wise move hiring Nora Cavanaugh from Brimmer's Fine Antiques after Al Brimmer died."

"Brimmer was a good man." Parker stirred his straw in his glass of iced tea. "He trained Nora well and he was good to her after that playboy husband of hers broke her heart."

Drake loosened his tie before adding, "When I went to see Brimmer at the hospital after that bad heart attack, he asked me if we'd consider hiring Nora if he passed on. He said his kids would sell out his business, that none of them wanted it, but that he'd like to know Nora would have a good place to work." He hesitated. "He died soon after. You probably remember the day I came to talk with you and Ann about hiring Nora."

"Yes." Parker nodded. "Ann knew she was ill by that time, and she knew we would soon need someone else in the store. She met Nora and liked her. Ann saw Nora had an eye for decorating and arranging in the store, strong office organizational skills, and good people skills, all of which she knew we'd need with her health declining. She helped to train Nora before she grew too ill to come into the store anymore." Parker paused, looking out over the water—lost for a moment in old memories.

"The three of us—you, Nora, and me—make a good team at Westcott's." Drake chuckled. "Along with Andrew." Andrew was Nora's seven-year-old son, who spent a lot of time at Westcott's and with Drake and Parker. "Andrew loves the store, already has a natural knack for antiquing."

"You've taught him a lot."

"So have you." Drake sent him a grin. "He's real worried about Claire and her girls possibly spending the summer at your beach house at Edisto."

"Why?" Parker asked.

"He's afraid with them there you won't take him to spend

weekends at the island any more," Drake explained. "That he won't get to hang out at the beach house this summer, ride down to the beach in your boat, fish a little with you now and then. You know."

"Did he tell you that?"

"No. Nora did."

"I'll still take Andrew to Edisto. Claire will like him, and he'll enjoy the girls."

"He'll be relieved to hear that." Drake paused. "Nora says it's meant a lot to him having the two of us as male figures in his life."

"You've been good to take him on buying trips with you, out to your place for the weekend sometimes, to the movies and such."

"I take him to the symphony, too. The kid loves classical music. He can sit over at my house and listen to it for hours."

Parker knew his mouth dropped open. "No kidding? I wouldn't have expected that of a seven-year-old. Does he play an instrument?"

Drake shook his head. "Not that I know of. He just has a real appreciation for it. Hears things in the music even I don't hear."

"A future music critic?"

"No, simply an appreciator of fine music and fine things. Nora says he got that from her people, the Quinns. Her mother was musical and her father an architect with a gift for working with wood. Her grandmother owned a furniture business in that little town in Maine where she came from. Nora spent a lot of time there growing up. Said her grandparents carried a lot of antiques in the store. It's where she learned the basics."

"I know she told me she came here with a college friend to spend the summer near the beach, got a job at Brimmer's, then met her husband in a whirlwind romance, married, and stayed."

Drake clenched a fist. "Yes, and realized too late Hayden Cavanaugh was a drunk half the time, a womanizer the other half."

"I guess everyone faces some sort of sorrow in their lives, but we move on."

"Yeah, and we need to move on." Drake grinned, pushing back from the table. "You haven't even been to the house yet, and I know you're tired. I need to get home, too. We could both use an early night. A furniture shipment is coming in the morning, and it's Saturday, as well. It will be a busy day for both of us."

They settled their bill and then walked back to the store to pick up their cars. "When will Claire come down to the coast?" Drake asked before they parted.

"Possibly as soon as next weekend, or maybe not until the end of the month," Parker answered. "She wasn't sure when she could get all her affairs resolved, get packed, and get the girls out of school. But she promised she'd call me before she headed south."

Parker slipped back into Westcott's after Drake left, just to walk around a last time in the familiar store, enjoying—as always—the look of the fine old building filled with beautiful antiques. The store predominantly handled furniture but they utilized period accessories to add ambience to the look of the store's interior— old china, fine glassware and vintage silver on the dining room tables, timeless pieces tucked into china cabinets and gracing the tops of richly polished dressers and breakfronts, an antique quilt draped over an old chest, statuary and handsome lamps adding a further historic flavor.

A well-worn stairway led upstairs to the second floor, railed all around with an open view to the showroom below. Around the upstairs walls, Westcott's kept more pieces, large ones that showed better against the wall, like armoires, tall chests, and mirrors. Room settings could be tucked into the corners and china plates and paintings hung on the high walls. At the top of the stairs an opening in an interior wall looked into an office. Whoever worked in the office could see any customers on the upstairs floor, and slip out through the door nearby to answer questions if needed.

Parker let himself into his office off a back hall in the store now to look around, to check his desk for any notes or messages he wanted to place in priority to handle in the morning. The furniture delivery would arrive out back in the early hours to be loaded into the old freight elevator and brought up to the show room floors or the third floor storage area. When items sold in the store, other items awaited in the storeroom to be brought down to fill the space. He'd noted downstairs that a vintage floral set of china had sold, to be replaced by a lavish set of early Spode dinnerware—showing Nora's artistry in how every detail on the table had been arranged.

He locked up and headed for the house then, following Craven to East Street and then traveling quiet back roads to River Street, a side street off Bayard that looked out over the Beaufort River before the wide river turned at the Bellamy Curve. Even after all these years, Parker never drove up to the imposing plantation house without being awed.

It was such a striking, gracious old piece of history. The side of him that loved antiques appreciated the stately white home on the water, with its broad porches, windows shuttered in forest green, and its high chimneys jutting up from the weathered green roof, reminiscent of a past time. A white picket fence surrounded the property, helping to discourage tourists from wandering through the yard. The historic streets on The Point, with their gracious homes and gardens, were heavily visited by tourists but River Street, a little further away from the major tourist area, received less traffic.

The neighbor's black lab, Congress, wiggled his way under the fence as Parker pulled his car into the driveway.

"Hey, big guy," he said to the dog, petting him as he bounded up to the car. Parker's next door neighbors, the Comptons, had given up long ago trying to keep Congress in when he wanted to get out. The dog, generally obedient and content to stay in his own yard or inside the Comptons' house, considered Parker part of his personal property. One way or the other, he would find a way to visit equally between the two homes when Parker was home. Parker decided long ago it was the easiest route for dog ownership a guy could hope for. Congress visited him but the Comptons assumed all the expense of ownership.

He unloaded the car and headed into the house, the dog at his heels. "I assume you've been keeping a watch on things," he said to the dog as he headed toward the front entry hall and up the old stairway rising to the second floor. The dog's toenails clicked on the wood floor behind him.

Waterview, the name of the house built by the Westcott family in Beaufort's prosperous Antebellum era, had its main rooms downstairs, its bedrooms upstairs. Over the years the family modernized certain areas of the home, of course, while carefully keeping its authenticity and character. Parker still slept in the same bedroom he and Ann had shared, a large upstairs room on the back of the house with its own bath and a giant walk-in closet. On the occasions when members of his family or out-of-town friends visited, there were three other bedrooms and several baths to choose from.

Parker, living alone in the old house, seldom used the formal rooms—a big parlor and dining room downstairs—but he loved the sunny kitchen, filled with windows looking out toward the river, and the screened porch off the kitchen where he often sat in the evenings to read and relax. The other room he used the most was a comfortable library-sitting room, a cozy space where he kept his home office, a television, stereo, and personal items.

Following a familiar pattern, Parker and the dog made their way to the kitchen now. He poured out a few bites of dry dog food for Congress, filled his water dish, and then poked in the refrigerator to see what he could find to make a drink for himself to take out on the porch.

When Ann had been alive, she'd taught him many Southern drinks to make with seltzer water or ginger ale, decorated with slices of limes, lemons, or oranges, and doctored with pineapple or orange juice. When guests came, she often added a touch of wine to her spritzers. Ann always fixed her drinks in a frosty glass with a swizzle stick. Over the years she'd collected many pretty antique glass swizzle sticks, including a set with glass birds on the end that Parker particularly liked. He dropped a parrot-topped stick into his lime seltzer drink now and headed out to the porch with a stack of mail and newspapers his housekeeper Florence had left on the kitchen counter for him.

After dumping the papers on a side table, he turned on the paddle fan overhead to stir the breeze and settled into one of the wicker chairs on the open porch with its vistas of the Beaufort River.

"That's a fine view for a man to look at every evening," he told Congress, scratching the dog under his neck. The backyard opened onto a marshy area, often alive with water birds. A long deck led out through the marsh to a dock on the river, where Parker kept a boat. He could boat down to his beach house at Edisto quicker than he could make the drive to it. The Beaufort River led through several waterways before merging into the South Edisto River that led directly into Saint Helena Sound beside Edisto Island. Off the Sound on Big Bay Creek lay a marina where Parker kept his boat when at the island. Nearby, at a friend's place, he kept an old jeep that served to get him to the beach house and around on the paved and unpaved streets on Edisto.

"We may be enjoying a little more company this summer," he told the dog, who'd settled down on the tile floor with his head on Parker's foot.

In many ways Parker enjoyed the dog's company. He'd told the Comptons so. Congress kept him entertained, helping to fill the loss of Ann's vibrant personality in his life.

He thought of Ann now. "I remembered what you told me about Claire this week," he said, believing Ann listened in on him and kept up with him. "I'm going to try to talk Claire into staying at the island until she can envision some sort of life for herself and the girls, besides simply moving in with either her parents or mine. I promised Charles I'd look out for her, you know. I guess he knew she might be pulled in several directions. Especially by her parents. She may yield and head back to live with them yet. We'll see."

He leaned back against the chair, tired from the long day on the road. "I can't be down at the island much, so you watch out for Claire and the girls, would you, Ann? This is going to be a difficult time for her."

CHAPTER 5

Claire and the girls did not get away to Edisto the next Saturday as planned, but they did finally get away on Monday. Some unexpected issues had to be resolved and packing the house took longer than Claire expected with all the continuing stream of company dropping by the parsonage.

In addition, she had to take the cats to the vet to get pills to help them sleep on the trip to the beach, and she spent almost a whole day trying to find two cat carriers she felt she could afford. In the end a friend offered a large rabbit cage she no longer needed, with a plastic bottom, long enough for both kittens. Because of its size Claire could put a small litter box in one end and a blanket in the other for the kittens to sleep on.

On Sunday afternoon as she finalized packing the car for the trip, the arguments about who would ride "shot gun" in the front seat began.

"It's *my* turn to sit in the front seat," Suki said, her mouth set in a pout. "You *always* get to sit up front, Mary Helen."

"I'm the oldest. I need to help Mommy with the map because *you* can't read."

"Mary Helen, is that kind?" Claire asked, stopping in the middle of packing a box of beach toys.

"It's true." Mary Helen held up her head stubbornly.

"We're supposed to share," Suki insisted. "That's fair."

Exasperated after a while as the argument bounced back and forth, Claire heaved a sigh. "Girls, I'm tired of hearing you argue.

I've decided that neither of you will sit in the front. I'm going to put the kittens' carrier on the front seat. Both of you will sit in the back, which will work out better anyway, so you can share toys and play together while we travel."

After a little grumbling, this plan seemed to resolve the dispute.

"Have you girls packed your travel bags to put in the backseat?" she asked, trying to get them to focus on something else. "Remember you can only take what fits in your tote bags—the ones I made for you with your names on them. The rest of your toys and things go in the back of the station wagon or remain here until we move. Our car only has so much room in it."

Claire felt grateful to Charles today for buying a Country Squire station wagon last year from Mr. Watson in the church. Glen Watson owned the Ford dealership in town and he'd offered Charles an opportunity to pick up a dealer's car with low mileage. It helped having the extra space now as Claire worked to pack what they would need for a few weeks or longer into the car. A neighbor helped Claire yesterday put the rooftop cargo box on top of the station wagon, ideal for bulky items—beach chairs, toys, umbrellas, and such, the kinds of things always hard to cram into the back of the wagon.

As Claire made the girls carry out some final items to the car, Mary Helen complained. "Daddy didn't make us pack the car for trips."

Claire rolled her eyes. "No, and I didn't appreciate before how much work that was for him."

"I'm tired," Suki said, dropping a suitcase to the ground by the car with a thump.

"If you girls are too tired to help pack the car, we can wait another day before leaving," Claire answered, watching their eyes pop.

"No, we'll help," Mary Helen said quickly.

Suki offered a smile meant to be cooperative. "My tote bag is all packed and ready, Mommy."

"That's good. What did you put in it?"

She wrinkled her nose, thinking. "Books to read, the color book and crayons Mrs. Gentry gave me, some My Little Ponies, Old Maid cards…"

"I packed my Go Fish cards, too," Mary Helen interrupted, "and we both put in our new Etch-a-Sketches that Ruthie and Bea's mother gave us." She paused. "We couldn't get our Cabbage Patch dolls in our tote bags, except sort of stuck in the top. Is that all right?"

Suki looked stricken. "We *can't* leave our dolls—my Evie Dawn and Mary Helen's Ruby June."

Claire smiled. The Cabbage Patch dolls the girls received for Christmas had quickly become favorites. They'd even come with full names and birth certificates. "Of course you can't leave your dolls. Remember to pack some of their clothes in your tote bags, too. You'll want them at the beach."

"Will you make our dolls a swimsuit?" Suki asked. "They really *need* one."

"Sure," Claire answered. "Ann's sewing machine is still at the beach house. I want to make some sun-suits for you and Mary Helen, too."

"Will you put pretty smocking on mine?" Mary Helen asked.

"Mine, too," Suki added.

"I'll put smocking on both. It will give me something to do while I watch you girls play on the beach."

"I *love* the beach. Will you carry me out in the deep water like Daddy?" Suki asked. "I'm afraid of the big waves by myself."

"Of course," Claire answered, shifting bags and boxes in the back of the station wagon to tuck in a few more items. "But you're older now and taller. You'll probably be able to walk out further in the waves than before."

"But I'll still need my water wings or my tube on," she answered, always the cautious one, unlike Mary Helen.

"Mommy, did you pack my canvas float?" Mary Helen asked. "I want to ride on the waves like I did last year."

"I think I remembered everything," Claire told them. "If I forgot anything, we can buy it when we get to the island."

Somehow they got the car loaded and Claire got two excited little girls into bed that night. She sat on the sofa in the living room to rest, after finishing a last cleaning of the house, and then dialed Parker's home phone.

"Parker here," he said, answering the phone much like Charles used to.

"Hi, it's Claire. I just wanted to phone and tell you the girls and I are finally heading to the beach in the morning."

"That's good. Kizzy Helton cleaned the house Friday to get things ready for you."

"That wasn't necessary, Parker. I can clean house."

He chuckled. "Kizzy would be real upset if you did that. She's taken care of our house at Edisto for years. She makes her living cleaning homes on the island and feels quite possessive about our place. I wouldn't want to change that for her."

"I guess not."

"Listen, I probably won't be able to get down to the island until the weekend," Parker said. "But if you encounter any problems, give me a call or call one of the neighbors. They all know you're coming and they're watching for you."

"That's nice. I'll look forward to seeing them again."

Claire thought about his last words after she hung up. The beach house on Edisto Island lay on Point Street at the island's south end, between several houses where locals lived full time, the Comptons, the Whaleys, and the Mikells. Across the street, and up and down the road in both directions, most of the homes were rentals. Parker's beach home, named Oleanders for the many flowering oleander shrubs around the house's foundation, lay between the Comptons' and Whaleys' homes with the Mikells' place just beyond. Over the years, visiting the island so often with Charles, and then with Charles and the girls, Claire had met all these families. It comforted her to know she would soon be seeing old friends again.

The next morning shortly before eight, Claire left for South Carolina and the beach. It felt sad in some ways pulling out of the driveway of the parsonage, vacating the old house, and leaving

Charles behind in the Trinity cemetery.

"I'm glad Daddy's going with us," Suki said, looking back, probably with similar thoughts. "Maybe he's riding along on the top of the car with us." She giggled, lightening Claire's heart with her words.

"I'll bet Daddy can fly like Superman now." Mary Helen raised her arms to demonstrate. "It would be cool to be able to fly."

The girls chatted and played happily as they started out. The kittens, loaded into the carrier beside Claire, meowed for a time and then settled down to sleep. Not surprisingly, both girls fell asleep not far up the road. They often slept through most long car trips.

Claire listened to the radio and her own thoughts as she followed the interstate over the mountain out of Tennessee and into North Carolina. The girls woke when she made a stop at a rest area inside the North Carolina line.

"How much further is it?" Suki asked, a familiar question often asked when they traveled.

On the big map on the wall in the visitor center, Claire showed them how far they'd come and how much further they had to go.

"That's *far*," Suki said, looking at the long line of roadway remaining.

"We'll be there before you know it," Claire replied.

The afternoon moved slower. Claire sang with the girls to keep them entertained, told them stories, and played car games like "I Spy" to pass the time. They stopped at a rest area in South Carolina for a picnic lunch, and the girls ran and played for a time to stretch their legs. The kittens seemed glad for a rest from the movement of the car, too, and for the food and water Claire offered them. She wished she could let them out to stretch their legs, too, but simply couldn't risk it. Even with a leash they might pull away from the girls and run off, creating a worse trauma. Claire had only sparingly used the sedative the vet provided, hoping the kittens would simply sleep through most of the trip. So far, they'd mewed a little but seemed to be handling the trip well.

"I want to *be* there already," Suki said a short time after they got in the car again.

"Me, too," said Mary Helen, sighing.

The girls complained and grew more quarrelsome at this point, tired from a long day of traveling.

"Tell us a story," Suki said.

Claire did, grateful the girls fell asleep again not long after. At nearly four in the afternoon, after turning off busy Highway 17 to travel on the quieter two-lane highway leading to Edisto Island on the coast, Claire said, "You girls might want to wake up now. We're almost to the draw bridge coming into Edisto."

They both sat up, excited and looking out the window.

"The bridge means we're almost there," Mary Helen said, bouncing in her seat now.

The Dawhoo Bridge lay across the Intracoastal Waterway. An old swing bridge, it could be shifted to one side to let passing boats through. An operator sat in a small box near the top of the bridge, watching the river for boats and then opening and shutting the bridge as needed. The girls were excited today because the bridge was closed to traffic, letting a shrimp boat pass through. Seagulls flew noisily around the boat hoping to get a treat from the catch.

"The boat's name is The Lady Bee." Mary Helen pointed through the car window. "See it painted on the side. Do boats always have names?"

"Many boats do," Claire answered.

"Beach houses can have names, too." Suki said. "What is our house's name?"

"Oleanders," Claire reminded her. "For all the flowering shrubs around the house, pretty rosy red and light pink oleanders."

"Pink like the house's roof," Mary Helen added.

"That's right." Claire smiled at her. "You have a good memory."

After a short wait, they were able to drive over the bridge, passing through sweeps of marshland with salt grass on either side. Giggling, the girls pointed to the old tree in the marsh, decorated with odds and ends of beach toys. It had been there for as long as

Claire could remember, displaying new items every year.

They soon drove through the historic section of the island, the car passing under massive live oak trees draped with Spanish moss and past old churches and buildings that had been on Edisto since earlier days.

Mary Helen began pointing out familiar spots now. "There's Bo Pigs where we like to eat and the big white Presbyterian Church we visited." She pressed her nose against the window. "There's the Old Post Office Restaurant and the snake place. What's the big word on the sign, Mommy?"

"Serpentarium," she answered. "It's a place where snakes and reptiles are kept for display and study, sort of like a snake zoo."

"Yukky. I don't want to go there," Suki said. "I don't *like* snakes. We won't see snakes at Edisto, will we?"

Claire glanced back to see a worried look on her face. "It's very unlikely, unless we take a boat tour back in the marshes."

"We might see an alligator though," Mary Helen told her.

"At our beach?" Suki squeaked out the words.

"No," Claire reassured her. "But we might see them in the water in the marshes or in the lagoons when riding our bikes in the Fairfield Resort."

"Look there's the old swinging bed!" Mary Helen pointed.

Claire laughed to see the old mattress suspended from chains from a big oak tree in front of one of the island houses. Sometimes they saw children playing on it, but today it simply swung gently in the breeze.

They passed familiar street names as they drew closer to the beach, Botany Bay Road and Oyster Factory Road, and then stores, shops, a bank, and the island's post office.

The girls were babbling with excitement as they wound their way down toward the beach now, passing the IGA grocery store, the only major grocery on the island, and the entrance to the Edisto Island State Park.

"We're here. We're here," Mary Helen announced, laughing. "I can see the ocean!"

"Me, too," Suki said. "It's so pretty."

Turning right by the park entrance and the Pavilion Restaurant, they headed up Palmetto Boulevard along the Atlantic Ocean. Between the beach houses to their left they could glimpse and hear the waves of the Atlantic Ocean crashing on the sandy beach.

Before Palmetto Boulevard reached the end of the island—the island only about eleven miles from end to end—they turned left to find Point Street, an unpaved side road, and then began to watch for Oleanders.

"There it is," cried Mary Helen at last, pointing, and Claire thought she felt as excited as the girls to see the familiar house tucked back from the road.

"I love, *love* our beach house," said Suki.

"It isn't *ours*," corrected Mary Helen. "But Parker said we could stay a long time, all summer if we want."

The beach house was a white cape cod home, with two dormers on the front roofline and a sweeping stairway winding up to a broad, covered front porch. The house had a soft pink, weathered roof and a shiny black front door and shutters. Like most homes on the island, Oleanders was built on stilts, well above ground, with enough room under the house for cars to park. Scraggly beach grass grew in the yard, along with an assortment of wild flowers scattered here and there. Palm trees waved in the ocean breeze around the yard and a big moss-draped oak grew to one side of the house, somehow surviving all the storms and weather of a beachside property.

Claire pulled into the driveway and then into one of the garage areas under the house, grateful to be here at last.

Despite the unpacking to be done, they had to walk down to the beach first to see the ocean for a minute. It was an old ritual.

A sandy path wound through tall grasses and dunes to drop down to the smooth beach. Only a few scattered umbrellas dotted the beach this early in May, although the weather was warm and balmy. They could see the waves more clearly now, rolling in to wash up the beach, leaving white foam behind, with pipers darting in and out of the receding water and gulls riding the sea breeze in the sky above—a lovely sight.

"Can we go swimming, Mommy?" Suki asked, pulling on Claire's hand.

Claire ruffled her hair. "We'll have days and days to swim and play at the beach, but right now we need to take the kittens inside to settle in and we have to unload the car. Work before play, remember?"

She heard Mary Helen sigh as they turned around to head back up the path to the car.

Claire carried the two kittens in first and put their carrier in the downstairs bathroom between her bedroom and a small sitting room, taking time to talk to the cats and pet them both. She opened their carrier so they could climb out, but shut the bathroom door as she left, not wanting either kitten to dash out of the house while she and the girls opened and shut doors unloading.

As Claire started to get the first suitcases out of the back of the station wagon, she saw Pete and Elaine Whaley and their children walking over from the house next door.

"Welcome back," Elaine called, coming to hug Claire while Jane and Emma raced to greet Mary Helen and Suki.

"We were so sorry to hear about Charles," Pete added, leaning over to give her a hug, too. He was a big man, fit and muscular with a rascally smile.

"Parker called to say you'd be coming tonight, so we wanted to help you unload and settle in." Elaine pushed a wisp of curly red-brown hair back from her face. "We also insist you come over to eat with us tonight. Pete is making his famous low country shrimp boil. I'm whipping up a salad on the side, and Tom and Chuck said they'd help crank homemade ice cream for dessert."

Claire greeted the Whaley children then—Tom at sixteen, taller than she remembered, his brown hair sun-kissed, Chuck, eleven, with his familiar grin and lighter hair, and the girls—Jane, who was Mary Helen's age, with red-brown hair like her mother's and a sunny smile, and Emma, the youngest, a year older than Suki, sweet-faced, her hair long and curly. It felt good to see them all again, tanned, smiling and happy.

With so many to help, they unloaded the car in a hurry. Then Elaine took the girls to her house with her, giving Claire a chance to unpack in quiet and to rest briefly after the long driving day.

Claire walked through the old beach house, seeing that little had changed. The downstairs, with its long living area down the middle of the house, led into an open dining space and branched off to a well-equipped kitchen on the left. A large master bedroom—Parker's room—lay behind it with a big private bath. On the other side of the living area lay a guest bedroom, always Claire and Charles's room when they visited, with a second bathroom and a cozy sitting room with views out to the ocean. Overhead big paddle fans moved the air softly in all the rooms.

Ann, with her excellent taste, had used a mix of old and new pieces throughout the house with lots of warm colors to make the house homey and comfortable. The predominant color scheme was a mixture of soft lime greens, coral pinks and red, with many of the walls in the bedrooms stenciled. Well-worn quilts draped the beds with colorful bed skirts below them. Pretty old chests and other pieces of fine furniture filled out the house. It was a fun house, stuffed with pillows, books, shells, and an eclectic mix of accessories—many with a story or a meaning attached.

Upstairs, the girls' rooms held cute twin bed sets in each and more fanciful furnishings. The big screened porch on the back of the house—probably Claire's favorite room—was packed with wicker pieces, old rockers, an assortment of tables, and rows of conch shells lining the deck railings.

Walking out on the screened porch and looking out to the sea, Claire felt a few tears slip out. Charles had loved it here. It felt sad to come again without him but it would have been sadder to stay on in the big parsonage by the church. She closed her eyes listening to the waves roll in, hearing the seagulls' calls on the wind, and feeling the soft sea breeze float in around her.

"It will be better for me and the girls to be here at the beach house right now, Charles," she said softly. "Parker was right. We need a little time for ourselves to heal, a space of quiet and peace, before moving on again."

Hearing the Whaleys next door—probably out on their porch, too—their laughter and talk carrying on the breeze, Claire headed out the door and down the steps to walk over to join them. For the girls' sake she would try to be happier, despite her sorrow, to help them and to help herself move on.

CHAPTER 6

Late May 1985

Parker had driven down to the beach house for several brief visits since Claire and the girls arrived, but today, with the Memorial Day weekend ahead, he was off for the entire weekend. He and Drake had recently hired an area college student to work at the store for the summer. Drake was training her this weekend, giving Parker extra free time at last.

He drove the convertible today with the top down, bringing groceries and some gifts for the girls. They waved at him from the screened porch as he pulled up.

Claire held the door open for him as he walked up the steps. He carried a small duffle, his gifts in a plastic bag, and an armful of groceries.

"Here, let me take one of those grocery bags into the kitchen." She took one of the bags and then peeped inside it. "You said a friend gave you flounder he'd caught when fishing."

"Yes, but the fish is in the cooler in the car, along with some shrimp. I thought I'd throw it all on the grill later."

"That sounds good." She followed him inside. "At the store yesterday, I bought fresh green beans and all the makings for a grits and cheese casserole and I made a devil's food cake."

"We'll eat well tonight." He helped her put the groceries away and then went out to the car to retrieve the cooler.

"You're early today. It's only nine thirty in the morning," Claire said as he came back into the kitchen.

"I wanted to get ahead of the holiday traffic." Taking the seafood out of the cooler he put it away in the refrigerator and then rinsed out the cooler.

Claire folded up the empty grocery sacks and put them under the sink. "We just finished breakfast. Did you have some before you came? I can make a quick omelet for you."

"No, I ate already, but I'd love a cup of coffee." He glanced toward the coffee pot.

"I'll pour you a cup. Go out on the porch and talk with the girls."

He carried his gift sack out with him. "I brought you girls a little gift." He opened the bag and pulled out two colorful plastic buckets, each packed with sand castle toys.

"Oh, boy!" Mary Helen began digging into hers with excitement. "We can make a great sand castle with these toys, Suki, with a big wall, a moat around it, and everything. Our little mermaid dolls can live in it."

"Can we go down to the beach right now and start it?" Suki asked, her eyes bright. "We've finished our breakfast."

Claire nodded as she came out to the porch with a mug of coffee for Parker. "Put on your swimsuits, flip flops, and sun lotion. You both know how to do that now. And take a towel to sit on. Parker and I will come down to watch in a little while, but until then you girls play where we can see you from the porch. And don't go in the water until we come down. Remember the beach rules."

"The tide is coming in now, too. Don't build your sand castle too low on the beach," Parker advised.

Suki nodded. "Or the waves will wash it away."

"We'll remember," Mary Helen said, heading into the house to change clothes. "We'll build our castle past the water line to keep it safe."

By the time the girls dashed back downstairs, Claire had heated a sweet roll for Parker and carried it out to the porch, along with a cup of coffee for herself as well. She slathered sun cream on the girls' backs—always a hard place to reach—before sending them out the door, giggling and excited.

"Looks like the sand toys were a hit," Parker said, picking up his sweet roll to take a bite.

Claire sat down at the table on the porch, smiling and following his glance to the girls scampering down the sandy path to the beach.

He watched her for a minute while her eyes followed the girls. She was a lovely woman—tall where Ann had been short—her dark brunette hair thick and long, her eyes a light chocolate brown flecked with white. In shorts today, she'd propped her long legs, tanned from her days on the beach, on a nearby chair. Claire had always exhibited a quiet grace and ease, and when she smiled, as she did now watching the girls, it lit up her whole face.

"It's good to see you smiling," he said, putting his sweet roll down and reaching for the hot coffee.

Claire sighed. "I have my moments, of course, but it's hard to stay too unhappy with the girls around."

"Their zest for life is infectious." Parker chuckled. "I'm looking forward to the weekend with them."

She fidgeted with her hands. "I feel bad that we're here on a holiday weekend like this. Wouldn't you have invited friends or family down if we weren't here?"

He shook his head. "I wouldn't have come to Oleanders at all if you and the girls weren't here. Ask Elaine. I've hardly come to the beach house since Ann died except a few times to bring Andrew."

"I like Andrew and I enjoyed meeting him earlier in the month when you brought him for the weekend." She frowned. "I'm sorry all the children were somewhat unkind to him, leaving him out of their play and then running off and deserting him."

"It's okay. Andrew is a somewhat quiet kid and at seven he's right in the middle between them in age. He's too young to interest the older children and hardly an ideal companion for the younger two."

"I did talk to them about it."

He sipped at his coffee. "I know you did, and you pushed on them to apologize. You made them all feel guilty."

She crossed her arms. "They needed to feel guilty."

"Perhaps." He considered the idea. "It's all right, though. Andrew has friends in Beaufort; he's not a social misfit—simply an outsider here, and he does make the numbers uneven. Chuck and J.T., both a few years older than Andrew, have been best friends since preschool. Andrew can hardly keep up with them or with Jane and Mary Helen, as active and adventurous as those two are. Little Suki at five and Emma, barely six, are younger than Andrew, wanting to play dolls or tea party most of the time." He saw her smile.

"I suppose you're right," she conceded, "but I believe that children should all find a way to play together with kindness and consideration for each other. I try to find games they *can* play together and I encourage them not to pair off too much."

"That's your early childhood education training kicking in. You are really good with the children." He finished off the last bite of sweet roll. "Elaine Whaley and Lula Mikell came into the store in Beaufort last week and said you were a natural with the kids, that their children always wanted to play over here with you all the time. They said you taught them games, sang and read with them, went on walks and bike rides with them, and took them over to the Edisto Zesto for ice creams."

"I like children and I like spending time with them."

"Well they're fascinated with all those fanciful stories you've created for them, too, and they love how you're always keep coming up with more new stories to tell them—even drawing sketches and pictures to go with them." He scratched his head. "I can't remember the storylines exactly."

She waved a hand. "Oh, I've been making up more stories about the Polka Dot kids. I used to play out those stories as a child with my friends; it's nothing special. I like to sketch and draw, and children love illustrations. I think pictures help stories come to life for children and make them more fun."

"Well, I'd say you're succeeding. You've already developed a small fan club here at Edisto," he commented. "Elaine Whaley loves how you work with Chuck, Jane, and Emma, and I could tell Lula Mikell was impressed with how much J.T. likes hanging around Oleanders since you came. She said she hasn't heard him say 'I'm bored' in weeks."

Claire smiled as she stood up to look toward the beach to see the girls better. "Mary Helen and Suki watch for the other kids to all come home from school every day. They're excited school is out now so they'll see more of their friends."

Parker's eyes wandered to a small, framed photo of Charles on a side table. "I read an article in a magazine about aneurysms the other day and I started thinking about Charles," he said. "The article said seventy-five percent show no symptoms at all, so there is seldom any warning."

Claire sat back down. "I've thought back many times, Parker, trying to remember if I saw anything that might have alerted me to trouble. As far as I remember Charles was vibrant and healthy in every way." She paused. "In some ways I like remembering him that way, and in other ways I wish I'd had more time, even if he'd lingered longer like Ann did."

"Ann's cancer crept up suddenly, too. Cancer like Ann had in the liver and bile ducts, and leading into the liver, shows few early symptoms. She was in stage four before we even realized something was wrong beyond a little fatigue and weight loss. I feel bad we didn't notice the jaundice more, that yellowing of her skin, but she was always so tan that it showed little. She seemed so healthy—working, laughing, busy. That diagnosis came as such a shock to us." He heaved a big sigh. "At that point not much could be done so Ann opted to simply enjoy what time she had left. She kept working while she could. She enjoyed training Nora Cavanaugh in the store and loved playing with Andrew. He was at a cute age then, about three years old when Nora came to work with us. You know we could never have children, so Ann really enjoyed Andrew, like she did your girls."

"Death is a nasty thing," Claire said, hugging herself as if chilled.

Parker felt guilty then for bringing up the subject. "I'm sorry I started talking about sickness and brought back sad memories to you."

She leaned over to pat his cheek. "No, it's a blessing when you bring it up sometimes so we can talk about it. Most people tiptoe around the subject. They're afraid they'll say something wrong, so they don't say anything at all." She glanced out toward the girls again, checking on them. "Sometimes when the girls are asleep, I play some of Charles's preaching tapes, just to hear his voice, to bring him back a little."

"I'd like to hear some of those." He turned his coffee cup in his hands, thinking back. "Charles was so charismatic, so dynamic. Having grown up with him it always surprised me to hear him preach later. It was if another person got a hold of him when he got in the pulpit."

Her mouth quirked in a small smile. "It was hardly another person that took hold when Charles preached. He used to tell me, 'I hope I can get out of the way so God can say what He wants to.'"

Parker leaned back in his chair. "That sounds like him. I liked watching that part of Charles develop, that man so relying on God, so sold out to the Lord. His messages were always motivational, never shallow or dry, and often convicting. Remember what he called the Bible?"

"Yes. The Handbook, The Instructional Manual, the Guidebook, the Textbook, God's Storybook. You never knew from Sunday to Sunday." Her eyes grew soft. "He'd say: 'Hold up your Instructional Manual. That tells you how to operate in this life. We're going to talk about that today...' And off he'd go. He made everyone use their Bibles. 'Look at Psalms 18, starting at verse 6', he'd say, and then he'd stop while everyone looked it up."

Parker looked toward Charles's picture, enjoying Claire's story. "I remember Charles said the people at Trinity weren't quite used to his methodology when he first started preaching there."

"No, but they soon came around. He got them excited. Trinity was a church that had been through problems and a split when we moved there from the small church in Sevierville where Charles served before. He helped the people at Trinity get zealous again, energized them to reach out into their community to bring people in. More than anything else he got them to read their Bibles more, to pray, and to want to be used of God, and that's what really made the difference."

"He changed their hearts, built their faith."

"Yes, he did." Claire stood to look out toward the sea. "He changed my heart toward the Lord, too. I had a very ritualistic relationship with God before I met Charles." She stopped, hesitating.

"There's no need to hesitate. Charles turned my relationship with God around ninety degrees, too—and Ann's. He had a true gifting."

"Perhaps." She sat down again. "But not in his earlier life."

"You're right about that. The zeal came later," Parker agreed. "Remember I grew up with him; I knew him longer than you."

"So you did," she said, sending him that warm smile again.

An old memory touched his mind. "Charles told me once that he picked the ministry at first for good intellectual reasons. 'But I was lucky,' he told me. 'God overlooked my arrogance and presumption in self-defining myself to be a man of God and called me along the way. I don't like to think what kind of minister I'd have been without His intervention. He shook up my conventional attitudes and showed me He wasn't a God-in-a-box.'"

Claire laughed a little at his words and Parker liked the sound of it. "I heard him share that often, too, especially when giving his testimony. He said it was powerful to share your experiences in faith, that we should do it more often, and that we should live to our fullest every minute of our lives."

They sat quietly for a minute.

"He's right," Parker said, "and this sunny day is getting away from us. Let's go down to the beach with the girls. I'd like to see what sort of sand castle they've started building."

Claire stood and began to gather up the cups and plates still on the table. "Keep an eye on the girls for a minute while I put these dishes in the sink and put my swimsuit on. Then I'll watch while you do the same. I don't like to leave the girls down on the beach without someone watching at any time."

"I understand," he said.

Parker took a few moments to think back on their words while Claire went to get ready for the beach. They'd shared a good talk, remembering Charles together. On another visit, they'd laughed about memories of Ann. He'd thought it would hurt more to share, to talk, and to remember, but it had felt better to do so. He still felt better for that talk.

"I'm glad you came," he told Clare when she returned. "It's been good to remember and share together."

"Yes, it has," she agreed. "I don't think we should lock all our feelings and remembrances away."

"No, we shouldn't," he agreed, getting up to go look for his own swimsuit, and knowing he'd done exactly that after Ann died.

Down at the beach, Parker helped Claire to put up the beach umbrella. Then he went back to the house to bring out a couple of chairs.

Claire put more sun lotion on the girls while he was gone and then some on herself, passing the bottle to him. While she settled into a striped beach chair, he helped the girls finish their sand castle and then they all waded out into the surf to wash the sand off and to play.

Both girls swam well but, at their young years, they still needed to be watched carefully—and taught more about the beach. Parker enjoyed this job, rattling off his beach knowledge, helping them to make new discoveries. Everything with children was always so fresh and new.

After their time playing in the ocean, they all took a walk down the beach to dry off and to enjoy the day. The girls scampered ahead of them, picking up shells, dashing in and out of the foam of the waves, pointing out sandpipers, and stopping to watch a long row of pelicans fly across the water in a neat line.

"Look, one swooped down to get a fish," Mary Helen called to them, pointing.

When they got back, Claire walked up to the house to make sandwiches and brought them down to the beach. After their lunch, Parker made little bread balls of the leftover bread and tossed them into the air for the seagulls to catch, making the girls laugh.

Parker set up a second umbrella after lunch, and Claire put a blanket under it for the girls. They read and played under it with their little mermaid dolls, getting out of the sun for a while and resting.

"What are those little dolls called?" Parker asked.

"They're called Sea Wees," Claire told him. "They're plastic and they can get wet, unlike most dolls. The girls love to brush out their hair and to play pretend games with them in the swimming pool or here at the beach."

"Have you visited with all the neighbors now?"

"We shared dinner with the Mikells and the Whaleys a few times, but Elaine and Lula are both busy—Elaine working at their realty and Lula helping John at their bike and boat rental shop. With the tourists coming in now I'll probably see less of both families." She paused to watch a row of pelicans fly overhead.

"Isabel and Ezra Compton came over to visit one night, too, and of course I had to take Mary Helen to Isabel's shop The Little Mermaid on one of the first days we arrived at Edisto. She absolutely loves that store. Suki, too."

"It's a cute place, full of children's things. I'm not surprised that the girls like it." Parker paused, before asking, "What have you been doing with yourself since you've been here?"

She smiled across at him. "Don't worry that I've been bored or lonely. Not with the girls and all the other children around. I've helped Mary Helen and Suki finish their year-end schoolwork during part of each day, and we've had fun revisiting all our favorite places on the island—enjoying them before all the summer tourists begin to come. It's nice seeing things while it's quieter here."

Parker glanced down the beach. "By tomorrow the beach will be busy with the holiday weekend."

"Yes, but you know it's never too crowded at Edisto. That's part of its charm. I hope it will always stay special in that way. Where else can you go where there are no multi-storied hotels packed along the beachfront, all stuffed with people? Edisto is simply beach homes and the villas in Fairfield. Fairfield is a beautiful resort, too, built on the remains of the old Oristo resort and the land of an earlier plantation. I'm so proud they kept the graceful, old live oaks throughout, preserved the loveliness of the land. Even the lagoons they created and the rental villas and homes are so pretty. The girls and I love to ride our bikes through the resort and on the bike trail around the island. This is a special place, Parker. You and Ann are blessed to own a home here."

He knew she was right but he also knew he hadn't appreciated it much in the last years since losing Ann.

"Thanks for pushing on me to come to Edisto for a time," she said. "It was the right choice for me. It has helped me being here. I've needed this time—and perhaps this place—to grieve in my own way. To begin to think about what the girls and I will do next."

He didn't push her to tell him what that might entail.

Suki had rolled over onto the blanket and fallen asleep, so Claire and Mary Helen took a little walk down the beach together, leaving Parker to keep guard. A shadow caused him to glance up to see a familiar face smiling at him.

"Well, hello, Parker Avery, I haven't seen you down here in a long time." Miles Lawrence reached out a hand to shake his. Miles's mother Eudora, now widowed, owned the beach house three doors down from Oleanders, just past the Comptons' place. Eudora seldom came to the house anymore, but Miles or his brother Carlton came now and then.

"I haven't seen you for a long time either," Parker said, taking in Miles' tall blond good looks. "Are you still teaching at the College of Charleston?"

"I am," he said. "I stopped in at Westcott's one day with mother when we were in Beaufort but I missed seeing you."

Miles dropped into Claire's empty chair. "This summer I may be down here at the beach house a little more. I have a textbook due and I need a quiet place to work on it." He glanced behind them toward Parker's home and then toward Suki sleeping on the quilt under the umbrella. "Will you be down here more often, too?"

"A little more." Parker's eyes moved to Claire and Mary Helen walking up the beach. "My brother's wife and her two girls are staying here for a time, perhaps the summer. Maybe longer. She recently lost her husband. It's a difficult time for her."

He glanced toward Claire. "I'm sorry for your loss. And hers."

"Thank you."

Miles was quiet for a moment and then began to whistle softly.

Parker gave him a quizzical look.

"I was whistling the old classic song "The Girl From Ipanema"— you remember it. That's what I think of when I see a tall, tan, young, and lovely woman like that walking down the beach."

With a little surprise Parker realized he was talking about Claire.

"She's got such grace, sort of a soft, natural poise." Miles studied her. "She looks like an un-awakened woman in some ways though. Fascinating."

Parker scowled at him. "Claire is my brother's wife, Miles."

"Well, of course." Miles smiled at him. "I'm a psychologist, if you remember. I study people, their personalities, their dynamics. It fascinates me. Don't take any offense at my interest. It's professional."

Parker doubted that, but he let it go as Miles stood now, seeing Claire approaching. Parker made the introductions and watched Miles's eyes rove over Claire's face—and more. A stab of what felt a lot like possessive jealousy, mixed with protectiveness, rolled over Parker. Of course he knew Charles's wife was beautiful, just as Ann had been beautiful in her way.

He listened to Miles talk—that smooth, Charlestonian Southern voice of his charming Claire and Mary Helen. Miles was one of those men with a way with women. Parker had never noticed that much before.

By the time Miles said goodbye and strolled back up the beach, Parker was seething inside and for no good reason. Whatever was wrong with him? Surely he couldn't be developing feelings for his brother's wife? His brother's *recently widowed* wife! He'd obviously been out of the dating scene for too long to suddenly begin noticing Claire through Miles Lawrence's eyes.

"What an interesting man," Claire said, sitting back down beside him. "And very charming."

Charming indeed, Parker thought with an inner snarl, but he carefully didn't offer a remark back.

CHAPTER 7

June 1985

A week later, while Claire sat adding decorative smocking to two sundresses she was making for the girls, she saw Elaine Whaley and Lula Mikell coming up the beach path. Claire sat outside today under the rustic cabana, a small, thatch-roofed beach hut situated a few feet off the sandy pathway between Oleanders and the ocean. Ann's parents had built the hut years ago, a picturesque, covered oasis close to the beach. A few weathered wooden Adirondack chairs sat inside the hut in a semicircle with a battered picnic table nearby.

Claire could hear the children's voices where they played a few feet away from her—Mary Helen and Suki, Elaine's three younger children, Chuck, Jane, and Emma, and Lula's boy J.T., the same age as Chuck. The teens, Tom Whaley and Ryder Mikell, were on the beach today, too, keeping watch over their younger siblings while playing volleyball with a net they'd set up and ogling the girls that walked by.

"I've always loved this old porch," Lula said, climbing the few steps to reach its plank floor. She settled into a chair beside Claire's, while Elaine pulled another over closer to them.

"Are there drinks in the cooler?" Elaine asked.

"Yes, help yourself," Claire said. She studied the difference in the two women while they picked out drinks and chattered. Both were fit and athletic-looking, Elaine with curly, reddish-brown hair always tossed by the sea breeze, hazel eyes, and a sprinkling of freckles, Lula—slightly younger—with sun-streaked brown hair in a short cut brushing her shoulders, eyes china blue and her skin well tanned. Neither women were beauties, although attractive, but both always exhibited gracious, Southern manners and spoke with the low country accents of women born and raised on the island.

Elaine pushed her sunglasses up on her head as she settled into a chair with her canned cola. "We're in a pickle, Claire," she said. "I don't mind to admit it."

"What's wrong?" Claire asked, laying her sewing aside for a minute, seeing both women upset.

"Our babysitter for the summer bailed on us," Lula said with a heavy sigh, dropping her sunglasses on a small table beside her. "That's why our older boys are out on the beach today keeping watch on the kids."

"It's really made for extra work for Pete and me at the realty office with our older son not there every day." Elaine leaned back in her chair and crossed her legs. "Now that Tom's sixteen and can drive, he does all sorts of errands for us at the office, taking keys to people who lock themselves out, checking on problems with the rentals, following up on the cleaning staff to be sure the units are ready to rent again. Pete's been teaching him to work on the desk and handle the phones now, too, checking renters in and out. We really need him at the office."

Lula jumped into the conversation. "We miss Ryder at our business, too." She glanced toward Claire. "You know we own Mikell's Island Rental, renting bikes, boats and kayaks, golf carts, and other beach supplies. Summer is our busiest season. Ryder works with Carlos, one of our employees, to do all the bike deliveries and pickups for us every day. Like Tom, Ryder works in the shop and outside where we keep many of the rentals. He helps tourists decide on a bike, adjusts the seats for them, puts a basket on if they want to rent one, or adds a child's seat on the back. John and I struggled all day today zipping in and out of the store, trying to do our jobs and his."

Claire smoothed back a strand of hair the sea breeze had blown from the big clip she'd pinned her hair up with today. "You should have called me. I'd have watched the younger ones so Ryder and Tom could work." She saw Elaine and Lula eye each other.

Elaine leaned forward. "If you really mean that, Claire, we'd love to ask a favor. Lula and I wondered if you could watch our younger ones, Chuck, J.T., Jane and Emma, until we can track down a new sitter."

"It really inconvenienced us that the Bladen's daughter Jessica dumped out on us." Lula made a face. "She got a better paying job in Charleston through a friend, plus a free place to stay."

"Naturally she'd rather party and kick up her heels in Charleston versus staying at home with her folks for the summer. In a way you can't blame her, but she gave us *no* notice. Just waltzed out on us." Elaine straightened the visor she wore, the words Whaley Realty embroidered across it.

"I remember being that age and wishing I could leave the island for the summer." Lula sighed.

Claire considered their request, not sure how to answer.

Elaine leaned toward her again. "If you would do this for even a few days each week, we wouldn't lose the boys every day. It really would be a tremendous help to us. Lula and I will pay you what we planned to pay Jessica and throw in some island discount coupons, too."

She named the hourly figure they'd paid Jessica, which sounded lavish to Claire. Did sitters get that much today? She'd certainly never paid that to get someone to sit for the girls in Sweetwater.

Lula sighed. "I know it's a lot to ask with all you're going through, Claire, getting over the loss of your husband, wanting a little quiet vacation time here at the island…"

"We know Chuck and J.T. can be a handful, too—those two daredevils," Elaine interrupted. "Even Jane and Emma often get whiney and start little childish spats that sometimes get really annoying."

"It's four kids to keep an eye on, plus your two," Lula added. "That's six children at once. It's not an easy job to consider."

Elaine heaved a big sigh and turned to Lula. "Surely if we ask around we can find someone to do this, Lula, without bothering Claire. Now that we're here I feel simply awful even asking her to consider it."

Claire smiled. "Why should you feel awful to ask me? The children already spend so much time with me. They come over most every day anyway to play and I enjoy them."

Lula's eyes lit up. "You'd really consider it? J.T. begged me to ask you. He was never enthusiastic about Jessica sitting for him this summer. He practically whooped when I told him she bolted to Charleston."

Elaine rolled her eyes. "Chuck said she stayed on the phone half the time while she babysat. She flirted with all the boys when down at the beach, too." She shrugged. "But I suppose that's what teenage girls do."

"*And* teenage boys." Lula pointed toward the beach where Tom and Ryder preened for a group of young girls in bikinis walking by. "The sooner those two Romeos get back to work the better. I don't want any complaints from the tourists about them."

Elaine smiled. "We acted as bad as those boys when we were younger, simpering and flirting with the tourists every summer. With the island so small, it was exciting to connect with all those cute boys coming to vacation at the beach."

"Perhaps so." Lula leaned her head back against her chair again and giggled. "Did you spend your summers flirting with boys somewhere, Claire?"

"I usually spent my summers at camp or at my Grandmother Levene Hampton's gray-shingled home on Martha's Vineyard," Claire replied.

"Oh, I've always heard about Martha's Vineyard." Lula's eyes lit up. "Is it beautiful there?"

"Yes, but in a different way from Edisto."

The subject shifted from flirting to travel. But soon Elaine and Lula began to talk about the children again. They discussed the hours and times they wanted Claire to keep them, the rules they expected their children to follow, where to contact them during the day, and other details—most not needed since the children had already reiterated these rules to Claire before.

"You don't need to pay me to help until you find someone to take care of the children," Claire put in.

Lula looked appalled. "Elaine and I wouldn't consider you doing it for nothing. Fair is fair. We've paid sitters for years, working as we do."

"You're *definitely* getting paid," Elaine agreed. "So don't even think about arguing that point. We'll write everything down for you about the kids. That's easier than us trying to tell you everything right now and expecting you to remember it all."

Lula stood up then. "I need to round up my two and head toward the house. We need to help John close the store. Then we're going to dinner at my mother's." She glanced at Claire. "You might remember my mother lives here on the island."

After Lula left, Elaine sat back in her chair, draining out the last of her cola. "Tell me honestly if you think this is too much for you, watching all these kids for a week or so. We probably wouldn't have asked if the kids hadn't suggested it. They literally begged us to ask you." She grinned. "You've got a Pied Piper's way with children, Claire Avery. They seem to mind you in a remarkable way, too. I don't know how you do it."

"I told Parker this weekend I really like children and enjoy spending time with them."

"Well, I'll sell you mine cheap." Elaine laughed. "You know I'm kidding," she added. "But Lula and I *really* do appreciate you helping us out in this situation. Promise you'll tell me if it's too much for you or if it becomes a problem."

Claire held up a hand. "I promise."

Isabel Compton waved to them from her porch next door and then walked over to join them. A mid years woman in her early fifties, she had dark, gray-streaked hair she wound at the base of her neck in a bun and merry gray eyes. She wore one of the colorful, long print skirts she favored with a knit top over it that said in lovely script on the front: *I Used To Be A Mermaid.*

Elaine laughed when Isabel drew close enough for her to read the words. "I'll bet you get some interesting comments about that shirt, don't you?"

"I do," Isabel said, settling into the chair Lula vacated. "It gives me a great opportunity to tell anyone who makes a comment about my store, The Little Mermaid." She smoothed the shirt with one hand. "Naturally I tell them we sell shirts just like mine in the store in all sizes and several colors. I'm a walking advertisement."

Claire and Elaine both giggled.

Isabel leaned over then to pick up the sundress Claire had been smocking. "This is exquisite." She studied it. "If you want to make some side money, darling, just bring me any of these you have time to make—or any of those sweet sundresses your girls wear with the smocking across the top. I could sell any of those pretty items and make us both a little extra money."

Elaine studied the checked sundress, smocked with yellow ducklings. "Emma and Jane would love one of these. They're always talking about how much they like the sundresses Mary Helen and Suki wear."

"Did you talk Claire into watching the kids?" Isabel asked Elaine, direct as always. She turned to Claire. "I knew Elaine and Lula were in a bad situation with that flighty Jessica bailing out on them."

"Thankfully, Claire said yes," Elaine answered. "The blessed woman."

Isabel smiled at Claire. "You are one of the good ones. We all love you and hope you'll simply stay with us now that you're widowed. It would be a good place for the girls to grow up." She studied the sundress again. "Maybe if we can keep you, I can wheedle you into making more of these for the shop."

"Mary Helen loves your store, Isabel," Claire replied. "You have a good way with children yourself."

Isabel shook her head. "I'm not so sure about that, but I *love* that Mary Helen of yours. When I took her down to the store with me last week, she rearranged three shelves of goods until they were all more appealing to customers, redesigned one of my store windows, and made the cutest jewelry display for me. That child has a natural gift for retail. She talked to the people who came in the store like she was nineteen instead of nine. I'd like to steal that one away from you. She feels like myself at the same age."

"That's a nice compliment." Claire took the sundress back from Isabel.

"No, it's simply the truth." Isabel glanced toward the beach where the girls and Chuck still played, all probably looking for shark's teeth in the sand. "One of the reasons I walked over this afternoon was to see if you'd let me take Mary Helen to the shop with me again one day."

"I'm sure she'd love it."

Isabel, always a little restless, picked up a sketchbook of Claire's from the picnic table that Claire had weighted down with a big conch shell. "Did you draw and paint these pictures?" she asked, flipping through the little designs Claire had sketched and later embellished with soft watercolors.

Claire nodded. "I like to doodle a little, keep my hands busy."

Isabel shook her head. "Dear one, this isn't doodling. You have a gift." She passed the sketchbook to Elaine. "Look at this one of the girls playing down on the beach."

"Oh, my." Elaine leaned closer to look at it. "It's really good."

"It's more than good. If we matted and framed some of these paintings, I could sell them in the shop." She leafed through the sketchbook. "You could ink some of these little calligraphy quotes and thoughts below them to make them even more special and unique."

Claire seemed stunned at the idea of her work being saleable. She wanted to ask: *Do you really think anyone would buy them?* But she held her tongue. Isabel Compton never joked about business.

Seeming to key in on Claire's surprise, Isabel leaned over to pat her cheek. "Miles Lawrence said you were an untapped treasure."

Claire knew her eyes flew wide at the remark.

"When did you meet the charming Mr. Lawrence?" Elaine asked. "I haven't seen him down here at the beach in ages."

"He's spending some time here this summer trying to get a textbook finished he has a contract on." Isabel continued looking through Claire's sketchbook as she talked. "He likes my husband Ezra, who's in practice as a psychiatrist near Charleston. They like to talk shop, pick people apart, share stories."

"I thought psychiatrists and psychologists were ethically required to be discreet about their patients," Elaine said.

"Oh, of course they are." Isabel waved away Elaine's comment. "The two just talk in generalities and debate the merits of different counseling techniques, Behaviorist versus Gestalt, that sort of thing. Bores the average person to tears. I leave the room and go read another chapter in a nice romance novel."

Claire laughed. She always enjoyed Isabel.

Tom walked up the path from the beach with Chuck and the girls trailing behind him, all dragging beach towels and toys piled in plastic totes.

"Mom, I have a game tonight. A bunch of us guys are practicing a little scrimmage up at the football field at Country Day School. We need to get home so I can eat something and get ready." Seeing Claire, Tom asked, "Did Ms. Claire say she would keep all the little chipmunks?"

"I'm not a chipmunk!" Jane claimed, hearing him.

Elaine sent Tom a warning look. "Claire graciously said yes— until we can find a sitter." She got up and helped the girls with the towels and toys they struggled to carry. Saying goodbye to all, she started across the yard to her house next door—called simply the Whaley House, after generations of Whaleys who had called it home.

"You were sweet to help Lula and Elaine out," Isabel said after they left.

Mary Helen leaned against Claire's leg. "Are you really going to look out for all the kids since their sitter quit?" she asked, picking up quickly on the adult conversation.

"Yes, I am for a time. I hope you and Suki don't mind."

"No, it will be fun." Suki danced up and down, obviously pleased, and Mary Helen smiled broadly.

"Looks like your girls are happy about the plan." Isabel pushed up from her chair. "I suppose I'd better amble back to my place. I just saw Ezra's car pull in the driveway."

"I like Isabel," Mary Helen said as she walked out of earshot.

"She likes you, too, and wants you to come back to the shop with her another day, if you'd like."

"Can I really?" Mary Helen put both hands up in a prayerful gesture.

"Of course. Isabel says you're a wonderful help in the store." Claire began to gather her sewing, sketchbooks and art supplies into her tote bag.

Suki's mouth formed into a pout. "Can I go, too?"

Before Mary Helen could pop a reply, Claire answered. "It would be a long day for you, sweets, but you and I can drop by the store and perhaps do something special you'd like to do that day."

Mary Helen frowned. "Won't you be keeping the kids every day?"

"Not all day every day. Times when Elaine is off, she'll watch them and the same with Lula. I'll fill in around their work schedules."

"Then we can still have special times all by ourselves," said Suki, who sometimes—more than the others—got lost in the crowd, being the youngest.

"We'll always make some special time for ourselves," Claire answered, giving Suki a hug. "Right now we need to go make supper."

"What are we having?" Mary Helen asked, picking up beach toys and towels to head toward the house.

"Left over spaghetti from last night and a salad."

This got an enthusiastic response, especially after ice cream for dessert was added into the mix.

After supper, the girls were invited to the Whaleys next door to watch a movie with Emma and Jane. Elaine had picked up the movie *Annie* at the video rental store for the girls to watch, a 1982 musical Mary Helen and Suki were eager to see again.

Claire took the opportunity to take a walk down the beach by herself. The moon, full for the last night or two, ran a long, shining ribbon of light across the ocean as darkness fell.

She passed others strolling on the beach and a few kids still playing in the edge of the waves as she walked up the shore toward the Fairfield Cabana, a spot where teens often clustered around the porch visiting. Claire loved the quiet of the evening. The sound of the waves, washing up on the beach, created such a peaceful feeling in the soul.

As she walked she thought about Charles and then about what she could do to entertain the children over the next days.

"A penny for your thoughts," she heard a voice say, and turned to see Miles Lawrence behind her.

Claire paused. "It's a nice night for a walk," she said.

He moved to walk along beside her. "Yes, it is, but you didn't answer my question."

"I wasn't thinking about anything special. How is your book coming?" she asked, remembering why he'd come to the beach to stay for a time.

"I'm writing a new textbook on theories and techniques for psychotherapy and counseling—actually an update of an older textbook written by a colleague who passed on. I've taught the course using the book for years, so I seemed a natural choice to revise it. I've also written other texts for the same educational publisher."

"I see." She gave him a small smile. "Tell me how you feel about that?" she asked.

He laughed out loud. "You've had some counseling background to hit me with that one, Claire Avery."

She smiled more broadly. "My husband Charles took some counseling courses to help him in the ministry and he shared a lot of what he learned with me. He practiced some of the techniques on me. I remember many of them included a lot of repetition of that particular question."

"Amazing how well it works when even lay people know it." He stopped to pick up a shell. "I guess everyone likes to talk about themselves and how they feel if given the opportunity."

She changed the subject, glancing toward the shell in his hand. "That's an oyster shell. Even though many people think it's ugly with all the little shells, humps, and bumps clinging to its back, I like the oyster shell."

He turned those probing blue eyes toward hers again. "I see you've read Anne Morrow Lindbergh's book *Gift From the Sea*. You probably identify with the oyster shell at your point in life. It's an appropriate shell to represent a married woman with children and many responsibilities and obligations."

"I'm fond of Lindbergh's book," she answered. "It's a favorite of mine."

"Lindbergh's little book is a wise text." Miles turned the shell over in his hand, studying it as he walked. "Who are you underneath all the shells and barnacles clinging to you, Claire Avery?"

Claire didn't reply. She wasn't sure she liked this man's probing.

"You're not sure," he answered for her when she didn't respond. "And you dislike me somewhat for asking."

Claire frowned. "Who are *you* under your shells and barnacles?" she asked, turning the tables on him.

"A professor, a counselor, a man with only the shells and barnacles I've specifically *chosen* to carry." He stopped as Claire paused to look out across the water at the moon growing brighter in the darkening sky.

Miles moved closer to her then. "I am certainly a man who appreciates a beautiful woman, too." His voice grew soft on those last words.

Shocked, Claire stepped away, looking up the beach to see how much further the path to her beach house was.

He chuckled. "Don't panic, pretty woman. I'm turning off here." He pointed to the path ahead. "This is our house at Edisto— Heron's Watch, named for the widow's watch above it."

Claire, still uncomfortable, wasn't sure what to say.

"Even a woman recently widowed should like to hear a man say she is beautiful. Is there anything wrong with the truth?"

She considered his words, but had no answer. "I hope the work on your book goes well," she said instead, starting away from him toward Oleanders.

He caught her hand, surprising her. "Think while you're here at the beach about who you are Claire Avery. Who are you besides a wife, a mother—and considering your past—a woman who everyone in the church probably had expectations of and who, by necessity, carried out many obligatory roles?"

"You hardly know me," she said, pulling her hand away.

"I may know you better than you think." He smiled at her, a knowing, self-assured smile that disconcerted her.

Claire turned, wanting to put distance between herself and this probing, arrogant man. Who did he think he was analyzing her like a bug here on the beach? Flirting with her subtly? Didn't he know she'd only recently buried her husband?

He let her go, not saying more, but as she glanced back a final time, he called softly, "The one who finds herself frees herself, Claire Avery."

She all but ran up the beach then, eager to get away.

Sitting on the screened porch afterward, hugging herself as if chilled, Claire couldn't help but think about her odd conversation with Miles Lawrence and about his knowing words. There was something elusively drawing about him that disturbed her. When he looked at her, the feelings he stirred in her troubled her even more, for they were feelings a woman should only consider for a man she was attracted to.

CHAPTER 8

August 1985

The summer weeks seemed to speed by. Parker felt shocked when he flipped the calendar in the beach house to the month of August.

"Hard to believe it's August already," he said to Claire, who was fixing sandwiches for lunch at the counter in the kitchen.

She didn't reply at once, and he saw her frown over his words.

"Yes, the summer has flown by," she said at last, not adding more.

Parker sensed in the last weeks a restlessness growing in Claire that he couldn't put his finger on. She seemed troubled and often distracted with her own thoughts whenever he came down to the beach.

"It was nice you could bring Andrew down this weekend," she said, making an effort to be cordial. "He seems to be growing more comfortable with the children."

"Andrew especially loves sitting and listening to Suki play the piano in the evenings." He glanced toward the piano in the living room where Ann used to play in the past. "Has Suki taken a lot of lessons?"

"I've been teaching her," Claire told him, getting a bag of chips from a shelf to put on the counter. "She's only five, but she plays primarily by ear. From an early age, she doodled around on the piano with sounds and chords, mimicking songs she heard or making up her own little melodies."

She paused before continuing, taking a jar of pickles from the refrigerator. "Charles and I thought of it as only fun for her at first but gradually began to realize her songs and melodies were growing more complex. Charles did some reading and said he thought we shouldn't push her too hard into lessons right away. He read that music teachers often look down on playing piano by ear, like Suki did so easily. However, we knew she needed to learn to read music, to learn theory, and to train her gift more, so I started teaching her basics." Claire smiled. "She gets annoyed at how much slower her playing is when she has to follow the sheet music."

"I'm always surprised at how much time she spends at the piano for such a little girl. That playing and practicing can only keep improving her natural gift. It especially interests me how frequently she sits down to play at the piano without anyone asking her to." Parker leaned against the counter beside Claire. "I've never heard you ask her to practice once."

"I've never needed to. She simply loves to play and make music." Claire laughed. "On the other hand, when I ask her to clean her room it's a different matter entirely."

Parker laughed with her. "Suki has a good ear for pitch. Most people gain this ability over time playing an instrument, but not many show a musical aptitude this early, or as naturally, as Suki does."

"Sometimes it worries me," Claire said, turning to him. "When a child holds a gift of any kind, either an intellectual, musical or artistic gift, a parent wants to encourage it and nourish it without squelching their talent or pushing the child too much. I've tried to read more about musical giftings."

"I don't think you need to worry. Even as a baby, Suki loved anything musical—a musical mobile, a chiming toy, records you played for Mary Helen. I remember her crawling into the room as a baby whenever music came on the television or record player."

"I suppose she did."

"Suki came with a natural, inborn love for music. She'll find her way with it. Try not to worry about it."

"Thanks." She loaded the plate of sandwiches, chips, pickles, carrots, and celery sticks onto a tray. "Take these out on the porch to the table and call the children in. I'll bring the drinks out. Mary Helen, Suki, and Andrew are playing a children's game they love, called Rock School, on the front porch steps. I told them not to go far. You and I can eat inside in the kitchen. I have leftover homemade vegetable soup for us from last night and some fresh bread."

When Parker came back inside, he saw Claire had already put their soup on the table, along with bread and relishes.

He sat down, offered grace, and dug in. He always enjoyed getting homemade meals on the weekends with Claire and the girls.

Watching her frown a little over her lunch, he finally asked, "What is bothering you, Claire? I can tell something is on your mind."

"I've received several critical calls from my mother lately. She clearly let me know of her disapproval in my staying so long here at the beach." Claire propped her chin on her hand and sighed. "She keeps telling me I should be settling the girls into a new life, looking for a job, thinking to the future. She often speaks casually of Charles's death, as though I should view it like a coat outgrown. She says I should be leaving the past behind by now, moving on, getting on with things, and making a new life versus ruminating down here."

"Ruminating?" He almost laughed.

"Don't laugh." She gave him a cautionary look. "It is time for me to make plans to head back to Arlington."

"Claire, I told you before that you don't need to go back to Arlington this fall unless you want to. You can stay here. The children can go to school on the island. The Edisto Beach Primary School is small but it's a good school with a good reputation. I know several of the teachers there."

"Elaine told me the same thing," she said, picking at a slice of bread on her plate. "But I can't stay here forever. I worked some this summer, taking care of Elaine and Lula's kids through most of June and July, and then I worked at The Little Mermaid for Isabel when she sprained her ankle." She smiled. "Mary Helen loved that. She went with me every day to the store, while I usually left Suki at Isabel's next door. Isabel said Suki played the piano for her and they listened to classical music together. Suki loved it; she learned about Beethoven, Bach, and all those composers. Isabel and Ezra own a nice collection of classical records, and Ezra brought home library books about the composers for Isabel to read to Suki."

"I'm sure there are other jobs you could find on the island or nearby if you wanted to stay."

He watched her hesitate, twisting her hands, before replying. "A few people have mentioned that it's hardly proper for me to stay longer at my husband's brother's home, especially with you coming down so many weekends."

Parker knew his mouth dropped open. "You mean someone suggested it's improper because we're both widowed?"

Claire looked down at her lap.

Vexed now, Parker asked, "Who's been saying things like that to you?"

She hesitated. "My mother, but also yours. When Edith talked to me the last time, she said we needed to think about how it looked—two single people spending so much time together. She said a lot of people wouldn't see it as proper."

He snorted. "That sounds like my mother. You shouldn't pay any attention to what she says or to what your mother says either."

"Both do have a point, Parker." A worry line formed across her forehead. "Even some of the children asked me if we were going to get married. If my girls begin to go to school here this fall, with us still living in your home, there might be more talk. I wouldn't want that for the children's sake or ours."

"You're my brother's wife, Claire." Parker's temper flared.

She waved a hand at him. "I know that, but I'm also a single woman living rent free in a man's home. That's how some people see it."

"I don't think we should pay any attention to that sort of nonsense." Parker sat back in his chair, annoyed.

"It's been good of you to let us stay here so long." Claire stood and began to clear plates and bowls from the table. "Let me take some cookies out to the children now. I baked oatmeal cookies this morning. You'll want a few, too."

Parker's eyes followed her as she took cookies outside and stood talking and laughing with the children for a few minutes. His heart wrenched at the idea of her leaving. He knew he was beginning to care for her far more than he should. And he hated the idea that his mother—and hers—had introduced the notion to Claire that it wasn't proper for her to stay longer in his home. His mother alluded to the same thing to him a few times, as well, but he'd sluffed it off. He knew his and Claire's relationship was innocent except for his own feelings and he'd kept them well hidden. He knew, too, Claire wasn't ready for another relationship and he honestly had no idea if she could ever view him as anything other than Charles's brother.

She came back in and put a plate of cookies on the table for them. "Do you want ice cream, too?" she asked.

"No, this is fine," he said, reaching for a couple of cookies.

"Everyone seems to have ideas for my life," Claire said, sitting back down and picking up their former conversation. "My mother, my sisters, your mother. Even Leona, my best friend back in Sweetwater, wrote to tell me about a possible job opening in one of the schools there. She sent me a picture of a little house for rent not far from her place and the church. She said she thought the girls would be happy staying where they had friends, and knew the school, church, and town. She made a very good case for why I should return."

"Do you want to go back to Sweetwater?"

She closed her eyes. "I simply don't know what I want. Isn't that sad? Everyone seems to know what's best for me, but I can't seem to know myself. I've prayed and prayed about it. But I don't seem to get any answers."

Parker wanted to push her to stay, to offer her all the reasons why he felt she should, but he hated to add himself to the growing list of those who seemed to know Claire's best life course and direction better than she did.

"You'll find your way," Parker said instead. "What seems most right to you and for the girls is what you should do."

"Thank you. I'm glad someone has confidence in me." She smiled at him, making him glad he hadn't said more.

"Are we still going to Fort Sumter in Charleston today?" Mary Helen asked, poking her head in the door with Andrew and Suki behind her with wide eyes. "You *said* after lunch."

Parker grinned. "I did say after lunch, so as soon as you're ready we'll go." Parker grinned watching the three children erupt with excitement. He'd taken them to many different tourist and historic spots over the summer, thinking they were old enough now to appreciate them.

Claire went into action, giving instructions about getting teeth brushed, changing into socks and tennis shoes instead of beach flip flops, and reminding them to put on sun lotion. Parker knew she'd been teaching the girls about Fort Sumter this week so they would know some of its history before they left.

A short time later he and Claire had loaded the three children into the back of his convertible and were on their way.

"How far is it to the fort?" Suki asked.

"About forty-five minutes to Charleston by car. We'll park near Concord Street and get on the Fort Sumter Tour boat that will take us across to the island that Fort Sumter is on."

"When was Fort Sumter built?" Claire asked as they drove through the marshlands heading away from the island.

"Before the Civil War," Andrew answered.

"Very good." Claire turned to smile at Andrew. "It was built in the 1800s, not long before South Carolina seceded from the Union."

"I've been coaching him," Parker said, looking in the rear view mirror with affection at the tanned, fair-haired, blue-eyed boy he'd watch grow from only a small tyke.

"What does 'secede' mean?" Suki asked.

"The south didn't want to be a part of the United States anymore," Mary Helen told her. "Secede means they told the north they were quitting."

"The South and North got mad at each other over slavery," Andrew added. "That's what started the Civil War and the first shots of the war were fired from Fort Sumter."

"Fort Sumter is famous because it's where the Civil War began," Parker said. "The first battle at Fort Sumter was in April, 1861. The Confederate soldiers fired on a Union Garrison. In the second battle the Union soldiers tried to take the fort back, but failed. Fort Sumter stayed in Confederate hands until 1865 when General Sherman marched through South Carolina with his Union army."

"He burned up a lot of people's homes and a lot of great antiques," Andrew put in. "Drake showed me places where really pretty plantations got burned all the way to the ground, just for meanness."

Parker chuckled. "I think the Union army tried to make a statement by doing that but most historians today think Sherman's destruction was unnecessary."

"Mean things always happen in wars," Mary Helen put in. "Daddy said even in needed wars that mean things happen."

"That's true, "Claire agreed. "Fort Sumter was in ruins after the war but the U.S. Army gradually worked to restore it. Then in the late 1800s it was used as a lighthouse station and eventually given to Charleston for a museum."

"I want to see the big cannons," Andrew said.

"Me, too, and Jane said the ride on the ferry boat was really fun." Mary Helen stretched a hand out the window to feel the breeze.

"Remember the rules we talked about," Clare reminded them. "We all stay together at all times. No leaning over the boat railings, no running around on the boat or at the fort. When the narrator on the boat is talking and when we get to the fort and the ranger gives his talk, we'll all be quiet and listen. Then we can look around the fort together."

Parker thought the children too young to enjoy all the aspects of history surrounding Fort Sumter, but he knew they'd enjoy the ride to the island and the adventure of seeing a historic spot.

Fortunately, it was a sunny, pleasant day for a sightseeing trip to the old fort, the day not too hot with clear blue skies.

"It's really nice of Parker to take us to the fort today," Claire said, glancing back at the children.

"Thanks, Uncle Parker," Mary Helen said, catching her hint. "You've taken us to so many cool places this summer like that big lighthouse and some pretty plantation homes."

"The lighthouse we visited was at Hunting Island," Claire reminded her, "and the plantation houses were Magnolia Plantation and Gardens, Middleton Place, Drayton Hall, and the Boone Hall Plantation where parts of *Gone With the Wind* were filmed."

"We've been to a *lot* of old houses," Suki put in.

Parker saw Claire hide a smirk.

"As an antiques dealer, I do like old houses and their furnishings," he decided to admit, remembering that after several visits to historic homes, the girls began to clamor for more interesting sites.

"We went to Savannah, too, to see the parks and the shops," Andrew added. "We went to that neat festival in Beaufort, too, with the fireworks at the Fourth of July."

For many of the trips Parker brought Andrew along. Through their shared outings the girls had grown fonder of him, although the other children still didn't always welcome his company or include him in their play. Watching the children as much as he did now, Parker could see that Andrew's interest in music, his bookishness and quieter, more serious nature set him apart from the more rambunctious, outgoing, and extroverted Whaley and Mikell kids. Plus Chuck and J.T., the other boys in the group, were several years older than Andrew.

"I think we're going to have a nice day," Claire said, smiling at him.

The afternoon passed happily. The children especially enjoyed the boat ride to Fort Sumter and poking through the gift shops on Concord Street and inside the fort. After returning from the fort, they walked along Charleston's historic downtown streets past stately Antebellum homes to White Point Gardens, a gracious waterfront park near the Charleston Harbor, and to the seawall and promenade at the tip of the peninsula known as The Battery. Along the Battery promenade they could look across the water to see the fort they just visited far out in the Charleston Harbor.

Although Parker and Ann often enjoyed elegant dining in downtown Charleston, eating at fine restaurants like 82 Queen in the French Quarter or Poogan's Porch near The Battery, these restaurants hardly seemed appropriate for three children nine years old and under. So Parker loaded them into his car after their walk around the city and drove them back to Edisto to eat dinner at the Planter's Oak Restaurant in the middle of the Fairfield Resort. The Planter's Oak served excellent food in a charming atmosphere with a big live oak tree right in the middle of the restaurant. Parker and Claire ordered shrimp and grits with salad and the children fried shrimp or burgers from the children's menu.

Back at the house, they all took a walk up the beach in the twilight. It was one of Parker's favorite times of day at Edisto, cool and quiet, the sea calmer, the beach less noisy. People strolled along slowly, savoring the end of the day, watching for the moon to send ripples of light across the water.

They walked down the island to the end of The Point, where the beach began to turn to follow along the Saint Helena Sound. Parker loved the broader beach in this area, the spaciousness and larger property lots, and the views across to nearby islands.

The children chattered, darting down to the waves to wade or to look for shells exposed as the tide went out. Tired from the long day, he and Claire walked along quietly, enjoying the evening, comfortable.

As they drew closer to Oleanders again, Parker saw a group of local volunteers ahead on the beach, directing tourists away from a nest of sea turtles hatching. He'd noticed the wooden stakes and yellow tape around the nest in the dunes earlier and saw a few people gathering around the area.

"What's going on?" Mary Helen asked, noticing the growing crowd.

"Baby sea turtles are making their way to the sea," Parker said, pointing to a depression in the sand below a grassy dune.

He and Claire caught the children's hands to keep them back as they spotted the newly hatched turtles starting down the beach.

"Oh, I can see little turtles coming out," Suki said with excitement.

"How do they know how to crawl to the sea without their mothers?" Mary Helen asked, watching them. "They're so tiny."

"It's instinct," Parker explained. "Just as the large mother sea turtle knows to swim here to Edisto to lay her eggs, protected under the dune, the little turtles know when it's time to hatch out and head back to sea."

"I've counted fifteen already," said Andrew. "How many will there be?"

"It can vary," Parker replied. "But a mother turtle can lay up to 120 eggs in one nest."

"Wow. That's a lot." Suki's mouth dropped open.

Claire laughed, a warm sound. "Some sea turtles can live to be 150 years old, too, and those tiny turtles making their way to sea might grow to be giant turtles that weigh as much as 200 pounds or more. It's incredible to think about, isn't it?"

Andrew nodded. "I saw one of those big mother turtles once. They're huge. I read you're not supposed to bother them if you see them trying to make a nest or lay their eggs or anything."

"I'll bet the moon on the ocean helps them see better in the dark," Mary Helen said.

"I'm sure it does," Claire answered.

They watched the little turtles, struggling through the sand with their fins, making their way with determination to the water. It didn't take long for all the babies to find their way to the sea, where they crawled into the waves, struggling against the surf to keep moving forward.

"Oh," Suki said with regret after a time. "The last ones are crawling into the ocean and swimming away now."

Parker noted one of the volunteers had filmed the event, and a ranger stood around talking and answering questions now from the visitors who'd stopped to witness the turtles making their way to the sea.

"That state park ranger in the uniform, who works with the volunteers, said about a hundred turtles climbed out of the nest tonight and crawled to the ocean." Andrew brushed a strand of hair out of his eyes.

Parker nodded. "I heard him say one of the volunteers on the island spotted activity in the nest earlier, alerting them it might be time for the turtles to hatch. They knew the date when this nest was laid and that fact helped them know when to begin checking the nest area every evening. It's unusual to get to watch sea turtles hatch, even for professionals."

He heard Claire sigh. "What a lovely memory for us after an already nice day." She hugged the girls and then Andrew and Parker. "We'll hold this special time soft in our hearts for a long, long time, remembering the night we got to watch baby sea turtles make their way to the ocean."

Parker's heart felt full in that moment, and he hoped, desperately perhaps, that Claire wouldn't leave Edisto to go north to her family at summer's end. But he knew there was nothing he could do or say to stop her.

CHAPTER 9

"I really wish you and the girls would stay at the island this fall," Elaine said as they sat at the cabana one afternoon watching the children play.

The beach provided a glorious playground the children seldom tired of. In between times, they biked around the island's lovely bike trails or on its quiet side streets, read books or colored pictures on the screened porch, created make-believe games, jumped rope, played hide-and-seek, night tag, rock school, and other favorite games. Claire and her girls, usually with some of the other children tagging along with them, walked to the small island library every week, only a few blocks away on Palmetto Boulevard. They stopped for an ice cream at the Edisto Zesto on the way home or bought a snack at Whaley's store.

"It's hard to think about leaving," Claire admitted. "One part of me feels like I should stay while the other part thinks I should go back home to Arlington."

Elaine pushed her sunglasses down to look at Claire more directly. "It's still bothering you that your mother and Charles's mother suggested it wasn't right for you to stay at Parker's with both of you single now."

Claire looked away from Elaine's gaze. "That's only one factor."

"Well, it's a silly one. You know Parker's beach house simply sits empty and forlorn year round except for an occasional weekend when he comes down to the island. We all love that he's come more often with you here this summer. You and the girls have been good for him. He's walked through a hard time, too, you know."

"I do know, but I feel awful freeloading on his goodness."

Elaine laughed. "Honey, Parker is a wealthy man. He doesn't rent the house so I don't see how you can think of yourself as freeloading. Pay him a little rent if it makes you feel better. I can look for another place for you to rent, too, if you prefer, or find you a house to buy. Your monthly payments would be lower on a place you owned. If I set my mind to it, I could find you a real bargain."

Claire sighed. "I'm not ready to consider buying a home yet. I need to find a job first and then think about where I want to live."

"Well, we'll miss you if you decide to leave." Elaine stood to call her children to start home for the evening. "I know it will break Jane and Emma's hearts to see the girls go. They've really bonded over the summer. Even the boys have become fond of your girls—and of your wonderful stories." She smiled at that last remark. "You may need to send them more installments about the Polka Dot kids' adventures by mail. You've really gotten them caught up in the story of that family."

Claire looked down at the sketchbook in her lap where she'd been working on drawings for a new episode for the Polka Dot family. The children clamoring for more stories all summer had kept her mind and hands busy coming up with new ideas.

After Elaine left, Claire called Mary Helen and Suki in from the beach. Then she left them to play in the cabana while she went in to start supper.

Glancing out the window later, she saw Miles talking to them.

"Thank goodness I came in before he stopped by," she mumbled to herself. Miles Lawrence had found more and more occasions to drop by to visit with her and the girls over the summer. Often he sat with Claire at the cabana or with her under the beach umbrella while the girls played on the beach. His visits always disturbed her. He probed at her using his psychologist's skills, pushing her to answer questions she didn't want to think about, pressuring her to examine herself more closely than she was used to doing. Frankly, he flirted with her, too, whenever they were together, making her feel odd and ill at ease.

She turned back to her dinner preparations, glad once again she'd managed to miss this visit with him.

"Miles stopped by to visit with us," Mary Helen told her later when the girls came in. "He's *s-o-o* nice," she said with a girlish sigh. "And so handsome, too. Me and Jane both like him."

"It's Jane and I," Claire corrected, but she knew what Mary Helen meant. Miles possessed very charming ways.

"I like him, too." Suki climbed up into her chair at the table, where Claire had put dinner out. "He kisses our hands and tells us we're beautiful."

"Miles teaches at some college in Charleston," Mary Helen said, helping herself to chicken casserole, salad, and corn. "Where does he live in Charleston, Mommy?"

"Miles teaches psychology courses at the College of Charleston. We've seen the campus on visits to the city." She helped Suki put food on her plate. "He lives in an apartment above the garage beside his mother's big home downtown. It's one of those lovely historic houses like we saw walking down to The Battery with Parker last week."

"When we went to the fort in the harbor?" Suki asked.

"Yes," Claire answered. "That's right. Many people who have homes on Edisto, or on the other barrier islands along the coast, also have homes in Charleston, Beaufort, or cities nearby."

"Some people from other states own beach houses here, too," Suki added. "Lots of them rent their places when they're not here."

"That's right."

Suki wrinkled her nose. "Chuck and J.T. can name *all* the beach homes on The Point and they laughed at me and Emma because we can't."

Claire raised an eyebrow toward Mary Helen.

"She's sort of right," Mary Helen explained. "Chuck and J.T. can name all the houses on the beach side of The Point from before Murray Street to just after LaRoche. There are fifteen. They can name them in order starting with the house called The Beginning of Paradise—isn't that a neat name?—to the house called Turnabout. It's like a game. The big boys Tom and Ryder can say them really fast and even backwards. Chuck and J.T. can name them all without any mistakes and Jane knows most of them now, too. It's like a cool thing if you can say them. J.T. says it shows you're a real insider who lives here and not an outsider."

"I can't say them all." Suki made a face.

"You could if you worked at it." Claire smiled at her. "It's like memorizing other things you know, like your ABCs or your numbers."

"I know numbers to one hundred now." Suki lifted her chin with pride.

"I'd like to memorize all the houses like a real insider, too." Mary Helen paused and sent Claire a questioning look. "Are we going to stay here this fall, go to school, and everything? Me and Suki really want to stay."

Claire got up to get dessert. "I don't know yet if we will stay Mary Helen, but I'm sure we'll come back to visit sometimes even if we don't."

"That won't be the same," Suki said in a small voice.

"It doesn't matter what we want," Mary Helen told her in a sulky tone. "Kids never get to decide *anything*."

"I always try to listen to what you girls want, Mary Helen, but there are big factors to consider about where we need to live now that Daddy is gone. I'm trying hard to make the right decisions."

Two doubtful faces told Claire she hadn't convinced them of the truth in her words. How could she when she was uncertain herself of what to do?

Later that evening Claire gratefully snagged some quiet time for herself when John and Lula Mikell took the younger children, J.T., Chuck, Jane, Emma, Mary Helen, and Suki, for a boat ride back in the marshes and to see the sunset. John loved any excuse to get out on the water in one of their boats.

Claire sat on the porch, trying to decide what to do about her life, wishing her prayers had provided clear answers and direction. Surely she should be able to figure out the right course. Looking toward the sky over the water, she wished, perhaps foolishly, that God would simply skywrite the best answer for her there, making it clear what she should do.

As darkness began to fall Claire remembered she'd left her stack of sketchbooks down at the cabana, so she let herself out the screened door to head down the sandy path to retrieve them. But they weren't there. She remembered leaving them on the table. Troubled, she looked around the perimeters of the cabana, in the grasses, and even walked around the yard behind the beach house, to see if the wind might have blown them a distance, before heading back to the cabana again.

"Looking for something?" a voice called, and she looked up to see Miles walking up the path. He was carrying her sketchbooks under his arm.

She put a hand to her heart in gratitude. "Oh, thank you. I see you found my sketchbooks. I was looking for them."

"Mary Helen showed them to me earlier, and I asked her if I could take them home to look through them."

Claire felt herself blush. "She didn't tell me that."

"Mary Helen told me how much she and the children like your stories about the Polka Dot kids." Miles sat down in one of the chairs in the cabana and flipped open one of her sketchbooks to a scene embellished with soft watercolors, the storyline written underneath in Claire's neat calligraphy lettering.

Feeling awkward to stand with Miles sitting down now, Claire settled into the chair across from him. "I keep the children a lot and the stories entertain them."

He thumbed through the sketchbook, smiling. He really was a handsome man, with rich golden blond hair, a good physique, deep blue eyes, and an easy grace about his ways. But he made her edgy and ill at ease.

"Mary Helen told me about your stories, how you wrote them and drew the illustrations for them. I'd seen a few of the small drawings you sketch here at the cabana. I knew you showed talent, but these are very good, Claire."

She shrugged. "Thank you. I enjoy working with my hands."

"There you go again diminishing yourself, putting your talent down, not seeing its value or worth." He leaned toward her, studying her. "Even Mary Helen tells me your work is good, that the children like your little books and stories more than the ones from the library."

"Children are easy to please," she answered and then watched his smile curl into a smirk.

"I've told you since early summer you are an untapped treasure," he said on a soft note. "You don't see your own gifts and talents."

Claire frowned at him. "Perhaps not."

She reached toward him to get her sketchbooks. "However, I'm glad you found these and I thank you." She stood after taking her books back. "I really need to go in. The girls will be coming back soon. Lula may try to call me. She and John took the children out on the boat tonight."

Miles stood, also. "I keep a copier at the beach house. I made copies of all these sketchbooks to send to a friend of mine in the publishing business. I think they might sell as books other children could enjoy."

Claire knew her mouth dropped open. "You had no right to do that, Miles Lawrence."

He leaned toward her. "Are you more afraid they'll fail or succeed, Claire Avery? What if you have real talent, real saleable talent? Would you rise to the occasion to pursue it? Could you handle the discipline involved or the possible responsibility and recognition? It might make demands on you."

"You're always probing at me," she snapped in anger. "Do you enjoy it? Do you like upsetting me?"

"I like making you think about yourself." He gave her a knowing smile, unfazed by her irritation. "I like making you look at who you are besides a wife and a mother. You define yourself in too narrow a sphere. You don't recognize any of your talents as possibilities for expanding who you are. Yet each of them holds the potential for showing you a whole new dimension of your being."

"I hate that you're always trying to analyze me. It makes me uncomfortable."

He moved closer. "I make you uncomfortable, too, because I look at you as a woman, a beautiful, desirable, and attractive woman. I know you feel the attraction between us. I certainly do."

Before Claire knew what he was doing, Miles leaned in and kissed her, and not just a chaste little kiss either, but a passionate one.

She was so stunned she gasped, dropping her sketchbooks as Miles pulled her closer to kiss her again.

"Miles stop!" She pushed away from him, shaking now and feeling tears well up in her eyes. "I've only recently lost my husband. Please."

He put a hand to her cheek. "And yet you've also just discovered another dimension of yourself, found that you have a passion lurking inside that you hardly knew existed."

She jerked away from him—and from his words—wishing she could smack him, but instead she gathered up her sketchbooks and fled, only wanting desperately to get away from him.

Somehow Claire got through the evening afterwards, struggling to act normal with the girls when they came home. But after she tucked them into bed, she cried herself to sleep, distressed over her earlier encounter with Miles. Angry at him for kissing her, angry and confused with herself for responding, for not jerking away immediately and slapping him. What sort of woman was she to make him think she might welcome his advances? Riddled with guilt, she rubbed at her mouth, remembering Charles and her love for him. Feeling dirty and horrible. Whatever was wrong with her?

Tired the next morning, Claire slept later than usual and then settled the girls into some schoolwork in their rooms to keep them busy after breakfast. She wished for someone she could talk with about what had happened, but it would be too humiliating to do so. What would anyone think? And what should she do the next time she ran into Miles?

She heard a car pull in the driveway while she worked around the house cleaning, trying to stay busy and work off her feelings. She groaned at the sound, hoping it wasn't Elaine, Lula, or Isabel. She wasn't ready to talk to anyone yet today. To her surprise it was her father.

"Dad?" She voiced her disbelief as he let himself in the screened door on the back of the beach house. "Is it really you? What are you doing here? Is Mother with you?" She looked behind him.

"It's only me." He smiled and came to gather her into a hug.

She felt like crying to feel his familiar warmth this morning, to smell that spicy scent of his favorite cologne.

Claire pulled back to look at him. "What are you doing here?"

"I had business with a banker friend in Savannah and decided to drive down the coast from Arlington for my meeting so I could stop by and see you on the way home. I've been worried about you."

The girls, hearing their grandfather's voice, came running with excitement into the room to hug him. After a little girlish chatter, Mary Helen and Suki insisted on taking him around the house and down to the beach to show him everything. To Claire's surprise, he threw his suit jacket over a chair and complied.

She fixed lunch for them afterwards and then her father changed into shorts and took a walk on the beach with the girls. Claire carried the big umbrella and a couple of chairs down to the beach, charmed with this aspect of her father that he would give time and interest to her daughters.

After the walk, her father sat down with Claire under the umbrella to watch the girls play in the ocean, both of them laughing as they danced in and out of the waves along the shore.

"It's lovely here. I can see why you like it," he said, relaxing and stretching his legs out. "The island and the house make me think of my parents' place at Martha's Vineyard. I loved to go there for the summer as a boy and to the beach on holidays. You always liked it there, too. I was glad you enjoyed it so much for Mother's sake, especially after my father died."

Clare knew her surprise showed.

He smiled at her. "Verna never liked the house at the Vineyard, nor did she get along well with my mother, but I was always pleased for Mother's sake you were more like her. You look like her with that dark hair of yours. I never look at you without remembering Mother."

Claire studied him, trying to figure out this new aspect of her father. "You never came to the beach much at the Vineyard except to bring me."

"I had work to do by then and Verna to please. But I enjoyed the short stays when I took you to the island and later picked you up. You enjoyed happy times there in the summers, didn't you?"

"Yes, I did." She smiled at him, remembering those soft idyllic summers with her grandmother, walking around the island, learning to paint, free to be herself without pressure and criticism from her mother and sisters.

"After the summer it was always time for you to head back to school, work, and back to duty—like for me when younger. Idyllic vacations always come to an end, don't they Claire?" He turned to look at her. "It's time for you to get back to work and duty, too. This has been a good time for healing, but it's time for you to think of your future and your girls' future."

Claire turned her eyes out to the sea, not sure how to answer.

"A friend of mine who is an attorney needs a receptionist for his office starting in a week or two. He'll pay well, and it's work you can do. Answering the phone, doing some typing, setting appointments, filing—simple office tasks. If you like, you can put your name into the school system for a teaching job when one opens. But Frank Kozak would be grateful for you coming to work for him. He likes a pretty girl out front, and he needs someone smart, poised, and cultured for the clientele he serves."

Her father picked up a small shell beside his chair to study it. "The girls need a good school to go to, Claire. I've investigated the school on the island. It's small, three or so teachers, each teaching more than one grade, meeting in a converted beach house. The public middle school and high school are forty-eight miles away in Walterboro, not remotely convenient. I think Mary Helen and Suki should have more. I'll send them to the private school you went to in our neighborhood. You know you loved that school, had friends there like Rachel Pearsons—Rachel Everley now—that you still keep in touch with. There are advantages in Arlington for the girls they won't have here. Your youngest needs piano lessons, and your older girl is smart—she needs a school that will challenge her."

"The island school does has a fine reputation, although small," Claire put in. "I've met some of the teachers. They are really dedicated. And after finishing the primary grades, most of the island children attend The Country Day private school, less than thirty minutes away." She paused. "There are good people here on the island. The girls have been happy."

"It feels like a good place, but it *is* a small island." He sent Claire a direct look. "Plus the house you are staying in is your husband's brother's home. It should be your *own* family helping you at a time like this. It doesn't look right for you to continue taking Parker's charity."

Claire winced at the words.

"I'm sorry if I hurt your feelings saying that but you know it's true. Now that you've lost your husband, you need to find a route to make your own way—for your pride's sake and because you owe it to your girls. I could take care of you financially so you could continue to sit quietly at home—I have the money to do so—but I don't think that's best for you."

"I know I need to find work," Claire admitted. "It's nice of your friend to offer to hire me without meeting me."

"It's a good opportunity." He hesitated. "I know you and your mother will grate on each other's nerves and that you'll want your own place eventually. You're very different people."

Claire knew her eyes popped open at that.

He chuckled. "I'd be blind and deaf if I hadn't noticed the differences between the two of you. You'll face a bit of a challenge with Verna, but you're a woman now. You don't need to be bulldozed by her anymore." He tossed the shell out toward the sea. "Verna is busy and out of the house much of the time, too, involved in her social groups, charities, and helping with the baton studio she co-owns with Marilyn and Marjorie. It's become quite a successful business, which I'm glad to see."

Claire tried to think what to say.

"Verna plans to put you in your old room upstairs and Mary Helen and Suki in the twins' former bedroom down the hall. All the upstairs rooms have been redecorated—Verna likes to do that—and she turned the old playroom into a sitting room, which she says will be nice for the three of you to enjoy. So you'll basically have the upstairs to yourselves. Verna and I always stay downstairs when we're home. You will have privacy, Claire. I know that's important once you've been on your own." He paused. "What problems do you see? Let's talk about them."

Claire smoothed back a strand of her hair caught by the sea breeze. "The girls will be heartbroken if we can't bring the cats. Mother was opposed to that. She says she's allergic."

He laughed. "She's not. She just always said that because she didn't want animals in the house. You can bring them. I'll talk to her. We'll put a sort of gate at the top of the stairs so they'll stay in your area. Does that sound fair? Then you won't have to hear her carry on about cat dander on her skirt or a scratch on an antique chair or something."

Claire flicked at a sand fly that had settled on her leg. "Who will keep the girls after school if I'm working? Suki will get out early with kindergarten. Even though the school is only a few blocks away, someone will need to pick her up or walk her home. When Mary Helen gets out of school later, she will need someone to watch after her, too."

"Aggie Houston still works for us." He grinned. "She can't wait to take care of your girls—said to tell you so. She's older, but capable and reliable. You know that. She told me to tell you she'll pick up the girls at school and take good care of them."

Claire, touched at his words, felt tears well up. "I loved Aggie.

She was wonderful to me, taught me to sew, to cook."

"Well, then." He patted her arm. "You'll feel good to have her helping you with the girls."

He picked up her hand again to kiss it. "We do love you, Claire. Let us help you in this hard time as you reestablish your life. I know Verna can be rather outspoken and not always kind, but she wants the best for you and the girls. She's worked hard to redecorate the upstairs. And she's bubbling with ideas about the girls. She's already found a good piano teacher for Suki. Verna says Suki shows a natural talent."

"She does," Claire answered.

The girls ran up to show their grandfather some shiny shells that they'd found, chattering to him happily. Claire watched them interact with a catch in her throat. She could tell her father was fond of them.

"So what do you say?" he asked, once the girls raced off back to the waves again.

"I think it's time for our summer to end," she said.

He nodded. "Good. Here's my plan about that." He shifted his chair out of the sun. "I drove instead of flying so I could drive back with you. We can caravan. I'll help you pack, and the trip will be easier for you having two cars to carry everything. I took the liberty of talking to Charles's attorney, Ben Harrison, in Sweetwater. He said he would meet the movers I've tentatively scheduled to be sure they pack and load all your furnishings and boxes at the parsonage. A neighbor of yours, Leona I think, told Ben Harrison she would help, as well. The movers will bring everything to Arlington and we'll put it all in a storage facility nearby. If there's anything you need, you can drive over at any time to retrieve it."

He took Claire's hand again. "Unfortunately, I need to get back to work at the first of the week, so we'll need to set out as soon as you can pack. It's an eight-hour trip to Arlington, more realistically nine with stops, but I think if we get an early start, we can make it in a day. How would that work for you?"

It gave Claire little time to think much about the changes ahead, but perhaps heading out quickly would be best. *And I won't have to see Miles again*, she thought. She felt a vast relief at that thought. "Could you give me two days to get ready?" she asked. "We can leave on Saturday. I think the girls and I can get packed, clean up the house, and be ready to go by then."

"That sounds excellent." Her father squeezed her hand. "This is for the best. You'll see. Arlington is your home. You'll have fun introducing your girls to all the places you love there, getting them registered and settled into your old school, taking them to the parks nearby. You know Aggie is a wonderful cook and a fine housekeeper. She'll spoil you and the girls."

After the emotional and confusing time with Miles last night, the idea of an escape sounded wonderful. And Claire did need to make some sort of decision for her future. Her father had been good enough to find her a job, make arrangements for her furnishings and boxes to be moved from Sweetwater. He'd been sweet enough to drive down, when he usually always flew on his business trips, simply to help her move. It touched and amazed her he'd done that.

"I should warn you. The girls are going to be upset to leave," she said, her eyes moving to them giggling and racing along the edge of the seashore, trying to escape the waves coming in.

"I'll talk to them. They'll be fine," he said. "I'll take care of it." And somehow Claire knew he would. Her father could be a powerful and persuasive force when he wanted to get something done. It was why he'd been so successful in business.

"I'll speak to Parker, too," he added. "I want to thank him for all he's done for you and the girls. I'll let him know, as well, that anytime he wants to come to Arlington, he's always welcome."

Claire leaned back in her chair, not sure what else to say. It was so easy sometimes, when your emotions were a wreck and when you didn't have your own clear answers, to simply let someone else strong lead the way. Arlington had been her home for all her young years growing up. It was familiar. Surely she and the girls could settle in there and be happy.

CHAPTER 10

November 1985

The fall months dragged by after Claire left the island to go back to Arlington. Parker threw himself into his work to keep his mind occupied. He walked Congress for miles around Beaufort's streets, spent more time on the boat with Drake fishing, and went to several national antiques conventions that he usually avoided.

He seldom went to the beach house, much to Andrew's disappointment, but the boy was back in school for the fall and busier, too, with his friends.

However, after a big storm along the coast, Parker headed down to Oleanders to fix loose shutters and boards and to pick up debris scattered around the property. Elaine had called to tell him he might want to come and check on things.

Walking through the house after he arrived, Parker felt guilty that his mind pictured Claire and the girls here now instead of Ann. The thought didn't improve his mood.

Elaine found him an hour or two later sweeping the carport and storage area underneath the house. "None of us experienced much damage thankfully," she said, stopping at the end of the driveway. She held up a white paper sack. "I brought you some lunch from the deli. I figured you might not have eaten yet."

"Thanks." He noticed the second bag in her hand.

"I picked up lunch for myself, too. I'm on break from the office. I thought you might like some company."

Actually, he didn't want any, hoping to finish up and head back to Beaufort as quickly as possible, but good manners prevailed. He leaned his broom against a post. "Let's go up on the porch to eat at the table. I could use a break."

Parker trailed behind Elaine up the stairs to the screened porch and then headed into the house to get a couple of canned drinks and two glasses of ice while she spread their lunch out on the table.

"I sure miss Claire," she said with a big sigh after they both sat down. "It's not the same around here without her."

"Yeah, well it was time for her to get on with her life." Parker bit into a roast beef and cheese sandwich.

"I wish I believed that." Elaine picked at her own lunch. "Do you think she's happy back in Arlington?"

He shrugged. "She's called a time or two, dropped me a few notes. She sounded happy."

Isabel Compton walked up the steps, opening the screened door to join them before Elaine could add more. "I thought I saw your car over here," she said to Parker. "I wanted to walk over to ask about Claire and the girls."

"I'd say you and Elaine know as much about how Claire is doing as I do." Parker practically snapped the words and then immediately regretted it as both the women's eyes lifted in surprise.

He sighed. "I'm worried about her, too," he admitted and then turned to Isabel. "Can I get you a soda or some water?"

"No, I'm good," she said, settling into a chair and crossing her leg. "I simply don't like it that Claire took off so suddenly. I've worried her father pressured her. She didn't say so but she acted odd the last time I saw her."

"She did act odd," Elaine agreed. "Sort of skittery and anxious."

"Claire probably had a lot on her mind," Parker said, although he'd noticed the same thing when he came to say goodbye.

Elaine and Isabel gave him two of those studied looks again. Women always wanted to talk a thing to death.

"Her father talked to me before they left," Parker said, trying to think what they wanted to hear. "He thanked me for letting Claire stay here for a time, told me about her new job. He invited me to come up to Arlington if I ever wanted to. Said I'd be welcome."

"I think you should go, Parker. I think Claire and the girls are miserable there." Elaine pulled a note out of her pocket. "Mary Helen has been writing little notes to Jane, and she got this one a few days ago and shared it with me. Shall I read it?"

He nodded, interested himself now.

"*Dear Jane,*" she read. "*I hope you are okay. We are awful. I hate it here and so does Suki. Mommy tries to pretend she likes it, but I know she doesn't. Our Grandmother is mean. She says mean things to me and Suki and to mother. Grandfather is nice but he works all the time. We don't ever do things with him. Aggie takes care of us and is nice but the house is big and fussy and we have to be careful about everything and how we look all the time. I wish we were back at Edisto. I miss everybody. Don't tell mommy I wrote we are sad. She says we need to try to be happy. ... Love, Mary Helen Avery.*"

"God bless that child's heart," Isabel said, wiping tears from her eyes. "That hurts me to hear it."

Elaine folded up the letter. "Jane showed me a few other letters from Mary Helen from before with little drawings and childish notes from Suki tucked in. None are cheerful. Even Suki's drawings show sad faces."

"Well, we need to do something." Isabel leaned toward Parker. "You need to go up there to Arlington and get her and the girls."

Parker bristled. "I can hardly make Claire and the girls leave her parents' home. She certainly hasn't indicated to me that she wants to come back here to Edisto either."

Elaine put a hand on one hip. "She would never ask you if she could come back, Parker, but if you asked her it might make a difference."

"I can hardly rush up there and tell her I miss her. I'm her husband's brother. It's not my place." He scowled, causing eyebrows to raise again.

"Parker does have a point," Isabel said, after a moment. "He needs a reason to go visit Claire and he needs a viable opportunity to offer her to make it seem sensible for her to come back. Claire has her pride after all. She'll want to think we need her, not that we're feeling sorry for her."

"You're right. I could certainly tell her the kids would love for her to come back so they can stay with her after school again," Elaine offered.

"Parker could mention that, but I have a better idea." Isabel gave them a smug smile. "I'm losing my store manager. Virginia Armond is getting married again and moving off island. I could use someone like Claire to manage The Little Mermaid. Claire is smart, sensible, personable, and creative. I don't think she's happy working with that lawyer in Arlington. It's too sterile an environment for her. At my store, Claire can sew or draw if the store's not busy. I don't care. Ezra and I would like to take a cruise this winter. If I knew Claire would take care of the store, I could take off and enjoy myself."

"That would be perfect." Elaine beamed.

Isabel leaned toward Parker. "Why don't you go up there and see how she is. You *have* been invited. If she's unhappy, tell her I need her at The Little Mermaid. You can tell her, too, that not a soul gives a fribble about her living at your house. She can pay you a little rent if it would make her feel better, but it's silly for her to do so. Only your mothers ever suggested there was anything inappropriate about her staying at your house anyway. Everyone else thought it lovely, knowing how much she, Charles, and the girls always loved staying at Oleanders."

Parker considered it. "I guess I could go up to DC for some business and stop over to see Claire and the girls in Arlington. See how they are."

"I'd be grateful to you for doing so. I don't like to think of those girls unhappy," Isabel said, drumming her fingers on the table.

"Will you go, Parker?" Elaine asked, a hopeful look in her eyes.

He finished off his sandwich, thinking. "Claire may not want to come back, regardless of what Mary Helen may be writing. You haven't seen Claire's family's home. It's very elegant."

"I've seen pictures of it." Elaine dismissed the idea. "Claire's not impressed with that sort of thing, although it is a beautiful place.

However, I do remember Claire sharing enough about her mother and sisters in that quiet way of hers for me to know I probably wouldn't like any of them."

Parker grinned. "I've met her mother and sisters. They're a piece of work, I can tell you. Unless they've made a dramatic personality change, I'd find them disagreeable to be around for long. Mary Helen is probably right that they're making Claire unhappy."

"So you'll go?" Elaine asked.

"I will," he said at last. "If Claire is unhappy at her parents' but doesn't want to come back to Edisto, I can help her find an apartment. I know some people around DC where I used to work at Chevalier's. I can talk to them and find her something affordable if she's purposed to stay in the area. Even that change would help."

"Well, not to my way of thinking." Isabel crossed her arms. "I want Claire and the girls back here. I've taken an interest in them."

Back in Beaufort later, Parker wrestled with himself about going to Arlington to see Claire. It might make it worse for him to see her again. In fact, he felt certain it would. He needed to get past his feelings for her. And he certainly didn't want to risk revealing them in any way to her.

Parker knew no one to talk with about this situation either. Drake already encouraged him to go to DC and Arlington to check on Claire and the girls if he wanted to, but Parker could hardly confide more personal feelings to him.

"You did promise Charles you'd keep a watch on her," Drake reminded him. "It wouldn't hurt for you to make a trip to DC for business and then stop in to visit her and the girls while there. You can take Claire out to dinner somewhere so she'll talk more candidly without her family around."

A few days later, still wrestling with himself about whether to go, Parker glanced up to see Miles Lawrence walking into Westcott Antiques. After glancing around the store for a moment Miles waved to Parker where he worked shelving a set of Depression glassware into an old china cabinet.

"I was looking for you," Miles said as he walked closer, reaching out a hand to shake Parker's. "How are you?"

"Well, thank you. And you?"

"Fine." Miles glanced around. "Is there somewhere we can talk privately for a moment? Do you have someone who can watch the store for you?"

"Sure. I'll page Nora to come down from upstairs. We can go to my office to talk. Is anything wrong?"

"Not exactly—just something I need to talk with you about."

Intrigued, Parker buzzed Nora from the front desk to come down to cover the store. After she arrived and offered a few cordial remarks to Miles, they headed to Parker's office. As expected for an antiques store like Westcott's, it was graciously furnished. Miles settled into the corner of a comfortable settee, crossing his ankle over his knee. Parker dropped into the chair across from him.

"Thank you for taking time to speak with me. This is about Claire Avery."

Parker lifted an eyebrow.

"I know she went back to Arlington where her family lives. Ezra and Isabel mentioned it. I suppose they might have her address, but I decided I would like to talk to someone in her family before I approach her."

Not sure what to say, Parker waited.

"I took an interest in Claire while she visited at the island. I like to see people reach for their best potential, become more self-actualized. You know." He waved a hand casually. "Her girls showed me some of her sketchbooks with those Polka Dot kids' stories and drawings in them. Did you ever see them?"

Parker tried to remember. "She painted a lot of beach scenes while at the island, wrote bits of stories for the children and drew some illustrations for them."

"This was different. From what Mary Helen told me, Claire created the idea for this Polka Dot family when younger and then later elaborated on it to make stories about them to entertain her girls and the other children at Edisto this summer."

"Claire did take care of Elaine and Lula's kids for about two months when their sitter bailed on them."

"You seem to be missing my point." Miles scowled. "This work was very good—strong storylines, charming concept overall, excellent illustrations. Mary Helen let me take Claire's sketchbooks home one afternoon and I found myself thoroughly entertained. On impulse, I duplicated them on the copier I keep in my office at the beach house. The next time I drove down to Savannah I took them to David Whittier when we shared lunch together. He's from New York originally, owns Whittier Publishing. I met him when he came to the college to speak one fall. We got acquainted, had some things in common." Miles shrugged. "I stop in to see him occasionally when I'm in Savannah."

"So you took him Claire's work for him to see," Parker repeated.

"Yes, I did. Then quite frankly I forgot about it. My textbook was due to my publisher at the end of summer. Fall term started at the college. Life got busy and Claire had left." He waved a hand again. "I was a little stunned when I got a letter from one of David Whittier's editors yesterday." He pulled it out of the inside pocket of his jacket. "The editor's name is Nancy Franklin. She generally makes the company's acquisitions for their children's book imprint Colorstone Press."

He handed the letter to Parker. "Whittier wants to contract Claire's Polka Dot kids' books. You can read the letter. It's directed to Claire but David sent it to me to pass on, since they didn't have Claire's address. This Nancy Franklin wants to meet with Claire, talk to her about making her stories into a series of books. It will mean some dedicated work for Claire. Whittier has a staff artist who will do the book illustrations but the artist wants to work with Claire to capture her concept in the artwork." Miles paused. "It's a very big opportunity for Claire."

"I assume she doesn't know about this," Parker said, running his eyes over the letter.

"No and naturally they thought she lived near our family place on Edisto and that I'd simply pass the letter on. As I explained, she *was* living on the island when I dropped off the material to David in August. You can see in the letter that they want her contact information, which I didn't provide earlier."

"Did Claire know you gave this material to Whittier Publishing?"

He shifted in his seat. "I told her and she wasn't happy with me about it. She has no concept of her potential, Parker. I think it embarrassed her that I would assume she possessed talent that would interest a publisher."

Parker glanced over the letter again. "I know little about publishing, but since you do publish academically, perhaps you can tell me what this might entail for Claire if she was interested in pursuing it."

"Basically they want to meet with Claire, from what the letter says, and explain it more clearly at that time. They definitely want to write contract. That is stated emphatically. They would probably work with Claire to decide on which story or stories to initiate first in book form. I'd say the editor Nancy Franklin, David, and other staff members already have this planned out."

Miles shifted in his seat before continuing. "Claire would need to work with them to edit the stories, perhaps pulling them together for book content. I'm not sure. It's not my field. But there would be focused work involved with it for Claire, meetings with her editor, then mailings back and forth, and meetings with the illustrator. Copy edits later, then proofs." He shrugged. "I would expect they'll push the first title heavily after publication and want Claire to do some book signings around the area. They'll explain that, I'm sure. Of course, they'll want her to keep working on the books to follow, too. Apparently they have several in mind for the first contract. If things go well, they could want more."

"Would this bring any significant income to Claire?" Parker asked.

"Of course. There would be an advance and then royalties. Whittier is a well-known publisher with a second office in New York. Authors, on average, don't get rich off their work, but many can—in time—make a good living at it if all goes well. Certainly a nice part-time income." He smiled. "For Claire it could be very rewarding and affirming, too. This opportunity might speak to he clearly that she holds talent worth pursuing professionally. Clair has never seen that."

"No, I don't think she has." Parker didn't add that he hadn either. He found himself curious now to look at her drawings an stories more carefully.

"I thought it might be more appropriate for you to talk to Clair about this opportunity than me. Claire was somewhat annoye with me before she left." He waved a hand again, obviously a affectation of his. "And you are family, her husband's brother. "

Miles pulled out another sheet of paper from his coat pocket an unfolded it. "Here is some further information about the publishe their address, and David Whittier's phone number if you need it."

Parker took the informational sheet Miles held out and the glanced over the letter to Claire once again. "It seems clear th editor, Nancy Franklin, wants Claire to contact her right away."

"Yes. That's why I drove down to Beaufort to bring this to yo today. Claire should get back with them within a few days to le them know she's interested and to make plans to travel to Savanna to meet with them soon. She shouldn't diddle around and lose thi opportunity. Most aspiring authors would give a great deal for chance like this."

Parker smoothed a hand over the papers on his lap. "It woul seem that Claire has you to thank for this opportunity. Wouldn you enjoy being the one to share it with her?"

He smiled at Parker then. "I find Claire Avery not only talente and interesting but *tempting*. Do you know what I mean?"

"Yes, I do." Parker snapped out the words, frowning. "But I thin I mentioned to you before that Claire is only recently widowed."

"I remember that conversation." Another smile tugged at th corner of Miles's mouth. "But although Claire Avery is widowe she isn't dead. Eventually that passionate side of her will surfac again. However, I don't think it's time for that yet, so it's probabl best I keep a little distance."

He stood up as he finished those words. "Will you handle this?

he asked. "I could ask Isabel if you prefer. She's fond of Claire and the girls."

Parker stood, following Miles's lead and biting off a few additional angry words he decided not to voice. "No, you don't need to ask Isabel. I'll contact Claire and instead of calling her I'll take the letter to her in person. I'd planned to drive up at the first of the week for business in DC and to stop to see Claire and the girls. Now, I think I'll head north tomorrow. Claire will be off work for the weekend and we can talk about this."

Miles's eyes met Parker's. "Do encourage her to say yes. This would be good for Claire."

"Yes, I can see that," Parker said. "I'll do my best to help her see what a fine opportunity this is."

When Miles left, Parker read over the letter again and then smiled as a new thought came to him. This was exactly the incentive he needed to get Claire back to the island. If he found she was truly unhappy in Arlington, as he suspected, he'd push even more to see it happen, too.

Whistling now, Parker decided to head to the small book store down the street from Westcott's to see what he could learn about children's books and about Whittier Publishing. Perhaps he'd pick up a few special books to take to the girls while there. Suddenly, his life ahead looked a lot sunnier.

CHAPTER 11

Claire felt pleased to see the sun shining out the window today and to know the temperature was expected to rise into the sixties. She and the girls could walk in the park nearby and get outside after a week of rainy and chilly weather. Too many of their weekends recently, when she'd been off work, had been cold, gray, and grim.

"Yippee." Mary Helen bounced into the room interrupting her thoughts. "Grandmother Verna, Aunt Marjorie, and Aunt Marilyn just left for that baton competition in Florida and they'll be gone five whole days. Grandfather is taking them to the airport now, then going to play golf. He told me to tell you to have a nice day."

Suki, trailing close behind Mary Helen, sighed. "Grandmother said I have to practice piano *every day* while she's gone."

Claire felt sad to hear those words. "But you love the piano," she said, smoothing a hand through her daughter's soft, baby fine hair.

"Not anymore," Mary Helen said. "Suki's teacher is real strict and mean and never smiles. I sit and wait when Suki has her lessons sometimes. Miss Najinski fusses at her all the time, says everything she's learned is wrong. And when Suki plays her own songs or changes anything in the music, she gets real mad and raps the piano with her little stick."

Claire's eyes popped in surprise. "She doesn't hit you, does she Suki?"

Suki shook her head. "No, but she scares me. And she doesn't like any of my songs."

Claire knew this meant the songs that flowed from Suki naturally when she sat down at the piano to play by ear.

Mary Helen made a face. "Miss Najinski puts her lipstick on all around the outside of her lips, not just inside them. It's funny looking. And her house is full of glass things and old stuff everywhere. Suki and I can hardly find a place to sit down when we have to wait. Aggie sits outside on the porch or waits in the car if it's cold. She won't *even* come inside. She doesn't like Miss Najinski and Miss Najinski doesn't like her."

"Why is that?"

"I heard Aggie tell her daughter on the phone it's because she's black and because she's help."

Claire sighed. "I'm sorry if Miss Najinski has been unkind to Aggie. You both know it isn't right to judge people by their color or to treat people disrespectfully based on the color of their skin."

"Miss Najinski is not a very nice person, Mother. I don't like her, either." Mary Helen made a face.

"I'll talk to Aggie and to Miss Najinski," Claire promised.

She knew Suki hadn't been happy with her music teacher but didn't realize the child this unhappy—or that there were problems with Aggie. Claire was always at work when Suki took her lessons, so she hadn't met Miss Najinski. Obviously, she would need to talk with her or to possibly find another teacher. She didn't want Suki to lose her love for music, even if she had to cross swords with her mother over this.

Suki sat on the floor and kicked off her shoes. "With Grandmother gone I don't have to wear these shoes all weekend. And until Grandmother gets back, I can be Suki and not Sarah Katherine."

"Don't you like those shoes?" Claire asked. Verna bought them for Suki when she took the girls shopping one day recently.

Mary Helen sighed. "They're *brown*, Mother."

Claire noted Mary Helen's use of the word Mother now. Verna had discouraged the girls from calling her Mommy.

"I hate brown," Suki said. "But Grandmother said brown is good for play shoes. I wanted the red ones."

"She never lets us get what we want in anything," Mary Helen complained. "I told her Suki didn't like brown shoes or brown dresses or brown clothes, and Grandmother called that silly. She said brown was a perfectly good and sensible color and that she wasn't catering to girlish whims. I don't see why it matters so much for play shoes. We have to wear black-and-white saddle shoes for school with our uniforms and black patents for church. You'd think we could wear any shoes we like for play or at least the color we want."

The style of Suki's shoes, Mary Janes with double straps, was one Suki usually liked but Claire had been too busy and too tired to notice they were brown or to remember Suki's odd distaste for brown clothing.

Mary Helen sat down and pulled off her shoes, too. "Aggie read us *Cinderella* after school yesterday and Suki said it was about us. She said Grandmother was the mean stepmother and Aunt Marjorie and Aunt Marilyn the mean stepsisters."

"That's not kind, girls," Claire chided. "Grandmother means well, and Marjorie and Marilyn are seldom here. Neither you or Suki are mistreated like Cinderella."

"I don't know why you keep trying to make us think they're nice when they're mean. Even Marjorie and Marilyn's kids are mean." Mary Helen flounced into a chair. "They act mean to you, too. They say rude, mean things to you and they talk about you behind your back. Me and Suki heard them."

Tears welled in Suki's eyes. "Why can't we go back to Edisto, Mommy? Everyone was nice to us there."

"This is where we live now." Claire sat down on the sofa in the sitting room where they spent most of their time. It was decorated too elaborately for Claire's taste, the sofa and chairs upholstered in brocades and velvets with deep fringe around the bottoms the kittens continually attacked. Heavy gold-framed portraits hung on the walls, also, giving the room too formal an air.

After their first weeks in Arlington, Claire rummaged in the attic to find some items to brighten the room—an old toy trunk from her girlhood days, some gay pillows, books and puzzles, and to her delight her old dollhouse with the Polka Dot dolls still packed inside in a box. The girls loved playing with the old wooden dolls that made up the fictitious Polkman family. Several of the dolls originally came dressed in clothes of polka dot fabric and Aggie long ago helped Claire create more in other fabrics to match. After that Claire's young imagination enjoyed a heyday, naming all the dolls, creating personalities for them, and making up stories and adventures involving them. She'd entertained herself many days playing with these dolls and now she and the girls were enjoying them all over again.

Mary Helen and Suki sat in front of the big dollhouse now, playing "pretend" with all the Polka Dot family.

Suki looked up with a smile Claire felt glad to see. "I can name all the dolls now, Mommy." She always forgot to say Mother, which annoyed Verna.

"Let's hear you name them," Claire said, moving to sit closer.

Suki began to lay out the dolls in a row, pointing to them as she recited. "This is Grampa and Gramma Polkman, this is Papa and Mama Polkman, and these are the children—Patrick and Patricia, the two oldest, and then Porter, Peter, Polly, Penney, and Baby Punkin."

"Very good." Claire leaned over to give her a kiss on the forehead.

"Why did you call them the Polkmans?" Mary Helen asked.

"I made it up from the words 'polka dot,' like the fabric of their clothes. It's fun when the names all sound the same, too— Polkman, Peter, Polly." She looked toward the window, where the sun shone brightly. "If you'd like we can walk to Monument Park. It's nice outside."

"Can we take the Farnsworth Fairies? And will you show us where you and Rachel used to play with them?" Mary Helen asked.

Suki clapped her hands. "Yes, please?"

Claire had also found a small cedar keepsake box containing her resin fairy collection in the attic. The fairies were tiny, each only a few inches tall, but all made of a sturdy material that resisted rain and weather. Her Grandmother Claire Levene Hampton sent them to her for her birthday one year, along with five little fairy houses of similar material. Claire supposed the fairies and houses were actually intended for inclusion in outdoor plant and garden displays, but she'd used them as play toys as her grandmother knew she would, quickly naming all the fairies and creating imaginative tales for them. Even with the fairies somewhat battered from love and play, the girls were delighted with them.

"I love the Farnsworth Fairies' names," Mary Helen said a short time later as they headed down the sidewalk of Bennington Street toward Monument Park, a few blocks away. Mary Helen proudly carried the collection of fairies in an old Tinkerbell tote bag, once Claire's.

Augusta Hills, a moneyed area of Arlington, had lovely tree-shaded sidewalks throughout, weaving in front of imposing homes with verdant lawns and immaculate landscaping. Claire's parents' house, a two-storied Federal style brick colonial with neat, symmetrical black shutters marching across its old brick front, nestled in a beautiful neighborhood with many parks, quaint tearooms, shops, churches, and schools nearby. Claire knew she should be happy that she and the girls had such a nice place to live.

Mary Helen recited off the Farnsworth Fairies' names, with Suki's help, as they walked along. "The girls are Fleuradew the queen, Loraleaf, Meadowlark, and Pearlshine."

"You forgot Moonbeam," Suki put in. "And the king of the boy fairies is Cloverdan."

"The other boy fairies are Mulberry, Bendweed, Pinegreen, and Glenwillow," Mary Helen finished.

"I love all the names you make up, Mommy," Suki said, taking her hand.

Claire smiled at her. "I was a very imaginative child. So are you."

"You make up great stories. I told Miles that," Mary Helen added.

Claire wrinkled her nose at that name. She'd overreacted at Miles's advances those months ago at the beach, but the memory still confused her, as did many of the conversations she'd held with

Miles. He wasn't an easy man to know or be with, unlike Charles or Parker. She missed Parker. She'd grown used to his company over the summer at Edisto, enjoyed their outings, their walks on the beach, the ease of talking with him. He was much like Charles in many ways but different, too, as brothers usually are.

She sighed. There was no reason to look back. She'd closed that door. She could only think ahead now and try to make the best of the life she had.

Following a nice afternoon at the park and lunch at a cute Tea Room across from Monument Park, Claire and the girls headed back to her family's home. With the day still fair and mild, Mary Helen and Suki begged to play in the fenced back yard behind the house with their kittens. Claire settled them in the yard and then went into the kitchen to find Aggie.

"I hope you're not planning dinner," Claire said, climbing onto an old stool in the kitchen. "Daddy called to say he planned to eat at the club with some of his golfing friends and the girls and I lunched at the Tea Room. We won't be hungry for much tonight." She smiled as Aggie turned from the counter. "Why don't you go on home early. I'll fix dinner for myself and the girls."

Aggie came over to pat her cheek. "You're still the same considerate girl I remember. You can be certain your mother would never offer to send me home early to put my feet up."

Concerned, Claire put a hand on Aggie's arm. "There isn't anything wrong is there? If you weren't well, you'd tell me, wouldn't you?"

"I'm fine, child. I'm just in my seventies now. Some days I wear out a little faster than I did as a young, spry thing."

"You know you could retire," Claire said.

"And why would I do that? I know this house and this family. What would I be doing with myself sitting around my house all day?" She smiled at Claire, before turning to put away dishes from the dishwasher again.

Claire loved spending time with Aggie. Warm-hearted, positive, cheerful, and encouraging, Aggie so often made Claire's life happier. The years had been kind to her and except for a little more weight than Claire remembered and a few more wrinkles she looked almost exactly the same.

"I know I have you to thank for saving my dollhouse, many of my old toys, and that box of fairy figures," Claire said. "Mother never was one to save things."

"I thought there might come a day you'd want those things for your own children." Aggie turned to smile at her. "I sure do love those sweet little girls of yours. They do you credit, both of them."

"They're not happy here, Aggie. Both were complaining again today."

Aggie shook her head. "They didn't grow up with Verna like you did. Getting along with Verna takes some getting used to, like living with a pet snake that might turn and bite you. Verna views those who are gentle and kind as weak and spineless and those who aren't outspoken and aggressive as mealy-mouthed and having no gumption. And that's only the icing of it."

"Mary Helen said you read them *Cinderella* yesterday and that Suki said Mother and the twins were like Cinderella's mother and stepsisters."

Aggie hooted with laughter. "Lord, I nearly laughed out loud over that. Children do see things clear as clear sometimes, don't they?"

Claire sighed. "Mary Helen also told me Suki wasn't happy with her piano teacher. Why didn't you tell me there was a problem?"

"Weren't my place, and I figured the child would tell you herself sooner or later."

"She said Miss Najinski acted rude to you."

"Humph. It's more that we neither one care for each other."

"Did Miss Najinski say anything rude to you because of your race? If so I'll speak to her."

"Pooh, child, don't you go fighting my battles. I can deal with the Miss Najinskis of this world. I've had a long life of dealing with such as that."

"I hate things like that. I hate prejudice."

Aggie took some hot cookies out of the oven, their cinnamon smell filling the air. "I know you do, child. You've got a good heart. Most folks are beginning to work their way past prejudices, but I figure there will always be some that can't or won't. You keep your heart right about that sort of thing and teach your girls right. We all know there will come an accounting for such things later when we move on to glory."

Claire sighed. "Charles used to say that."

Aggie smiled. "I sure did like him. A fine man. I'm grieved you had to lose him so young. It's a shame."

"You lost your husband, too."

"Yes, I did, and I raised our three children on up by myself. Women soldier on. That's what we do when life goes wrong." She put two cookies on a napkin and passed them to Claire. "These cookies are one of your old favorites, snicker doodles. Those girls of yours like them, too."

"It will be a treat for the girls later. I make so many of the wonderful recipes you taught me. I'm not sure if I ever thanked you enough for teaching me to cook, sew, embroider, and to take care of a home."

"You always liked making and doing—and creating things, like those stories and drawings. I sure did enjoy those, and it seems the girls do, too. They talk about them." She stopped to sit down on another stool. "I don't mean to step out of place, but I wouldn't be settling in here for too long. You endured things in this home that weren't healthy for you many a time, but that doesn't mean you need to hang up your permanent shingle here again. You know what I mean."

"I do, but I need some time to save some money for a down payment for a place of our own. I'm waiting, too, hoping I will get a job offer teaching kindergarten in one of the schools in the area. Then I'd like to move close to where I'll work, so the girls can go to the same school where I teach."

"Sounds like you've been doing some thinking."

"I have."

"I've been praying for your happiness and future." Aggie turned brown eyes to look at Claire thoughtfully. "I feel like God's working on something. He always has a plan. Sometimes we don't understand it or see it all at once, but in time we look back and see how every little thing fitted together in some way to our good. God always works things for good to those that love Him. You know that, Claire—even the evil things old satan sends our way God turns for our good. You keep remembering that."

"I will." Claire felt tears well in her eyes at Aggie's words.

"Aw, now, I didn't mean to make you cry. Those are good words and promises I know you've heard."

"Yes, but I needed to hear them again. I miss Charles in that way. He was so positive, so certain in his beliefs. I'd like to be more certain and sure in my beliefs."

She paused. "I'd like to feel more confident that God hears my prayers. Sometimes it seems like I pray and pray but get no answers at all."

Aggie stood up and began to stack cooled cookies into a decorative tin. "My mother always said when it seems like you're not hearing nothing that's when God's busy doing the most."

Claire smiled. "I hope you're right."

"For sure I am. Me and the Good Lord have walked together a lot of years now. I trust in Him. You should, too." She glanced at the clock. "I need to walk on down to the corner to catch the bus home now."

"Aggie, I know Daddy gave you a car. Why don't you drive?"

"I could, but I like the bus. I don't care to worry with the traffic and all those crazy folks on the road. While I'm on the bus it gives me time to think on things and to look out the window and see the pretty things in the world I forget to notice when I'm driving."

She walked over to give Claire a hug. "Don't you be worrying about me. I drive when I need to or when the weather's bad. I'm not wanting for anything."

Claire saw Aggie off and then began to look around the kitchen, thinking about what she'd cook for the girls for supper. The front doorbell interrupted her thoughts. She headed down the hallway to answer the door and to her surprise, when she looked through the door's peephole, she saw Parker standing on the front porch.

CHAPTER 12

Parker had left early from Beaufort on Saturday morning to drive to Arlington, making good time and arriving a little after four. He decided to drive directly to Claire's family's home before checking into the hotel where he always stayed in the Washington DC area.

He felt glad to see the delight on Claire's face when she opened the door to him. To his further pleasure, she threw herself into his arms giving him a warm hug.

"Parker, how wonderful to see you!" She pulled back to smile at him. "What are you doing here? Do you have business in DC?"

"I do, and I couldn't resist the chance to see you and the girls while here. How have you been?"

"Fine." She dropped her eyes from his. "Can you come in for a visit? The girls will want to see you."

"I can do better than that. I made reservations for dinner for the four of us at a restaurant not far away that I think Mary Helen and Suki will love. I hope you haven't eaten."

She led him into the house. "No, we haven't and it's kind of you to plan a dinner outing for us."

Parker glanced around at the formality of the home as he followed her to the kitchen. He saw no signs that children lived anywhere in the spaces he passed through.

"The girls are outside playing with the kittens," she told him. "We'd better go find them. They'll be excited to see you again."

She paused before putting her hand on the door leading into the backyard. "What time is the dinner reservation you made?"

"I made it early for five-thirty, thinking that would be best for the girls." He glanced at his watch. "Will that give you time to get ready? The restaurant is only fifteen or twenty minutes away. If we get there early, I'm sure they'd go ahead and seat us, too. I picked a restaurant where we wouldn't encounter a lot of Saturday evening night life."

She glanced at his navy corduroy sports coat and khaki slacks. "You're not dressed too formally, so if we wear casual dresses, will that be okay?"

"That will be perfect."

Parker enjoyed a few minutes hugging and greeting the girls—and checking out how much the kittens had grown—before Claire headed Mary Helen and Suki upstairs to dress. A short time later, they all pulled up at the parking lot of the restaurant he'd chosen, one of those new fondue restaurants becoming so popular.

He'd asked that their table be a quiet one when he made the reservation, and the waitress led them to a booth toward the back—exactly the type of table he had in mind, where they could visit and talk more privately.

Mary Helen and Suki looked around with wide eyes.

"We haven't eaten here before," Mary Helen said. "What kind of food do they have?"

"Can I get macaroni and cheese?" Suki asked, sliding into the booth ahead of Parker.

He laughed. "No, we're ordering what the restaurant calls the Four-Course Experience tonight. I want you girls to be adventurous with Claire and myself to try something new and fun. This is a fondue restaurant." He pointed toward a table they could see not too far away. "They bring fondue pots of different kinds and we spear and cook our own food in them."

Mary Helen's eyes widened. "That looks super fun," she said, craning to look around Claire to watch the party at the other table, already eating.

"I've read about fondue restaurants but haven't visited one yet." Claire looked over the menu. "What is our first course in this adventure of yours, Parker?"

"They bring a hot cheese fondue first that we can dip bread chunks, apple pieces, and raw vegetables in. Then they serve salads, followed by the main course. I'd like to order the land and sea selection for us, if it's okay. It includes beef, shrimp, and chicken to cook, along with mushrooms, potatoes, and broccoli on the side." He grinned. "The last pot is a chocolate fondue for dessert. We get an assortment of cakes, brownie bits, strawberries, bananas, and marshmallows to dip into hot chocolate for our finale."

"Yummm," Mary Helen said. "That is going to be so cool."

And it was. The girls loved the adventure of spearing and cooking their own dinner in the different fondue pots, and with the wide selection of food items, everyone found favorites to try.

"It's always fun with you," Suki said at one point, leaning up against Parker's side. "We miss you and Edisto. I wish we'd never left because me and Mary Helen hate it here."

Claire's eyes flew wide with embarrassment. "Suki, that wasn't a very nice thing to say. You know your grandparents are very good to us."

"She *always* says things like that," Mary Helen said, rolling her eyes. "She won't tell you her mother is mean to us, but I will. She's not a very nice person."

Parker tried to hide a smirk.

"The girls are having a little difficulty adjusting to a lifestyle that's somewhat different for us," Claire said, pasting an awkward smile on her face.

"How's your work with the attorney going?" Parker asked, shifting the subject a little.

"It's a nice office and Frank Kozak is very kind to me. I'm lucky to have such a good job," Claire answered.

"That means she doesn't really like it," Mary Helen added. "Me and Suki hear her crying some nights so we know she hates it. She's trying to get a job teaching again."

Claire's face flushed crimson.

"We're all sad living here," Suki put in, slipping her hand into Parker's. "Can we come back and stay with you at Edisto? You told Mommy we could stay if we wanted to. I heard you. Me and Mary Helen *want* to go back." Tears dripped down the child's face.

Parker wrapped an arm around her. "Everyone at Edisto misses you and Mary Helen, too. In fact Isabel Compton really needs you to come back." He looked toward Claire. "She's losing her store manager Virginia Armond, who's getting married again, and she's hoping you might come back to the island and manage the store for her. Isabel said she'd feel very happy to have you running The Little Mermaid, that you were personable, organized, and competent." He paused. "She doesn't know anyone else to ask right now. You know the island's small. It would be hard for her to work the store alone. And she and Ezra had planned a cruise later. They'll probably need to cancel it now." He let his words drift off.

"Oh, boy!" Mary Helen exclaimed. "We can work at The Little Mermaid." She turned to her mother. "I can help you, Mommy. I can. It will be fun!"

"I can help, too," Suki said.

"The Comptons are comfortable financially, and Isabel pays her store manager well." Parker named a figure he knew would sweeten the pot. "Isabel said to tell you she'd be happy for you to sew, paint, or work on your stories whenever the store is slow. That's often the case in the off-season months."

"That's very kind of Isabel to think of me," Claire said.

Parker watched her face, knowing she felt tempted but didn't want to let the girls know exactly how much.

He smiled at her. "You can think about it. Elaine said she'd love for you to keep the kids again, too, but I think working at the Mermaid would be better with more stability." He paused. "As for where to live, I see no reason why you and the girls couldn't live at Oleanders again. Elaine and Isabel both said the idea that it might be improper for you to stay in my vacation home was absurd. They said to tell you everyone at the island thought it lovely you and the

girls could stay at Oleanders where you'd shared so many happ
vacations. I really don't think anyone, except our mothers, saw
anything inappropriate in you being at the house."

"Why would it be in-propriate?" Suki asked, mispronouncing th
word.

"Because Grandmother said it wasn't nice for Mother to live i
someone else's house when she's not married to them."

"Why?" Suki wrinkled her nose trying to figure out that idea
"Uncle Parker is our family."

Mary Helen shrugged. "It's just another way Grandmother i
mean. She wanted Mother to move back home—probably so sh
could boss her around again and try to run our lives."

Claire lifted her chin. "Mary Helen, you need to watch you
tongue and mind your manners."

"Well, there's nothing wrong with us living in Uncle Parker'
beach house," Mary Helen replied defiantly. "He hardly ever use
it because he has his big house in Beaufort. And he loved Dadd
and said he wanted to help us be happy after Daddy died."

Out of the mouths of babes, Parker thought. "Mary Helen is right
Claire. I think Charles would be distressed to think of the three o
you unhappy. Won't you consider Isabel's offer?"

"It's a lot to think about," Claire answered. "I need to conside
my whole future, too, and not only what might make us happies
right now."

Parker played his ace. "There's another important reason wh
you and the girls need to come back to Edisto at this time. Th
publishing company Miles sent your Polka Dot stories to i
interested in publishing them. Their main office is in Savannah
They need you to come to Savannah to meet with the editor an
art director to talk about the books. You will need time to work o
them and a quiet place in which to do it. Edisto would be perfect.

Claire's mouth dropped open and her eyes grew wide. Her han
shaking, she dropped her fork with a clatter to the table. "Wha
did you say?"

"Uncle Parker said a *real* publisher wants to make your Polka Do kids stories into books," Mary Helen answered, jumping up and down in her seat. "That is so neat!"

"Does that mean you'll be a real author, Mommy?" Suki asked, her eyes wide.

"It means she *could* be if she's willing to seize this opportunity," Parker added, smiling at Claire.

"I don't know what to say," Claire said, shaking her head in disbelief.

"Remember Miles said your stories were really, really good. Mommy. and that his publisher friend might like them," Mary Helen reminded her.

"Despite his peculiarities, Miles does exhibit some good attributes," Parker added. "We owe him a big thank you for this opportunity for you. Claire, this publisher is a very respected one. I did some checking."

"How did you learn about this?" Claire asked, finally getting over her shock.

"Miles came to the store in Beaufort yesterday to bring me a letter for you from the publisher. Since I'd planned to come to DC for a meeting on Monday anyway, I decided to come early to bring you the letter in person," he replied, fudging the truth only a little. "You can read it when we get back to the house, and we can talk about it more then."

The waitress brought their ticket and they gathered their things to leave.

Claire moved closer to Parker as they walked toward the register, the girls skipping ahead. "You should have called me about this, Parker, so it wouldn't have caught me off guard so much."

He grinned at her. "And missed the chance to see you shocked and speechless? Not in a million years."

She punched his arm. "I should be mad at you, but I'm simply too stunned to be mad right now."

The evening hours after their return to the house passed happily. Parker updated the girls on all the happenings at the island, and they shared with him, too, about their months in Arlington. Not every memory was bad, and they'd taken many sightseeing trips into the Capitol and to points of interest in the area.

Claire fell somewhat quiet through the evening, and Parker knew she was thinking about their earlier conversation and the letter from Whittier she'd read when they returned to the house.

Parker felt grateful to find Claire's family out for the evening and even more grateful to learn her mother would be away for a few days. Claire didn't need Verna Hampton's opinions and interference while trying to come to terms with this new opportunity for her life.

After getting the girls to bed, Claire came back downstairs to the family room where she'd left Parker. She sat down beside him on the couch and burst into tears. Parker wrapped an arm around her and let her cry for a time.

"You've been unhappy," he said at last.

"Wretchedly," she admitted. "I thought I could adjust to living with my family again, that it would be different now that I'm grown, but I was wrong. Somehow, despite all my best intentions, I simply lapsed back into that old, timid Claire I used to be growing up. Mother took over my life as she'd always done and she began to take over my girls' lives. I didn't know what to do so I simply went along, hoping every day things would somehow get better."

"You should have called me," Parker said, pulling a handkerchief out of his jacket pocket to hand to her.

"What could I have said? I hated to admit to anyone my family is so difficult, that I can't hold my own with them or stand up to my own mother—especially for the sake of my girls." She sniffed. "I could hardly run back to my husband's brother's home with my tail between my legs, either. It's not as though you're my actual brother, even though you feel like a dear brother. You're Charles's brother, not mine."

The words "dear brother" weren't exactly the ones Parker hoped to hear. But he knew it more than he could realistically hope for.

Claire picked up the letter from the publisher from the coffee table to read it over again. "Parker, this is a wonderful opportunity and hardly one I deserve."

"No need to diminish your talents with me," Parker said. "If a big publisher like Whittier is interested in your work, you can believe with a certainty your work holds merit."

"What will happen at a meeting with them?" she asked.

He told her what Miles said. "I'm sure Whittier will explain everything clearly as soon as you meet with them, but it's a solid offer. They want to write contract with you. Why would you hesitate?"

"I don't know," she said honestly, shaking her head. "It just doesn't seem real, and I need to think about the girls, too, in relation to any decisions I might make. I can't consider anything that would keep me from being a good mother to Mary Helen and Suki."

"As if there's any chance of that happening." Parker sent her a fond look.

"What do you think I should do?" Claire asked, chewing on her lip.

Parker bit his tongue over his answer. "I think you should do what is best for you. If you are happy, the girls will be happy."

"Is it that simple?"

"It might not be if you were a selfish person, but that isn't the case here."

Claire leaned her head back against the sofa. "I've prayed and prayed that God would show me what He wanted me to do with my life, what would be best for me and the girls. Aggie said today that sometimes when we're praying the hardest and not getting answers, that God is working the most to bring the answer we need."

Parker chuckled. "Does God need to skywrite it across the sky for you?"

She looked at him in surprise. "I had that same thought at the beach shortly before I left, wishing foolishly that He would."

"Sometimes prayers get answered, Claire. I hope you will say yes to the opportunity with Whittier and to work for Isabel. If the writing picks up and becomes more of a job than you expect,

Isabel can begin to look for another manager. I know she would understand. She doesn't know about this opportunity with Whittier yet. But you can be sure she, Elaine, Lula, and all your other friends will be thrilled for you." He laughed. "I can hear Isabel Compton now planning a book signing for The Little Mermaid the minute your first book publishes."

Claire's lips twitched in a smile. "I simply can't take all this in. But I do think I will need to go back to Edisto. It would be hard to write here. I doubt Mother would be supportive and even Daddy might see this as an unstable opportunity. I doubt either could envision me as an author or even as a store manager."

"Perhaps you will surprise them both—and possibly yourself."

She laughed softly. "Now you sound like Miles Lawrence. He was always pushing on me to discover myself."

"He is a psychologist and a counselor, Claire." He hesitated. "I'm sorry I didn't see your talents more clearly and encourage them myself."

"I doubt they were particularly obvious to anyone." Claire looked over the letter again. "When should I contact this editor Nancy Franklin? It's the weekend now."

"I think Monday morning would be soon enough to call her." He glanced over her shoulder at the letter. "She'll expect you to suggest a time for a meeting in Savannah when you call. How soon can you pack and be ready to leave for Edisto? I'm sure Isabel or Elaine can arrange to keep the girls while you drive down to Savannah, or I can go with you if you'd like."

"No, I think I should do this on my own. I need to start being my own person and to stop leaning on others so much."

He nodded, deciding not to add a response.

Claire put a hand to her face, tapping her cheek and thinking. "Would it be cowardly if the girls and I pack up and leave on Monday or Tuesday? My mother and sisters are gone and they won't be back until midweek. It would save a lot of recriminations and difficulties for me, and for the girls, to be gone before my mother returns home."

Parker chuckled. "I think that's an excellent idea. Whittier will probably want you to drive down for a meeting later this week or next and I'm sure Isabel would love to begin training you at the store as soon as possible. You have the perfect excuse to leave more quickly than you might otherwise."

"I'm beginning to feel like a very impulsive person, packing up at the drop of a hat to make major moves." She ran a hand through her hair. "I'll be running out on my job with Frank Kozak rather suddenly, too. It might be kinder to give him two weeks notice at least."

Parker waited, letting Claire think this through on her own.

She tapped her finger on her cheek again, mulling it over. "However, I think Frank would understand if I explained."

Parker crossed his ankle over his knee. "You could also add that you have a relative visiting right now to help you pack and move. I need to pop over to Chevalier's for my meeting in DC on Monday morning, but we could leave after that on Monday or early Tuesday morning."

A little smile slipped across Claire's face after a moment. "How lovely to think I'll be back at Edisto again this very week." She folded up the letter and put it back in the envelope. "Let's plan on Tuesday," she said in a decisive tone, her face practically glowing. "That will give me Monday to contact the publisher, to go to Frank's office to explain in person why I need to leave, and time to visit the girls' school to get their records and talk to their teachers."

"That sounds good to me."

She sighed deeply. "I'll still need to talk to my father, too."

"Talk to your father about what?" Conrad Hampton said, coming into the room. He stopped inside the door, surprised to see Parker. "Well, hello, Parker. Glad to see you here for a visit. Sorry I was out, but I don't believe Claire told me you were coming."

Parker stood to shake Claire's father's hand. "I had business in DC at the first of the week and decided to come early to see Claire and the girls." He looked toward Claire. "I had the pleasure of bringing Claire the news of two wonderful job opportunities—

one at Edisto and one through a publisher in Savannah. I'll le
her tell you more, but I will tell you I'm delighted she's decided t
accept both. I'll be helping her move back to the island at the firs
of the week. She and the girls can stay at Oleanders for a time o
for as long as they want. I seldom use the house. You know I ow
a large home and a demanding business in Beaufort." He pause
"I hope you'll be excited for Claire."

Parker watched Conrad scowl at his words. He knew the ma
wasn't used to someone else taking charge of situations, but he fel
Claire had experienced enough emotion for the day without facin
an overly difficult time with her father. Best for Conrad to kno
up front her decision was made.

Claire stood to give her father a hug. "It's been an eventfu
evening. Parker was good enough to bring the news about thes
jobs in person. Both need to be acted on quickly or they might b
lost. I want to say yes, Dad."

She paused to twist her hands, watching his face. "I hope you'
understand. Parker has graciously agreed to help me move bacl
to the island while he's here. Just as it was easier for me to mak
the trip to Arlington with your help, it will be easier for me to
make the trip back with Parker's help. I'm grateful for such a kin
and generous brother-in-law to help me take advantage of thes
wonderful opportunities."

She turned to Parker. "It's late and I'm sure you need to go chec
into your hotel in DC. Enjoy time with your old friends in DC
tomorrow and then stop by, if you'd like, tomorrow evening fo
dinner with Daddy and me. I'll cook, since Aggie is off on Sunday
You, Daddy, and I will have a nice chance to talk together then."

Parker felt a grudging respect for Claire, taking control of th
situation.

She came to give Parker a light hug. "Thank you for the nic
dinner out. The girls enjoyed it so much. We are truly grateful t
you for all the support you've been to us since Charles's death
I'm sure Charles is looking down from heaven with gratitude, too
You're a very good brother."

Recognizing his cue to leave, Parker shrugged into his jacket and said his goodbyes. It was best, he knew, for Claire to talk over her new opportunities, and her own heart's desires, with her father without him there. He would see her tomorrow, after all, and, thankfully, much more often from now on.

CHAPTER 13

May 1986

Claire opened the mailbox in front of The Little Mermaid to pull out a stack of bills and circulars left the afternoon before. Walking back up the sidewalk toward the front door, she smiled to see more May shrubs and flowers popping into bloom around the little store's property. It seemed incredible to realize a year had passed now since Charles's death.

The Little Mermaid, where Claire had worked since coming back to the island from Arlington, had originally been a vacation cottage belonging to Isabel Compton's family, longtime residents of the island. When Isabel inherited the house, she and Ezra moved back to Edisto from Charleston so Isabel could turn the place into a business. Isabel renovated the interior into a children's store and then painted the exterior in fanciful colors—bright indigo blue with light aqua shutters and mustard yellow trim. Behind the white picket fence around the yard stood statues of mermaids, cute signs, and mermaid flags, many for sale.

Claire paused to straighten the brass mermaid Welcome sign by the front door before letting herself back inside. She loved The Little Mermaid, almost as much as Mary Helen and Isabel, and she'd enjoyed her months working here. The main store sprawled across one big area with shelving and displays to divide it into sections. Isabel's main lines of merchandise, geared to children, consisted of mermaid toys, collectibles, jewelry, and clothing, along with beach items, colorful art prints, pillows, dolls, books, decorative statuary, even lamps and painted children's furniture.

With Isabel's creative eye for arrangement, simply walking into the store made customers smile with delight.

Although The Little Mermaid was not a large store, Isabel had packed every space efficiently with merchandise, even the screened porch to one side, filling it with whimsical items in a garden-like setting. Behind the front register and check out desk, a door led to a private office and then into a kitchen area, with a bath to one side and a small sun porch at its rear. When Mary Helen and Suki came to the shop after school, they ate their snacks in the kitchen, and then colored and read on the sun porch or played in the back yard until Claire got off work. Isabel or Bettie Lou Pope, the store's other employee, came to cover the evening hours. Retired from the retail business, Bettie Lou loved working part-time at the Mermaid to keep herself busy.

"Good morning," Isabel called, letting herself in the store, the brass bell on the door jangling as she came in. "Have you made coffee?"

"Yes. It's in the kitchen." Claire paused, glancing at the desk calendar. "I didn't think you worked today."

The older woman smiled. "I'm not on the schedule, but I thought you might need a little company."

Claire glanced away.

"Elaine mentioned to me that this was the day you buried Charles a year ago." She headed toward the kitchen. "I brought homemade cinnamon rolls. They make any day better."

She came out of the kitchen a few minutes later carrying a tray with a plate of warm, fragrant rolls on it and two cups of coffee. "Come sit a minute," she said. "You know the tourists aren't even out of bed yet."

Isabel moved from the register to the small table and chairs tucked in front of the window by the door. "I put this little table here for the children to color on while their parents shopped or for grandpas and daddies to sit at to read the newspaper, but I think I've enjoyed it more than any of them." She placed her tray on the table, pulling up the blinds to let the morning sun stream in before settling into a cushioned chair.

"I'm really all right, Isabel," Claire said coming to join her. "You didn't need to come in this morning."

"Perhaps I wanted some company," Isabel said in her businesslike way. She put a cinnamon roll on a napkin for Claire and pushed it her way. "You need to humor me and eat this. Ezra almost fainted to see me baking in the kitchen this morning. Despite his teasing, however, you can be sure he carried several of these rolls to his office when he left."

Claire knew Isabel usually made a quick breakfast for herself at the shop or, if she ate at home, that Ezra cooked breakfast. "Ummm, these are good," Claire said after biting into a roll.

"It's an old island recipe I learned from my grandmother." She cut her own roll neatly with a fork. "I *can* actually cook very well when I make up my mind to it, but since Ezra enjoys the kitchen so much, I usually leave most of the meals to him."

Claire had eaten some of Ezra's meals and knew he was a fine cook. She smiled at Isabel. "Suki likes to putter in the kitchen much more than Mary Helen does."

"Mary Helen is so much like me. I hope you don't mind me saying so."

"I see the similarities, and despite the fact that you don't have children you do have a way with them, especially my girls."

"Claire, you have very gifted girls, which makes them a pleasure to spend time with. I'm sure they got those creative genes from you." She reached for her coffee mug, which of course had a mermaid on it and the words: *If you can't be yourself, be a mermaid.*

"That's a new one." Claire grinned, pointing to it.

"Isn't it great?" Isabel held the aqua mug up to admire it. "I bet it will sell like hotcakes. Mary Helen found it in one of our catalogs. Your mug, too."

Claire looked at the words on hers and read them out loud, "*I'm through adulting; let's be mermaids.*" She laughed. "I like it."

"There, I've made you laugh and fed you fattening cinnamon rolls. What more can you want?" Isabel, not often demonstrative, reached over to pat Claire's cheek. "I'm so proud about your books. Have they set a specific publication date for the first one to come out?"

"Whittier said the first week of October. They want the books out for fall and holiday shopping."

"Good idea." She nodded. "What are they titling the first one?

"Simply *The Polka Dot Kids*. The next will be *The Polka Dot Kids at the Beach*."

Isabel's eyes brightened. "Won't that go great here in the store!"'

Claire propped her chin on her hand. "I worried about the art at first," she admitted. "I'd created my own illustrations to go with the stories and I feared a new artist's work wouldn't match the settings I'd always envisioned. But Whittier's art director, Leland Menya, chose this lovely illustrator, Vanessa Yardley, whose light, sweet watercolors are simply perfect. She worked from many of my own sketches to capture the personalities I intended."

Isabel snorted. "I don't know why publishers are so stuffy about not letting authors illustrate their own books. Your illustrations were lovely."

"I feel lucky to have any input about the art at all, "Claire replied. "It was the point I hesitated over the most before I signed contract."

"Well, good for you for standing up for what you wanted." Isabel finished her roll and pushed her plate back. "Will you do a book tour once the book publishes this fall?"

Claire sighed. "They want me to do signings almost until Christmas."

"Three months is normal for book tours. What worries you about that?"

"The girls and my work here."

Isabel put a hand on her hip. "Late fall and winter are the dead season months on the island. Bettie Lou and I can handle any days or weekends you might need to travel to a bookstore. I doubt you'll need to spend the night in most instances. Publishers usually set signings near the area where an author lives. They'll probably want you to sign in some of the major cities along the coast—Savannah,

Charleston, Myrtle Beach—maybe inland to a few of the larger cities. Of course, they'll want you to schedule signings in areas where you're known, too, like here and in Beaufort. I'll naturally want to host a little event at the Mermaid."

Claire sighed. "I guess I'll need to get used to that sort of thing. Whittier is already talking about publishing some of the Farnsworth Fairy stories in the future, too."

Isabel clapped her hands. "You haven't told me that. What wonderful news!" She studied Claire's face. "Why aren't you happy about this, dear?"

Claire leaned forward and put a hand over Isabel's. "I am happy, but it seems so impossible to believe sometimes. What if no one likes my books? What if they don't sell well or if Whittier is disappointed in me?"

Isabel squeezed her hand. "And what if everyone loves them? What if they are a wonderful success? Why not believe for the best? Have faith in yourself and your work."

Claire sighed. "You sound like Miles."

"Miles and Ezra both say you don't have enough confidence in your own abilities and talents. They're right, you know. You need to work on that. Get some of those positive thinking books at the library and start pumping yourself up more. My mother always said, 'If you don't believe in yourself in this world, who will?' She taught me to be spunky and self-confident and I'm grateful for it."

Claire laughed. "I think you came into this world spunky and self-confident, Isabel. I can't imagine you any other way."

Isabel sat back in her chair. "Well, then you'd be wrong. I grew up in one of those big, old plantation houses down a shady side road on the island, beautiful but isolated. I read and dreamed but was a shy little thing as a girl, not spending much time around others. Mother saw I needed more confidence, so she set me up a vegetable stand out on the road with one of our servants, Sassy, who wove sweetgrass baskets. She told me any money I made I could keep for my own. It was my first retail experience and Sassy taught me a lot while I worked with her under one of those big shady oaks along the highway."

She laughed at her own memories. "Do you know why Edisto *still* has those lovely big oaks draped with Spanish moss all along the highway?"

"I never really thought about it. Is there a reason?"

"There is indeed and it was because of a woman. In the early 1900s, Jean Wilkinson, one of Frank and Violet Wilkinson's girls, was engaged to the engineer building the new highway into the island. She told him flat out if he cut down the live oaks along the highway as intended, that she wouldn't marry him. She held fast to her stand, too, and he changed his plans and kept the trees." She grinned. "You think of that plucky woman every time you drive in and out of Edisto from now on. A strong, determined woman can do about anything she wants to if she sets her mind to it."

"That's a great story." Claire finished her coffee. "I look forward to telling it to the girls later." She paused. "Is it because of Sassy and her sweetgrass baskets that you named your beach house Sweetgrass?"

"Yes." Isabel got up and began to put their mugs and dishes back on the tray. "I still have some of Sassy's old baskets, too, and I surely cherish them."

Looking out the window, Claire saw a group of women heading up the sidewalk to the store. "I see some shoppers coming. Why don't you go home and enjoy your day? I'll be fine on my own. I'm not grieving, simply remembering Charles with love and feeling grateful for how good God has been to make a new, happy life for me and the girls." She walked over to hug Isabel. "I'm so grateful for all the love and interest you've shown to me and my girls, and I thank you for giving me this job."

Isabel patted Claire's cheek again. "I've been the more blessed. Not having children, it's been like gaining a daughter and two lovely granddaughters having you here with me at the Mermaid." She picked up the tray to head to the kitchen. "I'll put these dishes away and then head home. My friend Lucy Baines wants to drive to Charleston to shop and have lunch today. I'll go now that I know you're okay."

She turned to grin at Claire. "You talk those women into buying a few of our new mugs and if they have grandchildren, you show them those hand-smocked dresses of yours I talked you into putting in the store." Laughing, she headed back to the kitchen, and Claire got up from the table to greet the women coming into the store.

Later that evening while she and the girls were eating their dinner out on the screened porch at Oleanders, Miles Lawrence walked up the sandy path from the beach and let himself into the porch. He'd become a more frequent visitor this spring, and Claire felt a little more comfortable around him, knowing he'd been responsible for her books finding a publishing home.

"Hi, Miles." Mary Helen waved. Claire watched the usual worshipful expression cross her daughter's face as Miles strolled into the room to pull up a chair at the table. He did have a way with women—and with girls.

Suki held out her hand. "Will you kiss my hand?"

"I'm always happy to kiss the hand of a pretty girl," he said, kissing her hand and making Suki giggle.

"Have you eaten dinner?" Claire asked.

Suki's eyes brightened. "We're having Tater Tot Casserole."

Claire watched his eyes move to the casserole dish on the table.

"It's one of Mary Helen and Suki's favorites—ground beef, frozen potatoes, cheese, and soup," she said. "You're welcome to some if you'd like. I generally try to cook things the girls like best."

He flashed a slow, easy smile. "I've enjoyed several of your girls' favorite meals here. Today though I ate an early dinner with a colleague after class at the college, but I will take a glass of that mint tea." He pointed at hers.

"I'll get you one," Claire offered, heading into the kitchen.

Miles occasionally stopped by when he drove down to his family's beach house for the weekend. Sometimes he brought his mother, Eudora, with him and a few times his brother and family had come up from Savannah to visit. Miles still made Claire feel antsy and uneasy so she felt grateful his visits were sporadic.

After dinner, the girls begged to play night tag outside with the other children for a time. Claire stayed on the screened porch to keep an eye on them. Miles lingered, too. They moved from the table to sit in two rockers looking out toward the ocean, the lights dim on the porch now, the paddle fan swishing softly as it turned overhead.

"Did you finish the edits on your book?" Miles asked, rocking his chair gently with one foot.

"Yes," Claire answered. "There weren't many changes to make, but I appreciated your advice about how to approach them."

He chuckled. "Which advice was that?"

"You said not to over-react to changes requested, but to try each one to see if it might make the story better. Actually, my editor made the same suggestion. She said if I made any changes that didn't feel right, I could change them back and explain why I wanted to keep the original." Claire smiled at him. "Most of the time, the changes improved the story once I got over feeling prickly about it."

He laughed a rich laugh. "I know that feeling. It happens with editing for academic work, too."

Claire had to admit she did like talking about writing with Miles. So few of her friends understood the peculiar issues an author deals with. As a writer as well as a professor, Miles always did.

"What are you working on now besides your teaching?" she asked.

"I've been asked to write a short supplementary text for a gender course this summer." He chuckled. "That should prove to be an interesting experience."

"Why?" she asked.

"Because of the continually fascinating differences between men and women, despite inequality in most areas basically resolved now."

"Do you really think inequalities *are* resolved in most areas?" she asked, surprised.

"Don't you?" He turned the question back on her.

"No," she answered, shaking her head.

"That calls for an explanation, Ms. Avery. Those are the words I would say to one of my students in class."

Claire saw his smile flash in the dark. "I'm *not* one of your students, Miles. Although I do feel you often *grade* my answers."

He laughed out loud. "What an excellent and spunky comeback, Claire Avery. I do think you are making progress toward becoming a more outspoken individual."

"Is that good?"

He looked at her curiously. "Why wouldn't it be?"

"If being outspoken hurts someone," she answered. "If it discourages them or makes them feel diminished or unimportant."

"That's often a part of learning."

"I don't agree." She shook her head. "I'm a teacher, too. I think a teacher should encourage students to want to learn, should make them feel that their contributions, no matter how small, are important. A teacher's goal should be to lift up, not put down."

"Interesting." He turned toward her. "And do I put *you* down, Claire Avery?"

She crossed her arms. "We were talking about education in general."

"Were we?" he asked, sending her a smug smile.

"There you go again picking at me." She got up to look outdoors, to see if the girls were staying nearby as asked.

"You still have trouble responding when challenged, but I do see improvement," he observed.

She whirled around to face him. "I am *not* your patient."

"No, but I find you an interesting study."

Claire started toward the door, annoyed. "I need to go out and call the girls now. It's late and it's getting dark."

Miles moved quickly to catch her arm before she started out the door. "I still make you uncomfortable, don't I, Claire Avery?"

"Do you need to ask?" She turned to glare at him. "You purposely try to provoke me."

He leaned closer, looking at her with those intense blue eyes of his. His voice dropped. "Better that I provoke you a little than respond to you as I'd like to." He ran a finger slowly down her cheek and neck.

Claire jerked away, opening the screen door and heading down the steps. "Good night, Mr. Lawrence. I think our visit is at an end." She heard his soft laugh follow her into the darkness.

Later that night after she settled the girls into bed, she thought again about her encounter with Miles. She knew he was attracted to her. But was she equally attracted to him? It seemed hard to know amid all the feelings he stirred up in her whenever he came around.

Turning in bed, she touched a finger to Charles's picture by her bedside. He'd been such an easier, gentler, and kinder man to be around than Miles Lawrence. She sighed. She so missed him. However, in all truth Claire knew, as well, that Miles pushed her in ways Charles never did, believed she could do more than she thought she could and be more. She knew Miles had impacted her life positively and influenced her to make changes in the way she thought about herself, despite his odd methods. Perhaps if she spent more time with him, she could get to know him better. The girls certainly loved him and they seemed to show no awkward feelings around him at all. That should tell her something, shouldn't it?

Closing her eyes, Claire could almost hear Charles's advice to her, *Read your Bible for the answers of life and go to prayer to seek God's guidance.* Knowing the wisdom of that counsel, Claire pulled her Bible off the bedside table, praying that what she read would help her with her relationship with Miles and with other matters in her life. She'd relied too much on her own understanding lately. And it wasn't the best way to live.

CHAPTER 14

With only a few customers milling around the store this Friday in late May, Parker let his thoughts drift ahead to the small gathering of friends planned at his home tonight, one of the first in a very long time. He smiled over the words "small gathering"—words he'd learned from Ann. Back at the farm in Tennessee, his mother would say, "We're having some folks over to eat tonight." Same concept, of course. Parker had invited Drake, Nora, Andrew, Claire and the girls to share dinner with him at Waterview. Even nicer, Parker had talked Claire into staying over so they could attend the Gullah Festival in Beaufort on Saturday.

"Good morning, Parker," Nora called, walking down the stairs from the office and interrupting his thoughts. With short russet brown hair, a fresh, winning smile, and a gift for gab, the customers always loved Nora. "I thought Claire was dropping the girls off for the day while she drove to Savannah for a meeting with Whittier."

"She is." Parker glanced at his watch. "I'm expecting them any time."

Her lips twitched in a smile. "Do you think you can keep up with those two little girls on your own all afternoon?"

"Actually, I'm looking forward to it." Parker leaned against the counter. "I'm going to take them on a walking tour around Beaufort."

She moved a blue and white Chinese vase to center it on an antique table. "Andrew is so jealous the girls have a school holiday today and get to spend the afternoon with you. But he's looking forward to dinner at your house tonight." She paused. "Is there anything else I can do to help with that?"

He shook his head. "No, you and Drake are doing enough bringing food to help out."

"I'm only bringing a linguini salad to go with the shrimp and corn you're boiling." She grinned. "I admit I'm eager to try the crab cakes Drake is making, too. Andrew says he is a really good cook."

"He is a great cook, which cannot be said of me. I can boil shrimp and corn with the best of them though," Parker said, sorting through some fliers while he talked. "I can also chop lettuce into neat wedges and drizzle Thousand Island dressing over them so they look like restaurant items."

She laughed. "What is Claire bringing for dessert? Does she need help since she'll be in Savannah all day?"

"No. She told me all the ingredients to buy for strawberry shortcake she plans to make at the house after she gets back."

"I'm glad she and the girls can stay over. I know they'll enjoy the Gullah Festival tomorrow. I read this is the first year for it; I hope it will go well and become a regular Beaufort event."

Parker stacked the mail on the counter to carry to his office later. "With Rosalie Pazant and her daughters behind it, it can't help but be a success. Drake is on the board and helping, too. I think it's a great idea to have a festival focused on the African American Gullah heritage."

Nora smiled. "Andrew, Drake, and I look forward to tagging along with you, Claire, and the girls tomorrow. It should be fun. Drake said the festival includes singing, dancing, arts, crafts, and storytelling."

"*And* food vendors," Parker added.

"I'm certain Andrew looks forward to that." Nora pointed toward the door. "Here come Claire and the girls now." She put a hand on his arm. "Don't worry about the store this afternoon. Drake and I have the hours covered until close, and tomorrow he's letting our new summer employee, Marlo Holland, cover while we all go to the festival. She's personable and smart. I think she'll be a good help this summer when our tourist traffic picks up."

Mary Helen and Suki danced into the store, Claire following close behind. Parker's eyes moved discreetly over Claire. She looked beautiful in a navy skirt, crisp white blouse, and a striking, embroidered vest she probably made herself. Her long hair was tied back in a businesslike style and she wore dressier sandals than usual. Since Claire started working at The Little Mermaid, she'd updated her wardrobe and begun to develop a more personal style, different from her look as a pastor's wife before.

"You look really nice," Parker told her after swinging both the girls around in a welcoming hug.

"Thank you." She twisted her hands, showing Parker she felt a little nervous about her scheduled meeting in Savannah. "I appreciate you taking care of the girls while I drive down to meet with Nancy Franklin and David Whittier. With Memorial Day coming up, Isabel, Elaine, and Lula were busy with tourists coming in for the weekend." She paused. "Are you sure it's not an imposition for you to keep them?" She glanced around the store at the customers milling through different areas.

Nora jumped in to reassure her. "Don't worry about the store. Drake and I will take care of things. Parker needs a day off now and then."

Nora changed the subject as she sat down on the stool by the register. "Andrew and I are so excited about having dinner on the river at Parker's tonight with all of you and about going to the Gullah Festival tomorrow. Andrew said his class is learning about the Gullah heritage and culture in school this week."

"The girls and I read about that, too," Claire said. "It was really interesting." Glancing at her watch, she added, "I guess I'd better leave so I won't be late." She squatted down to hug Suki and Mary Helen. "You girls behave yourselves and mind your Uncle Parker in everything he asks of you."

"We will," they parroted.

After waving goodbye to their mother, the girls were eager to set off for the day. Claire had dressed them in shorts sets and tennis shoes for walking, and they each carried a child's shoulder bag.

"I have monies in my purse to buy something with," Suki said, pointing to the red purse she wore around her neck. Partial to red, she also wore red shorts and red tennis shoes today.

"Isabel gave us five dollars each for helping at The Little Mermaid," Mary Helen added. She wore bright turquoise blue today, so at least Parker would be able to spot both girls if needed from a distance. Not surprisingly, Mary Helen's purse said *I Love Mermaids* on it.

They started their walking tour by heading up Craven Street to pass by the old Gothic-style Arsenal, built of brick and yellow-washed tabby. For young girls the military history of the building was only briefly interesting.

Parker had stopped by the visitor center earlier to pick up a walking tour map, so in front of The Arsenal he showed them on the map where they were headed next. "We'll walk down Scott Street to Bay Street, Beaufort's main street along the river. It's where all the shops are."

"I want to buy jelly bracelets like Gracie Byrd has," Mary Helen said as they strolled down the sidewalk.

"Me, too," Suki added.

Parker scratched his head. "What are jelly bracelets?"

"They're plastic bracelets kids like to wear," Mary Helen explained. "Gracie Byrd has more than anybody."

"Who is Gracie Byrd?"

"She's in school with us," Suki answered. "She doesn't like Mary Helen."

Parker lifted an eyebrow, glancing at Mary Helen. "Is there a reason for that?"

"Gracie Byrd likes J.T. Mikell for a boyfriend and she doesn't like it that I'm friends with him. J.T. doesn't like Gracie at all so he kissed me at the Edisto Zesto one day to make her mad."

"It made her *real* mad, too." Suki shook her head up and down. "She stomped Mary Helen's foot."

Parker tried not to laugh. "I thought boyfriends were for when girls grow up more."

"They are." Mary Helen tossed her head. "And J.T. Mikell is *not* my boyfriend. He makes me mad all the time."

"I see," Parker said. Deciding to change the subject, he pointed ahead as they reached Bay Street. "On the corner is the John Mark Verdier House. It's one of the oldest homes in Beaufort, built in 1804."

"It's not as pretty as Oleanders or your house," Mary Helen said looking up at the two-storied Federal style building.

Parker tried to think what might interest the girls about the house. "The Verdier family who built the house had to abandon it in 1861 during the Civil War. The house was taken over by Union soldiers for their headquarters. After the war, the Verdier family managed to buy the house back again."

Mary Helen wrinkled her nose. "How come they had to buy it back if it was theirs?"

"Most families who owned homes in Beaufort lost their homes in the Civil War. Only a few were able to buy their homes and properties back."

"That's not fair." Mary Helen crossed her arms. "It's no wonder a lot of people in the South are still mad about the war if the North stole stuff from them."

"It's not right to steal." Suki shook her head back and forth.

"It was a difficult time," Parker said, not sure how to explain the entire Civil War to two small girls on a downtown street corner in Beaufort.

"Let's walk down Bay Street and look into some of the stores," he said instead, moving on.

Shopping proved to be a hit for the girls. They loved exploring the quaint gift stores, walking through art galleries and specialty shops. They found bright, colorful jelly bracelets in one of the children's stores, which the girls bought and immediately decorated both of their arms with.

In an artisan shop, Parker bought them handmade hemp

necklaces. Claire warned him about indulging the girls in too many gifts or treats while shopping, but he hoped he wouldn't get chastised for buying them a small necklace each. Suki chose one with a shell pendant and Mary Helen one with a crescent moon.

"We can wear these and our jellies to school on Monday," Suki said.

For lunch, Parker took the girls to a cute sandwich shop and ice cream parlor off Bay Street. He thought they'd enjoy it more than visiting one of the nicer restaurants, and he was right. They loved spending time deciding which of the multitudes of ice cream flavors to try for dessert.

Near the end of Bay Street the girls got to pet one of the horses used on the carriage ride tours. Parker considered taking them on one of the tours, but he knew the tours were lengthy and full of facts unlikely to appeal much to small children. Knowing the girls would enjoy the park along the waterfront, though, he led them through the park on their way back. Mary Helen and Suki played under the trees as they walked and enjoyed looking at the boats coming up the river. They got as excited about squirrels and seabirds as historic homes and sites. Parker decided it didn't take a lot to make a happy day for kids.

Starting back toward Westcott Antiques after a rest in the park, Parker cut across to Cataret Street to take the girls to The Chocolate Tree, a shop that made chocolates and other candies on site. He let them pick out several treats, including pieces of homemade taffy to tuck in their purses for later.

"Mommy told us Ann is buried in a cemetery in downtown Beaufort," Mary Helen said as they left the store. "Is it far from here? We've seen Daddy's grave, but not Ann's."

While Parker hesitated, surprised at this turn in the conversation, Suki added, "Mommy said Ann's cemetery is beside the church you go to and that the church is real pretty, like Trinity where Daddy pastored."

"You're right. The Baptist Church of Beaufort looks somewhat like Trinity Methodist with big white pillars in front. It's near

Westcott's," he added. "We can walk over to the church on our way back. The cemetery has lovely, quiet pathways and we can go inside the church to see the sanctuary."

"We can take pictures for Mommy," Mary Helen said. She'd brought a small camera and taken several photographs throughout the day.

"I'm sure Claire would like that. The church is a very old one," he told them as they walked along Beaufort's shady side streets. "Thomas Jefferson was president when it formally began. During the Civil War the church was used as a hospital."

"Did the North steal it, too?" Mary Helen asked.

"The Northern army took over many buildings to use for hospitals and other purposes," Parker answered. "It took our church a long time to recover from the war but now the church is beautiful again."

At the cemetery Parker walked them down a quiet pathway to Ann's gravesite.

Suki put a small hand on the top of the monument. "I like that Ann has a dove bird on her headstone. That's nice."

"She asked for that," Parker said, remembering.

"I wish people didn't have to die." Mary Helen sighed, rubbing her arm. "I know we all die when we get old, because our bodies wear out, and then we get a new spirit body in heaven. Daddy preached about that. But it makes me mad when good, sweet people like Ann and Daddy die young."

"Me, too," said Suki, tracing her fingers over the dove etched in the monument. She looked up at Parker. "Do you think you and Mommy will ever get married again? I know lots of people do."

Parker couldn't think what to answer to this unexpected question.

"Mommy's pretty," Mary Helen said. "Isabel said maybe she might want to get married again someday."

"Miles thinks Mommy is pretty." Suki scuffed a toe in the grass. "Maybe Mommy will marry Miles."

Mary Helen's eyes widened. "That would be cool." She looked toward Parker. "Do you think she will?"

"I have no idea, Mary Helen, but I think any matter like that is personal and something you should talk to your mother about and not me." Inside Parker felt a stab to his heart at the very thought. He knew Miles had been spending more time visiting with Claire and the girls, but he hadn't realized it had grown serious enough to start the girls speculating about more.

"Listen." Suki put a hand on his arm, interrupting his thoughts. "I hear someone playing music."

Parker smiled, glad for the distraction. "That's the church organ. The organist is probably practicing."

Suki's eyes widened. "Can we go inside to see?"

"Yes, I think the sanctuary is open. We can go inside." He led the way to the church with its tall white steeple rising into the sky.

They climbed the steps and slipped into the sanctuary, a lavish one with balconies on two sides, a beautiful altar, and an elaborate gold chandelier.

"The pews look like little boxes with walls around," Mary Helen remarked, glancing into one of the pews toward the back of the church.

"Members once paid to rent these pew boxes," Parker said.

Mary Helen looked horrified. "They *paid* for a seat in the church?"

He tried not to laugh. "It was common in early church history for people to rent or even buy a pew or a pew box for their family."

Her mouth dropped open. "Do they still do that?"

"No," he answered. Looking around for Suki he saw her down at the front of the church now, leaning on a pew watching the organist play.

Hearing their voices, the man at the organ stopped after a moment to turn around toward them.

"That's not church music," Suki announced to him.

"No, it's not."

"It's *Claire de Lune* by Debussy," she said.

The man's eyes widened. "How old are you?"

"Six years old," she answered. "How old are you?"

He laughed. "In my forties." He glanced toward Parker and Mary

Helen. "I'm John Morgan Dillon, the organist here at the church. I go by Morgan." His eyes narrowed, studying Parker. "I think we've met before."

"I'm Parker Avery," he answered. "I'm a member here at the church and I own Westcott Antiques a block or two away on Craven."

"Ah, yes. I knew I'd met you and I remember your wife Ann." Morgan got up from the organ to walk down closer to them.

"We just visited her grave," Mary Helen said.

"These are my nieces, Mary Helen and Suki." Parker made the introductions. "I've been giving them a little tour of Beaufort today."

Morgan nodded at both.

"How come you were playing *Claire de Lune* and not church music?" Suki asked. She'd walked over to run her fingers over the keys of the big grand piano near the altar as she asked her question.

"I'm helping to start the Beaufort Symphony Orchestra and I'm playing with them at a performance later this month. After I practiced my church music, I decided to practice some of my classical pieces."

"Suki can play that piece you were playing," Mary Helen said.

"Can she?" Morgan looked doubtful.

"Not on the organ," Suki said, shaking her head.

Mary Helen sat down in one of the pews. "Play it for him, Suki."

"Okay," she answered readily, sitting down at the piano and starting to play before Parker could say anything.

As Parker heard the music filling the air, he sat down beside Mary Helen, stunned as always at Suki's gift. Glancing at the organist, he saw him watching Suki with astonishment, too.

"How long have you been taking piano lessons?" he asked when Suki finished.

Mary Helen answered for her. "Suki's heard that piece so many times she just knows it. She likes to play. Mommy taught her some music and she took lessons with mean Miss Najinski last year, but we don't live near her anymore. We live at Edisto now."

"Why didn't you like Miss Najinski?" Morgan asked Suki.

Suki dropped her eyes, her hands straying over the keys of the piano. "She didn't like my songs."

"She didn't like the songs Suki played from out of her heart," Mary Helen explained.

"She plays mostly by ear?" Morgan asked Parker.

He nodded. "She's very gifted."

"She needs to be taking lessons with that talent," he replied.

Suki frowned at him. "Teachers are mean."

"Not all teachers." Morgan walked over to slide onto the piano bench beside her. Putting his fingers on the keys, he began to play.

Parker watched a smile flicker across Suki's face as she watched his hands. He stopped after a little while.

"What is that song?" Suki asked.

"You like it?"

"Yes, it's a happy fun song."

"It's called *Waltz of the Flowers* by Tchaikovsky."

Suki smiled at him. "I can see fairies dancing in the flowers when I hear it."

"Would you like to learn to play it?"

She nodded.

"I can teach you," he said. Morgan trailed his fingers along the keys as he talked. "When I was a boy I could play by ear, too, but when I learned to play with music, I could play so many more things. You can do both, too, Suki, and both are good ways to play."

Her eyes brightened.

Morgan turned to Parker. "I teach in the Music Performance Department of the Baptist College at Charleston—the Horton School of Music—but I live here in Beaufort. I would teach Suki if her mother could bring her to me once a week. Occasionally I take on a special student I take an interest in." He looked at Suki. "I would count it a privilege to be your teacher."

She studied him, taking in his glasses, kindly face, and then looked at his hands again. "Okay, if my mommy will let me and if you don't hit the piano with a little stick when you don't like my songs."

Morgan's eyes shot wide.

"Suki had a rather unfortunate experience with the teacher her grandmother chose for her when living in Arlington," Parker said, making an attempt to explain. "She evidently chose to use her director's baton in a poor way."

"She hit her stick on the piano when Suki didn't play like she wanted," Mary Helen said.

Morgan turned to Suki. "I will never hit the piano with a stick. We'll talk together about any pieces we play and about what we learn together."

She nodded, seemingly relieved.

"Let me get one of my cards for you," Morgan said. "I have some in my office. I'd also like to get your contact information."

He stood up again and Parker noted he was a tall, blond, fit man with wire-rimmed glasses and an imposing posture. Parker liked him, but more important, Suki seemed to like him. They trailed behind Morgan through a couple of hallways to a small office, exchanged information and then talked a little longer.

Morgan handed Parker several tickets as they started to leave. "These are four complimentary tickets to the symphony later this month. I hope you, the girls, and their mother can attend. I think Suki would like to hear the orchestra, and I will be playing. She'll be able to see what people can do with the piano if they study and learn theory and composition, as well as playing the songs they hear with their hearts."

Leaving the church a short time later, Mary Helen said, "He's nice."

Suki looked up at Parker. "Do you think Mommy will bring me to take piano lessons with Mr. Dillon? I like him."

"So do I." Parker smoothed a hand over her hair. "We'll talk to your mother about the lessons together, okay?"

Mary Helen looked back at the church. "Daddy always said God works it out so you meet people you are supposed to. Maybe He worked it out so Suki could meet Mr. Dillon today."

"Perhaps He did," Parker replied.

She nodded. "I think He worked it out so we could stay at Oleanders and for us to meet Isabel to work at The Little Mermaid, too. Isabel says some day I can own a store like she does, that I have good *retail* gifts."

Parker hid a smile. "Isabel would know about retail gifts. She certainly has them in spades."

"You do, too," Mary Helen told him. "But I don't think I want to work with old furniture and stuff like you do. I mean I know you love it, but I don't think it's my thing."

Parker laughed. "I knew it was my thing from the time I was a boy."

She tipped her head to one side. "Do you think God always knows who we're meant to be from when we're little?"

"Maybe," Parker answered honestly. "But it takes some people a lot longer to figure out if that's true and to learn to listen to those nudgings."

"Are we going to your house now?" Suki asked.

"Yes, we are, and you girls can help me set up chairs and tables on the back patio and then play outdoors until your mother comes."

"Can we play with Congress?" Mary Helen asked.

"I'm sure he'd love it," Parker answered, knowing the dog fond of Mary Helen and Suki.

As they strolled down the sidewalks of Beaufort toward the store, the girls each holding one of his hands, Parker smiled, thinking back over what a wonderful day he'd spent with these two small women.

CHAPTER 15

With summer starting, Lula, Elaine, Isabel, and Claire all had a day off from work on the same day, and Lula insisted on having everyone over to her house for lunch on the back porch. Lula and John Mikell's house, called Point Place, a newer home than most on the island's south point, was slate gray with white trim and broad open porches across the back.

The children were having lunch on one end of the porch on a big picnic table while Lula, Elaine, Isabel and Claire ate at a round metal table with cushioned chairs under a shady eave at the other end of the porch.

"Everything is absolutely lovely," Isabel said, spreading a cloth napkin over her lap. "You outdid yourself making such a nice lunch for us."

Lula laughed. "I eat my meals either on the run or with John and the boys who wouldn't notice a pretty tablecloth, napkins, or good china if I put them out. It's a treat for me to provide lunch for someone who will appreciate my efforts."

"I feel exactly the same way," Elaine said. "Pete and the kids sit down to a meal, wolf down the food, and leave. Sometimes I'm not even sure they notice what I fix." She paused. "But this is so nice, a pretty floral tablecloth, napkins to match, beautiful china and girly food—quiche, asparagus, salad with mandarin oranges, homemade yeast rolls, real butter, and peach tea. Plus that lovely coconut cake you made. I feel so special."

"Me, too," Claire said. "But I wish you'd have let us bring something."

Lula waved a hand. "All of you have hosted dinners, shrimp boils, beach cookouts, and more. It was my turn."

"Well, it's charming to see all of you in colorful skirts and sundresses, too, for a change," Isabel added. "We must get one of the boys to take our photo. Someday when we're old, we'll remember this lovely day out on Lula's porch."

They settled in to eat then, enjoying their lunch.

"I guess you heard they voted down the ordinance proposal to build higher buildings on Edisto again," Elaine announced after a time.

"Good. I always worry every time that comes up." Isabel glanced out to the sea, where the waves rolled in one after the other with that sweet sound only heard at the beach. "It would totally change the character of Edisto if that ever passed."

"It's all about greed," Lula put in. "Big high rises pack in more people and make more money for the owners. No one is giving thought to what is best for the environment when they plan those."

Claire shook her head in agreement. "I think Charles and I fell in love with Edisto because it has retained its natural beauty. It doesn't have high rises or motels with lavish swimming pools packed along the beach front—simply beach houses on quiet streets and villas and homes tucked around the Fairfield Resort. I love how they planned the resort so tastefully, keeping the lovely oaks and developing the entire resort and golf course around winding roads lined with flowers, shrubs, and so many beautiful spots."

"It took a few fights to see that the character and beauty of the old resort prevailed at Fairfield. Fortunately, locals had much to do with the resort's development. That always helps." Elaine poured herself another glass of tea.

"A few duplex units and two-level condos are starting to develop around the island, but the limits and restrictions will help to keep Edisto safe from becoming simply another commercial vacation mecca if we all keep standing firm to keep it that way," Isabel added.

Claire passed more raspberry dressing to Elaine for her salad. "I love how the island was planned with beach access areas every few blocks. With so many access points to the beach and ample parking, tourists don't need to park on the streets or cut through the yards of the beach homes."

Isabel laughed. "Of course there are always those tourists every now and then who will trek right through your property or actually ask to use your outdoor showers or your bathroom."

Claire's mouth dropped open. "You can't be serious?"

Elaine waved a hand. "Honey, you haven't lived here long enough to know some of the odd things people can do. In the realty business, I could tell you some stories for a truth."

"What's the worst problem you have with renters?" Isabel asked.

"Theft," Elaine answered. "And property damage."

"They steal things from the rentals?" Claire asked, shocked.

"All the time," Elaine said. "Just the other day, they stole the ironing board and vacuum cleaner from out of one of the Fairfield villas we rent."

"We need to watch for theft in the store, too," Lula said, passing a plate with more quiche slices around the table. "People steal all sorts of things and sadly they steal the bikes people rent from us, too. Tourists forget to be careful to lock them up at the beach during the day or at night while they're sleeping. And then they get mad at us when they're responsible for the loss."

"Well, our problems are small at The Little Mermaid compared to the ones at your businesses," Isabel said. "I remember how shocked Claire was when I caught shoplifters heading out of the store one day."

"Did you call the police?" Elaine asked.

"I did. Those two women had loaded their tote bags up and even hid things under their clothes."

"They seemed so nice." Claire sighed. "But it taught me how watchful I need to be at the store. If Isabel hadn't been there, those two women would have waltzed out with hundreds of dollars of merchandise."

"Ah, the woes of retailers," Elaine said, putting a hand dramatically to her forehead.

"Let's talk about something more fun." Lula looked at Claire. "I think Miles Lawrence has a major crush on you."

Claire blushed. "Miles is kind to the girls and to me. But Lula, I'm a recent widow. I'm not ready to consider another relationship. Charles was a wonderful man, and I still miss him."

"Don't tease Claire," Isabel cautioned. "Miles is *definitely* interested. That's obvious but Claire has not encouraged him beyond going to a concert and a movie with him in Charleston." She grinned. "Although I heard he was dazzling and romantic on those occasions."

"He is *so* handsome." Lula put a hand over her heart. "Where did he take you, Claire?"

"To a concert at the college his mother couldn't attend at the last minute—he'd already bought the tickets—and to dinner and a movie one night when the girls spent the night at Elaine's. That's all." She eyed her friends. "Don't make more of this than there is."

"I wonder why he's never married?" Elaine asked.

"*And* why he still lives with his mother," Lula added. "I always worry about men who live with their mothers after they're grown."

"He doesn't *live* with Eudora. He lives in the large apartment over the garage next to Eudora's antebellum house," Isabel corrected. "Ezra and I always thought it rather nice of him to stay close to Eudora after his father Bronson died. Besides, with Eudora's other son Carlton well settled in Savannah, it will probably be Miles who inherits the Lawrence-Beauregard home in Charleston. It's been in Eudora's family for years. It's right in the heart of downtown Charleston, too. I'm sure Miles values it, and he probably couldn't afford to buy a place like that as a professor."

"Well, John thinks Miles is a mama's boy," Elaine put in.

"He is close to his mother, while most men aren't." Isabel tapped her chin thoughtfully. "But I don't think there's anything queer about it. Ezra says Eudora has favored and spoiled him, but the two have always gotten along surprisingly well."

"I would *hate* to live with my parents or with John's." Lula made a face. "I certainly love them, but they're so bossy and often difficult."

Elaine grinned. "You and your mother are total opposites. I think she'd faint to ride on a jet ski like you do or to canoe into the marsh. You always were a tomboy and still are an outdoor girl."

Isabel waved a hand. "Yes, and that's why it's so charming to see you hostessing this lovely little ladies luncheon. You must give a picture to your mother Avalou." Isabel teased. "She'd be so proud."

They all laughed over this and then got into a discussion about Lula's mother before moving on to chat about other things.

Claire enjoyed the lunch at Lula's. She'd become fast friends with Elaine, Lula, and Isabel over the last year. She'd made other friends, as well, especially through her work at the Mermaid. Edisto was a small island and most of the locals eventually became acquainted, although Claire was, of course, still an outsider compared to many born and raised on the island like Lula, Elaine, and Isabel.

That evening, Elaine took Mary Helen and Suki and her own girls, Jane and Emma, to the new animated *My Little Pony* movie in Charleston. Claire opted out, wanting to work on her writing. She didn't get many quiet evenings to herself.

"I work so many hours that I don't get a chance to do much for my girls," Elaine told her. "I'm sure the movie will be a little silly, but the girls will love it. We're going to the early show and I promised them we'd run over to the mall after to get a hamburger and to buy a new My Little Pony for each of them."

Claire handed her two twenty-dollar bills. "Here's some money for my girls' movie, dinner, and their ponies. They are so excited about this evening. Are you sure you can handle all four girls on your own?"

"Absolutely, and keep your money." She pushed it back into Claire's hand. "As often as you help me with my children, it's the least I can do to cover this small trip."

Claire frowned. "It's too much for you to cover—movie, dinner, and new toys, Elaine."

"Fine, fine. I'll take one of those twenties to help with the movie tickets but I'm covering the rest and the dinner."

With the house quiet after they left, Claire settled in to write on the next Polka Dot kids book. The first was in production stages now but the second needed to be completed by early fall. She fixed a simple supper of tuna salad in a fresh tomato for herself during a work break, and then as the sun began to set, decided to take a walk on the beach. The girls weren't due back for another hour so she had time to walk and stretch her legs after sitting at the typewriter for so long.

Miles waved to her as she passed in front of his house, walking down from the porch to join her on the beach. "Heading out for a walk or coming back?" he asked.

"Just heading out," she answered.

"Where are the girls?" he looked behind her.

"They're at a movie with Elaine, Jane, and Emma."

He moved into step beside her as they walked up the beach. "What are they seeing?"

She smiled. "The new animated *My Little Pony* movie."

He rolled his eyes. "I can see why you opted out on that."

"Actually, I probably would love it," she said. "It features the voices of Cloris Leachman, Danny Devito, and Madeline Kahn, which I'm sure enhanced it. Besides I like animated films and Disney movies, too."

"I'd like to see Rodney Dangerfield in *Back to School.*"

Claire looked at him in surprise. "I wouldn't have expected you to like a slapstick comedy like that."

"Well, you'd be wrong. I enjoy a good spoof on the college world. I enjoyed *Short Circuit*, too."

"About the robot that comes to life? I heard that was cute."

"It was." He pointed toward the moon, changing the subject. "The moon is almost full tonight."

"Yes, it's pretty." Several other couples strolled by. "It's a nice night to be out, but I miss the quieter days when the tourists aren't here, don't you?"

"The tourist trade is what keeps this island alive all year."

"I know that, but I need to watch the girls more carefully with so many people on the beach now. And all the stores and restaurants are more crowded. I've gotten spoiled to the quieter pace."

"It will return." He stopped to pick up an oyster shell. "How's your new life as an author coming along?"

She glanced at the shell in his hand. "Are you thinking of that author role as another encumbrance for me to carry, like all the other barnacles and broken shells attached to that oyster shell?"

"What I like is the idea that this new encumbrance—or addition to your life as an author—will grow and enhance who you are individually."

She slowed to look at him. "You make it sound like my life as a mother and wife took away from me rather than adding to me. You'd be wrong about that. Charles enhanced and grew me, and his love changed me in a positive way. The same is true for the girls. Being a mother enriched and expanded who I am, adding depth and dimension to my life."

"Do you think so?" He looked doubtful.

She lifted her chin. "I *know* so. You haven't been married and you haven't had children yet, so in this area your view is more limited than mine."

He chuckled. "I read a lot, and I counsel with married couples."

"Probably the people who come to talk with you are troubled in their marriage, looking for answers."

"Perhaps." He flashed her a smile. "I do love how you've become more outspoken and sure of yourself."

"There you go again, analyzing me." She punched at him. "I never do that to you."

"What do you wonder about me?"

"Well." She paused. "Having come to know you better, I wonder about your childhood, how you grew up, why you decided to study psychology. I sometimes wonder why you haven't married yet. It's not as though you're not smart and attractive. And you're very charming when you want to be."

He laughed out loud. "I'm delighted to know you've been

thinking about me, Claire Avery. I certainly think about you often enough."

She blushed, annoyed at how he'd twisted her interest around. "You know that's not what I meant."

"Perhaps." He stopped to pick up another shell. "Look at this shell. He laid it out on his palm. It's a double sunrise shell with both sides of the shell still attached together. It's rare to find one at Edisto. Do you remember what Lindbergh wrote that this shell stood for?"

"Young love and romance. The time of being a new couple."

"You keep this one." He took her hand and put the shell in it. "To remember we're a new couple."

She shook her head. "Miles, I'm recently widowed ..."

"You've told me," he interrupted. "But we *are* interested in each other, nevertheless. And we *are* friends, aren't we?"

He laughed softly as she took her time considering his words.

"I suppose we are friends," she said then, tucking the shell gently in her shirt pocket. "And I do appreciate all you did to help my books find a publisher. I'm indebted to you."

"It isn't indebted I'm interested in, Claire Avery."

She managed to change the conversational topic again, pointing out a group of boys riding the waves to the beach, and then they talked about changes around the island with the number of tourists growing daily.

It was dark when they made their way up the pathway to Oleanders. Miles insisted on seeing her home before he walked back to his own place.

"It was nice of you to walk me to the house," Claire said, feeling nervous and twitchy now with them standing in the dark by the steps leading up to the screen porch. "I hope the work on your book continues to go well."

"I'm sure it will." He moved closer, and Claire found that with the stair rail behind her she couldn't step back. As she began to move sideways instead, Miles reached out to put his hands on her arms. "Look at me, Claire."

Uncomfortable, she lifted her eyes. "I really need to go in …"

"You have become important to me, Claire Avery. You haunt my thoughts and often my dreams. I know you are attracted to me as I am to you." He held up a hand to stop her as she started to speak. "I know it worries you, that you feel you're betraying your husband's memory to care about someone else so soon. But it's been over a year now. I don't think your husband would want you to never experience love or passion again."

Claire swallowed, not sure what to say. She could feel her heartbeat kicking up, and she wet her lips as Miles continued to look into her eyes, smiling softly. Then he leaned forward and kissed her. Claire found herself caught up in a swirl of passion, surprising her.

Somehow she found herself in his arms, pressed against him, his hands finding ways to stroke her hair, neck, back, and arms. But oh, so very gently and sweetly. She felt like a little bird, trapped, unable to move or fly away as he kissed her more deeply, reminding her of the thrill of passion, which she found she'd almost forgotten.

"We might just be falling in love, Claire Avery," he whispered against her mouth. "A lovely emotion to experience, don't you think?"

She pulled away. "I don't know what to think, Miles," she said in a choked voice. "It feels too soon. It doesn't feel right."

Claire saw his smile flash in the dark. "It feels very right to me." Then he pulled her close to kiss her again, making her senses spin.

Oh, what's wrong with me? Claire wondered. *Why am I enjoying this?* But even as the questions rolled through her mind she found her fingers threading through Miles's hair, touching his face, feeling the strength of his back as her hands moved, seemingly with a mind of their own, to slide over the back of his shirt. *Could they actually be falling in love? And should they be?* It was too complicated to consider, especially when all her senses were waking up to Miles's kisses and touch.

She heard the phone ring in the house, waking her to reality.

"It's the phone," she managed to say, pulling away, and practically scrambling up the stairs. "I need to get it."

But the ringing quit before she got to the screen door at the top of the steps. She glanced back and her eyes locked with Miles's eyes.

"Don't be afraid of your feelings, Claire. Or of me." He smiled then, blew her a kiss, and walked away.

Claire stood, frozen in place for a moment, and then opened the door to let herself inside. On the screened porch, she watched Miles walk back up the beach. At the path to his house, he turned before walking up the sandy trail and waved to her.

Embarrassed, she slipped back into the darkness of the porch, wondering again at all the feelings he'd aroused in her tonight. Troubled, she spent time in prayer before the girls came back. *Should it be time for her to love again? And was Miles the right man for her to love?* She simply wasn't sure of the answers.

CHAPTER 16

July 1986

With the Fourth of July past, the sultry days of mid July moved forward at their slow, hot, Southern pace into the dog days of summer. On Sundays Claire came to Beaufort to attend church with Parker now and to share lunch before taking Suki to her afternoon piano lesson with Morgan Dillon. Claire and Morgan had settled on Sunday afternoons as the best time for both of them around their busy work lives.

Back at Parker's house this Sunday, Parker and Claire worked together in the kitchen preparing lunch while the girls played outdoors in the backyard with Congress.

"They're very fond of that black Labrador," Claire commented after looking out the kitchen window to check on them.

"I'd say the feeling is mutual." Parker paused in tearing up lettuce for a salad to glance Claire's way. "What's in your casserole?"

"I call it Crunchy Chicken Casserole. It's full of chicken chunks, chopped celery and onions, water chestnuts, and sliced almonds, all mixed in cream of chicken soup and mayonnaise with herbed breadcrumbs on top. It's nice for a hot summer day like this." She finished spreading crumbs over the casserole, dotted it with butter, and popped it in the oven. "I think this casserole is all we'll need with a salad and ice cream for dessert."

"Sundays are a treat for me now with you cooking a nice lunch after church every week."

She turned to smile at him. "I'm very grateful you introduced Suki to Morgan Dillon. She loves working with him." Claire paused. "It's also good for us to be back in church again. Charles, the girls, and I often came to church with you and Ann in the past, and I like your church."

"It's not the same denomination Charles preached in."

"Neither is it the denomination I grew up in." She shrugged. "But I think the heart and spirit of a church is more important than the particular denomination."

"Suki and Mary Helen like it, too." Parker chuckled. "However, I'm still getting used to sitting so close to the front every week. Suki insisted, wanting to see Morgan at the piano and organ better."

Claire rinsed and wiped her hands on a kitchen towel. "If you're finished with that salad, we can sit on the back porch for about twenty minutes until the casserole is ready. I can keep an eye on the girls better."

Parker put plastic wrap over his finished salad, placed the bowl in the refrigerator, and retrieved two bottles of Perrier while there. He handed one to Claire as he joined her on the porch.

She sipped the cold sparkling water, looking out over the lush green yard, the marsh, and beyond to the Beaufort River. "You live in such a beautiful place and you truly enjoy the best of both worlds with a home in the city and a beach house at Edisto."

"Sometimes the marvel of it still surprises me."

Claire smothered a smile. "Ann always said you experienced a hard time accepting her family had so much money and property."

"Like Charles, I grew up simply."

She leaned back in her chair and shifted the subject. "Everything in your house looks the same as when Ann was alive. You haven't made many changes."

"Should I have?" He turned toward her with the question. "I always thought Ann possessed a good eye for decorating."

"She did and the house is gracious throughout. I like it that you kept the character of the home's historic period without over-modernizing, too."

"Ann and her parents insisted on it. She and I added bathrooms and upgraded the kitchen, but that's about all, except for buying more outdoor furniture for entertaining."

"Who keeps the yard up?"

"A local man named Willie James Nicely takes care of the property. His wife Florence comes and cleans the house while he works outside. They've worked here a long time." He crossed an ankle over his knee. "I'm glad. I admit I don't like yard and garden work much—a bone of contention to my parents that I didn't."

"Knowing them as I do, I doubt you exaggerate."

Parker saw her smirk. "How are things coming along with Whittier and your books?"

Claire pushed a strand of hair from her face. "It's exciting but hard. I still can't believe sometimes that my first children's book comes out this fall. I hope it will do well."

"I doubt Whittier would have chosen to publish it if they didn't think it would."

She bit her lip. "Sometimes I worry about disappointing them if it doesn't sell well—and disappointing others so excited for me."

"You shouldn't doubt yourself when you're doing what you love. It will work out, and if not life will offer you something else useful to do, something else to give your love and talents to. No one who loves you will think less of you for trying."

She smiled at him. "That's a nice thought."

"It's a true thought."

Claire glanced at her watch and then stood up to call out to the girls in the yard to come in for lunch.

They waved and began to gather up the few toys they'd taken outside.

At lunch, after the blessing, the four gathered around the table in the kitchen alcove to eat.

Mary Helen looked up from her plate after a time. "I like the minister at your church, Parker, but I liked Daddy better."

Parker grinned. "Actually so did I. Your father possessed an exceptional ministry gift."

"I like Mr. Dillon's playing though," Suki added.

"Yes, he's very good. I enjoy him, too." Parker reached for one of the rolls Claire had baked with the casserole.

"Your church has altar calls so people can come up if they aren't saved yet," Mary Helen said between bites. "Daddy did that a few times at Trinity but the church leaders didn't like it much."

Claire choked on her salad. "How do you know that, Mary Helen?"

She shrugged. "I heard Daddy and some men talking. My Sunday school teacher said Methodists like to get saved private-like."

Parker laughed out loud.

"Different churches do things different ways in their services," Claire told her.

Mary Helen picked croutons out of her salad to eat them. "I know that, Mommy. I was only noticing, that's all. Daddy said the important thing was that people *get* saved, not how. He told me lots about the services he helped with in Haiti when he traveled. They were *really* different. At one of our kids' night meetings, he even showed a film of one."

Suki interrupted. "The people jumped up and down, danced, sang, played drums and everything. It looked fun."

"There are many ways to praise and worship God," Claire said.

Mary Helen changed the subject. "I like your house, Parker. But our bedrooms at Oleanders are better for kids. Me and Suki sleep in the same room when we are here, the one with the two twin beds, because Suki doesn't want to sleep in that room with the high fussy bed."

Claire gasped. "Mary Helen, it isn't nice to criticize others' homes."

Mary Helen rolled her eyes. "I'm not *criticizing*. It's just that Parker has lots of old antique stuff in his house. And that bed is so high we can't get in or out of it without a stool. Why is that, Parker?"

"In the past beds were built high off the floor so trundle beds or trunks could be stored underneath," he explained, grinning. "Beds were often considered an opportunity to show off one's wealth then, so people built them lavish in appearance with ornate carvings, often decorated with gold, silver, or inlaid wood. With beds so high, a small step stool was usually kept beside the bed to help people climb in and out."

"I don't *like* to climb in and out of bed on a stool," Suki complained. "It's scary when it's dark at night. And if you roll out of bed, it's a big fall."

Parker tried to keep a straight face. "I suppose lower beds are more advantageous, and two of the guest room beds are built rather high off the floor."

"The highest one is the bed with the big top over it and the drapes around the sides," Mary Helen told him.

He laughed then. "That bed is called a canopied bed. Most women like those with the draperies all around."

Mary Helen put a hand on her hip. "It's pretty but too tall for sleeping in. Like Suki, I don't like to climb out of bed on a stool at night, especially when I need to go to the bathroom."

Suki's eyes brightened. "But me and Mary Helen like to play pretend-house in that bed with the drapes."

Claire looked shocked. "Beds are not to play in, girls."

Parker waved a hand. "Oh, I don't mind. Maybe I need to create a more fun-like girls' bedroom since you two come to stay here more often now."

"You certainly don't need to go to that trouble or expense," Claire said, sending both girls a stern look. "The room the girls share is lovely just as it is, like all of your house."

"We love to come to your house, Parker," Mary Helen said, picking up on her mother's cue and trying to redeem her manners. "We love all the big porches and the huge yard."

"I love your piano in the front room," Suki added, beaming a sunshine smile at him.

"You girls finish your lunch," Claire said, artfully changing the subject and then shifting the conversation to a new topic.

A short time later, after cleaning up from lunch, Claire, Parker, and Mary Helen dropped Suki off at the church sanctuary with Morgan for her piano lesson. They walked into the cemetery to leave flowers on Ann's grave and then across the street so Mary

Helen could play in the playground by the church's Enrichment Center. A bench under a shady tree offered a nice spot for Parker and Claire to sit while they kept an eye on her.

Claire glanced back toward the cemetery and sighed. "Do you ever think you might marry again?"

Parker felt his heart kick up a notch. "Possibly. Why do you ask?"

She smiled. "You're very handsome and I've seen women try to attract your interest. Like at church today, or at times at the beach or your store. I've wondered sometimes if Nora doesn't have a crush on you. You've been so good to Andrew. I know she appreciates it."

Stunned, he answered quickly. "Nora and I are strong friends, but there are no feelings like that between us."

"Or with Nora and Drake? I can tell she really likes him, too."

"The three of us work together, Claire. We're colleagues and friends. That's all." He studied her. "What brought these questions on? Has Nora said something to you or has someone else?"

"No, I guess I was simply thinking about whether either of us would ever marry again." She picked at her skirt as she answered.

Noticing she was acting nervous, Parker said, "You have your admirers, too. You might wish to marry again yourself some day."

She lifted her eyes to meet his. "Do you think Charles would mind if I did marry again someday?"

Ah, so that's what this is about, he thought. "No. I don't think Ann or Charles would mind if either of us married again someday. I wouldn't have wanted Ann to remain single for the rest of her life if I'd died earlier. Would you have wanted Charles to never marry again?"

"Oh, no, of course not." She put a hand to her heart in surprise. "I'd want him to have another chance at happiness."

He smiled at her. "Well, there's your answer. He would want the same for you."

She shifted on the bench. "I wonder if it will be as easy to know you've found the right person the second time. Do you think you will know?"

"Yes. Absolutely," he answered. "I believe I will know, but I might be slower to express my feelings, more cautious. I would want someone with similar values, someone I could share my life with and be comfortable with, someone I could trust and be friends with as well as lovers. I believe I learned the first time how important those things are, despite other differences."

"It's so hard to know." Claire twisted her hands in her lap as if thinking and Parker knew from those words it wasn't him she was thinking of at all.

He thought of bringing up Miles's name to see if she wanted to talk about him or confide more, but then he checked himself. He didn't really want to hear about her feelings for Miles Lawrence, and it hurt him to think she might be serious enough about Miles to want to discuss marriage.

Mary Helen ran over to chatter with them before Claire could ask further questions, much to Parker's relief.

"Can we walk at the park on the river before we go back to Edisto?" Mary Helen asked. "Suki and I love to play in that park and watch the boats come down the river."

"We need to head back to the island," Claire told her. "We'll go to the park another day."

Parker felt relieved that Mary Helen's bubbling conversation filled the space between them while they walked across the street to get Suki. His heart hurt over their earlier words. He ached inside to think he might lose their company and that it might be Miles in future spending the weekends with them and sharing in their lives.

After Claire and the girls left the house later, Parker walked around through all the rooms thinking back over the day. He realized the house, filled with antiques and collectibles, didn't offer a homey, family appeal. Only a few of the rooms spoke of ease and comfort, and he could see that all the upstairs guest rooms looked more like rooms in a bed and breakfast or an antiques showroom than bedrooms a person might feel relaxed and comfortable in. Especially a child. He knew, as well, that he purposely hadn't changed anything since Ann died, even the bedspread on his bed.

Congress walked along behind him, the dog's nails clicking on the hardwood floors.

"I guess I need to make some changes," Parker said to the dog, standing in one of the guest bedroom doorways. "Perhaps Claire and the girls were gently suggesting the idea earlier." He walked into the guest room, running a hand over an elaborate side chair. "I'll talk to Drake and Nora about changing out some of the household furnishings to make the place more appealing, more family oriented. Ann always wanted our home to reflect the business, to be a showcase for Westcott Antiques. But it doesn't need to be quite so formal now, I guess."

Walking back downstairs to look for the Sunday newspaper, he reached a hand down to pet the black lab's head. "I'll find a way to get Claire involved in helping me make the changes. It might help her see I'm ready to move on, shift her thoughts in this direction. Besides, women like to put their own stamp and signature on a home. I've seen that at play in the business all these years. Perhaps getting Claire involved in changes at Waterview might help turn her heart my way."

Parker heard Charles's words in his mind then, *Do your best and trust God for the rest.* That's really all he could do at this point.

CHAPTER 17

The month of July ended with a lengthy heat wave along the coast of South Carolina, but when a week of cooler temperatures arrived in early August, Claire decided to take the girls shopping in Charleston for clothes and school supplies. She wouldn't have many more days off work this month and both girls needed new shoes and a few new outfits.

"Remember I don't want *brown* shoes," Suki told her on the way to town. "Or any brown dresses."

"You've made that perfectly clear to me several times." Claire smiled at her. "I don't think we'll buy more than a few dresses for school anyway. Since you girls don't wear uniforms at Edisto Primary, pants and shirts will be more practical. You often sit on the floor for reading circle and story hours, and with the weather nice most all year, you play outdoors nearly every day, too. We might buy a new dress or two for church, but I think pants and tops will be better for school wear, don't you?"

"Yes, but I want one school dress with leggings. Those are cool now," Mary Helen told her. "And I want some stirrup pants with a long top."

"Gracie Byrd has stirrup pants," Suki said.

Claire rolled her eyes. "I think both of you notice entirely too much what Gracie Byrd has or does not have. Why is that?"

"Because she always brags and makes you notice it," Mary Helen explained.

"People usually brag when they have low self-esteem and don't really think well of themselves. They brag to try to impress others."

Claire slowed the car for a stoplight as she replied. "Perhaps you and Suki might want to try harder in future to see that Gracie Byrd doesn't succeed quite so well. Try not to notice her bragging so much."

"That will be hard because she's *always* doing it," Mary Helen said. frowning.

Claire sighed, giving up on the argument.

By noon, a little late, they'd finished their shopping at the Citadel Mall. Claire had talked the girls out of buying faddish parachute pants and Members Only jackets but gave in to a pair of leg warmers for each—a foolish fashion item to her way of thinking with the weather so warm in the South.

"Can we go to the Charleston City Market?" Mary Helen asked. "I love looking at all the handmade crafts and things. It's so fun."

"Yes, can we?" Suki put her hands up in a prayerful gesture.

"All right," Claire agreed. "But let's eat at a simple restaurant on the way into town. It's expensive to eat downtown."

"Arby's is close and they have a kids' menu," Mary Helen said. "I like their roast beef sandwiches and curly fries."

"I want chicken tenders and chocolate milk," Suki put in.

Claire smiled. "That's a good idea. I like Arby's, too."

A short time later with lunch behind them, Claire found a spot to park near the City Market in Charleston. She and the girls made their way then to the historic four-blocks-long market to enjoy looking at all the vendors lining the inside of the building. Admittedly, Claire loved the City Market, too, and it was always a fun place to spend an afternoon.

After two hours exploring the market, Claire and the girls walked down to White Point Garden on the Cooper River.

"I loved watching the sweetgrass weavers make their baskets," Mary Helen said. They sat on a bench in the park not far from the Cooper River, enjoying homemade cookies from the market and lemonade bought at a small shop along the way.

Suki sat in the grass beside their bench playing with her new Nesting Dolls. Each colorfully painted wooden doll fit neatly inside another until the various sized dolls formed one larger doll at the end. "These are so cute, Mommy. Thanks for getting them for me and Mary Helen."

"You're welcome." Claire finished off her lemonade, glad to enjoy it after the walk in the afternoon heat from the City Market. "Besides it's nice to take home a present from a happy day."

Mary Helen opened her purse to take out her nesting dolls, too, her set painted blue with gay flowers while Suki's was red. "I liked seeing the lady paint other dolls like these while we watched. She said she painted our dolls yesterday."

"Can we take them to school for Show n' Tell, Mommy?" Suki's face brightened with the thought.

"Of course."

Mary Helen turned to Claire, changing the subject. "Do you still have your Charleston map?"

"Yes." Claire took it from her purse and laid it open. "We're here at White Point Garden only a few blocks from the City Market." She pointed to both spots.

Mary Helen leaned over the map to study it. "Miles lives right here." She pointed to a street only a block or two away. "We could go by to see him."

"How do you know where Miles lives?" Claire slanted Mary Helen a sharp glance.

She lifted her chin. "He *told* me. He gave me his school card and wrote his address on the back for me, and he said to come see him when we came to Charleston the next time." She fished the card out of her purse and handed it to Claire.

Claire studied the business card from Miles's college.

"Can we go?" Suki begged. "I want to see where Miles lives."

"I think we should call before dropping by Miles's home," Claire replied. "Besides, his home phone isn't on this card. We'll plan a trip to see him another day, girls."

"Mom, he *said* to come by anytime we were in Charleston," Mary Helen insisted. "He might not even be there anyway, but we can see where he lives."

"We could just *walk* by," Suki added, always the child to come up with a compromise.

Claire couldn't help smiling. "I suppose we might walk by."

Miles's street was only a few blocks away, right on the way to their car, and, like the girls, she was curious to see his home. "We can walk past his home on our way back to our car, but we won't stop."

"Yea!" Mary Helen said, starting to pick up their napkins and cups to put them in the nearby trash.

They walked up Meeting Street from White Point Garden, crossing Tradd and then turned right on Elliott Street, a quiet side street. They passed a church, several condos and a few colorful row houses before finding the house number on Miles's card.

"There it is." Mary Helen pointed across the street.

Like many downtown Charleston homes, the side of the Antebellum house faced the street, plants spilling gaily from the second story window boxes, the formal front of the home tucked neatly behind a gated wall. The yellow stucco home, with its maroon shutters and door and its ornate balconies, linked to a two-storied garage beside it. A doorway by the garage, with a maroon awning, gave entry to an apartment above it.

"I see the number eleven by that door," Mary Helen said, pointing to the entry by the garage. "That must be where Miles lives and the big house must be Mrs. Eudora's."

The girls had met Miles's mother Eudora Lawrence at the beach a number of times over the last year. Although not a warm or friendly woman—and a bit snobby to Claire's way of thinking—Eudora had nevertheless been relatively congenial to them.

Suki tilted her head to look up at the tall house. "I don't think this house is as pretty as Miles's house at the beach."

"It's old and probably full of lots of antiques and stuff, too." Mary Helen wrinkled her nose.

Claire smiled. She loved and appreciated gracious Southern architecture and beautiful antique furniture but the girls didn't always hold the same views, especially Mary Helen.

"Couldn't we go and knock on the door since we're here?" Mary Helen asked. "Miles might be home, and we could say hello."

Suki gave Claire an appealing glance. "Please? Miles might be sad if he knew we came to his street but didn't stop to say hello."

Claire hated to think Eudora or Miles would look out their windows to see them lurking across the street and staring at their home. At the thought, she all but shoved the girls to a point further up the road to sit on a bench in front of a small business. Here, somewhat hidden behind a street post, she could think about what to do. Dropping in uninvited simply didn't feel right.

"I really think we should wait and call before we visit..." she began, trying to help the girls understand, but she paused as she saw Miles's door open.

A young woman came out, turning to talk to someone inside and causing Claire to pull back even tighter out of sight.

Suki started to get up, but Claire grabbed her hand. "Stay here and be quiet. That isn't Eudora."

"Maybe she's the cleaning lady," Suki said, looking around the post.

"Maybe," Claire said, but the woman looked entirely too young and trendy to be a cleaning woman. More like a student. Claire smiled to herself at the thought: *Probably one of Mile's students stopping by to drop off a paper.*

This explanation stopped dead as Miles stepped out of the house, his shirt unbuttoned, his hair tousled, and wrapped the girl in his arms to kiss her. The girl kissed him back with obvious passion, plastering herself against him and wrapping a leg around him to get closer.

Claire gasped. "Let's go, girls," she whispered in a low voice, grabbing both the girls' hands and starting down the street the way they'd come earlier. "This isn't a good time for us to visit."

Claire pulled them along, practically running, until they came to Meeting Street again.

"My shoe's untied," Suki complained, trying to keep up.

Claire slowed hearing her words. They were far enough away

now for her to stop and check Suki's shoe. Miles hadn't seen them. *Thank goodness.*

As Claire dropped to one knee to tie Suki's shoe, she looked up to see tears running down Mary Helen's face.

Suki started to cry, too, seeing Mary Helen's tears. "Who was that lady, Mommy?" Suki asked. "And why was Miles kissing her? I thought he loved *us.* Me and Mary Helen saw him kissing you one day when you didn't know, and Miles said he wished he could be our daddy. I thought we would get married again to Miles."

Claire, so upset herself, couldn't think what to say.

Mary Helen rubbed at the tears still running down her face. "Don't you watch television shows about men like Miles," she snapped. "Miles is a cheater and not a nice man."

"Are you sure?" Suki asked, confused.

"We saw what we saw." Mary Helen crossed her arms. "It isn't like we heard gossip and aren't sure about it. We *saw* Miles kissing that woman." She began to cry again with the words.

Despite herself, Claire started to cry, too. She simply couldn't help it. "People can be disappointing," she said at last, not knowing what else to say.

"Maybe, but people can be mean, too. It's mean to lead little girls along and pretend you want to be their daddy when theirs died." Mary Helen stomped her foot. "I *hate* him."

"It's wrong to hate," Claire put in.

"Maybe not always." Suki sighed. "Miles was bad and hurted our feelings. He hurt you, too, Mommy. He kissed you, and he kissed me and Mary Helen, too, and he pretended like he loved us when he really didn't."

"She's right." Mary Helen sniffed. "He took you on dates, too."

Again, Claire tried to think what to say but couldn't find any words.

"Why would Miles do that, Mommy?" Suki asked around her tears. "I thought he was nice. He told us we were beautiful, and he helped you get your books published. How could he be so nice if he's bad?"

"I don't know all the answers, girls," Claire said, fishing tissues out of her purse to pass around.

Mary Helen flashed angry eyes her way. "You won't ever let him kiss you again, will you?"

"No, of course not, Mary Helen, and you and Suki should have talked to me about seeing Miles kiss me before." She paused. "I must admit I thought his feelings had grown more serious than I realize they are now."

"He's a scumbag creep." Mary Helen kicked at a potted plant on the street beside them. "That was only a *girl* he was kissing, too, and Miles is old."

Claire saw little point in arguing with that truth.

"We need to go home," she said instead, starting back up the street again, not even chastising Mary Helen for kicking the planter.

Suki took her hand. "Does this mean Miles won't be our friend anymore?"

Mary Helen glared at her. "That's a dumb thing to ask, Suki. Why would you *want* to be friends with Miles anymore at all? We know he's not a nice person now. I will *never, ever* be his friend again."

"Will you stomp on his foot like Gracie Byrd did yours?"

The words almost made Claire smile.

"No, but I hope he doesn't ever come to our house again because I won't let him in. We lost our daddy and were sad and he *pretended* like he loved us. That's bad and I won't *ever* forget it." Mary Helen walked ahead of them up the street with angry strides.

Claire couldn't even think what to say to comfort her.

Their ride back home to the island was quiet, the girls sniffling and crying and Claire, despite her best intentions, often joining them. She felt so humiliated and foolish.

Later in the evening when the girls went out to play night tag with the other children, Claire slipped into her room, lay down on her bed and sobbed.

"From what I heard you're wasting tears over someone who isn't worth them." Isabel's voice came from the doorway. She came over to sit down by Claire on the bed.

"What are you doing here?"

"Mary Helen came over to get me." Isabel chuckled. "She said you needed a mommy but that yours was too mean to call."

Claire couldn't help a small laugh.

"There. See you're feeling better already." Isabel stood up. "Let's go drink a glass of iced tea out on the porch and listen to the ocean. The girls need to see that you're better. It scares them to see you cry like this." She patted Claire on the hip. "It scares me to see it, too. You go wash your face. I'll fix the tea."

After washing her face and tidying up, Claire slipped out to join Isabel on the screened porch. Seeing the girls playing at the cabana, she waved to them.

"I'm sorry to be such a mess," Claire said, sitting down and taking the glass of tea Isabel passed to her.

"You have a right to be upset from what Mary Helen told Ezra and me."

Claire groaned. "I am so embarrassed."

"Don't be. It was best you learned what you did *before* you became further involved with the man or before you married him. Be grateful."

"I feel so shocked though," Claire admitted. "I hate, too, that both the girls were with me."

"That was for the best, too. Miles had all three of you charmed. Ezra and me as well. I'll admit it." She wrinkled her nose. "I'd heard talk that Miles was somewhat of a ladies man, but I thought that simply meant he hadn't found the right woman to care for yet. A lot of men sow their wild oats, so to speak, until they do." She paused. "But they don't continue sowing their wild oats after. That shows a problem they'll probably carry around for a lifetime."

"Maybe once I get over hurting I can be grateful." Claire closed her eyes and leaned her head back against the back of the rocking chair. "I'm not quite there yet. Honestly, Isabel, that young girl didn't look over eighteen, although she might have been a year or two beyond that. But she was only a girl."

Isabel looked out into the night. "Ezra drove into Charleston to give Miles *what for*. I thought you should know that. He was really mad."

"Oh, my. Ezra shouldn't have done that." Claire put a hand to her heart.

"Nonsense. We've come to feel about you like a daughter." She lifted her chin, annoyed. "Miles took advantage of your vulnerability and of the girls', too. Ezra didn't want him cruising down to the beach tomorrow not knowing anything was different, putting you in the awkward position of trying to explain to him what you saw."

Claire shook her head. "I hadn't even thought that far ahead or considered what I might say."

"Ezra is going to suggest that Miles make himself scarce at Edisto for a time, and I'm sure he'll make it very clear to him that no one is eager to see his face around here any time soon, either."

They sat in the quiet, listening to the waves roll in onto the beach, feeling the peace of the evening settle over them.

"This is such a peaceful place," Claire said after a time.

"That it is." Isabel reached across to pat Claire's hand on the arm of the rocker. "Keep in mind that every woman makes a mistake about a man every now and then, Claire. Don't make too much of it and don't beat yourself up over it for longer than you need to. Shake the dust off your feet and move on."

Isabel paused and sniggered. "I'd say Mary Helen has the best take on it. She said she hoped both Miles's houses burned down and that the slutty girl dumped him and made him feel like a rat pig. She said she hoped when he came crawling back to apologize that she was here so she could slam the door in his face and tell him what she thought of him."

Claire shook her head. "Oh, my. I do worry about Mary Helen's temper sometimes. She can be so outspoken."

"I rather like her spunk myself."

Claire rubbed her neck. "Still, there could be an explanation we don't know about," she said, trying to be fair.

"That's where I admire Mary Helen's take more. I'd say Miles showed his true colors and we should take his word for it."

"You're probably right." Claire felt tears start again. "It's only that I'm so embarrassed."

"Don't you start crying on me again," Isabel warned. "I swear that jackass isn't worth one more tear of yours. You better tell yourself that, too."

"Miles said he thought we were probably falling in love."

"A man like that will say what he needs to in order get what he wants. Lying becomes a comfortable pattern." She stirred the ice cubes in her glass with her straw. "You've read enough books to know the type."

Claire looked out toward the sea, letting the sound of the waves comfort her.

"Had you fallen in love with him?" Isabel asked after a space.

Claire turned to give her a little smile. "Only around the edges, Isabel. From the very first Miles made me uncomfortable, even with the attraction I felt. Perhaps that offered a warning I should have paid more attention to. I tried to pray about it but never got a clear answer."

Isabel flashed her a grin. "I'd say God answered. His ways of doing that aren't always what we have in mind, but they do tend to clarify things. My mother always used to say: *The truth wills out.* I'd say it did here for you and the girls today. Mary Helen in particular told me she'd never have a minute's use in her life for a cheating man in the future. That they hurt too much."

Claire shook her head. "Mary Helen was so charmed by Miles. He had certainly stolen her heart. I hate especially that he hurt her and Suki. Those girls didn't need more pain and disappointment at this time in their lives."

"No one needs betrayal and lies at any time in their lives, Claire. It always hurts."

A new thought hit her mind. "Do you think Miles will try to come and see me?"

Isabel bristled. "In time I imagine he will. His sort always comes back around with charm and a lie to cover for their wrong. I hope you'll have the good sense to show him the door if he does." She laughed. "That is *if* Mary Helen lets him in. Even little Suki said she would stomp his foot if he came here because he made you cry."

"That sweet child." Claire blinked back tears again.

"You're a kind, trusting woman, Claire Avery, but be sure you don't let that compassionate side of yours rear its head and let Miles Lawrence back around you and your girls in future. I don't want to see any of you hurt again, you hear?"

"Yes, ma'am, I hear." She reached over to take Isabel's hand. "You were kind to come and comfort me tonight. I'd have said I didn't want or need company, but I did."

"All bad things are easier born with a friend." Isabel squeezed her hand. "Hurts and bad times pass. You've learned that before. You'll see it to be true again."

"Yes. I know you're right." Claire turned to Isabel. "How can I best help the girls through this?"

"Like the old saying: *When the going gets tough, the tough keep going.* You just keep living your life to show them how strong women keep moving on when life gets hard. It's a lesson that will teach them a lot for their own futures ahead. No one escapes pain and hurt and betrayal. As much as you hope it won't touch the girls, Claire, it will someday. And they'll remember and draw strength from how you moved through your times of facing it—like this time. Make them proud, girl."

"I'll try," she said and meant it. She would stay tough and she would keep going. And somehow she would heal from this hurt.

CHAPTER 18

Elaine called Parker that night to tell him about what happened between Miles and Claire. "I know Claire would be too embarrassed to tell you about it," Elaine explained. "But because you're her family, Pete and I wanted you to know, especially because the girls were involved. They'd started dreaming Miles might be their new father." He heard Elaine sniffling between words. "I hate so much that Miles hurt Claire and those girls. They didn't need this right now after losing Charles only last year."

No, they didn't, Parker thought, hanging up the phone. He glanced at the clock. After ten already. Too late to head to the island to see how Claire was doing. Too late to call, too. What would he say to Claire anyway? She'd be embarrassed to learn Elaine called him, no matter Elaine's good intentions.

Parker sat on the screened porch, looking across the marshes in the dark, watching the lights of ships and buildings wink in the night sky. Guilt niggled at the back of his mind. Guilt that he felt glad deep down inside that the relationship with Miles had ended. He shouldn't, of course. He should only want Claire's happiness. But he'd never felt Miles the right man for her, the man to replace Charles. He shook his head. Who could replace Charles anyway? He had been a sterling man of strong character, close to God, beloved by all his congregations. Impacting lives. Changing people. What did Parker have to offer in comparison to that? He hadn't even noticed, as Miles did so clearly and he practically a stranger, that Claire possessed a strong writing gift. As far as Parker knew,

Charles hadn't seen Claire's gift either. Certainly, he'd never mentioned it. Had he even known? Or had he simply thought of it as only a nice hobby? Parker could only wonder.

He got up to go to bed at last.

Any ideas he'd nurtured about beginning to let Claire know he cared for her would need to be shifted to the back burner now. She'd be leery about her emotions after this situation, fearful of trusting any man for a time. So would the girls. He sighed at the thought.

Be their anchor, he seemed to hear in the back of his mind. Parker looked around the room, almost expecting to see someone. The words had sounded almost audible. Charles? God? Or maybe Ann? He couldn't be clear. But it was wise counsel, he knew.

Getting into his bed a little later, he opened his Bible to read a few scriptures before settling down to sleep. He flipped the Bible at random to Ecclesiastes. "To everything there is a season," he read, "and a time to every purpose under the heaven… A time to weep, and a time to laugh, a time to mourn and a time to dance." He smiled. He hoped that was true, that there might be a season someday for he and Claire, a time for them to laugh and dance, to both love deeply again.

The next morning he called to tell Drake he wanted to take the day off. It wasn't a morning he needed to be at the store anyway except to help process some orders. Drake and Nora could take care of things.

He headed instead to Charleston. He'd made a quick call to Miles's college department, checking on his teaching schedule, and he knew when to find him coming out of class.

The old historic college, founded in the 1700s, sprawled amid the downtown streets of Charleston, the majority of the buildings between King and Coming streets, from east to west, and Vanderhost and Beufain, north to south. Parker found a place to park his car beyond Marion Square and walked in to the campus. Walking always helped clear his thoughts and give him a more open mind. He needed that for speaking to Miles today.

Parker propped against a wall where he could keep an eye on the entrance to the building where Miles was finishing his morning Social Psychology class about now. If he missed the man coming out, the psychology department offices weren't far away. Students soon began to wander out of the old building, dispersing in different directions, and then after a space, Parker spotted Miles coming out. As he walked down the stairs, Miles glanced up from talking with a student—a female student, Parker noticed—and he spotted Parker. Miles nodded to him, pausing to finish talking with the student, and then headed Parker's way.

"Parker," he said, drawing closer. "I don't suppose you've come to offer to take me to lunch. There's a nice café only a couple of blocks from here."

"What I have to say won't take long."

Miles shifted the satchel hanging over one shoulder. "I've already had a harsh lecture from Dr. Ezra Compton last night. You're a day late to be the first to rebuke me for supposedly leading Claire Avery on." He gestured to a park bench by the sidewalk. "Could we sit down? I've been on my feet lecturing."

Parker followed Miles to the bench, but he stood instead of sitting down with him. "Tell me what happened. I've heard what others said."

"That's broad-minded of you to ask," he said, crossing one ankle over his knee. Miles wore a gray suit, white shirt, and a smart bow tie and looked impeccable, the morning sun dappling over his blond hair. Parker saw several girls and women glance his way. He certainly possessed that unmistakable charisma some men seemed to have.

Miles rubbed a hand across his eyes. "I told you once before that I found Claire Avery extremely attractive and intriguing. She has a natural softness about her, a rare innocence, and an un-awakened quality that drew me. Of course she is beautiful, too, but completely unaware of her own appeal." He smiled. "It's a tempting combination for a man like me."

"And what kind of man is that?"

He shrugged. "A psychologist interested in people, a counselor who enjoys bringing out the inherent potential in others, and a man who simply enjoys women." Miles offered Parker a smile. "Women like me, Parker, and I like women. In general, I am very good with women. They enjoy me; I enjoy them."

"You knew Claire's situation," Parker reminded him.

"Yes, but from the first she intrigued me. I told you that on the first day I met her if you remember."

"I think I cautioned you about that interest, too, even that first day."

"Perhaps you did." Miles ran a hand through his hair and sighed. "I grew fond of Claire and her girls though. They made me wish, at certain moments, for a family of my own. For a different life, one I'm not cut out for."

"You led her on. You led the girls on."

"I might have, without fully realizing it. As I said, she and the girls made me entertain some new fantasies. Some sweet ones."

Parker clenched a fist. "If we weren't out here in a public place, I'd like to hit you hard for that. Claire, Mary Helen, and Suki aren't toys for you or anyone else to entertain themselves with. They're recovering from a hard loss. They were vulnerable. You knew that."

"So Ezra said and as a shrink I guess he should know. He told me emphatically, with anger I might add, that I should have recognized that aspect more clearly about Claire. Admittedly, I let my vision get clouded in the matter. I do regret it." He sighed. "I will say, however, that I did not realize Claire or the girls thought I'd indicated to them I was interested in marriage. I never told Claire I loved her. We never made love. I only kissed her a time or two. Frankly, I never even indicated that I was serious about her. I stopped in to visit with her when down at the beach, perhaps flirted with her and the girls, and took Claire out on two casual dates, to a concert and to a movie. I had no idea she or the girls had moved our relationship in their minds to a higher level than what it had progressed to."

Parker studied the man. "It's obvious you live by a looser moral code that Claire is used to—or that I and most of Claire's friends are used to. I wish I'd seen that about you to have warned Claire."

He laughed. "She wouldn't have believed you. Women tend to believe what they want to about men. They seldom see relationships realistically."

Irritated, Parker scowled now. "Everyone who knows Claire thinks you've acted like a cad, but you don't seem to see that. That shows me it's you who doesn't see relationships realistically. Maybe you need to work on that, Miles."

He paused. "I will ask you to stay away from Claire and the girls. I hope you can see the necessity for that. Claire is hurt and embarrassed. She thought of you as someone more trustworthy and honorable than you are, and evidently she felt that you spoke and acted in ways indicating you were more interested in her than you actually were. You need to examine your own heart to look back and see what you did to create that impression. Claire isn't stupid. I'm sure you said and did things that made her think you were forming a serious interest in her. Evidently, you said things to the girls to create the same impression in them. In some ways I think that's even worse than leading Claire on as you did."

"Are we finished?" Miles looked at his watch and stood. "I need to catch lunch and look over my notes before my next class."

"Make yourself scarce at Edisto for a time, Miles."

He laughed. "Are you threatening to act in an uncivil way and hit me if I don't Parker? I thought you had more dignity."

Parker studied him for a minute, annoyed with how little repentance the man acknowledged for how he'd hurt a kind woman and two sweet little girls. "When you care about someone you throw dignity to the wind," he said after a few moments, and then he belted Miles in the jaw, watching him crumble to the ground in surprise before he turned to walk away.

Parker whistled on the way back to his car.

"I probably shouldn't have hit him," he told Claire and the girls later in the day, after driving over to Edisto when Claire got off work at The Little Mermaid. He'd called and invited them out to dinner. Now they sat at The Old Post Office, one of Edisto's nicer restaurants, waiting for their dinner order to come.

Mary Helen practically jumped in her seat with excitement at his words. "I wish I'd been there to hit him, too."

"Mary Helen." Claire chided her.

"Well, I think Parker was brave to hit Miles." Mary Helen stuck her chin up with the words. "Miles deserved it."

"I've thought about this situation a lot," Claire said. "Miles never declared his love for me, only hinted at the idea, and we weren't engaged or anything. I think I read more into his actions than I should have."

Mary Helen crossed her arms. "I hate how you always try to blame yourself for stuff when other people act awful. Like Parker and Ezra said, Miles led us on, Mommy. He let us all think he cared more than he did."

Suki nodded. "He told me he wished he could be my daddy. That wasn't nice to say unless he meant it."

"The girls have a point," Parker said, trying to hide a grin.

"I suppose, but I've felt so foolish over this whole thing. I should have been more discerning about Miles's character."

"No one else was," Mary Helen put in. "Even Ezra and he's a psychiatrist and he knew Miles better than we did."

Parker smiled at Claire. "She's right again."

Mary Helen leaned forward, propping her elbows on the table. "Ezra said when he went to talk to Miles at his house that Eudora came in and got mad at him and took up for Miles."

Claire turned her eyes to her daughter. "How do you know that, Mary Helen?"

She shrugged. "I heard Isabel talking about it."

"Mommies should fuss at their kids when they do bad things," Suki piped in. "Wasn't Mrs. Eudora mad at him?"

"No, and Ezra said that was *very telling*, whatever that means." Mary Helen wrinkled her nose. "Miles's mother said that many of the Lawrence men had a gift for attracting women and it was hardly their fault. She said Miles's father had been the same way."

"Mary Helen, this is not gossip you should be repeating." Claire blushed.

"It does explain things a little, though, doesn't it?" Parker couldn't help grinning.

"Don't encourage her." Claire glared at him, so Parker busied himself attacking the salad the waitress sat in front of him.

They all grew quiet while the waitress chatted with them and passed salads around, refilling their tea glasses and putting fresh bread on the table.

"This is such a nice restaurant," Claire said changing the subject.

"I thought you girls deserved a treat after a stressful week," Parker said. "Besides I love to come here to eat but I don't like coming alone. The food is worth driving over from Beaufort to enjoy."

Claire smiled at him, kicking up his heartbeat.

The conversation shifted as they ate their salads. The girls caught Parker up on their news and told him about things they'd bought for school when shopping.

"We got new notebooks and My Little Pony pencils and a big new box of crayons," Suki told him.

Their food arrived then, Firecracker Flounder for himself, Fried Oysters for Mary Helen, Pecan Crusted Chicken Strips for Suki, and Veal Edistonian for Claire, all served with The Old Post Office's fabulous cheese grits and green beans, the restaurant's vegetable of the day.

They ate, laughed, and talked casually, and it did Parker's heart good to see them happier after being so hurt this week.

For dessert Parker and Claire ordered Key Lime Pie and the girls got Blueberry Cobbler. It was a nice evening, and Parker felt glad he could stay over at Oleanders since it was Friday. He'd planned things for them to do on Saturday to keep them all busy so they wouldn't have time to dwell on Miles's actions.

On Saturday morning after breakfast, Parker suggested they all bike around the Edisto bike trail that wound its way in a loop around the backside of the island. The girls loved the idea and they soon rode from The Point over to catch the bike trail passing Whaley's and the Edisto Zesto. Suki, now six and a more experienced biker, could ride and keep up better than last year at five. Mary Helen and Suki rode ahead of him and Claire, where they could easily keep a watch on them.

"The girls and I love playing Bingo at the Lions Club," Claire said as they passed the building, not far from the girls' school.

"It's been an island tradition for a long time."

The trail entered the quieter paved bike trail now, following under moss-draped oaks behind the back yards of beach homes. They slowed to pass other bikers along the way, the trail a little busier with summer in full swing on the island. However, in any season, the ride was always a peaceful, pleasant one.

Toward the end of the island, instead of following the trail on its marked route along Dock Site Road, they cut into the backside of the Fairfield Resort. Parker wanted to stop by the resort office to pick up passes a friend had offered him for a day at the resort's swimming pool.

"I love going to the Fairfield pool," Mary Helen said as they rode along the quiet roads in the resort. "Can we stop at the little store by the Planter's Oak Restaurant to get a treat?"

"Sure," Parker answered. Even he liked the cute store tucked on a small hill across from the restaurant.

"I'll pack a lunch we can take to the pool with us," Claire said, thinking ahead. "There are picnic tables beside the pool where we can eat."

"I want to play putt-putt, too," Mary Helen added while bouncing her bike over a speed bump. "Can we do that with your passes, Uncle Parker?"

"Sure, but keep in mind I'm very good at putt-putt—just a warning."

Claire laughed. "You might be surprised at how good these girls are. Elaine and Pete bring us over to play often. They own and manage a couple of rentals here in the resort and are Fairfield members. The girls are getting pretty good at the game."

"We love to ride the little tram, too," Suki added, as they parked their bikes at the small store.

The Market, a small, picturesque resort store, carried a few basic food supplies, beach products, sun lotion, drinks, and snacks. The girls each picked out a candy bar and a canned drink, as did Claire and Parker. Then they walked over to sit in the rocking chairs on the porch of the Planter's Oak Restaurant to enjoy them.

Back at Oleanders after their ride, they changed into swim clothes, packed a picnic lunch, put drinks in a small cooler, and headed to Fairfield's swimming pool in Parker's car. The pool, a pretty kidney shaped one, sat in a scenic spot by Kingfisher Lake on Sea Cloud Circle. A putt-putt course, recreation center, bike rental shop, and playground spread around the pool area. This central spot in the resort also served as the main pickup area for the Fairfield tram, which carried tourists down to the Fairfield Beach Cabana and back. Biking through Fairfield earlier, they'd spotted tourists waiting for the tram at different points, carrying towels and sand toys, looking forward to a day on the beach.

"I've heard tourists whine, saying they expected this resort to be right on the ocean," Claire said, as they sat around a table under a big umbrella later enjoying their lunch.

"So have I," Parker added. "But none of the resort's materials suggest the resort is ocean side and all the island maps show exactly where the resort is located."

"People are lazy," Mary Helen put in. "They want to walk out their door and be right on the beach. They want someone else to put up their umbrellas and set up their beach chairs. Lots of tourists never even walk up the beach at all, ride bikes, or play in the ocean."

"Why do they come then?" Suki asked, looking confused.

"I don't know." Mary Helen shrugged. "I guess they like to look at the ocean or putter around in the shops and eat seafood."

Claire smiled. "Those who don't want to be active should go to one of the high rises on the more commercial beaches. They can sit on a little balcony high in a big hotel and look at the ocean from a safe distance all day."

Mary Helen laughed. "A lady asked me yesterday where the restrooms were on the beach. I told her there weren't any and she looked shocked."

"Edisto isn't for everyone," Parker said. "Many visitors don't like the fact that it's a forty-five minute drive from the island to either Charleston or Beaufort. They'd rather vacation closer to a big city, its many restaurants, stores, and attractions."

"People are stupid about using umbrellas and sun lotion, too," Mary Helen said. "I told this man yesterday his kids were getting red and sunburned and he told me to mind my own business."

Claire smiled. "It isn't your business to tell people how to take care of their children."

"Well, *somebody* should tell them." She pointed at two little girls playing on a big float in the pool. "Those little girls are already red from being out in the sun too long. They're going to be crying tonight. Sunburns *hurt.*"

"When you get a sunburn, it hurts to play on the beach the next day, too." Suki paused, watching the girls. "Do you think I should tell them to put on some cream, Mommy?"

"No. Unfortunately, people have to learn how to best enjoy beach vacations on their own. Some lessons simply need to be learned the hard way," Claire answered.

"Like learning what a rat fink Miles Lawrence is." Mary Helen frowned at the thought.

"Remember we talked about the importance of forgiveness and moving on," Claire reminded her.

"God says to *always* forgive," Suki parroted. "Even when it's hard."

"You can forgive because it's the right thing to do, but that doesn't mean you have to forget." Mary Helen crossed her arms. "Like Mommy said, when you learn lessons the *hard* way, you remember them. After you get a really bad sunburn, you remember better to use sun lotion and an umbrella at the beach. After you love someone like Miles Lawrence, you learn to be careful about charming, handsome men that girls cluster around, and you learn for yourself some men are cheaters and not the kind of men you can trust."

"Are all *pretty* men bad?" Suki asked.

Parker laughed. "No. It isn't looks that make a person bad. Their behavior and character are what cause that."

"Gracie Byrd is pretty and she acts bad *a lot*," Suki added.

Mary Helen snorted at her sister's comment. "Yes, and I already *don't* trust Gracie Byrd either."

Claire sighed. "Both you girls care entirely too much about what Gracie Byrd does and thinks."

Parker decided to change the subject. "Since we need a break from the pool after lunch, how about a game of putt-putt?"

The girls enthusiastically responded, and they soon cleaned up their picnic area, gathered their towels and beach toys, and headed over to start a game on the resort's shady course.

For dinner, despite Claire's arguments about Parker spending more money to treat them again, he insisted on taking them to the Dockside Restaurant across from the resort's entrance after they'd showered and dressed from their afternoon at the pool.

By going early, they got a nice table by the window in the upstairs restaurant, looking out over Big Bay Creek. Parker and Claire chose seafood items from the menu but the girls wanted hamburgers for a change.

"I love watching the shrimp boats come home on the creek," Mary Helen said, pointing out the window as a boat headed into a dock area not far up the creek from the restaurant.

"It's a nice time of day," Claire agreed. "Look. I see two other boats coming downstream, too." She pointed to a yacht and a small fishing boat heading up the backwater creek. She turned to Parker. "You often bring your boat to the island, don't you?"

"It's actually faster from Beaufort to Edisto by boat. You've ridden over to the island with me before." Parker dipped a hush puppy into tarter sauce. "I drive my car over most of the time, though, because I need to run errands or shop on my way over. My little jeep I keep at Edisto is fun to drive around on the island, but I don't like to get out in highway traffic in it."

"I like your boat. It's fun," Mary Helen said around bites of her hamburger. "J. T. loves boats. He can't wait until he is big enough to drive one all by himself. He says he's going to buy a boat of his own when he gets big."

"All the Mikells love the water." Parker smiled over the words. "With such a love for the ocean and the outdoors, they chose the perfect business, running a bike and boat rental shop."

They finished dinner, talking casually, and then returned to Oleanders. The girls, tired from their long day, went to sleep quickly after only a book or two from Parker.

He came to look for Claire after reading to the girls and found her sitting outside on the porch. He settled into the rocking chair beside hers.

"The moon is full tonight," she said, pointing to the silvery white ball in the night sky. "I love the dancing trail of light it makes across the ocean below, don't you?"

"Yes. You notice the moon's beauty so much more at the beach." Parker settled back against the rocker, tired himself from the long day.

A small silence fell before Claire spoke again. "Thanks for keeping the girls and me keep busy these last two days. I know you consciously planned a lot of activities so we wouldn't have time to dwell on our episode with Miles." She paused, a little smile twitching her lips. "Did you really hit him?"

"I didn't intend to," he admitted. "I went to talk to him, angry I admit, but I also wanted to understand. I wanted to know how he saw things, why he did what he did, if he felt remorse."

Parker told Claire some of the things Miles said.

She listened. "I didn't say so in front of the girls, but Miles did say he thought we were falling in love. Another time he said more along the same line and talked about what a sweet family he thought the four of us would make. I didn't really imagine Miles's intentions more than he presented them to me, Parker, even though I've tried to say so in front of the girls to help them feel better about what happened. I actually held back on expressing my own feelings to Miles, so unclear about them and believing it too soon for me to enter a serious relationship so soon after Charles's death." She paused. "It was Miles who painted pictures of being in love and talked of the possibility of marriage. Not only to me. He spoke that way often to the girls, too. I hate most of all that he hurt them and damaged their trust."

Parker pushed his rocking chair back and forth on the wooden porch thinking about her words. "It seems from what Mary Helen said that Miles grew up around an example of philandering by his own father, with his mother accepting it and not speaking out against it. It's sad to think she didn't see Miles's behavior with you and the girls as wrong."

"Isabel and Ezra told me that. I didn't know Mary Helen knew about it until she talked about it last night. That child manages to stay keenly on top of whatever the adults around her are saying."

"She's a sharp one." He looked out over the ocean. "She's taken this hard about Miles, more so than Suki."

"Mary Helen idolized Miles, had a deep girlish crush on him. I could see it in how she acted every time he came over. It worried me." She turned to Parker. "Do you think it will scar her? Hurt her trust and relationships in the future?"

"I doubt it," he answered. "It might make her more careful in placing her affections too readily, but that can't be a bad thing."

"Perhaps."

"What about you? Will this scar you?"

She looked at him in surprise. "Do you mean will it make me reluctant to love another man in future?"

He nodded.

She looked out toward the moon. "It might make me more careful. It's taught me that any relationship I might make in the future involves the girls more than I imagined before. I'll be more discreet about *any* interest I might have in future for their sakes. I don't want those girls hurt again." She turned her brown eyes toward his. "As you helped me see before, I don't think it wrong for either of us to hope love will come our way again some day. I do believe Charles and Ann would want that. Don't you?"

"Yes," he said, tucking her words away to remember, wishing he knew a way to tell her those feelings had already come for him.

CHAPTER 19

September 1986

Summer drifted into fall, and before Claire knew it she found herself caught up in the pre-excitement of her first book coming out. Although her publicist at Whittier worked diligently on early marketing and publicity for the book, Claire soon learned that many promotional efforts fell to her. Isabel, more accustomed to planning events and handling marketing, proved a great help to Claire, jumping in with zeal to help Claire set book signings and schedule events.

"This really isn't your job," Claire argued at the store one day, worrying over the time Isabel spent helping with calls and scheduling.

She waved a hand dismissively. "This is fun. We're all so excited for you. Let me help and quit fussing."

Parker lent a hand, too, scheduling a photographer friend of his to do a photo shoot of Claire and the girls at Edisto. Delighted with the idea, Rae Litz, the Sales and Marketing Director at Whittier, and Marty Richmond, Claire's publicist, suggested Claire and the girls wear romantic white dresses and straw boater hats with ribbon bands for the shoot. Claire hadn't expected Whittier to want photos of the girls, too, but they maintained since Claire wrote children's books the press would be interested in the girls and their part in how the Polka Dot kids books came into creation.

The idea proved a huge success, and an early write-up appeared in a major women's magazine featuring the photographer's lyrical photos of Claire and the girls in their sweet white dresses down by the sea.

"Look! We're in a *real* magazine," Mary Helen exclaimed, waving the magazine Isabel brought to the store in Claire's face after she and Suki came in from school.

Claire studied the photos and full-page article with pleasure again. "It's a very nice write-up, isn't it?"

"It's *better* than nice, Mom. That article will sell books for you," Mary Helen said.

Isabel smirked. "She's right, you know. That's my little retail girl talking."

"Can we go to one of your book signings with you?" Suki asked, her eyes wide with the thought of it.

"Well, I don't know." Claire frowned.

"Oh, let them go with you to a few signings," Isabel said as Claire hesitated. "You can wear your lovely white dresses again. It will help to sell more books, and readers will love it."

"We'll see," Claire said evasively. "But only if Whittier thinks it's all right and only if the events aren't too far away and on Saturday, not a school day."

In a meeting at Whittier later in the week at Savannah, Claire asked about the girls possibly attending one or two of her signings. Everyone agreed that including the girls in a few events would boost interest and sales.

Isabel sent Claire a smug smile when she heard about it. "I told you it was a good idea," she said. "With a little coaching about how to act, they'll do great, too. You'll see."

"Here's what the new book will look like." Claire pulled an early galley copy, or ARC, out of her purse for Isabel to see.

"What a fabulous book cover." Isabel snatched the book out of Claire's hand to study it. "I absolutely love it."

"I'm so glad you like it." Claire smiled. "Vanessa Yardley and I talked about what might be appealing for a cover design. I told her I thought all the Polkman family should be on the cover— Mama and Papa Polkman, Grampa and Gramma, and all seven kids. In my stories they always crammed into an old Volkswagen van together that Papa Polkman had pulled the top off of. So that's what Vanessa created—all of them jammed into an old van, laughing and having fun. It's better than my old sketches."

"Is this the family's house you envisioned in the background?" She pointed at it.

"Yes." Claire studied it. "For my stories, I described the Polkmans' house somewhat like my old dollhouse, tall, narrow and stacked four stories high. Look how cute Vanessa made it, sunny yellow with bright blue shutters."

"Well, a book cover always makes a book, one way or the another—and especially for a picture book. Children will love this happy, colorful cover. I know I do. It's absolutely charming."

Claire ran her hand over the large hardback book. "I can't believe this is happening to me. It still seems like a dream. A year ago I was at my parents' home in Arlington, despondent and unhappy with two miserable, unhappy girls. I feel so grateful."

Isabel whisked her feather duster over a glass shelf before pausing to turn back to Claire. "You know, we do have Miles Lawrence to thank for this in part. Ironic, isn't it? He saw a potential in you no one else saw."

Claire leaned against the counter by the register. "Yes, and that's why I went to see Miles earlier this week."

Isabel dropped the duster in surprise. "What? You haven't told me this."

"I haven't told anyone," Claire admitted.

"Well, this is big news and I need to sit down to hear it." Isabel gestured to the table by the window. "Come sit down and tell me all about this. We'll be lucky if anyone comes in the store on a midweek afternoon in September. You know how quiet it gets off-season."

Claire settled into a chair across from Isabel at the window. She still held the galley of her book and smoothed her hand over it. "When I got the box of galley copies earlier this week, I decided to go to see Miles. I realized, as you said, that I had him to thank for my book becoming a reality."

"Did you go to his house?" Isabel leaned forward.

"No, I didn't want to encounter Eudora. She's acts rude and huffy to the girls and me now whenever she visits at the beach. She obviously faults us because Miles isn't with her. She leans on him a lot, you know, and she likes him to drive her places. Elaine said she blames us that Miles has avoided coming down to the beach house with her."

Isabel rolled her eyes. "Eudora certainly views things as she wants them to be. Ezra and I never picked up on that in the past about her, but he says we should have. He sees patterns now."

Claire continued her story. "Anyway, wanting to avoid Eudora, I went to the college, like Parker did, and found Miles coming out of class."

"What did he say when he saw you?"

"He was surprised, but he covered quickly and then exhibited his usual charm. I gave him one of the galley copies of my book and thanked him."

"How very professional and dignified of you, Claire Avery. You make me proud." Isabel reached across the table to pat her hand.

"I felt nervous about seeing him again, but I soon realized, that despite his toying with our affections, he'd been a friend to us, too."

"What did he say?"

She laughed and shook her head. "He launched into typical analysis mode and said he felt proud to see how I could face my difficulties on my own so much better now. He said it showed remarkable progress from where I'd been when he first met me."

"What a jerk."

"Miles will be Miles." Claire laughed. "I don't know why I let my heart dominate my good sense about Miles. I saw his arrogance and a lot of his problems from the first."

"Did Miles show *any* graciousness about you coming all the way to Charleston to bring him your book?"

"Yes." She smiled at the memory. "He sat on a campus bench and looked through every page of the book, commenting on the art and the book layout, even remembering the storyline and laughing over how it had been represented through Vanessa's cute watercolor drawings."

"Have you told Parker about this meeting?"

"No and I haven't told the girls either. But I will." She paused. "I told Miles he was welcome to come back to the beach house with his mother whenever he wanted to, but I did suggest he not spend particular time at our house or with the girls. They don't need to form a reattachment to him."

Isabel snorted. "As if Mary Helen would!"

"She might in time. She cared deeply for Miles. A girl's first crushes aren't so easily forgotten. And Suki simply wants so much to be loved. She has a sweet, tender heart."

"I'll need to tell Ezra about this," Isabel said. "So he won't throw his weight around when Miles decides to show up at Edisto again. You'll need to tell Parker, too, for the same reason."

"I will." She smoothed her hand over the book cover again.

"I'm really excited about having your book launch here on Edisto so all your friends can come." She got up to resume her dusting.

"So am I." Claire went back to the register to sort mail. "I wouldn't have wanted it anyplace else."

"Elaine and Pete talked the Fairfield Resort management team into letting us use the Planter's Oak Restaurant for the launch event. I simply don't have room here." She turned to smile at Claire. "We can thank Elaine and Pete for working that out for us. They own property at the resort and had good contacts. It's the perfect place on the island for a launch event with that marvelous giant oak tree in the middle of the restaurant. Planter's is closed on Sundays, too, so it didn't interfere with their normal schedule to let us rent the restaurant in the afternoon for the book launch. Off-season like this, they were glad to get the rental fee."

Claire frowned. "I hate it that Parker insisted on paying the fee."

"That paltry fee was nothing to him, Claire, and he wanted to do something to be a part of this since all the rest of us are helping with the catering and decorations. We're going to offer a nice array of refreshments for the event and a few of the Planter's staff will help with setup and serving as part of their fee."

Isabel put down her duster and began to straighten items on the shelf. "I promised all the children you would do a reading of the book, but I imagine many of the grown-ups will want to sit in on it, too. There's a side area in the restaurant we can use for that."

"The plans for the launch sound so nice, and the restaurant has plenty of parking for all. So many people have told me they plan to come. I'm starting to get really excited."

"Me, too," Isabel admitted. "I've never hosted an author's book launch before. This will be an occasion for me to remember, too, and any ordered books we don't sell at the launch I'll put in the store to sell after."

Claire opened a date book by the register to glance at the circled events in it. "It looks like I'll be busy every weekend after the launch, all the way through mid December."

"You have a lovely book tour schedule in place with many signings at major bookstores and also at cute, independent stores like McIntosh Book Shoppe in Beaufort, E. Shaver Bookseller and The Book Lady Bookstore in Savannah, and lovely small bookstores in Atlanta, Charleston, Myrtle Beach, Columbia, Charlotte, and Asheville. You also have library events scheduled and signings at children's stores, like mine, where you'll get to sit and read to the children. You'll love doing that, Claire."

"Maybe, but it makes me nervous to think about it."

"Why?" Isabel turned to look at her. "You'll do fine. You'll simply be talking to people about your new book and the characters in it you made up. Think how lovely it will be to help people discover your charming Polka Dot family. You should look on every event as a gift and a privilege."

"I'm so grateful to have you for a friend in all this," Claire said. "You've done more for me than I can ever repay you for."

"Nonsense. Look at how you've helped me run my store." She swept a hand around in a broad gesture. "Without you, Ezra and I couldn't have taken that marvelous cruise in Europe this winter. It isn't easy to find responsible help you can leave your store with to be away that long. I'm indebted to you."

"I guess so."

"I *know* so."

"Do you ever worry about keeping the store going?" Claire asked.

"The building and property are mine, paid for. Ezra makes good money to cover the lean times, and I have some money of my own through my family. Even in the slow seasons, I sell enough to make my basic expenses and during the tourist seasons I sell lavishly enough to cover for the leaner times. You've seen that to be true. It's a profitable enough business, and I enjoy it."

Isabel glanced out the window. "Here come the girls from school. With as little store traffic as we've had this afternoon, you go on home with them and let me close up later. I hope the weekend will bring more business."

She walked over to study Claire's galley copy of *The Polka Dot Kids*. "Can I take this home to show Ezra?"

Claire put the book in her hands. "You take it home and keep it. I have more in a box at the house."

"I'm delighted!" Isabel leaned across the counter to give Claire a hug. "I look forward to showing it off to all my friends as well as to Ezra." She examined the book in her hands. "Of course, we'll soon need to create some promotional signs for the book launch coming up, including signs we can use for the store and signs to mail to stores where you'll be signing later if they need them."

"Many of the larger stores create their own signs and Whittier will help with mailing materials."

"Well, you and I will help to promote around whatever they choose to do." She turned with a smile as Mary Helen and Suki came in the door.

"There are my girls," she said with warmth. "I'm sending you home with your mother early today. Business is slow."

"Isn't Mother's book pretty?" Suki pointed to the book in Isabel's hands.

"It's fabulous, and we're going to sell tons of them in the store."

Mary Helen glanced at a display of mermaid dolls on the shelf.

"It would be great if Mother would write a series of mermaid books."

Isabel laughed. "So it would. You girls start encouraging her to tell you mermaid tales and maybe they'll turn into books later."

As Claire left with the girls, Isabel said, "Don't forget to talk with Parker about what we discussed. I think you should share with Elaine and Lula, too."

"I will," she said, following the girls out the door.

Claire found time to talk to Elaine and Lula over the next days but she didn't get a chance to speak to Parker until after church on Sunday.

With one of Drake's recipes, and with his help, Parker had made homemade chili in a Crockpot the day before and only needed to heat it up again after church. The temperature had cooled to the upper fifties for a few days, making the idea of chili more appealing.

While Parker stirred the chili, Claire chopped up celery and carrots for side relishes and made cornbread. "I haven't had chili in a long time," she said, taking plates and bowls from a kitchen cabinet to set on the table.

"It wasn't that hard, but I'm still glad Drake came by to help me with it. I'm trying to learn to cook more things. Drake says it's only a matter of following recipe directions but I hate debuting a new main dish not knowing how it will turn out."

Claire opened a drawer to get silverware. "When I married Charles I had very little experience or confidence in the kitchen. I'd grown up in a home with full-time help, you know, and Mother rarely if ever cooked. Aggie taught me to cook many basic recipes, for which I'm grateful, but I basically taught myself the rest. It was too humiliating to let people know I had such limited culinary skills as a minister's wife." She laughed. "You know how church life revolves around food—covered dish dinners, casseroles to the shut-ins, desserts for ladies meetings. It was a challenge, I can tell you."

He paused to study her. "I always forget you came from such a privileged background. When Ann and I first visited you and

Charles, after you married and Charles was assigned to that quaint stone church in Sevierville, you lived in a tiny house made of gray rock on the street behind the church."

She leaned against the counter, still holding a fistful of silverware.

"Charles and I called it the 'little gray manse.' It was made of mountain rock, like the church, and the manse and church both had bright red doors."

He grinned. "I remember that now."

"Charles served there five years. Mary Helen was born there near the Smoky Mountains. Then we moved to Sweetwater to Trinity United Methodist."

"At least you got a bigger house in Sweetwater, although a somewhat older and shabbier one."

"I was happy there, and those years sped by fast." She gave him a soft smile. "I just realized, thinking back, that you and I have known each other for over twelve years now. That's a long time."

"Yes, it is," he said. "A virtual eon."

She giggled and went to get the cornbread out of the oven. "Call the girls and we'll eat," she said.

We sound like an old married couple, Parker thought heading outside to call Mary Helen and Suki. He didn't say the words out loud, of course, but the thought was sweet.

Later in the day Claire showed him the galley copy of her new book and told him about driving to Charleston to see Miles. "Do you think I did the wrong thing, going to talk to him again?" she asked.

"No," he said, turning the book over in his hands and then looking through every page. "Miles helped to bring your work to a publisher. I can see why you wanted to thank him. I'd probably offer him a word of thanks myself if he were here right now." He looked across at her. "Miles did help to birth this beautiful book in a way, and it's fabulous. I'm so proud of you."

"Thanks." She leaned over to kiss his cheek. "I'm pleased you like it."

"I love it," he told her, wishing he could say more.

On the way home in the car, Claire told Mary Helen and Suki about going to see Miles. She could see Mary Helen's face settle into a scowl in the rearview mirror.

"I'm glad you didn't ask me and Suki to go with you. I still don't like Miles, and even if you were nice to him, I hope he won't come to our house ever again." Mary Helen snapped out the words.

"I doubt he will, but if you encounter him on the beach, you should be cordial, Mary Helen."

Claire could see her shake her head.

"I won't." she said. "I'm not as nice as you."

Suki, riding in the front seat, sighed. "I don't want to be nice to Miles, either, Mommy. He hurted us."

"Yes, but that doesn't mean it's all right for us to be rude to him or to hurt him in return." Claire slowed for a stop sign. "Remember that old saying we learned: *Treat everyone with politeness and thoughtfulness, even those who've been rude and unkind to you, not because what they did was right or because they are nice people, but because you are nice.*"

"I always thought that was a dumb saying," Mary Helen said mulishly.

"Daddy said we're supposed to love even our enemies," Suki said. "But it sounded easier to hear about in our Bible stories than it is to do it."

Claire bit back a smile. *Out of the mouths of babes*, she thought, *truth so often comes.*

CHAPTER 20

October 1986

On the first Monday of October, Parker met as usual with Drake for their weekly meeting at Westcott Antiques. He flipped the big wall calendar to the new month as he and Drake sat down to go over the week's agenda. Two yellow highlighted dates stood out amid store delivery dates and other scribbled notes on the calendar: Suki's piano recital this Sunday and Claire's book launch the following Sunday.

"Glad you noted those dates," Drake said, leaning back in his chair. "Nora, Andrew, and I look forward to those special occasions, too."

"They seemed worth noting, even here," Parker said, starting to flip through a pile of mail on his desk.

"Andrew is especially looking forward to Suki's recital," Drake added.

Parker grinned. "It's sweet how much interest Andrew takes in Suki's playing. When he visits at the beach house, or at Waterview when the girls come to Beaufort, Andrew sits right beside Suki on the piano bench, watching and listening to her play."

"I noticed that, too. He has an unusual appreciation for music."

"How's he doing with the piano lessons?" Parker asked, knowing Andrew started taking lessons a month ago.

"He seems to enjoy it, but he likes going to the symphony or listening to my classical records more." Drake shook his head. "He's kind of an odd kid with such intense musical interests."

"No less odd that you sneaking downtown to poke through antiques stores at his age."

Drake laughed. "There is that, and Andrew seems like a normal, well-adjusted kid in most every other way. He loves to fish and has a great pitching arm. I went with Nora to one of his ballgames this week."

Parker glanced at the small photo of Andrew and Nora on his bookshelf. "Nora's done a good job with Andrew, raising him alone."

"Yeah, she has," Drake agreed before their talk turned back to business.

On Sunday afternoon Parker remembered his earlier conversation with Drake as Andrew sat rapt beside Suki at the piano while she practiced a final time before her recital. Nora, Drake, and Andrew had arrived about an hour ago at Parker's house to attend the symphony with them. He, Drake, and Nora sat in the kitchen drinking fruit tea and talking now while Claire and Mary Helen finished getting dressed. They could see Suki and Andrew at the piano in the living room.

"Suki doesn't seem nervous at all," Nora commented, shaking her head.

Parker watched the child play effortlessly with a smile on her face.

"Suki never seems to feel nervous about playing for others."

"I'd be terrified to play in front of all those people." Nora got up to put her glass in the sink.

"Not if you were good at it." Drake glanced at his watch as she did. "We should probably head over to the theater. Suki needs to get there early."

Nora smiled at Parker. "Why don't you go upstairs to see if Claire and Mary Helen are ready to go?"

Parker nodded and walked toward the front of the house. He stopped to straighten his tie at the hall mirror, feeling stuffy as usual in the formal wear expected for an evening at the symphony. Hearing steps, he glanced up the stairs to see Claire starting down in a sleek black sheath, hugging her figure like a glove. He caught his breath at the sight, often forgetting how beautiful she was.

"Is my dress not all right?" Claire asked, noticing him staring.

"No. It's perfect." He put out a hand to help her down the last few stairs, smiling. "You look beautiful."

"Do I look nice, too, Uncle Parker?" Mary Helen asked, skipping down the stairs behind her mother in a black and white taffeta dress.

"I think you look *entirely* too grown up," Parker answered, knowing the words exactly what Mary Helen wanted to hear.

They all headed out the door then, Parker locking up behind them.

The University of South Carolina Beaufort Center for the Arts Theatre, where the Beaufort Orchestra performed its concerts, was only a short distance away downtown. Drake always bought season tickets, being a symphony buff, but with Suki now taking lessons from Morgan Dillon and Andrew studying with Oliver Cowan, one of Morgan's pianist friends, they all attended faithfully whenever the orchestra performed. Today the orchestra was giving a special concert, spotlighting young performers.

"Do you think Andrew feels bad that Suki is performing and not him?" Mary Helen whispered to her mother as they settled into their seats in the theatre a short time later.

"No. Andrew knows he's not ready for an event like this yet," she answered. "Only a few accomplished young performers are playing with the symphony tonight." She opened her program. "Here are their names and when each will play a short piece."

"Look. There's Suki's name." Mary Helen pointed. "Sarah Katherine Avery—age six—piano, playing *Fur Elise* by Ludwig van Beethoven."

She turned to Parker. "Suki wanted to play Tchaikovsky's *Waltz of the Flowers* but Morgan thought it was too hard for her yet."

"The Beethoven selection is slower in pace, a soft, gentle, and lyrical piece. You know Suki likes it," Claire answered.

Mary Helen fluffed out the skirt of her dress. "I know she

loves the little high trilly parts. Suki says they sound like bees or butterflies fluttering over flowers."

Drake laughed, hearing her comment. "The right hand melody in *Fur Elise* does sound rather joyous and fanciful."

Mary Helen read the other names out loud. "Marcos Donovan playing cello, Regina Blakely playing flute, and Hiro Katsuo playing the violin." She looked up. "Suki is the youngest one. The others are all lots older."

"Then that makes it more of an honor for her to be selected to play," Nora said as the lights began to dim.

The program began with a performance by the orchestra alone before the children began to come on stage. Each performed a small solo piece, soon joined by the orchestra as the piece continued.

Parker felt like a proud father as Suki walked out on stage in her pretty satin dress with its white fluffy skirt and neat black top.

Mary Helen leaned toward him. "Suki had Mommy make that red cummerbund for her dress. She said red is her lucky color."

The red satin cummerbund stood out prominently among the black and white of the orchestra's clothing as did Suki's fair hair and small size. She bowed neatly, her eyes scanning the audience, searching for them. After spotting them she looked out into the crowd, hesitated, her eyes widening, and then turned to climb onto the raised seat at the piano.

"Something's upset her. She's scared," Andrew said, his quiet voice carrying to Parker.

"I'm sure she'll be fine," Parker said.

But she wasn't.

She simply sat at the piano, even when the conductor gave her a short lead in to help her begin.

Parker saw the orchestra waiting now, looking for a cue for what to do, and heard people begin to whisper around the room.

Then Andrew got up and started down the aisle.

Nora gasped, but Drake put a hand over hers. "Let him go if he feels led. He knows Suki at the piano better than anyone."

Bold for eight, Andrew walked up the steps to the stage, across the long polished floor, and after reaching the big grand piano, he scooted onto the bench beside Suki. Then he said something to her. The audience and the orchestra heard a small giggle in the silence that had fallen across the room, and then Suki put her hands on the piano and began to play—calmly and beautifully—as if the tense moments before never occurred at all.

"Wonder what he said to her?" Claire whispered to Parker as the audience stood to their feet to applaud after Suki finished.

He shrugged, having no idea.

While the audience applauded, Andrew sat on the piano bench, smiling and watching Suki take her bow, not seeming to realize what he'd done was highly irregular. He'd stayed quietly beside her the entire time while she played, turning the pages for her.

"Suki needed him and he went, without a moment of questioning or fear," Drake commented, shaking his head in wonder as Suki and Andrew walked off the stage. "I'd say Andrew is the true hero of the evening."

Andrew was unimpressed with himself as they began to question him afterwards when they all went out to dinner together.

"What did you say to her?" Parker asked.

"I told her I could play for her if she was too scared." he said.

Suki laughed. "Andrew plays piano *awful*. It made me giggle to think about it and then I was okay."

"We're grateful to you for helping Suki tonight," Claire said.

Andrew shrugged. "I knew she would be good, and I wanted everyone to hear her play. She just had a little freeze."

"What made you freeze?" Mary Helen asked, curious.

Suki hesitated. "I saw Miles and his mean mother in the audience."

Claire caught her breath.

"I wish I'd seen him," Mary Helen said. "I'd have kicked him in the shin for coming and making you get nervous." She looked at Claire and frowned. "He and his creepy mother better not come to your book launch party next weekend. You didn't invite him, did you?"

"No."

"Good. Cause we want everything to be perfect for that party, Mom."

Everything did seem perfect the next weekend at the launch. The weather was fair and mild, the refreshments and decorations beautiful in the Planter's Oak Restaurant, and a wonderful crowd of friends turned out to help Claire celebrate the publication of her first book.

"Mary Helen certainly got her wish about everything being perfect for Claire's launch," Drake said, wandering over with Nora to where Parker leaned against a pillar.

"I'm pleased so many people came for Claire." Nora pulled a chair out from a small table beside them to sit down in it. "Look at that line of people waiting to get Claire to sign a copy of her book for them. Isn't that wonderful?"

"Yes, I'm really happy for her," Parker said.

"Claire's been charming and gracious to everyone all afternoon in her usual way. If she's tired you wouldn't even know it," Drake observed. "Look how she makes each person she talks to feel special."

"Yes, and I love that she and the girls dressed in their beautiful white dresses and the girls in their cute straw hats they wore for their photo shoots earlier." Nora sighed. "The girls look so sweet."

Changing the subject, she asked, "Are any of Claire's family here?"

Parker frowned. "No, but her father sent an arrangement of flowers to wish her congratulations."

Drake stroked his chin. "I don't think I saw any of your and Charles's family here, either."

Parker snorted. "You know how seldom they leave the farm for anything, even for a special time like this for Claire."

"Ah, the joys of familial love," Drake said with a sarcastic tone. "Surely you both know most of my family are a piece of work, too."

"I do like your sister, though," Nora said.

Drake laughed. "The other black sheep in the family?"

Parker's eyes narrowed to see a skirmish starting around Claire's signing table.

Drake saw it, too, leaning forward and frowning. "I think that kid just tripped Mary Helen and knocked her down."

"Excuse me," Parker said, pushing his way through the crowd.

"You did that on purpose, Gracie Byrd!" He heard Mary Helen cry as he drew closer. "And you knocked off my hat."

"Oh my, did I?" the blond-haired girl asked, putting her foot neatly on top of Mary Helen's pretty straw hat on the floor.

Tears welled in Mary Helen's eyes.

J.T. Mikell moved in before Parker could get through the crowd. "Here, let me help you up, Mary Helen." He pulled her to her feet and then retrieved her hat, dusting it off.

Turning, with an angry look in his eye, he grabbed a glass of punch from the signing table and poured it on the grinning girl, who was still gloating over Mary Helen's fall.

She gasped with surprise.

"Take that, Gracie Byrd, and see how it feels." J.T. pushed her to the floor then, too.

Mary Helen's mouth dropped open in surprise as the girl fell to the floor, wailing as her skirts flew up to show her panties.

"I'll get you J.T. Mikell," she threatened, scrambling to her feet.

Parker moved in at the same moment that Isabel Compton did, grabbing J.T. as Isabel grabbed Gracie before any more fighting occurred.

"Remember what this occasion is for," Isabel warned both of them. "A time to recognize Claire for her lovely new book and *not* a time for you children to act up and draw attention to yourselves."

Gracie and J.T.'s parents moved in then, getting into the fray.

Isabel shuffled them all away from Claire's signing area, while Parker went over to wrap an arm around Mary Helen. Claire joined him, leaving her table.

"Are you all right?" she asked Mary Helen, straightening the child's dress and smoothing a hand over her hair.

"I'm fine," she said, leaning against Parker. "Go back and sign your books, Mom. It was only a little accident with Gracie Byrd being mean. Parker will take care of me."

She glanced toward her table and then at Mary Helen carefully. "If you're sure."

"She'll be fine," Parker added. "Mary Helen and I will get ourselves a bite to eat and a glass of punch. Don't worry." He glanced toward the line at Claire's table. "You have people waiting."

"All right." She looked at Mary Helen and smiled. "We'll talk later, okay?"

Parker walked with Mary Helen to the refreshment table, snagged a couple of brownies and two bottles of water and then steered her outside to the restaurant's porch.

"What happened in there?" he asked after a few minutes, knowing with Mary Helen it was always best to wait until she cooled off a little to talk.

Finishing her brownie she flounced into a chair on the porch. "Gracie Byrd was jealous."

He raised an eyebrow.

"That's how she is, Uncle Parker. Mother was getting a lot of attention, and so was I, and Gracie likes to be the center of things. Then when the photographer lady snapped a photo of me with J.T. and said we made a cute couple Gracie Byrd got really mad."

Mary Helen rolled her eyes. "You remember I *told* you Gracie Byrd has a crush on J.T. Mikell. I guess seeing us get our picture made together frosted it for her. She stuck out her big foot and tripped me when I was walking back to Mom's table and then she pushed me to be sure I fell down hard. She even flipped my hat off and then stomped on it."

Parker tried to think what to say. "Is she always that aggressive?"

Mary Helen wrinkled her nose. "Only sometimes, but she's always a pill. You can see why I don't like her." She brushed off her dress. "She got my nice dress dirty."

"It looks all right," Parker assured her.

"I feel really bad I caused a problem at Mom's book launch." She heaved a big sigh.

"It seems to me that Gracie Byrd caused the problem." Parker grinned. "And J.T. acted very chivalrous on your behalf, don't you think?"

She shrugged her shoulders. "He just felt guilty because his creepy girlfriend caused trouble."

"That's not how I saw it."

Mary Helen looked past him. "Well, there's more trouble coming."

Parker turned to see Miles Lawrence heading up the sidewalk to the restaurant with his mother's arm tucked into his.

"Good evening Eudora and Miles," Parker said, stepping forward to block their path up the steps.

Miles, seeming to sense Parker's mood behind his cordial words, said, "Mother and I just wanted to stop by to wish Claire the best at her launch."

"You didn't get an invitation," Mary Helen said, coming to stand beside Parker. "And we don't want you here at our party."

Eudora lifted her chin. "That child has no manners. I'm sure Claire Avery will not mind us stopping by to pay our regards." She glared at Mary Helen. "After all, it was because of my son's intervention that Claire made contact with a publisher at all."

"Perhaps," Parker replied. "But I believe Claire told Miles that she'd prefer him not to spend time with her or her family any more."

Eudora put a hand on her hip. "Honestly, Parker Avery. Everyone on the island is here tonight. I can't believe Claire would not want us to simply stop by to pay our respects."

"We don't want you here," Mary Helen repeated, looking pointedly at Miles. "You hurt my mother and you hurt my little sister." She turned to Eudora. "And you don't even like us, so I don't know why you even want to be here anyway."

Eudora drew in a shocked breath and a small silence fell.

Miles spoke at last. "Perhaps it wasn't the best idea for us to come, Mother. I really wasn't aware formal invitations had been sent for an island event." He lifted an eyebrow over the words, knowing all of the Edisto invitations had been informal ones spread by word of mouth.

Mary Helen edged closer to Parker to ask softly. "You're not going to hit him again are you?"

Parker saw Miles smirk at her words and heard Eudora gasp.

Parker bit back a smile. "Miles, I could go and ask Claire if she'd be willing for you and your mother to attend, but I recall her specifically telling me last weekend she hadn't invited you and didn't think it would be a good idea to do so."

"Well, I never," Eudora huffed.

"I think you should go home now," Mary Helen said in a very grown up tone. "Me, Parker, Suki, and all Mommy's friends want this to be a happy time for her. You'll mess it up if you stay."

Miles eyes flicked over Mary Helen with surprise. "It seems we've walked into a little ill will we didn't expect, Mother," he said at last. "I think it best, under the circumstances, that we leave. I'll take you to dinner somewhere nice since you're already dressed for the evening. What do you say to that?'

She stuck her nose in the air and turned. "I'd say the company would be much better, that's what I'd say."

They walked away, and Parker felt Mary Helen tuck herself tight under his arm. He glanced down to see big tears rolling down her cheeks.

"Are you all right?" he asked, hugging her closer to his side.

"I didn't think it would hurt so much to see him again," she said. "But it did. I know now why Suki got upset when she saw him and Eudora in the audience at her performance and froze and couldn't play."

Parker looked after Miles and Eudora's retreating figures.

"I'm glad we were outside here when Miles came." Mary Helen tucked her hand into his. "Mommy would have acted nice about them coming, like she always does, but it would have hurt her and made a bad memory for her special time."

"I'm rather glad we were out here, too." He smiled down at Mary Helen. "Do you think you might like to go back in and join all the fun again now?"

"Yes, but you keep a watch on Gracie Byrd for me. I wish she'd go home, too, like Miles and his mean mother did."

Parker squeezed the child's hand. "Perhaps I'll find her parents and make that suggestion in a tactful way," he said as they headed back in to the restaurant.

Mary Helen grinned. "I like you, Uncle Parker."

"I like you, too," he said.

Isabel waved at them. "There you two are. We've been looking for you. The photographer wants more pictures of Claire and the girls." She came over to give Mary Helen a small hug. "Are you all right, child?"

"She's fine," Parker answered for her, winking at her before Isabel whisked her away.

CHAPTER 21

August 1987

"**I** can't believe the summer is nearly over again," Elaine said on a Sunday afternoon in late August almost a year later. "The tourist traffic is already falling off."

"I'm almost glad for that fact even though it means business slows." Lula laughed. "The summer months have been *so* busy at work. I've hardly had a minute to sit down and enjoy a little break like this with the two of you."

Elaine, Lula, and Claire sat outside under the cabana behind Oleanders keeping an eye on their children playing down on the beach.

Lula turned to smile at Claire. "It's been two years since you first came to the island after Charles died. Time has flown by, hasn't it? A lot has changed for you since then."

"That's true." Claire's eyes moved to her girls chasing along the beach with the other children, playing in the waves. "Mary Helen is getting so much taller now at eleven, and Suki will soon be seven. She's losing those sweet baby looks."

"They're all growing up like weeds," Elaine said.

Lula opened the cooler to get out a cold drink, nestled in the ice. "When will your new book come out, Claire?"

"In October like the one last year," she replied. "This one is *The Polka Dot Kids at the Beach*. Isabel can't wait to stock it at The Little Mermaid."

"Isabel says your first book has gone very well." Elaine picked out a cola for herself before Lula closed the cooler.

"I'm pleased and Whittier is pleased. The book didn't rocket to the best-seller list or win any great awards in the children's book industry, but it's sold well and the reviews are good. Whittier feels confident many more readers will discover the book series as more titles publish. I hope so."

"Are you working on the third Polka Dot book now?" Lula asked, propping her tan legs on an empty chair across from her.

"I am, and I'm writing the first of the Farnsworth Fairies series Whittier wants to publish next."

"Ah. That explains the sudden interest in fairies the girls have shown, and why they all made fairy wings and floated around the yard in them for days." Elaine shook her head. "However did you make those fairy wings for the girls, Claire? You are so creative."

"They're easy to make. You take two coat hangers, twist the tops together and pull each hanger into an oval shape. Then you cut off the legs of an old pair of tights, stretch them over the ovals, tape them into place, tape the hangers together, and use the scraps from the tights to make arm ties."

"You make it sound easy, but it wouldn't be for me. I also had to put my foot down to keep Jane and Emma from cutting up more than one pair of their school tights." Elaine giggled. "But I got my camera out to take pictures of all four girls dressed up in wings and fairy costumes. They even made wands. They looked so cute."

"I think you've contributed so much to our children's creativity since you came, Claire," Lula added. "Elaine and I are grateful for your influence not only with creative activities, but with the moral principles you've taught them. It's impacted even the older boys Ryder and Tom, as well as Chuck and J.T."

Claire knew her mouth dropped open in surprise.

"It's impacted me, too." Elaine smiled at Claire. "When growing up, faith was pushed down my throat in a way I always resented, but being around you has changed the way I feel about it."

"Claire passed along some good books, too, teaching about a deeper walk in the Lord, that helped my faith grow." Lula finished off the last of her cola and put the can on the table beside them. "You've been our island evangelist."

"Thank you. That's a very nice compliment." Claire sent a smile to each of them. "Charles had such a strong relationship with the Lord. I envied it and it made me seek to grow my own relationship deeper, to be more like his. He helped lead me into a stronger place in my faith."

Elaine stood up to holler at Chuck. He'd started a water fight with J.T. and Mary Helen that was quickly getting out of hand. "That's enough Chuck Whaley. You hear me?" she called. "If you don't quit that, I'm going to make all three of you sit on the porch for a while."

With reluctance, Claire watched them stop and then gallop into the waves, a new game in mind.

"Is your sister still coming today, Claire?" Lula asked, changing the subject.

Claire nodded.

"Considering the poor relationship you've had with your sisters, I'm surprised one of them is coming to see you at all," Elaine said with candor.

Claire couldn't help laughing. "I admit I felt stunned when Marilyn called to say she wanted to stop over on her way to Florida for a baton conference. We've never been close. It makes me wonder if Mother has put her up to coming. Mother has never gotten over me not staying in Arlington. She still believes living there would have been better for me and the girls."

"I think your mother just wanted to control you and the girls," Elaine put in, settling back into her chair.

Claire brushed a strand of hair back from her face. "I don't know, but she and Parker and Charles's mother still don't approve of me continuing to live here at Oleanders."

"That is so silly." Lula frowned.

"Well, I know I need to find a place of my own soon," Claire replied. "I've stayed here over two years now. Even if Parker seldom uses the house and doesn't rent it, the girls and I need our own place. I've been saving up." She turned to Elaine. "I hope you'll start looking for a place for us. I won't be able to afford beachfront, but I should be able to afford a smaller home off the beach. Sometimes after homes sit for a time without a sale, the owners let them go for a bargain. I looked at one house near The Little Mermaid on Jungle Road but it was really too large for us."

"I'll keep my eyes open," Elaine promised. "But I know Parker won't like the idea of you leaving Oleanders. He really believes it's what Charles would have wanted, you and the girls staying here. I tend to agree."

"Selfishly, we only want Claire to stay close by." Lula reached over to pat Claire's hand.

The three women went down to the beach then, to play with the children and walk along the beach, enjoying the day.

"What's the shell of the day?" Claire asked her girls later as the three of them took a walk up the beach toward The Point.

"We're collecting white moon shells today," Mary Helen told her.

"They're hard to find, "Suki added. "But I found two." She pulled them out of her shirt pocket. The girls had put on long button-front shirts now to protect their shoulders from the sun, even in the late afternoon.

"Is Aunt Marilyn really spending the night with us?" Mary Helen asked.

"She is and we need to turn around in a minute to head back. I need to start something for supper for us to eat."

"I hope she doesn't try to make us go back to Arlington to Grandmother's." Suki's mouth formed a pout over the words.

"It doesn't matter what she wants," Mary Helen said as they turned to walk back down the beach. "We're *not* going."

"You girls remember your manners and act cordial and polite while Marilyn visits with us," Claire warned. "She *is* my sister and your aunt, and she will be our guest."

"Okay." Mary Helen grumbled.

The evening with Marilyn turned out to be more pleasant than Claire and the girls expected. Marilyn loved Oleanders and the beach. She went along with the girls' idea to drive around the island so they could point out favorite places. They stopped at The Little Mermaid, where Marilyn bought gifts for her three children to take back home with her. Then they drove to the back of the island to watch the sun go down on the water. With surprise, Claire watched Marilyn make an effort to talk with the girls and to look at pictures they brought out showing trips they'd taken around the area and photos of Claire's book launch and signings.

"The girls are happy here," Marilyn said a little later when she and Claire sat out on the screened porch after the girls went to bed.

"They are."

"So are you." Marilyn turned to give Claire a smile. "You seem so at ease and comfortable here, and you look fabulous." She picked at the edge of her shorts. "I'm really happy about your books, too. Marjorie and I keep a couple of copies at the baton studio and all the children that come in really love them."

"Thank you for telling me that."

Marilyn looked out across the ocean, sighing, and Claire could see again the pinched expression and sad eyes she'd noticed before.

"Are you unhappy, Marilyn?" she asked at last.

Tears started in Marilyn's eyes. "My life is a wreck right now. You probably know I married Harold mostly because he was in the law firm linked to Daddy's bank, older than me, but such a good catch. Mother pushed the match on me, wanting me to be well set. I never loved Harold in a romantic way, but I liked him. I haven't had a bad life, Claire. Money, advantages, three children, and starting a business I love with Marjorie and Mother." She paused. "I think Harold loved me when we married, but love has to be nurtured to endure. Over time, he realized my heart wasn't really attached. Now he's met someone who is head over heels for him and he wants a divorce."

"I'm sorry." Claire handed her a tissue.

"It shouldn't hurt, but it does. Hearing Harold talk about this woman, seeing him with her, I can see they share an obvious warmth and happiness, a joy together Harold and I never had.

Somehow I yearn for that now. Isn't that silly?"

Claire wasn't sure what to say.

"Marjorie and Mother say I should make the divorce difficult for Harold. We had a nasty fight once and Harold hit me. It was basically accidental, a swinging out of his arm that connected to me. But Marjorie and Mother say I should use that against Harold. Make the divorce messy, cause trouble with Harold in his law firm and social circles. Make him pay." She turned anguished eyes to Claire. "That doesn't feel right to me. What do you think?"

Claire put a hand over her sister's. "I've been a minister's wife. Surely you know what answer I would give to that. To any nasty vengeance or lying. To deliberately try to hurt someone." She paused. "I'm sorry you and Harold couldn't find a way to love each other through all these years."

"So am I now." She shook her head, closing her eyes.

After a time Marilyn added, "You did the right thing not to stay in Arlington. You were always different from Mother, Marjorie, and me. I know we weren't always kind to you because we didn't understand you, and I'm sorry." She shrugged. "Mother never helped with that, never helped Marjorie and me to see any of your good attributes. I see those more now, Claire."

"Thank you. I know I was different."

"Mother put more stress on material things, on social standing and accomplishments. Those things do matter. I can't say they don't matter to me. But I'm beginning to realize other things matter, too." She gave Claire a candid look. "I could never be happy on a small island like this. It drove me crazy when we had to spend time at Grandmother Hampton's little beach house on Martha's Vineyard. I need a busy social life and I admit I like money and what it can buy and do, but I'd like to know some happiness, too. To maybe find love. It hurts to have Harold discarding me. It's made me realize I had feelings for him I never acknowledged. But now it's too late."

Claire listened and she and Marilyn talked about a lot of things that night. Realistically, Claire knew she couldn't change her sister, but she felt glad she'd begun to reestablish a relationship with her.

"You've become your own person," Marilyn told her at one point. "Even Mother is a little proud about your books, although she still can't understand why you're still staying at Parker's place on this small island away from it all. But I can see you and the girls are happy here."

Claire knew that was probably the closest to a compliment she would get from Marilyn. "I'm so happy you and Marjorie started your business and that it's been successful," Claire replied. "You can share your skills and your love for twirling with so many young girls."

"I do love it." She looked out toward the ocean, changing the subject. "I hope that storm out to sea doesn't hit the Daytona area where I'll be with the baton competition. The weather report we watched earlier on television said the storm was hurricane strength now and battering some of the Caribbean islands. Do you worry it might hit here, living on the beach like you do?"

"I've weathered a few bad storms here already, Marilyn, and the predictions show it moving more out to sea by morning. It may not even touch land except in lower Florida."

"I hope you're right." She leaned her head back against the rocking chair. "I drove down to the competition to take time to think. Harold's mother has my three children. Tyler, Rachel, and Vivian don't understand why their father has moved out and why he and I are getting a divorce. It's a difficult time. All my friends are tiptoeing around the issue, knowing Harold is already practically living with Courtney. That's her name. I hate even saying it."

She sighed. "A lot of my friends, married to men in Harold's firm and social circle, are sweetly dumping me. You know how those things go."

Claire didn't. But she nodded, trying to be understanding.

"You should come home sometime for a visit," Marilyn said, changing topics. "Your girls need to know their cousins, my three children and Marjorie's. I know Daddy would love to have you visit, too. I think he and Mother realize now you needed your own life, Claire."

"I'm sure we'll visit sometime in future," Claire said. "Any of you are welcome here, too. I hope you know that."

Marilyn stood up. "Let's go watch television," she said, never content to sit quietly with her own thoughts for too long. "Maybe the news will tell more about the hurricane. I think they're calling this one Francine."

By the time Marilyn left the following morning, the news about Hurricane Francine was a little more worrisome. It was now projected to move closer along the east coast, possibly touching land if it strengthened and if its course altered a little. With Edisto Island in the storm's possible path, the local news stations had started encouraging tourists to leave and head for home. A mandatory evacuation hadn't been ordered, but advisories were already out.

Edisto Primary School closed since many of the children planned to travel inland with their parents to friends or grandparents' homes. Isabel closed The Little Mermaid and later walked over to check on Claire where she sat on the steps behind the house, watching the ocean.

"Ezra and I are heading to his brother's place in Summerville. You and the girls are welcome to come with us." She hesitated, looking toward the waves now crashing higher on the beach. "It isn't fun to weather through a hurricane at the beach, Claire. We've stayed at our house through a few but, now that we're older, I don't want the stress and worry of it. Why don't you and the girls come with us?"

"That's kind of you, Isabel, but Elaine and Lula both offered to take us to stay with them if the weather report changes. Lula's mother has a plantation home with lots of room further back on the island and Elaine and Pete own Fairfield rentals where we can stay if we need to leave the beachfront. Most of the tourists are packing to head home as a precaution, which will leave a lot of empty rentals at the resort." She glanced toward the sky, still blue in many places between gray clouds. "We may not need to leave at all. The hurricane is still far away. It may go out to sea and not even come near the coast."

"When a bad storm comes to Edisto, the water rises in the creeks and marshes. It washes over the roads. You know how close the water is to the road in many areas driving in." Isabel grabbed hold of her straw hat, almost tossed off her head by the rising wind. "The bridge off the island also closes. It's too dangerous to open and shut it. My point to you is that the option to leave the island becomes impossible once a hurricane moves in close to us. Not being from Edisto, you might not know that."

Claire appreciated her friend's concerns. "Don't worry. I won't put the girls in danger. We'll leave Oleanders if things get bad."

She patted Claire's cheek. "The truth is *I'll* worry about you. I've never liked a storm, ever since childhood."

"You and Ezra take care driving over to Summerville," Claire said as Isabel started down the stairs holding onto her hat. "I heard on the news the evacuation traffic is terrible."

"Ezra knows some back roads. We'll be okay," she replied, starting across the yard to her own house.

The sound of hammering filled the air between the noise of the rising wind and the crashing of waves on the beach. Islanders always boarded up their houses before leaving the island. On a walk up the beach earlier, Claire had seen people taking in chairs, tables, grills, and beach items, moving their cars, kayaks, and boats away from the beach to safer places.

Following Elaine and Pete's advice, Claire put the girls' bikes, beach toys, chairs, and umbrellas into the storage area under the house and brought small items from the porches inside. The rocking chairs on the back porch rocked gently in the breeze from the sea, but things looked calm otherwise.

"What did Isabel want?" Mary Helen asked, coming out on the screened porch.

Claire told her.

"I want to go with Elaine if we need to leave so me and Suki can play with Jane and Emma." Mary Helen looked out toward the beach. "The waves are getting really huge." She laughed and pointed. "Some silly boys are trying to surf them, too."

"That is not only silly but dangerous." Claire frowned. "You and Suki stay inside until this storm passes by."

"We wouldn't be stupid enough to try to surf in those waves." Mary Helen walked closer to the edge of the porch to watch the boys. "Did you know that when a big hurricane hit the island a long time ago, only one house was left on the beach side of The Point. A family didn't leave in time to get off the island and they had to stay in their house all through the storm. Chuck said it scared them so bad, they sold it afterwards and moved away."

"Will Oleanders get blown away?" Suki asked, coming out of the house as Mary Helen finished her story. Claire noticed she chewed on a nail as she often did when nervous or upset.

"The storm is still hundreds of miles out to sea," Claire answered, smoothing a hand over Suki's hair. "The weather reporters say it's not expected to hit our coastal area. The bands of a hurricane are broad, however, like big circles around a little circle. Those bands bring lots of wind and rain as a hurricane travels. The early edges of those bands are starting to touch the coast now."

"Will it get scarier?" Suki asked, always a little frightened of big storms.

"It might," Claire said honestly. "Inevitably, we'll get heavy rains and strong wind."

That statement proved far truer than Claire realized. By afternoon, Hurricane Francine had changed course to head more directly toward the coast. All Edisto Beach nonresidents had been told to evacuate and locals advised to prepare for a strong storm, even though Edisto was not targeted by the weather service to get a direct hit.

"We're working around the island to secure our properties." Elaine called and told Claire. "All the kids are helping and we should be finished in about two hours. Then Pete and the boys are coming back to the beach house to board it up and pick up supplies we might need. When they finish they'll bring you and the girls over to one of our rental houses in Fairfield in a more protected and safe location. I'm heading over there now with the girls ahead of you. Pete thinks with the surf as high as it is already that water may roll up under our houses before this is over. When the worst of the wind hits it might blow off shutters, too, take out power, and potentially do a little damage."

Claire felt her heartbeat kick up.

"Pete said for you to pack a few things you'll need and to be ready. The Fairfield house has a generator and a big fireplace. We'll all play campout together and we'll be fine. Pete and I have weathered through a lot of hurricanes and storms at Edisto." She hesitated. "Try to stay calm, Claire. All reports still say Edisto is not expected to get a direct hit. The hurricane is supposed to plow by the island off coast and then swerve in toward land near the Outer Banks in North Carolina."

"I'll be ready. And you and the girls be careful heading to the resort."

After hanging up the phone, Claire began to pack bags for her and the girls. The wind howled outside with the storm growing closer. Waves rose in the air in giant peaks to crash high on the beach, the froth rolling up into the yard. A few times the power flickered and Claire could feel the beach house rock on its high stilts as gusts of wind blew in off the sea.

"I'm scared, Mommy," Mary Helen said, coming down the stairs with her bag. "And Suki's crying."

"I don't like it here in the storm, Mommy," Suki wailed, following Mary Helen downstairs. "Our house shakes and the cats are yowling. Ginger and Smokey are hiding under the bed and won't come out. How are we going to get them in their carrier? We can't leave them here."

Claire remembered then that the big cat carrier was in the storage area under the house. Wrapping herself in a raincoat, she made her way down the stairs in the sheeting rain to get it, soaked to the skin by the time she dragged it up the stairs and inside the house.

"We can't see the TV anymore," Mary Helen announced. "I tried it and it won't come on."

"Television reception often goes out in a bad storm," Claire explained. "Sometimes power does, too. Mary Helen, look for some flashlights and candles while I change into dry clothes. We want to be ready in case we lose power." She started toward her bedroom and then turned back. "And Suki, pack some cat food for the cats. Put it in Ziploc bags so it won't get wet."

Realizing how soaked she'd gotten simply walking downstairs, she added, "You girls find your rain boots to put on and your rain coats, too. An umbrella alone won't be much help."

"No kidding," Mary Helen added, looking out the window. "The rain is blowing sideways."

"I hope we don't die like Daddy," Suki said, sniffling, as Claire walked back to the bedroom.

Hearing her words, Claire added her own quiet prayer words. "Lord be with us and keep us safe. I know You never leave us or forsake us. Watch over us and watch over those we love here. I thank you for Your love and care, in Jesus name."

CHAPTER 22

Well inland from the coast, Waterview was safe from the storm stirring in the Atlantic, but Parker paced the floor of the house worrying about Claire and the girls. The magnitude of the hurricane had increased, and even with the worst of the storm hours away, the wind lashed against his house in Beaufort and rain fell in sheets. Oleanders sat right on the beach, unprotected from the elements.

Parker called Pete Whaley. "I'm heading down in the boat to get Claire and the girls. They've never weathered through a hurricane."

"You don't need to come. I'm boarding up our last property now and then going to pick up Claire and the girls. Elaine and I are taking them with us to one of our big rental houses in the back of Fairfield. We should all be safe there, even if the storm hits more directly."

"Thanks Pete, but I need to come to get them. I'll go crazy if I don't." He choked on the words. "I can't risk another loss."

Pete waited a minute to answer. "I understand. Maybe more than you know."

"It won't take me long to get there by boat." Parker threw a few supplies into a tote bag while he talked on the kitchen phone. "I'll be under a hardtop in the Whaler, safe from the weather, and I'll turn into Bay Creek to the marina long before I get close to the ocean and the surf." He paused. "I *need* to bring them back with me to know they're safe, Pete. It's going to be a bad night tonight.

Claire and the girls haven't seen a hurricane through. They'll be scared. It's different for you and Elaine. You've grown up on the island."

"You may be right, and by boat you'll be here in about thirty minutes." Pete hesitated. "Let me do this to help though. I'll go pick up Claire and the girls and bring them to the marina to you. Claire doesn't need to drive in this wind and rain, even that short distance. If you have to drive over in your jeep to pick them up after you get to the island, you'll all get soaked through on the trip." A fritz of static cut them off for a minute. "Claire will bring the cats, too. Do you have a place for them on the boat?"

"I'll tuck their carrier in the cabin along with Claire's and the girls' things to keep them out of the weather."

As soon as Parker hung up from talking with Pete, he threw on his rain gear and headed out the door to the boat. At the back of his property, a long wooden walkway led across the marsh to a covered dock on a curve of the Beaufort River. There the Whaler waited, securely tied under cover but rocking in the waves from the storm.

Parker had bought the craft only a year ago, trading his older boat which reminded him too much of Ann and all the trips they'd made to the island. The Whaler with its sleek deep V-hull, wide beam, and well-appointed cabin made travel down to the island, or fishing at sea or in coastal waterways, a pleasure. Today, he was glad for the boat's speed. Even in the rain with the river and coastal waterways rising from the incoming storm, the boat skimmed through the water like a dream.

Parker had fought with himself about racing to Claire's rescue all day. Now with the roads to the island closed, boating to Edisto offered his only alternative. Actually, it was faster anyway with the mass exodus of coastal traffic still backing up the highways.

Over and over he'd imagined what it might be like if he lost Claire and the girls, if the hurricane turned and slammed into the island. It could happen. The latest tracking showed the hurricane on a path skimming all too close to the South Carolina coast. One turn and it could sweep toward Edisto. He'd seen coastal storms do unpredictable things over the years.

Turning to head the boat into the South Edisto River, Parker faced the full realization at last of how much he loved Claire. He'd fought it for so long. Felt it was wrong. But here he was, racing to get her like a lovesick swain.

When he pulled into the marina, slowing the boat to ease it into a space by the dock, he saw Claire immediately, running toward him down the ramp. She threw herself into his arms as he stepped out of the boat.

"Parker, you crazy thing, coming to get us." She pulled back to look at him, the rain falling in sheets around them. "But I'm so glad you did. All I could think about all day was you, wishing you were with us, worrying if you were all right. I'm so happy to see you." She kissed him full on the mouth, laughing at the same time.

With joy, Parker kissed her back, realizing then that their first joyous kiss was turning into a more passionate one.

Claire pulled back, her eyes widening with surprise. "I'd better get the girls. They're inside with Pete. I said I'd watch for you to come."

Parker wanted to reach for her again, but he held back. "I'll go help you get your things," he said instead.

Mary Helen and Suki threw themselves into his arms, too, as he and Claire walked up the ramp and into the covered dining area behind the Dockside Restaurant. The girls hugged and kissed him with enthusiasm, while Pete stood to one side grinning.

"I guess these girls are glad to see you," Pete said. "I'll help you load up your gear."

They loaded the yowling, scared cats into the cabin area of the Whaler, dumping their bags there, too. Parker suggested Mary Helen and Suki might like to ride below in the cabin, but they insisted on coming up into the cockpit with him and Claire.

"We might have a bit of a choppy ride," he told them, as they buckled themselves into their seats after putting on life jackets. "But once we get away from the ocean, the ride will be smoother."

"I've been scared all day and wishing you would come," Suki told him.

Mary Helen frowned at her. "You didn't say anything to me about that."

Suki lifted her chin. "But I thought it and wished it."

"Actually so did I," Mary Helen admitted. She leaned over to give Parker another kiss. "You're our hero, Uncle Parker."

"It's always good to have a few heroes," Claire said with a small smile.

The wind and rain pelted the Whaler on the trip back, and they talked little, conscious of the storm at sea moving closer and closer to the land.

"Will that mean storm hurt our house at Edisto?" Suki asked.

"I hope not," Parker answered, steering the boat around a limb in the river. "The last weather report I heard still tracked the storm off the coast with a direct hit to Edisto not predicted. But as close as the hurricane is to land and with its high category, it's hard to know what damage it might bring."

They rode on in silence for most of the rest of the trip, listening to the rain slashing against the boat and the wind roaring through the trees along the sides of the bank.

Back at Beaufort at last Parker slowed the boat's motor to guide the Whaler under cover of the dock, then he climbed out to secure it tightly. Letting the girls lug their tote bags, Parker picked up the big carrier containing the cats. He'd wrapped it in a waterproof tarp, but the cats still didn't like the idea of being out in the rain again and meowed piteously as he made his way up the path to the house.

On the back porch leading into the kitchen, they all took off their wet slickers and boots, and then let themselves into the warmth of the kitchen.

Parker put the cats' litter box and food inside the laundry room and then opened the door of the crate so the cats could come out and explore. Mary Helen and Suki sat on the floor to comfort and talk to them.

"Poor little kitties," Suki soothed.

"I'll close off this room and the kitchen area for a little while until they settle down." Parker watched the cats slink slowly out of the crate sniffing around, their eyes still wide from their trip up the river. "They don't need to start exploring the whole house until they feel comfortable again."

Both cats were fully grown now, Ginger with her rich marmalade coat and Smokey with his soft gray tabby fur. Mary Helen gathered Smokey into her arms, petting him and crooning soft words to him while Suki stroked Ginger.

Claire leaned against the doorframe, watching as she patted her hair dry with a kitchen towel. "Don't you wish they could talk and tell us what they thought about that journey in your boat?"

He laughed. "No. I imagine it would be full of bitter complaints."

She smiled.

His eyes roamed over her noticing how wet she was. "Why don't you go upstairs and put some dry clothes on? You're soaked."

"I think I will." She glanced at his wet hair and then at the girls. "You and the girls need to dry off and change, too." She smiled. "Then I think I'll make a big pot of homemade soup, if I can find enough ingredients for it in your kitchen."

"I keep a lot more on hand now than I used to." His eyes met hers and he saw her flush and look away. She hadn't forgotten that kiss, nor had he.

Over the evening, they shared soup and homemade rolls for dinner, then all played Parchesi while the rain continued to beat against the house, the wind sometimes howling as the storm grew closer to the coast.

Claire went to stand at the window at one point to look out toward the river. "I can only imagine how fiercely this storm is hitting the island. I hope everyone is all right."

"We won't know for sure until the worst of the hurricane passes through in the night hours."

She put a hand to her mouth. "I would have been so terrified to be down there alone with the girls. I thought of that all day."

She turned to look at him. "Like Suki said, I kept wishing that you would come."

Parker let her lean against him and wrapped an arm gently around her, fearful of doing more. But still wanting to savor this small moment. *Was she beginning to care? Was she starting to realize new feelings for him, as he'd once discovered feelings for her?* Parker wondered, but he dared not ask.

The rain fell incessantly all evening and reports of flooding around the area began to hit the news. With no phone communication to Edisto possible now, Parker and Claire could only wonder about their friends still at the island. With many transformers blown out, telephone poles down, and hundreds of homes without power, the news continued to caution residents to stay home and not venture out on the highways, even in Beaufort.

As the wind rose when darkness fell, Parker headed outdoors to secure a shutter blown loose from the side of the house. A heavy wind gust literally blew him off his feet at one point.

Claire let him in the back door as he returned, her eyes anxious, her hands eager to help him out of his wet rain slicker. "Are you all right?" she asked. "I saw that wind throw you to the ground."

"I'm fine," he replied, smoothing a hand down her face before thinking, wanting to wipe away the worry lines.

He heard her draw in a breath, her eyes widening and her pupils dilating for a moment, before she looked away. *Could this be happening?* he asked himself, watching her wrestle with her emotions and wishing he could gather her in his arms and kiss her again. *But should he?* It didn't feel the right time for declarations in the middle of this crisis. Besides, it might only be the danger of the hurricane that had heightened her emotions.

"Are the girls sleeping okay through the storm?" he asked instead.

"Yes," she answered, seeming glad for a change in thought. "I checked on them before you went out. I think they were both so tired from the day they just crashed once I finally got them into bed."

"That's good," he said, starting back into the kitchen.

"Would you like some hot coffee?" she asked. "I can make a pot, and there's some coffee cake in your breadbox."

"Yes to both," he answered, letting his eyes rove over her familiar face, her dark thick hair loose and free tonight, her deep brown eyes revealing even the emotions she tried to hide. How precious she had become to him.

Claire hesitated as if unsure of what to say or do.

Realizing he couldn't continue to stand there simply staring at her, Parker said, "I think I'll go in the den to look at the television and see if there's any more news about the storm."

She turned and walked to the counter to begin spooning coffee into the coffeemaker. "The reports I saw earlier kept talking about impacts around the coastal area, but without any word about Edisto," she said. "Fripp Island and Hunting Island are experiencing flooding and have lost power. They're not far from Edisto by sea."

"No," he said, worried like her about what brunt Edisto might be taking from the hurricane.

A short time later, she settled onto the sofa in the den beside him with mugs of hot coffee and a slice of coffee cake each.

Parker took a sip of the coffee, grateful for its warmth.

"The stores are out of bread, milk, and bottled water," Claire commented as they listened to the news.

He grinned. "That always happens even if there's only a heavy storm advisory, much less a hurricane warning."

"Is Beaufort in danger? I hate to think of any of the beautiful old homes being damaged."

"Actually, the shape of the South Carolina coast has protected Beaufort historically from direct hits from hurricanes. The city is tucked away from the Atlantic Ocean. It's unlikely a hurricane will hit here. The only hurricane I remember hearing about that hit Beaufort was the storm of 1893. It felled trees and wreaked havoc downtown. No place near the coast is ever completely safe from the hit of a storm." He smiled at her. "But some of the locals call Beaufort 'God's nook,' a blessed place of safety."

"I hope you're right." She looked around in alarm as the power flickered.

"That's the wind blowing the lines." He resisted the temptation to put his hand on her leg to comfort her.

She glanced toward the window, uneasy. "Would you mind if we pray together?" she asked.

"I have been praying," he said. "Haven't you?"

"Yes." She twisted her hands. "But I mean pray together. It's powerful when two agree in prayer. We should pray not only for our safety and the safety of your home and property, but for safety and comfort for our friends on Edisto, for Oleanders, and for all this beautiful area."

He studied her. "That's what you and Charles would have done, isn't it?"

She nodded, not adding more.

"Ann and I would have prayed, too, Claire. Praying together was a big part of our marriage. We shared our faith, read the Bible and other devotional books, and tried to grow in faith together."

"I'm glad," she said, not looking up to meet his eyes.

Parker had offered blessings at meals when he visited at the island with Claire and the girls or when they visited at Waterview, but they hadn't prayed together other than that. He was sure Charles, as a pastor, would have prayed often with Claire and the girls. He shouldn't have hesitated to do so in the past. Now he knew it was critical to do so if they were to consider being a couple in the future.

The lights flickered in and out again, and Parker reached across to take Claire's hand. "Father, we thank you that we are here together. Thank you for allowing me to bring Claire, Mary Helen, and Suki to safety further inland from the hurricane raging at sea. We ask for your continuing protection, your guidance, your care. We pray for protection for our friends at Edisto, for the island we love, for Oleanders. Keep all safe."

He felt Claire squeeze his hand as he continued, felt the unity of her thoughts and prayers uniting with his. *How sweet this is*, he thought, as he finished his prayer at last and felt the peace settle over them. He wondered how many people realized the importance of this aspect in a couple's relationship.

Claire added some extra words of her own then, remembering to pray for The Little Mermaid where she worked, for Drake, Nora and Andrew, for Westcott Antiques, for their church and friends. Her voice and words soothed him.

She leaned against him later as they watched television and then drifted off to sleep in the quiet of the evening. Parker shifted her until her head lay on his lap, letting his hand smooth her hair as he might Mary Helen's or Suki's. She was so beautiful.

Parker flicked off the television with his remote, leaned his head back against the couch and soon fell asleep, too, waking later as Claire did as a crash from outdoors shook the house.

"What was that?" She jerked up to look toward the window.

Parker went to look outside. "The wind blew a tree down across the street, but fortunately it didn't hit the power lines or any houses. I'm sure even in Beaufort, there will be debris and downed trees to clean up tomorrow."

She stood up. "I need to check on the girls, and I think I'll go to bed, too. Both of us are tired."

Parker locked up the house, checked on the cats, and found his way to his own bedroom after a time. But he lay in bed thinking of Claire, knowing he hungered for more intimacy with her and a deeper relationship. He wanted to marry her, possess her, but he wondered if that could ever be possible. Would she even consider it with her husband's brother? And what would their families and friends think?

He drifted to sleep at last, pulling up the bedspread as the night cooled, smiling as he realized it one of the new items for the house Claire had helped him pick out. Her touch was beginning to show in more and more aspects of his life and his home. And certainly in his heart.

CHAPTER 23

September 1987

Less than a month later, Claire and Elaine Whaley walked up the beach together on a weekday morning.

"It's hard to believe a storm swept through here only a few weeks ago," Claire said looking up at the blue, cloudless sky.

"We were lucky." Elaine stopped to pick up a shell to examine it before dropping it again. "The hurricane stayed out to sea and lessened in category as it drew closer to the South Carolina coast. Several low-lying areas on the island flooded as you know, wind damaged a lot of houses and felled some trees. The surf rolled up under many of the homes on the beach, battering them hard in the wind, too, but nothing more."

"We got blessed," Claire added. "Even so it took Parker more than two weeks around his work at Westcott to clean up the damage at Oleanders."

"You and the girls helped, too."

"We did as much as we could. But it isn't our home and most of the decisions about the cleanup were Parker's to make."

Elaine passed her an odd look. "It *is* your home, Claire."

She looked away. "No, it isn't. And it's time for us to find our own place. I've been looking around the island and I saw one or two places I want to ask you about."

"You're serious about this." Elaine slowed to a stop, surprised.

"I am. You know I told you earlier this summer I needed to find my own place."

Elaine shrugged, walking on. "I remember you talking about it but you didn't indicate there was any hurry."

"It's a good time for me to move right now," she answered evasively. "The girls just started school again and if I buy something right away I'll have a month to move and get settled before my next book comes out."

As the beach widened at the island's point, they turned to start back in the other direction.

Claire picked up the conversation again. "I found one house I like on Lee Street and another on Myrtle Street on the St. Helena Sound side of the island. It's backyard faces the bike trail, which I think is nice. The house on Lee is quiet and private, too." She pushed a loose strand of hair back, tossed by the sea breeze. "The third property I like is in Fairfield on Barony, one of the quiet side streets in the residential area. The advantage of Fairfield would be the protection of being in the resort. The property is beautifully kept there."

"You really *are* serious about this," Elaine repeated, stopping to sit on one of the benches by a beach access point.

Claire sat down beside her. "I really need to do this, Elaine."

"You're pushing this issue more than normal for you. Has Parker said anything to you about moving? Are you having problems with him in some way?" Elaine probed.

"Of course not," Claire said but couldn't meet Elaine's eyes with the words.

"What do the girls think about this?" Elaine asked.

"They don't know. I thought it better to find a house first and then take them to see it. I'm sure they'll be excited about us purchasing our own place. We can get our own furniture out of storage, and it will be fun to buy other things we need and to decorate a new home."

Elaine shook her head. "You know Mary Helen and Suki won't be excited to leave Oleanders. They'll pitch a fit."

"They'll understand."

"I doubt it and neither do I understand it, but of course I'll help you if your mind is set on this and I can't talk you out of it."

"I do think this is best," she replied. But, of course, Elaine argued with her about it for most of the rest of the morning.

Claire faced a similar scene later when she went to work at The Little Mermaid and posed the idea to Isabel.

"I thought you could help me by keeping your eyes open for a new place for us," she added. "You know so many people on the island."

Isabel leaned on the counter by the register to look more closely at her. "You've been unhappy lately. I've seen it, but didn't comment about it with all the cleanup efforts we've had since the storm. I worried for a time the hurricane scared you and that you might consider moving off island."

"No, I love Edisto, and the girls love it." She looked away from Isabel's study of her.

"There's something you're not telling me. Has Miles Lawrence been bothering you again? Or has your harpy mother been calling to suggest it's inappropriate for you to live at Parker's place?"

Seeing this as a ready excuse, Claire said, "My family does disapprove of my continuing to live at Parker's home. They don't think it looks right and neither do Charles's family. Charles's mother has been somewhat outspoken about it to both Parker and me. I hate to cause trouble between Parker and his relatives."

Isabel waved a hand. "You know Parker doesn't care a fig about their opinion on this, and I didn't think you did either."

Claire rearranged some items on a nearby shelf in the store. "I've lived at Parker's home for over two years. It simply feels like time for me to buy my own place, and as I told Elaine I'd like to move this month if possible before my next book comes out in October. The island is less busy now; the girls are in school. It's a good time for it."

Isabel settled onto the stool behind the register. "I suppose from your comments you've already started looking at houses on the island."

"I have." Claire told her about the three she'd mentioned to

Elaine earlier. "Elaine took me to see all of them this morning before I came to work. I'm favoring the little house on Myrtle, on the quiet end of the island. It's painted green, called The Green Parrot. Isn't that a cute name? It has four bedrooms, one for each of the girls, the fourth an ideal office for me. Lovely oak trees shade it and a screened porch on back looks across the lawn to the bike trail. The girls will like that."

"You're kidding yourself if you think the girls will like this idea at all."

Claire crossed her arms. "It's not like I'm moving them off the island."

"They love Parker. And he loves them. This will hurt him."

She looked away. "I'm sure he will understand."

Isabel shook her head. "This doesn't feel right to me, but it is your life to live. You know Ezra and I will help you get settled if you decide to move. I know some furniture stores in Charleston where you can find some of the items you'll need. Is the rest of your stuff still stored in Arlington?"

"Not any more. Parker moved it to a storage facility in Beaufort he uses for excess pieces for Westcott's, things they don't have space for at the store." She offered Isabel a smile. "I'm sure the Westcott truck driver can deliver it. I have three bedroom suites, Charles's desk and office pieces, dishes, sheets, towels, and more. I'll only need living, dining, and porch furniture."

"Obviously, you've had this idea in your head for some time."

"It's *time* for me to move," Claire said, turning back to continue organizing the new items on the store shelf.

"At least I can be grateful you're staying on the island so you can still work for me."

Claire turned to smile at Isabel. "Surely you know I wouldn't leave the Mermaid."

"If you meet someone and marry, you will. But that would be different. I'd feel only happiness for you then." She laughed. "However, I hope he wouldn't take you and my girls too far away."

"I'm sure marrying again in the near future *isn't* in the cards for me," Claire said, feeling like she might weep over the words.

Later in the day Claire took the girls to see The Green Parrot. The more she thought about it, the more she felt this house right for them.

They biked over, Claire not mentioning to them she planned to stop and show them a house. Elaine had given her the key so she could get in without her. Claire often changed their bike route, so today she led the girls off trail to follow along Fort Street before cutting over to Myrtle to pass by the house.

"This is my Favorite House of the Day, girls," she said, stopping her bike in front of The Green Parrot. She and the girls often picked out a "favorite" of the day as they biked around the island.

"It's cute," Mary Helen said as the girls stopped their bikes, too.

"I like its name The Green Parrot," Suki added, reading the wooden sign that hung from the porch rail, decorated with a jaunty green parrot.

"I think it might win my vote for Favorite House of the Day, too," Mary Helen said, swatting at a mosquito trying to settle on her leg. "Suki and I both like it."

"Let's go walk around and look at it," Claire said. "The house is empty."

"It's for sale, too," Mary Helen pointed to the Whaley Realty sign in the yard. "So no one will come out to fuss at us if we walk around in the yard."

They walked through the shady yard then, the girls liking the big oak trees around the house and the tire swing hanging from a high tree limb.

"This is a neat house," Mary Helen said as they started back to their bikes again.

"I wish we could see inside," Suki added.

"We can." Claire pulled the key out of her pocket. "Elaine gave me the key to the house so we could go inside."

A suspicious look crossed Mary Helen's face. "Why would she do that?"

"Because I'm thinking about buying this house for us. It's time we had our own place."

Suki's mouth dropped open. "And leave Oleanders?"

"We can't stay there forever," Claire tried to explain. "It's Parker's home. He's been good to let us stay there since Daddy died, but we need to buy our own home now."

"Why?" Mary Helen glared at her.

Claire put a hand on one hip. "For many practical reasons—to build equity, to keep from imposing on Parker's hospitality. To have our own furniture and things again."

She sighed. "We need to do this, girls. I know you love Oleanders, but I'm not asking you to leave the island, your friends, or your school. Only to move a short bike-ride away from The Point to a home of our own. Would you look at the house and tell me what you think about it? If you don't like it, Elaine has shown me several others."

"At least we don't have to move to Grandmother's again, and we can bring the cats to this house. Smokey and Ginger will love the yard and the big trees they can climb in," Suki said, trying as always to find something positive to focus on.

"If we move, it will hurt Parker's feelings," Mary Helen pronounced.

"He'll understand," Claire replied, heading up the stairs to the front door. Like most beach homes, The Green Parrot was raised on stilts with a garage area, storage, and patio underneath.

Begrudgingly the girls followed and walked through the house with her. Despite their surprise at the idea of moving, they liked the house. Both girls picked out the room they'd want for their bedroom and had ideas for furnishing other areas. It helped that they weren't totally negative.

"It's a good house, but I wish it was on the beach," Mary Helen said wistfully as they walked out to explore the screened porch on the back.

"I can't afford beach front property," Claire said, deciding to be honest. "But you know Parker will be happy for us to use the beach and the cabana in front of his house anytime. Elaine, Lula, and

Isabel offered the same."

Mary Helen sighed. "But they won't be our neighbors anymore. It won't be the same at all."

"Anywhere we moved would be different. And we *need* to move, Mary Helen. It's the right thing for us to do after two years."

"Have you told Parker we're moving?" she asked.

"No, but I will. Probably this weekend when he comes down."

Mary Helen put a hand on one hip. "He won't like it."

"As I told Suki, I think he'll understand."

When they went back out to retrieve their bikes, Mary Helen asked, "Can we ride to the other houses you've looked at—just to see them?"

"Sure, we can do that. All are on this end of the island."

They biked by the other two homes, and after exploring them the girls agreed The Green Parrot was still their favorite.

"If we *have* to move, I guess it's all right," Mary Helen said as they parked their bikes under the house later after coming back to Oleanders.

When Claire returned the key to Elaine that evening, she asked her to approach the owners of the Parrot with an offer. By the next day it seemed like everyone on the island knew Claire was planning to move.

Isabel laughed as yet another of the locals left The Little Mermaid after asking Claire about it. "Russ and Irma Oswald seem real excited you're buying their house. They moved to Virginia to live near their kids in one of those retirement villages but they sure spread the word quickly to everyone that paperwork is in the works for a sale of their old home here."

Claire frowned. "I wish they hadn't said anything before it's final. We've only barely started negotiations."

"Are you thinking about changing your mind?"

"No. I simply wanted to keep it to myself until we wrote contract."

"Ah, well, people will be people. This is a small island. There are few secrets here."

The truth was, Claire hoped Parker hadn't heard the news. She planned to tell him when he came down for the weekend, but she dreaded doing so. Claire knew he'd be upset, and she worried Parker might see through her reasons about needing to move. *Oh, she hoped he didn't!*

It so embarrassed her, but ever since the night he'd come to rescue them from the storm, nothing had been the same. An uncomfortable tension hummed in the air between them. Their conversations felt awkward. Claire felt twitchy and uncomfortable in Parker's presence now, and she didn't know what to do about it. Somehow, she had fallen in love with her husband's brother.

She walked down the beach now worrying over it, wondering if moving across the island would even be far enough. She had to find a way to clamp down on these feelings so Parker wouldn't see them. It would be so awful if he knew after all he'd done for them since Charles's death.

Claire kicked at a shell as she walked along the beach. Whatever had she been thinking to kiss him like she did that night of the storm, and for him to kiss her back and then stare at her the way he did? She was sure he'd felt stunned and embarrassed. Claire remembered how quickly he'd changed the conversation right after. Hopefully, he looked back on the incident, and some of the soft moments later that night at his home, and simply chalked them all up to the emotion stirred up by the hurricane. She hoped so.

She kicked at another shell in frustration.

"Planning to kick all the shells on the beach back out to sea?" said a familiar voice behind her.

Claire turned her head slightly to see Miles Lawrence walking up beside her. *Great*, just what she needed—another problem tonight.

"Do you mind if I walk along with you?" he asked.

"No. It's all right."

"I'm pleased at how well your first book has done this year. David Whittier had only good things to say the last time we shared lunch in Savannah. He thinks your new book will go well, too. It comes out next month, doesn't it?"

"Yes," Claire answered. She realized as they walked along that Miles still made her uncomfortable but not in the same way. That old attraction to him was gone.

"I heard through the grapevine you might be buying a house of your own on the island."

"It seems *everyone* has heard that even though Elaine hasn't even written a contract yet."

He laughed. "Small things are big news on a little island like Edisto."

"Apparently."

"You seem annoyed," Miles observed. "Although you could still be annoyed at me, I don't think that's what you're upset about tonight. You were kicking shells out to sea long before I walked up to join you."

"I have a lot on my mind."

They walked along quietly for a few minutes.

"Have you told Parker about this move you're planning?" Miles asked after a time.

"I plan to this weekend," she said, trying not to add *as if it's any of your business.*

He laughed out loud. "You're right to dread it. He won't be happy about it."

"I do think it's my decision to make," she snipped back.

"Um. Um. Something's going on." Miles laughed. "Did Parker finally declare his love and kiss you, causing you to want to run away like you did when I first sneaked a kiss or two?"

Claire stopped to stare at him, her mouth dropping open.

"You should see your face. Obviously I got something right."

Claire hugged her arms to herself. "This is none of your business, Miles Lawrence. Stop trying to analyze my life."

"One of two things is obvious to me here, Claire Avery. Either Parker kissed you, which I might add would be about time, or you didn't know the man is in love with you. Surely the latter isn't true?"

Claire felt a flush spread up her neck and face. "You don't know what you're talking about."

"Don't I? Use your brain, Claire. The man warned me off from the first day I set eyes on you. He punched me out after I flirted with you. He threatened my mother and me, and he wouldn't even let us into your book launch last October to pay our respects. Every time I come down to the island, he still glares at me whenever he sees me, even though you and I are not interested in each other any more." He shook his head. "Only a man in love acts like that."

Claire looked out to sea, thinking over his words. "Parker just feels protective toward me. That's all." She started to walk on, Miles falling into step beside her. "And I didn't know you came to the book launch."

"You didn't invite me."

"No, I didn't. I thought it might upset the girls."

He chuckled. "It did. Mary Helen certainly gave me a piece of her mind."

Claire sighed. "I really don't need this drama tonight, Miles."

"I'd say not. You have your own little drama going with Parker Avery. I could tell by how you responded when I brought his name up." He laughed, that free, loose, know-it-all laugh of his. "I'll head on home now and just let you think about it."

He turned to start up the path to his beach house, but then turned back. "Parker Avery is a good man, Claire," he said in a changed tone. "Don't be a fool and overlook that."

More confused than ever, Claire made her way back to Oleanders. With the girls older now, she'd left them for a short time watching television to take a walk and to try to clear her thoughts. And now, Miles Lawrence's words had left her in a greater muddle than before. Could he be right? Did Parker care for her more than as only a sister-in-law he'd promised to look after? He'd never said anything to her to that effect. Never flirted with her. Never shown any signs of caring in a romantic way before the night of the storm. And ever since then, he'd acted like everything was just the same, even when he surely felt the awkwardness stirring between them.

What should she do? Claire simply didn't know. There was no one she could talk to about this, either. Certainly not Parker. And what if Miles was totally wrong about Parker? He wasn't exactly what Claire would think of as a wise expert about love. No, she was more likely right. And because of that, she needed to move out of Parker's house and soon.

CHAPTER 24

Parker dreaded heading down to the beach house this weekend. He still needed to finish repairing the cabana from its hit by the storm, so he could hardly make an excuse to stay away. Claire and the girls expected him, too.

"You've been moody the last few weeks," Nora commented at a break between customers at Westcott's. September often brought a sweep of tourist traffic to Beaufort and they'd been busy.

"I've had a lot on my mind with the cleanup around my place here and down at the island." Parker looked through some sales fliers by the register as he answered.

"Andrew enjoyed going down to help last weekend."

"He worked hard. He and the girls surprised me with all they did to help pick up limbs and debris strewn all over the yard."

"I heard it was a mess," she said. She paused in her task of arranging glassware in an antique cabinet to study him. "Are you having a problem in your relationship with Claire? Or is anything wrong in the business here at Westcott's you're not telling me about? You haven't been yourself since the storm. Drake noticed it, too."

Great, Parker thought. They'd been talking about him.

"I'm fine." He offered Nora a big smile. "I think I've simply felt bad about all the problems the people at the island experienced. It took days for the restoration of power and phone service. Homes and businesses were damaged, beautiful trees lost. The hurricane pushed sand under most all the houses on the beach front, leaving a big cleanup job behind. It hurt tourism and caused difficulties for many."

She nodded, seeming to accept his explanation.

The door opened to let in a group of new customers, moving the day along and moving Nora's thoughts away from probing into his behavior.

Truthfully, Parker didn't know what to do about the situation with Claire. Since the night of the hurricane, their relationship had definitely changed. He'd tried to move it back to the old level, but Claire felt awkward around him now. Parker felt sure she regretted her impulsive kiss to him that rainy night and was even more sure she now felt uncomfortable about his passionate kiss in return. What had he been thinking to kiss her like that and he her brother-in-law? He'd seen the shock and surprise on her face afterward. Even though the evening brought some sweet moments later that gave him hope for a change in Claire's feelings, she'd only acted twitchy and nervous with him ever sense.

Arriving at the island on Friday afternoon, he found Claire acting more nervous and uncomfortable than usual. Even the girls seemed to pick up on the tension, their eyes moving between him and Claire as he arrived.

"Pete said to call him when you got here," Claire told him. "He and Tom are coming over to help you work on the cabana. Elaine and I are whipping up a shrimp and rice casserole for dinner with green beans, rolls, and some other sides. She and Pete wanted us to eat with them over at their place after the work on the cabana is done."

Parker felt a sweep of gratitude they'd be sharing the evening with the Whaley family. It meant he and Claire wouldn't have to talk one-on-one much.

"It's good of Pete and Tom to offer to help me finish the repairs," he said in reply. "Pete is better with his hands than I am. The work will go faster."

Mary Helen sent him a smile. "Mr. Whaley said that since they enjoy using the cabana so much they should help fix it."

With Pete and Tom's help, and with extra help from Chuck, the quickly finished replacing the loose floorboards in the cabana fixing the roof, and repairing the steps. By the time Elaine called them to come over to the house for dinner, the job was done.

Elaine served dinner on the long table on their back porch with the weather pleasant. With a barrage of mix-and-match wooden chairs, the big table seated as many as twelve easily. Elaine, always informal in presentation, set the table for dinner with colorful plastic plates, cups, and throwaway plastic silverware.

They all talked about the weather, school, and odds and end as they passed dishes around so everyone could serve their own plates.

Emma, now eight, chattered away, telling them about a school matter and then said, "I wish Claire and Mary Helen and Suki weren't moving away from Oleanders." She turned towards Parker seated at one of the heads of the table. "Can't you talk her into staying, Parker?"

Stunned, Parker dropped the cup in his hand, spilling tea on the table.

Elaine jumped up to wipe it up with paper towels. "Don't worry Parker. It's only a little spill. I'll get you some more tea."

Parker's eyes found Claire's.

She bit her lip. "I was planning to tell you tonight that Elaine helped me find a house. It's time the girls and I stopped imposing on your hospitality."

Elaine came back out on the porch with a new glass of tea for Parker. "I had *nothing* to do with this Parker. I'd just like to clarify that. In fact, I tried to talk Claire out of moving. I know you love having her at Oleanders."

Parker couldn't seem to find any words.

"I *told* you Parker wouldn't like it." Mary Helen glared at her mother.

"Maybe we can stay," Suki offered hopefully.

Parker watched Claire twist her hands, a sign that she was obviously nervous. *How long had she been planning this*, he thought?

Conversation lapsed for a few moments as Parker continued to stare at Claire, trying to take in the idea of her moving.

He watched Claire swallow. "It's a nice little house over on Myrtle Street, a short distance beyond where Fort Street ends. A safe, quiet area of the island. It's the green house on the corner by Louise Street, called The Green Parrot. You probably know it."

Parker didn't trust himself to answer.

"Obviously this is a subject the two of you need to talk about later," Elaine offered, trying to move the evening along.

She and Pete picked up the conversation, introducing a new topic, getting the boys involved in talking about an upcoming football game at their school. And somehow Parker got through the meal.

He excused himself as soon as they ate dessert, saying he needed to go back to clean up at the cabana before dark fell.

Pete soon joined him. An easy-going guy, handsome and sun-browned with salt and pepper hair, he seemed to sense how upset Parker was and worked with him in silence for a time.

"Sorry Emma dropped the ball about Claire's move before she had time to talk with you about it. Emma didn't know you hadn't gotten the news yet."

"I gathered that." Parker dropped tools into a metal tool box and began picking up wood scraps to throw into a trash can he'd dragged down to the cabana earlier.

"You need to think about why Claire is doing this...." Pete began.

Parker interrupted, annoyed. "I have *no* idea why she is doing this." He knew he snapped out the words, his anger rising.

Pete shook his head. "You *do* know why she's doing this and you *do* know why *you're* so upset about it." He emphasized several words. "The real question is what are you going to do about it? I saw that kiss the night of the storm, Parker. A moment like that changes everything. Puts a relationship on a new level. Do you want to run with that change or run *from* it? That's the question you have to ask yourself."

Pete's eyes met his in a calm way. "I'm going to head on to the house and let you think this one through on your own." He clapped

Parker on the back. "Follow your heart, man. It usually knows the best way to go."

Parker finished the clean-up of the house, allowing the shock over Claire's news to gradually settle in. He thought a lot about Pete's words, too, trying to decide what he should do.

He noticed Claire and the girls walking back to Oleanders from the Whaleys' place, but he still didn't start toward the house. Instead, after cleaning up the last of the tools, lumber, and trash around the cabana, he headed up the beach to walk and think. He felt torn in half over Claire's announcement. She hadn't even discussed the idea with him. Why? He thought she'd come to trust him. That she leaned to him. Did she want so badly to get away from him now that she would locate a house, put in an offer on it, and not even tell him about it? Was she afraid of him? Did she despise him since that night in the hurricane?

Dark fell before he returned from walking miles down the beach and back. He saw Ezra Compton waiting for him as he drew nearer to Oleanders.

"Pete and Elaine have been worried about you," he said, motioning to a bench by the access path near Ezra and Isabel's house. "Sit down."

Parker complied, tired from walking. "So they called you thinking I needed a shrink." He choked on a laugh.

Ezra's eyes twinkled at the words. An older man, nearly bald, with a calm manner and discerning eyes, Ezra had been a good help to Parker in the years after Ann died. Difficult years to get through.

"I don't think you need a shrink," he said, "but I think you might need a friend. You keep your emotions and feelings locked in pretty tight from others, Parker."

"Meaning?"

Ezra's lips twitched. "Meaning Claire Avery probably has no idea you're in love with her. Probably few others do, either."

Parker gritted his teeth. "And you know this how?" He knew he sounded sarcastic but he couldn't help it.

Ezra's brows drew together in a frown. "Denying the obvious is not going to help you decide what to do in this situation. Can't you see that? You're a thoughtful, hesitant and cautious man, but there are times when action is needed." He paused. "An old quote says: 'If you wait too long for the perfect moment, the perfect moment will pass you by.' "

Parker glared at him. "Keep in mind this is my brother's widow we're talking about. I can't afford to be hasty. What would Charles have thought about this anyway? Or Ann? It feels wrong."

Ezra shook his head. "People hold a misguided concept that the dead want the living to suffer after they are gone. That they'd want to deny any second chance at happiness to the one left behind." He reached down to pick up a handful of sand, letting it slide through his fingers. "Time slips away, like this sand through my hand. Each man chooses for himself what he will let slip away and what he will choose to embrace. What do you want, Parker?"

Parker turned anguished eyes to Ezra's. "I want Claire. I've loved her for so long and held it in for so long that I don't know how to let my feelings out now. I don't know what to do, how to tell her. How not to look like a fool."

Ezra laughed then. "Every man feels like a fool when he tells a woman he loves her. It's a given, Parker. Didn't you feel that way when you told Ann those words?"

"Yes, but she hadn't been my brother's wife."

"Should Claire suffer for that? Should she be denied love because of that?"

Parker half closed his eyes. "Do you think it possible she might love me?"

"Why not? Are you not a good man?"

"Maybe not good enough for Claire."

"You mean maybe not as good as Charles."

His stomach felt like someone kicked him. "I know I'm not as good a man as Charles."

"I think Claire ought to get the opportunity to decide whether that is true or not." Ezra stood up. "I also think Claire is probably worried sick because you walked off from dinner and haven't come back in all this time."

"What will I say to her?"

Ezra grinned and shook his head. "Charles once told me I analyze life's issues and problems too much in my mind. He suggested that when I had a problem I should pray more. 'Why anguish over so many things,' he asked me one day, 'when God has the answers ready to give you?' Maybe you should take your brother's advice."

Like Pete, he patted Parker on the shoulder before walking on back up the path toward his house.

Parker looked out toward the moon over the sea, thinking about Ezra's words. "Lord, he's right," he said at last. "I haven't turned this over to You. I haven't given it to You in prayer. Help me to know what to do."

He prayed at length then for quite some time, walked a little more up the beach and back, and finally headed up the path to Oleanders. Some type of action was required, and he couldn't put it off any longer.

Parker saw Claire sitting in the old glider, her legs curled up under her, as soon as he let himself into the screened porch. She looked toward him, her eyes wide and distressed. "I'm sorry I didn't talk to you about the move earlier. I should have."

Both the girls, coloring pictures at the picnic table, turned worried eyes to him, too.

Parker went over to tousle both the girls' heads, and then leaned over to give both of them a kiss on the cheek. "I'm okay," he told them. "But I had some things to think about and I took a long walk to do it."

He caught Mary Helen's eyes with his. "Do you think you could see yourself and your sister to bed without Claire or me helping tonight? Maybe read your sister a book or two? I need to have a private talk with your mother."

Mary Helen nodded. "I can do that." She closed her color book. "Come on Suki. I'll read you the Frances books that you love. All three of them."

Suki's eyes lit. "Okay." She looked at Parker. "I can do my own bath and put on my pajamas all by myself now, too. I'm already seven."

"You're both growing up fast," he answered, giving both of them another kiss.

They headed upstairs while Parker went into the kitchen to fix two glasses of tea for himself and for Claire. He brought them back out to the porch and handed one to her.

Claire's words poured out in a rush before he could even sit down. "I know you're angry at me for not talking to you about planning to move. And again I'm so sorry. I truly planned to tell you about everything tonight and then you went out to work on the cabana with Pete and Tom and…." Her words fell off.

"Tell me about this house you're looking at," he said, sitting down in the glider beside her.

She did, her voice hitching now and then with her nerves. "It's a nice little place, Parker." She paused. "You've been so good to let the girls and I stay here in your house for so long. It was generous of you. I'll always be grateful to you for everything you've done for us. And we won't be far away."

When he didn't reply, she added on a softer note, "It's time for a change for us."

"It *is* time for a change." He turned to look at her, letting his eyes move slowly over her dark hair, her beautiful, expressive eyes, her flushed face, and then down over her sweet and familiar body, curved in all the right places.

Parker watched the color deepen in Claire's cheeks as his eyes roved with appreciation over her, heard her breath hitch. The air fairly crackled between them, making Parker smile.

"I have another house in mind for you to consider," he said then, watching surprise flash in her eyes.

"Well, I haven't signed the final contract yet," she said, wetting her lips as he continued to keep his eyes on hers. "I guess there *is* still time to look at another place."

Sitting this close to her, watching her twitch and shift, feeling the obvious strong current of mutual physical attraction between them, built Parker's confidence.

"Actually I have *two* houses in mind that would be perfect for you and the girls," he replied, beginning to enjoy Claire's discomfort, understanding it for the first time.

She twisted her fingers in her lap.

He reached for her hands, taking both of them in his, watching her eyes widen in surprise at the action. "Claire, both the homes I have in mind for you are mine, Waterview in Beaufort and Oleanders here at Edisto. I'm in love with you, Claire. I don't want you and the girls to move away to another home. I want you to make your home with me."

"You love me?" She croaked out the words in a whisper.

Parker moved one hand to touch her face. "I've loved you for a long time. Because the time wasn't right, because you'd only recently lost Charles, even when my feelings began to grow, I felt I couldn't tell you." He shook his head. "I think I held my feelings in check for so long I didn't know how to let them out even when the time was finally right."

Her breath hitched.

"When you ran down the ramp and kissed me that night of the storm, my heart soared. I kissed you back without thinking. I'd worried all day, tormenting myself that I might lose you and the girls to the hurricane. I didn't stop to think and analyze that night. I only felt."

He traced his hand through her hair, enjoying the silky feel of it. "That evening together was so sweet, but I found it hard to believe it was happening, to imagine you might be beginning to care for me as I did you. Now I have to ask if you might care. You're right; things have changed between us. I can't go on pretending I'm only a brother-in-law interested *only* in your well-being anymore. You know, too, that things have changed. Isn't that why you really looked for a house suddenly?"

She nodded, tears welling in her eyes.

"Oh, Claire, why are you crying? Have I made you unhappy

with all these words? If so, I'm truly sorry, but they needed to be spoken. I prayed and prayed out on the beach, and I knew I had to speak the truth when I came back."

She sniffed and then reached to wipe away her tears. "I'm crying because I'm so happy. I've fallen in love with you, too. It seemed wrong and I felt sure you couldn't feel as I did, so I decided I needed to move. Every time you came, I felt so awkward, so girlish and silly." She put a hand to his face. "Do you really love me?"

"With all my heart and soul," he said, and then he kissed her. Parker's heart hammered in his chest as emotions flared to life between them.

"Ah," he said. "If fireworks rocketed across the sky in celebration, I couldn't be happier right now." He moved his lips to kiss Claire's eyes, her cheeks, and then to move down to kiss her neck.

"We do have a full moon tonight, too," she whispered, kissing him back with joyous abandon. "That will be a sweet memory to cherish."

They kissed again, exploring their love, enjoying the passion rising between them, murmuring sweet words now and then. Both happy to express at last what they'd held back and thought was wrong.

"Do you think Ann and Charles would mind that we found each other?" Claire asked at last.

"No, as I told you that day in the cemetery, I think they'd want us to both have a chance to love again."

She dropped her eyes away from his.

"I know you were thinking about Miles that day in the cemetery," he said, lifting her chin. "You don't still hold feelings for him now, do you?"

"No," she assured him. "I actually saw Miles yesterday. He walked down the beach with me. I realized then he no longer held any attraction for me."

"I'm glad."

She giggled. "Miles knew I was upset about something, probed in his usual way and then said he wondered if you'd finally kissed me or told me you loved me. I was stunned at his words. I couldn't believe he might be right, but I wished he was."

Parker rested his forehead against hers. "Pete and Ezra both talked to me tonight, too. They both saw the situation between us more clearly than either of us did. That's rather sad, isn't it?"

"Perhaps, but we wanted to be careful and respectful to Ann and Charles's memory. That's sweet versus sad, don't you think?"

"That's a nice way to look at it. Makes me feel less an idiot." He drew away to take her hands in his again. "Will you mind living much of the time with me in Beaufort? I need to live in the city near the business. I can come here often, like I do now, on the weekends, and on days when I'm off. Would you and the girls mind living with me at Waterview most of the time?"

"I don't think the girls will mind, as long as we come here often. They love you, Parker. They'll be happy we plan to marry."

"I haven't proposed properly." Parker got down on one knee in front of the glider. "Claire, I love you and am asking you now if you will agree to marry me." He grinned at her. "You and the girls won't even have to change your last name. You can keep all those towels and pillowcases embroidered with an A."

Claire laughed. "I'd forgotten about those. And yes, yes, I'll marry you, Parker Avery. Thank you for loving me and thank you for asking me." Her smile fell and she frowned then. "Do you think our families will be upset we've fallen in love?"

He shrugged, getting up to sit beside her again. "We need to stop worrying about what our families think and to start focusing on our own happiness. As Charles would say, if we've prayed and we feel the Lord's favor is on our decisions, then the opinions of others shouldn't matter."

"I can remember him saying that often, too." Claire spoke softly. "I do think he would be happy for both of us."

"So do I." He reached for his tea glass on the table beside them.

Claire glanced toward the kitchen. "I made an apple pie earlier. Would you like me to fix you a piece?"

"Yes, but I'd like to go upstairs first and share our news with the girls. What do you think? You know they've been worried."

"They might be asleep by now, but that's a lovely thought. Even if we need to wake them, they'll be excited."

Parker stood and offered his hand, pulling Claire to her feet and then into his arms to kiss her again. He loved the feel of her pressed against him, reveled in the knowledge that he'd found love again, that she cared for him. That a lifetime lay ahead in which to love and share his days with Claire.

"What are you thinking?" she asked, her arms still wrapped around him.

"How happy I am," he answered. "How glad I am to think about a future with you and the girls in it."

She glanced toward the house. "I'll bet one of the first things Mary Helen suggests is bringing her own bedroom furniture to one of the rooms at Waterview."

He laughed. "That's fine with me. I expect a lot of changes to occur at Waterview as we turn it into a family home. Anything we take out of the house, I can sell at the store."

Claire gave him a little grin. "Three women will change your bachelor life significantly."

"I can't wait to start the changes," he said. "Can we get married soon?"

She cocked her head to one side. "I did think this would be a good month for a move before my new book comes out in October." A worry line crossed her brow. "I hope Isabel won't be too upset about us marrying. She'll need to find someone else to work at The Little Mermaid. I can still come over to work a few days part time, but I'll need to help the girls get settled into their new life and school in Beaufort."

"We'll work it all out," he said, taking her hand to start into the house. "I'll always count every day as a little miracle we both found each other and that we found a new way to happiness."

She paused. "I was so unhappy at my parents' home and I used to dream I could be *Claire at Edisto* again. Now I'll never have to leave."

RECIPES from *Claire at Edisto*

Aggie's Snickerdoodle Cookies

½ cup soft shortening
½ cup softened butter
2 eggs
1 ½ cups sugar
2 teaspoons vanilla
2 ¾ cups sifted flour

2 teaspoons cream of tartar
1 teaspoon soda
¼ teaspoon salt
Cinnamon-Sugar Mixture:
2 tablespoons sugar
2 teaspoons cinnamon

Directions:

Preheat oven to 400 degrees. With mixer cream together the shortening, butter, sugar, eggs and vanilla 4-5 minutes until smooth. Next blend in the flour, cream of tartar, soda, and salt. Chill the dough for about 20-30 minutes. Then roll dough into round balls the size of small walnuts. Stir together the sugar and cinnamon and roll the dough balls well in the mixture, twice if needed to coat well. Place two inches apart on ungreased baking sheets. Press down the center of each ball slightly to keep the cookies from puffing up in the middle while baking. Then bake for 8 to 10 minutes until the edges become a light golden brown. The cookies will still be slightly soft when removed from the oven but will harden when cooled. Store in airtight container. Makes about 4-5 dozen 2-inch cookies.

Claire's Crunchy Chicken Casserole

1 cup celery, peeled & sliced
½ cup onion, chopped small
1 can cream of chicken soup
½ cup mayonnaise
4 cubed chicken breasts

1 8-oz can sliced water
    chestnuts, drained
1 tablespoon butter
1 pkg (1/2 c) sliced almonds

Directions:

Microwave-cook chopped, cubed chicken breasts covered for appx 10 minutes until done in covered oven-proof Corning-type casserole dish. Drain liquid. Microwave celery, onion, and butter, covered, for 2-3 minutes until soft and lightly cooked. Add to chicken in casserole dish. Stir in chicken soup and mayonnaise. Sprinkle in a little garlic salt and black pepper to taste. Then stir in sliced almonds and sliced water chestnuts. *Topping:* Top casserole with a layer of London breadcrumbs or dry herb-seasoned stuffing mix and then drizzle with 2 tablespoons of melted butter. Then bake the casserole at 350 degrees, uncovered, for 30 minutes. Serve with rice and peas or a green salad.

Nora's Linguini Salad

- 1 16-oz box linguini pasta cooked and drained
- 1-2 16-oz bottles Kraft Italian dressing
- 1 pkg sliced fresh mushrooms
- 2-3 chpd Romano tomatoes
- 1 small pkg sliced pepperoni
- 1 sm chpd red onion
- 1/2 6-oz can black pitted olives, sliced
- 1 med sliced cucumber, remove skin
- 1 chpd green pepper

Directions:

Place linguini pasta in a large bowl. Add tomatoes, pepper, olives, cucumber, sliced mushrooms, and pepperoni. Toss all ingredients together, except chopped red onion, which can be added before serving. Add one bottle Italian dressing and stir into ingredients. Depending on taste, stir in part of second bottle of dressing. Marinate covered 1-2 hours in refrigerator. Before serving, toss in red onion if desired and add more dressing.

A Reading Group Guide

CLAIRE AT EDISTO

Lin Stepp

About This Guide

The questions on the following pages are included
to enhance your group's reading of
Lin Stepp's *Claire At Edisto*

DISCUSSION QUESTIONS

1. As this book begins Claire Avery is at her husband Charles's funeral. How did Charles die? What was his occupation and what did you learn about him in the early parts of this book and later? Facing the death of a loved one is always hard. What factors make this situation especially difficult for Claire? Why can't she stay in the home where she and her two girls live? What occupational and personal issues does she face? How does Charles's brother Parker help her at the funeral and after?

2. At the funeral, you meet Claire's family and Charles's family. What are your impressions of each? What do you think of Claire's plans to go to live with her family in Arlington, VA, for a time and what do you think of her father, mother, and twin sisters? How do Mary Helen and Suki feel about going to live in Arlington? What does Parker think? Why do you think Claire and the girls might have problems living with either family?

3. What factors bonded Parker and Charles as brothers in their large family? What is Parker's occupation and where does he live? What did Charles make Parker promise to do if anything ever happened to him? How did Parker's wife Ann die and how was Charles a strong support to him in that time? How were Ann and Claire different in personality? Why did Parker encourage Claire and the girls to come to stay at his beach house at Edisto for a time? Had they been there before?

4. Claire's girls, Mary Helen and Suki, are introduced in the book's first chapter. How old are they as the book begins and how are they different in looks and personality? How do the girls comfort and support Claire in dealing with Charles's death and how does Claire support them? How is their family faith a strong help? What scenes with Claire and the girls, early in the book and

later, remind you of scenes with your own children or child you may have worked with?

5. The book begins in Sweetwater, a small town in Tennes and then shifts in setting to Edisto Island, a remote barrier isl off the coast of South Carolina. Have you ever been to Ed Island? The island lies about halfway between Charles and Beaufort and scenes in both these cities play a part in story. Have you ever visited Charleston or Beaufort? Did recognize the scenes and places described in these locations the book you learn that Edisto is somewhat different from m popular beach vacation spots. How? Would these differer make Edisto more or less attractive to you?

6. Dealing with the grief of death is always hard. Pai mentions a book by Elizabeth Kubler Ross describing stages of grief. The five stages are: (1) Denial and diffic in believing the death has occurred; (2) Anger and pain, fee lost; (3) Bargaining, wishing things were as they were before Depression and sadness over the loss; and finally (5) Accepta of the reality that the loved one is gone and moving on. Altho these were not detailed in the book, did you see some of th emotional stages playing out? Which stage did Parker say l stayed in too long? Claire seems to drift through the sum after Charles' death, finding it hard to move on as in stage Have you seen these stages of grief playing out in your life c the lives of people you love?

7. Friendships mean so much in our lives. Parker has frie at the island and at Westcott Antiques with Drake Jenkins Nora Cavanaugh where he works. What did you learn ab Drake and Nora? How did Parker also become close to Nc son Andrew? Some of Parker's friends at the island also bec friends to Claire, especially Elaine Whaley, Lula Mikell,

Isabel Compton. How do you think each of these friends were a help to Claire?

8. Elaine's younger children Chuck, Jane, and Emma, and Lula's youngest J.T. soon become friends with Mary Helen and Suki. What sorts of games and activities did all these children enjoy living on a coastal island? Who was Gracie Byrd and how did she cause problems among the children? How did Claire get involved in keeping Lula and Elaine's children for part of the summer? What characteristics and talents of Claire's made her a good—and popular—sitter with the children? How did Andrew mix in with the children on his visits to Edisto? What special bond did he and Suki develop?

9. Who is Miles Lawrence and how does Claire meet him? What is Miles' occupation and where does he live and work? Miles is attracted to Claire and also intrigued by her as a psychologist. Why? How does he push Claire to examine her life in new ways? Why is this upsetting and confusing to Claire? What did you think about his methods, both professionally and personally? How does Miles gradually grow closer to Claire and her girls? What episode with Miles pushes Claire toward accepting her father's counsel to come home with him to Arlington?

10. Are Claire and the girls happy in their move to Arlington? Why or why not? Is Parker happy that Claire has moved back to live with her parents? How did Parker's feelings toward Claire change from the time of the funeral until she left Edisto? Why was he upset to have these feelings and reluctant to reveal them to anyone? When Elaine and Isabel learn that Claire and the girls are unhappy, they push Parker to go to Arlington to encourage her to come back to Edisto. What job does Isabel offer to encourage Claire to come back? What offer does Parker learn from Miles that he thinks may also help encourage Claire to come back?

11. Giftings and talents in children often show up early. What gifting did Suki have? When Charles and Claire recognized it how did they try to encourage it? What hindrances later came for Suki taking lessons with Ms. Najinski? How did Suki meet Morgan Dillon and begin taking lessons with him? What happened at her first big recital? Why did she freeze? How did Andrew help her in that moment? Early in the book, several people note that Mary Helen is really smart. In seriousness and fun, what gifting does Isabel later say Mary Helen has? How does this gift show when Mary Helen helps Isabel in her store The Little Mermaid? Did you have gifts and talents that showed up early in your life? Do you think they were well encouraged and celebrated? Do you think Claire's gifts and talents were celebrated in her early home life?

12. After Claire's return to Edisto from Arlington her first children's book is published by Whittier the next fall. What is this first book in her new series called? How had the idea for these books developed? What other books do you later learn her publisher is interested in? Where did the idea for these books evolve? Why is Claire worried about the publication of her book and her expected book tour? How does Isabel help her with this and with Claire's first book launch? Where is it held? What two problems happen at the book launch and how are they resolved?

13. Aggie Mosely Houston, the Hampton family housekeeper, played an important role in Claire's upbringing. Did you like Aggie? How did Aggie impact Claire's early life? What things did she teach her? When Claire returns to her family home, how is Aggie a support and help to her again? What personal and spiritual advice does she give Claire about her situation? Aggie claims God always has a plan, even if we don't understand it or see it all at once. Do you think that's true?

14. How does Claire move into a more serious relationship with Miles Lawrence when she returns to the island? Why do you think she and the girls are so attracted to Miles? What things does Miles do and say that lead Claire, Mary Helen, and Suki to all think he's more serious than he is? What happens to show them this isn't so? How is Isabel a help? In what way do Ezra and Parker both confront Miles?

15. Why did Claire's sister Marilyn come to visit with her toward the close of the book? How did Marilyn act differently from in the past? What did you learn about Marilyn and her life? What did she ask Claire's advice about? This visit, despite its positive aspects, continued to point out the differences between Claire and her family. Do you have family members whose beliefs and lives are very different from yours? How have these differences caused difficulties and misunderstandings over the years? Have you also seen small resolutions occur over time?

16. Isabel comes to see if Claire and the girls want to evacuate with her and Ezra as Hurricane Frances advances toward the South Carolina coast. What problems does Isabel warn Claire that might occur? What has Claire decided to do if the storm gets worse? What fears do Claire and the girls have as the danger increases and the storm draws closer? In Beaufort, as Parker's worries increase about Claire and the girls, what does he decide to do? How does Pete help with this? Have you ever been at the coast when a major hurricane hit? Would you stay or evacuate?

17. When an emotional scene occurs, when Parker comes to pick up Claire and the girls, their feelings for each other come out in the open? What are Parker's thoughts about it? What are Claire's? Why do they neither one talk about their feelings but instead try to go on as before? Why doesn't this work? How is their relationship changed after the hurricane? What does Claire

decide she needs to do? What does Parker do when he learns Claire plans to move? How does he act? Often when two people are swirling in the midst of emotions, they can't seem to see their personal situations clearly. How does Miles provoke Claire to consider her situation in another way? Why does she dismiss his advice? How do Ezra and Pete do the same for Parker? What happens when Parker finally shares with Claire how he feels?

18. What characters did you like most in this book? Why did you especially identify with these characters or like the scenes involving them? Knowing this is the first book in a continuing trilogy, what characters do you hope you might meet again in future books? Mary Helen, now grown, will be the main character in the second book RETURN TO EDISTO while Suki will be the main character in the third EDISTO SONG. What do you think Mary Helen and Suki will be like when they are older?

About the Author
Lin Stepp

Dr. Lin Stepp is a *New York Times, USA Today,* and *Publishers Weekly* Best-Selling international author. A native Tennessean, she also works as both a businesswoman and as an educator. Although not actively teaching now, she is still on adjunct faculty at Tusculum College where she taught research and a variety of psychology and counseling courses for almost twenty years. Her business background includes over twenty-five years in marketing, sales, production art, and regional publishing.

Stepp writes engaging, heart-warming contemporary Southern fiction with a strong sense of place and has twelve published novels each set in different locations around the Smoky Mountains. Her latest novels are *The Interlude* (2019), *Lost Inheritance* (2018) and *Daddy's Girl* (2017), with previous novels including *Welcome Back* (2016), *Saving Laurel Springs* (2015), *Makin' Miracles* (2015), and *Down by the River* (2014) published by Kensington of New York. Other earlier titles include: *Second Hand Rose* (2013), *Delia's Place* (2012), *For Six Good Reasons* (2011), *Tell Me About Orchard Hollow* (2010), and *The Foster Girls* (2009). In addition Stepp and her husband J.L. Stepp have co-authored a Smoky Mountains hiking guidebook titled *The Afternoon Hiker* (2014) and a Tennessee state parks guidebook *Discovering Tennessee State Parks* (2018).

For more about Stepp's work and to keep up with her monthly blog, ongoing appearances and signing events, see her website at: *www.linstepp.com*

CPSIA information can be obtained
at www.ICGtesting.com
Printed in the USA
BVHW030854240721
612636BV00006BA/177